OCEAN BEACH

Frank Cassese

No Record Press

2014

NO RECORD PRESS

www.norecordpress.com

First published in 2014 by
No Record Press

Cassese, Frank.
Ocean Beach/Frank Cassese.

ISBN 978-0-692-22750-3

Cover design by Geraldine Lau

Printed in the United States of America

For my mother

Death is not an event in life: we do not live to experience death. If we take eternity to mean not infinite temporal duration but timelessness, then eternal life belongs to those who live in the present.

— Ludwig Wittgenstein

One of the first signs of the beginnings of understanding is the wish to die. This life appears unbearable, another unattainable. One is no longer ashamed of wanting to die; one asks to be moved from the old cell, which one hates, to a new one, which one will only in time come to hate.

— Franz Kafka

If in heavy horrible dreams anxiety reaches its highest degree, it causes us to wake up, whereby all those monstrous horrors of the night vanish. The same thing happens in the dream of life when the highest degree of anxiety forces us to break it off.

— Arthur Schopenhauer

1

The Rite of Spring

The flesh is sad, alas, and I have read all the books.

— Stéphane Mallarmé

My life takes place in a room. It's a very clean room. Clean as in neat or tidy. Clean also as in not dirty. I spend the majority of my time here, and I sleep whenever possible, because I like to and because there's not a lot to do in the same room, day in and day out. I sleep so much that I am always tired, walking about in a dreamy daze, a continuous stupor, with slumber constantly in my head like an infectious melody that buzzes around unbidden but not entirely unwelcome, though I don't necessarily like it, maybe even hate it. And it's not sleeping so much as napping. Drowsiness or fatigue has little to do with it. I don't have to be tired to nap. In fact, I enjoy it more when I'm not.

The house that I live in is seated squarely in the middle of a one-acre plot of well-wooded land, surrounded by other houses of roughly the same dimensions and structural design, each with its own discriminating decorative aesthetic, making them seem like a set of highly competitive siblings struggling to outdo one another in the eyes of an absentee parent. There are two windows in my room, one that gives onto the front yard and the street, and another that faces the house next door. Since it is on the western side, my room is brightest toward dusk, and on clear, cloudless days, sunlight streaks through the slats of the blinds and drenches the walls with an eerie twilight brightness that lasts only a few minutes, until the sun retreats below the horizon. Then it gets dark quickly.

Down the long, vaulted hallway of the upper level, at the very end, is my sister's room. Severine. She was young, not more than five or six years old, when she began to sneak out after the lights were off, tiptoe through the carpeted corridor and crawl into my bed, braving the darkened passage to take refuge next to me, not wanting to tell my parents that she was afraid to sleep by herself, that whatever imaginary horrors haunted her room were somehow absent from mine. Even then it was hard for her to show her weaknesses, her fears, harder than it should have been. She was already being touted as something of a prodigy at the piano. At a time when the tastes of most American kids were limited to the slim spectrum of popular music running from schmaltzy soft rock to short-lived hair metal to early hip hop, she would sit for hours a day behind the piano practicing Bach and Bartók, religiously starting each session by warming up on *The Well-Tempered Clavier* and eventually working her way to Chopin, which has always been my favorite—the nocturnes. There was something about these pieces in particular and the way she interpreted them, their wistful melody lines meandering up into my room, where I was napping, reading, or watching afternoon sitcoms, that succeeded in drowning out the clamor, and tempering the turmoil, of adolescence, in making me forget, at least for a little while, that I existed.

She rarely said anything upon entering my room at night. She would climb into bed next to me and curl up in a fetal ball, redolent of Ivory Soap and Johnson's Baby Shampoo (which she continued to use long past babyhood) from her evening bath, warm and drowsy and eager to surrender consciousness. It got to be so regular that on those nights when she would fall asleep in her own bed before our parents had extinguished the lights, I would lie there waiting restlessly, on the qui vive, intermittently dozing and waking until finally she was there, and I could breathe easy. Only when I found her form squeezed against my own on the narrow single bedframe would I fall asleep for good. And if she didn't come, if my patience was not rewarded with her presence, I would repeat the dozing-waking cycle deep into the small hours until I gave up hope, succumbed to sad exhaustion, and settled for second-rate slumber, rising the next morning with an aching disappointment and the bitter, unrefreshed feeling of a lost night's sleep. I, too, was afraid to be in bed alone, but I never told her.

As we got older, we'd stay up for hours. Sometimes we didn't speak at all. Sometimes I just listened. She said no one listened like I did.

"People only hear," she used to say. "They filter out what they choose and hear what they want to, but they don't really listen."

"Nobody listens when you're fifteen," I told her. "You have to expect that. What could a fifteen-year-old have to say? What does a teenager know about the world?"

"What does anybody really know about the world? But no, that's not what I mean. I mean… That's why hardly anybody appreciates music anymore. Classical music. You can't just *hear* it. If you just hear it, you can't understand it, you can't feel it. And then it becomes worthless. Then it's only sounds."

She didn't speak like a child, like an adolescent; teenagers don't say the things she said.

"And this bothers you," I gibed, just a little, "that they can't *feel* it?"

"Yes."

"Why?"

"Because I can."

"Maybe they're just not able to, not capable. You expect too much from people."

She closed her eyes and burrowed her head into my chest. "Maybe. But they expect too much from me."

In truth, I do not like listening to people. It's mostly just noise, all this flapping of lips—tedious, mechanized cant—and it almost always seems rehearsed. Talk never changed anything, never made any lasting difference in the world. My talents are honed and put to good use within the silent seclusion of my room, my cloistral chamber, where I can fall asleep on command, sleepy or not, close my eyes and cut off everything, provisionally suspend existence at will. Except at night. It's trickier at night. And so I'll often stay up through the early morning hours, lying in bed or sitting at my desk, just sitting straight up in a chair and staring listlessly at the wall or the TV or the encompassing darkness, trying hard to think of nothing. Sometimes I walk around the house, touring each floor, sifting through boxes of old odds and ends in the basement—where I will occasionally come across a treasured trinket from my youth, a forgotten artifact of childhood—and combing the kitchen pantry for something to eat, whether I'm hungry or not. It's more about the search than the find.

I enjoy this roaming and rummaging when everyone else is asleep and nobody is there to interfere with me. It's a different world during those hours. The entire house becomes my room. My world.

Problems arise when I return to bed and find it empty, the rumpled sheets bereft of her sleeping form, the pillow bare without her hair fanned out over it like brilliant gilded streamers, and disquiet destroys the regnant silence of my nighttime world. I loved watching her sleep, the calm, leveled rhythm of her breathing. I could watch her for hours on end. If I could just do that and nothing more, just watch her, but forever—it would have to be forever, nothing less than forever—then, I think, I could be satisfied.

My life takes place in a room. In a twin bed with black sheets and a thick, fluffy gray and white marbled comforter large enough to cover the entire low-to-the-ground frame. I don't make my bed. There's no reason to, I'm so often in it. I prefer its unmade state, sheets wrinkled and pillows furrowed with the indentation of my head, a preformed mold ever ready to be filled. It feels as if the bed is always waiting for me, anticipating my return from the moment I leave it. Once I'm there, I don't like to think about getting up. First there's the physical facet, the complexity of movement required to rise, the mere thought of which serves to keep me where I am. Then there's the idea of actually leaving the bed, which is what I am most averse to, the very concept of being anywhere but in this bed, anyplace outside its sanctuary. In here, under the covers, everything is orderly and controlled, safe and secure, all threats to the sovereignty of my kingdom of sloth and siesta nicely neutralized. Out there, it's anything goes. And even though I know I'll eventually have to get up and do something, go somewhere, for those few sacred seconds before I tumble out of consciousness, those delicious moments of transience, everything is good, it all works, because I can lie there and let anything flit through my head, good or bad, heavenly or hateful, and each thought, without exception, will soon be blessedly forgotten for the time being, erased by the divine oblivion of unconsciousness.

I don't dream much. Or at least I don't remember if I do. When I am in bed, the world ceases to exist. This is sleep's greatest reward.

J'habite une seule chambre.

She is still referred to as Sev, or Sevy sometimes, as when she was a little girl, but even these less distinctive variations are infinitely more expressive than my plain, prosaic forename. She gets an elegant and exotic Gallic name, I get the utterly commonplace Peter. The advantage was hers from the beginning. I still wonder how my parents overlooked the barefaced injustice of this disparity, how they saw nothing awkward in naming one child Peter and the other Severine, unless they did it on purpose, deliberately creating this chasm of inequality from the moment we were labeled. There's no continuity between the two, as if we were issued from two different sets of parents, as if we weren't really brother and sister, or shouldn't have been.

There are variations of my name as well—Pete, Petey, sometimes simply P—but these condensed versions are even less appealing. I have always disliked my name. I have always felt a biting sense of embarrassment or displacement when being called, because I don't feel like a Peter. The associations bound with the name do not blend with who I am; the qualities Peter conjures do not apply to me. Like a sexy swimsuit model named Bertha or Marge. There's nothing inherently ugly or unsavory about these names. They just don't fit my image of a *bathing beauty*, as I don't fit Peter. It's as if I am playing a role, the wrong role, someone else's part. I am a stranger to my own name, an imposter who has lived under an assumed identity for so long that on occasion it almost feels like who I really am, but never who I want to be.

My sister, on the other hand, has always lived up to the promise of her name. Our parents fished out the right one for her; she was fated to be a Severine, an anomaly in a family rife with Vinnys, Tonys, Marys, and Johnnys. She defined her name, embodying it as though having emerged from the womb with a preternaturally precocious awareness of who she was, as perfect for it as I am imperfect for mine. I have loathed Peter from as far back as I can remember, even seeing it written, even hearing it pronounced, except when it came off her lips.

People frequently asked if we were twins. We were not. There was just shy of a year between us. It has often come to my mind that one of us was a mistake, my parents' attempt to atone for an earlier blunder or a simple slip-up too soon after their firstborn—a literal misconception.

Our parents liked our closeness—in age and otherwise—and remarks abounded among family, friends, and neighbors as to how well brother and sister got along, accompanied by complaints of the havoc caused in their own homes by feuding sons and daughters, spoiled suburban rug rats vying viciously for limited parental attention and resources. This was far from the case with us. Being as close in age as we were was convenient for everyone involved. We would play and nap and eat and bathe together, as though our togetherness were the essential aspect of the world. Rarely were we found apart. We grew together, as one. A sibling unit.

So I couldn't say where it started. There seemed to be no readily identifiable beginning. It was so natural a development.

There was no other course to take, no questioning. You don't question the implicit state of things, when things happen the way it seems they must.

Le cœur a ses raisons que la raison ne connaît point.

And throughout it all, I did my best—failing more often than not—to fight the instinct to shield her from foreign factors that might get in the way, because I wanted what we shared to remain natural and unforced, to continue unfolding the way it always had, the way it always should have. This was not that difficult, because she never expressed much interest in boys, though boys were all too often interested in her, an eventuality for which I was always prepared. If a friend of mine came to the house (a rare occurrence) and made a comment about her—which happened once and again as we crept into maturity, something like, *Hey, your sister have a boyfriend?* or the decidedly more direct, *Your sis is looking good, dude. How about introducing us?*—I would make a point of withholding future invitations. But these methods were purely prophylactic; there were really no considerable grounds for concern. Severine would not have wanted to be involved with any of my friends. I was just saving them from frustration, averting an uncomfortable situation for everyone. I've only ever had one friend worth keeping anyway.

Then there was Spencer. But that was later, and he was not my friend.

I was never much of a ladies' man—more of a Leopardi than a Lothario, when it comes to amorous relations—but the fair sex is absolutely alien to me now. It has been such a long time since I've been with a girl, years since I've had any intimate physical contact with a woman—at least with a woman who is not paid to play—that I have all but forgotten what sex is. The

10

female body has become an unknown quantity, an obscure and outlandish object of desire, a faintly remembered relic from a former life, merely conceptual with no corresponding corporeal reality. I know they are out there in great numbers, many of them ready and willing to mix and mingle and do what nature intended, but I don't even see them, in large part because I'm always in my room; and since they are not in my room, they might as well not exist.

Four or five years ago, when I was in college and actively attending classes, my parents suspected homosexual tendencies. We were sitting around the table eating beef stroganoff, and my father broke a piece of seeded pumpernickel and let the crumbs fall onto his plate and said, "What… no cute girls around?" I was taken aback, as he doesn't usually speak like this or about things like that. He's a philosophy professor, and his speech generally conforms to his métier, whether at home or in the classroom, brooking no breach in the consistency of his persona. (I believe that he believes this speaks to a certain *authenticity of being*—as I believe he would put it—though the very idea of authentic being is not something I believe he would admit to believing in.) Then he began chewing his bread and twirling some noodles around his fork, and I noticed my mother focusing intently on me from across the table. She, too, was chewing.

I said, "Nope," bit into a piece of bread, and began chewing as well.

"None?" my father continued keenly, slightly raising his pitch and an eyebrow to accentuate his piqued curiosity. "I find that hard to swallow. I see a lot of nice-looking young ladies on campus all the time." Teaching at the same university I attended put him in a position to make such an observation, and to point it out to me as though I were grievously flouting some crucial academic fact.

"Yes, I'm sure you do," I told him, "but that doesn't mean I do. Could be a question of perspective."

"They're in my classes," he persisted, "in the hallways, the cafeteria, the commons, the library. They exist, is the point. It's hard *not* to see them."

"We can never be certain of the existence of anyone or anything, not even ourselves. Isn't that what you've been telling me my whole life? You're going back on it now?"

"Peter," my mother interjected diplomatically, concerned enough to cease her chewing, "we want to ask you—and, well, we're completely fine with it if you're—it's just that—what we're asking is if—"

"You do like girls, don't you?" my father said, taking control, showing his hand. They waited anxiously for my response, unmoving, hopefully anticipating the appropriate answer to the question of their only son's sexual preference.

I said, "I don't really like much of anything, but yes, I *like* girls, in that sense, in the *biblical* sense." Despite the sarcasm, this was the nearest to the truth that I could have told them. There was an unspoken but measurable release of tension as everyone went on eating contentedly, and the subject was not broached again.

In a way, I choose this estrangement from girls and have no desire to find one, or more precisely, no desire to try. My friend Don puts it best. He's the only one who really knows about my sexual inactivity. He's the only one I have much contact or communion with. Nobody I know uses words like Don. "Doesn't matter," he says. "If you're talking about love, love is a myth and sex is just a grotesque and execrable exchange of liquids. It's all a heinous trap. Mother Nature's well-wrought ruse to get you to reproduce, to hoodwink you into furthering the species. Master and marionette. The libido is the string and we're the puppets. Now, heroin addicts," becoming more animated, "they're the ones that successfully screw the system, the ones who beat the bitch at her own game, because junk totally ousts the urge to fuck. You just want junk, you lose all interest in sex, and that, my friend, is why it's the only tried-and-true antidote to the sex drive, short of snipping off your prick. And don't think I haven't given this careful and extensive consideration. Heroin, I mean. Not cock-chopping."

He says this with his girlfriend, Susan, sitting next to him on the floor of his room as he packs the bowl of his bong and prepares to get high, which he does at least three or four times a day. She just shakes her head and laughs at him and demands the first hit, a concession always granted her. She usually smokes way too much, much too fast, and subsequently falls asleep. On Don, however, marijuana has the opposite effect, making him hypertalkative, a loquacious suburban sage with just enough knowledge on most subjects to be able to deliver a convincing and consistently entertaining discourse, while I—a perpetual abstainer on whom pot's most appreciable effects are a hazy headache and mild nausea—sit there sober and somber, bouncing all kinds of questions and ideas off him, his stoned but never dulled reasoning rarely failing to engage. In fact, he's often sharper when high.

"I think my father thinks that if I had a girlfriend my whole outlook would change," I say.

"That's a fair assessment. A little *punani* goes a long way."

"Ugh," Susan grumbles. "You know I hate that word."

"I do. But what I do not know is why. It means *beautiful blossom* in old Hawaiian." He seems legitimately distressed by her failure to appreciate the term.

"It's a disgusting word. Keep using it and see how often you get any."

Don huffs and shakes his head. "Fine." He looks at me. "A gash a day keeps the doctor away." Then he looks at Susan, who stares daggers at him.

"Asshole."

He motions me to go on. "You were saying..."

"I think my father thinks getting laid would radically alter my life for the better, like some of the major problems of the world would be solved if I somehow managed to find a willing partner for intercourse. Global warming. Peace in the Middle East."

"Regrowth of the rainforests, baldness," Susan contributes before puckering her lips inside the bong and sucking out a dense column of smoke with a long, potent yet feminine drag.

"Cancer. Erectile dysfunction. The common cold."

I've known Don most of my life. I can't remember not knowing him. If I had a brother, I prefer to think he would be like Don, a slightly older, slightly wiser sibling who could offer fraternal advice and protection, yet who was near enough in age to remain a peer, a pal, a close confidante. This is Don. We speak alike and even look somewhat alike, both of us deriving from similar Mediterranean ancestry: dark eyes, dark hair (though his is kinky and almost black—a *Wopfro*, as he sometimes calls it—betraying his Sicilian ancestry, while mine is a wavy chestnut), olive complexions, lean builds, height within an inch of each other's (though he never fails to round his up to an even 5'10", bestowing upon himself that imaginary half inch so often that he has come to believe it's really there). He's the only one I see any-more, barring my parents. He lives in the house where he grew up, across the street and three doors down from me, about as far from the refuge of my room as I dare to go, so when I do venture out it's to his place. Loyal to the creed of suburbia, every home in our development was strictly designed after the same model, and Don's bedroom corresponds exactly to mine, a mirror-image facsimile in the upper right corner of the second level; it's as close as I can get to my own room without actually being there. We usually just sit around talking, watching TV, snacking, play-ing video games. He is the only child of particularly permissive parents who essentially yield him unregulated autonomy, so being there is much like being at Don's apartment.

With his girlfriend tucked away in a pot-induced slumber, Don picks up the thread of his earlier speech, butane lighter at the ready. "You cannot have love in a post-Darwinian world, or rather, you can't take it seriously." He lights the contents of the bowl, presses his lips to the opening of the bong, sucks in, holds, releases, coughs lightly, and goes on. "But if you admit to your-self that you're a sucker, if you understand and accept that in the end all this yearning for love and romance is a veil for the most primordial of instincts, which is of course the search for a mate and the consequent process of sexual reproduction—if you fully grasp this, that you're nothing but nature's pawn, a pathetic little peon, a fucking motherfucking dupe, then you can keep love... as a euphemism." When he says *love*, his features crunch up as though he's just put something deplorably sour in his mouth, and he presents his case with the cool confidence of a scientist whose experimentally verifiable results are far above reproach. "You're programmed, you see? You're a computer chip. I mean, it's a simple, fundamental fact." He chops down hard at his fully flexed, upturned left palm with the knife edge of his right hand. "Everybody knows the practicality of it, but they're bamboozled into thinking there's this mystical, numinous thing that exists between two people having sex. There's nothing more magical or romantic about it than a couple of pigs fucking in the mud or two stray cats rutting in the woods behind your house. You're driven by nature, manipulative bitch that she is, to further the species, to be plagued by this… this torturous desire to copulate. It's a vast scheme, and it's perfectly engineered. When the attraction is there, *your* thingy hardens up and *she* gets lubricious so that *your* thingy can do its job and function according to the way nature, manipulative bitch that she is, has planned it. Even the pleasure you get from it is secondary. Necessary, yes, but not an end in itself, nothing more than a shifty means to get you to do nature's bidding. If fucking didn't feel so fucking good, you wouldn't do it, would you?"

I don't answer, thinking he means this rhetorically.

"I'm asking you," he prods.

"Oh. No, I guess I wouldn't."

"Of course you wouldn't. If sex didn't offer such intense pleasure that the lack of it is equivalent to pain and suffering, if the gratification weren't so singular and incomparable that we think about it almost all the time, there'd be no babies. The race would end. Nature would lose. And she cannot lose, the calculating cunt, the hateful harpy. She has implanted these horrible desires that can never be fully satiated so that we keep doing it until a baby is born, and then her designs are complete. She breeds us like dogs. We get a few seconds of intense pleasure, she multiplies herself infinitely. A lifetime of libidinous hunger for the commitment to continuance. Anything but a fair fucking exchange." He pauses, breathes, sucks his teeth. "Once you've propagated, your job is done, my friend. You can degenerate and get old and die with the knowledge that you've fulfilled your mission. Your services are no longer required, except to feed the maggots."

"Agreed. But knowing this doesn't help things. Whatever the reason, the drive is there. The world would stop tomorrow if the drive weren't there. You can't just stop wanting to fuck. It's impossible."

"True, true, but it does help put things in perspective. Think about the amount of time and energy we waste trying to find a hole to stick our dicks in. A disgusting little slimy hole, man. That's what it comes down to. The world turns because we're all trying to find holes for our penises." He raises his arms in triumphant culmination. "That's it. That's our raison d'être. No higher meaning, no transcendental purpose. We're here to fuck and that's it. That's the origin and the aspiration of the world. If you see it as nothing more than this, then the whole thing is less intimidating. It becomes laughable." He pauses. "Laughable." He laughs. Then he takes a hit, exhales, holds the bong away from him and looks at it with a sudden revulsion. "This weed is shit tonight, just to let you know. I really have to find a new source."

Susan groans in her sleep. We both turn to look at her, then turn back.

"I'm not the one smoking it."

"Understood. But just to let you know."

I watch a good deal of television now, but it was strongly discouraged when we were younger, at times prohibited—just as some parents don't allow their children junk food or soda—as though it were detrimental to our health. TV was antithetical to the ethos of our household. Life was in literature. By our mid-teens, we were able to rattle off maxims of La Rochefoucauld and lines of Mallarmé like well-trained *lycéens*, a practiced skill kept in top form by my father, who would drill us at the dinner table while Mahler, Schubert, or something else vaguely funereal was playing in the background. Having no basis for comparison, I accepted this as normal. Didn't everyone live like this?

He weaned us on the stuff early, reading symbolist poetry as a lullaby—Verlaine and Rimbaud instead of Bert and Ernie, *Les Contes de La Fontaine* in lieu of *Mother Goose*—teaching us French and Italian, which he christened "the twin gems of the Romance languages," even as we developed our native tongue, so that there would be as minor a gap as possible in comparative fluency.

"It's invaluable to know other languages," he'd trumpet. "It enriches the mind, expands the network of connections in the brain. Most Americans are lucky if they can speak *one* correctly. You'll thank me someday."

But above all there was Baudelaire. Baudelaire was gospel. We *had* to know our Baudelaire. My father would tell us how all French schoolchildren, even the less bright ones, could quote Baudelaire on demand.

"What do kids here know? Heavy metal lyrics? Comic books? Video games?"

So he would quiz us over dinner, abrogating my mother's best attempts to discuss more insouciant subjects while eating, methodically swirling his wine—never spilling a drop—as he asked us why the albatross cannot walk.

Ses ailes de géant l'empêchent de marcher, we would answer correctly in unison, and then we'd be happy because he was happy with us. We had passed. There would be appeased smiles all around. Even my father, who has always been frugal with smiles, would eke out a satisfied grin. *Well done*, he'd say. *Très bien.*

"And how about our friend Dante, hm?" As though we could get off that easy. "Nel mezzo del cammin di nostra vita... Peter..."

"Io... no. No, Io..." I swallowed. I knew this. I knew it by heart, but the words wouldn't come. They were there but hiding, teasing, taunting me. "Mi ritrovo... ritrovavo... I found... I found myself..." It must have been painful to watch.

"Mi ritrovai per una selva oscura..." The words rolled off her youthful tongue as though this were their original vocalization. And she saved me.

"Che la diritta via era smarrita," I finished unerringly, a light sweat broken over me.

My father looked at Severine, then at me, then somehow focused on both of us as though we were one entity. "Bene." And he smiled again. "Bene."

When he turned eighteen, my father had his name legally changed from Francis to Frank. Suffering with *Francis* through twelve years in the New York City public school system, where he found himself repeatedly embroiled in blacktop fisticuffs when some smart-mouthed bullies berated him for having a feminine-sounding name, he waited for this symbolic birthday to effect the long-awaited change so as to make it the first independent act of his newborn manhood. Our mutual distaste for our given names is one of the few things we have in common, though I would have stuck with Francis.

He is the black sheep of his family, one of three sons of southern Italian immigrants who spoke broken English at best, growing up humbly in Lower Manhattan slums, stuffed into overcrowded, underserved tenements, and hustling to survive the squalid streets, a common midcentury coming-to-America story. The brothers are now all successful in their respective fields. My father, the middle child, has a doctorate in modern continental philosophy and is the departmental chairman at his university. He is sandwiched between his younger brother, an administrative staff analyst in the New York City Department of Sanitation, and the eldest, currently serving the tail end of a five-year federal racketeering sentence. Considering his background, I always wondered how my father developed his interests, how he cultivated them while being raised by my grandparents, hardworking and single-minded people who had little time for books, and even less of an interest in them.

"When I couldn't buy my books, I stole them," he would tell me, a suggestion of pride in his voice, "like Genet. For him it was the *bouquinistes* along the quays of the Seine; for me it was the secondhand bookstores along Fourth Avenue, Book Row."

While his brothers were out working, playing ball, girl-chasing, running rackets, my father was home or at the library, buried in Hegel, Heidegger, and Kant, plowing through Proust and Joyce and Mann. They teased him lovingly, perhaps with a tinge of envy and a touch of apprehension at his inexplicable exoticism, dubbing him *il professore,* a nickname that stuck until he actually became one.

And so our childhood was filled with these things of which other children had little concept, estranging us from them and binding us closer to each other. We weren't completely reclusive, though; we had some acquaintances, people we'd say hello to in the halls, an occasional play date, a night at the movies or a few wasted hours at some sorrowful suburban pool hall or bleak bowling alley. But for the most part we kept to ourselves. We stayed together, always. There was no need for externals. No after-school sports, no cheerleading, no hanging out with the guys and ogling every prematurely developed female bust, no schoolgirl gossip sessions, no niches, no cliques, no best friends to whom we'd divulge all, no puppy love, ninth-grade crushes, or extended adolescent telephone conversations. Nothing but us.

And in our own way we did kid things. We had a playhouse in the backyard, a simple A-frame log cabin with ceilings just high enough for tots and a comparatively large unglazed casement fronting the rarely used patio of pale pink brickwork, on which the even more rarely used barbecue sat in utter neglect under a torn black tarpaulin. I always wanted a tree house, but that never came to pass—*too dangerous*—so instead we had this, our own snug space where I could read comics and Severine could peruse a discarded fashion magazine and imagine what she'd look like when she grew up, where we could lose ourselves in the mindless intricacy of a domino setup, a silly game of tag, a checkers match or a round of War that we would play on a wobbly wooden table while sitting on mismatched plastic chairs. Severine had some old Barbie dolls lying around. I took occasional target practice with my Lazer Tag pistol. It was not far from the main house, this second home of ours, but far enough to feel so, in a weedy, slightly forested area at the outer edge of our acreage, out of hearing distance from my father's deadly didacticism, his unceasing discourse. Philosophy had no place here. No linguistics or literature, deconstruction or phenomenology, postmodern aesthetics or metaphysics or logical positivism. Just two kids playing children's games, brother and sister, imperfectly manufactured intellects fashioned in his holy image, the Word become flesh.

Imagine we could stay here, Peter, and never go back. Imagine.

We would freeze in the winter.

Imagine though, if we could bring furniture and everything we need.

Yes, but we'd still be in the backyard.

True. That's true.

What's the matter, Sev?

I don't want to go back. I don't want to practice today.

Why not? You love the piano.

I just don't. Just not today. I don't want to today. I'm afraid.

Don't cry. Afraid of what?

I don't know. Just afraid. I just don't want to go back.

But we have to. We have to go back.

But imagine we didn't. Imagine we could live here. Here in the backyard, far away, in this little wooden house. It's big enough. Just imagine we could move in and not go back. And we could put furniture and an oven and a bed and all we would need. Nobody would know we're here.

Dad and Mom would know.

Imagine we could stay here forever.

Nothing is forever.

Peter?

Yes.

You think forever is the same as infinity?

Kind of, but not really.

So when you die, is it for infinity or forever?

Why do you want to know that?

Because I don't want to be dead forever.

It won't matter. You won't know.

But I'd like to know what it's like to die. I mean, I'd really like to feel it, you know.

Someday you will, don't worry.

But when you die you're dead, so you can't really know what it feels like to die. It's weird but… it's like sleep. You don't really enjoy sleeping, because you're not awake to enjoy it. You only know you feel better after you've slept, and you know you want it when you're tired, but while you're asleep you don't feel anything. I guess you can never know what the experience of dying is like, even when you die. I think I'd like to know what it feels like.

Too bad. You only get one crack at it.

Peter?

Yes.

I think if you died… I'd feel like I was dead.

I remember one muggy midsummer day when the cicadas were buzzing stridently and flying fast around the playhouse and we were chasing them with butterfly nets and laughing loudly like two little idiots, like someone else's children, until the somnolent sun was settling into place behind the trees and the cicadas quieted down and gave way to fireflies, which we also tried to capture, though they slipped effortlessly through our netting. When it got too dark to see and we were good and sweaty—and arid with thirst—we burst into the kitchen through the back door, at once fatigued and high on juvenile adrenaline. My father was there, unpacking a single mug from the dishwasher, inspecting its cleanliness before filling it with coffee, which he seemed to be drinking at all times, day and night. I grabbed two glasses from the cabinet and held them under the cold tap, then handed one to Severine. We drank ravenously. It was one of those times when plain old water is the best-tasting substance on earth, when you can feel the cool liquescence pulsing through your parched body while wondering how you ever lasted so long without it.

After I drained my glass and retook my breath, I saw my father leaning against the counter with his steaming stoneware mug, smiling at us.

"Long day in the desert?"

"It's like a hundred degrees out there," I said.

"It's not *like* anything. Either it's a hundred degrees or it's not." He lifted his mug and took a slow, cautious sip.

"Well, it feels like it is," Severine said.

My father nodded. His eyes swayed back and forth between us. He always had this way of looking at us that made me think he could read my mind, or worse, plant his own thoughts in it.

"You know," he said, suddenly good-humored, "there's a real solid chance that in each of your glasses there's at least one molecule of water that's passed through Plato's body."

My sister and I looked at each other, then down into our glasses as though we'd discovered flies floating on the surface.

"That's disgusting, Dad," I said.

"No. It's science. There are vastly more molecules of water per glass than there are glasses of water in the sea. Given enough time, you're bound to drink molecules that have passed through many other people. Probably anyone you could name throughout history, if you go back far enough to allow the hydrologic circuit to distribute its contents."

We stood there staring dumbly at him.

"Who knows who's in this mug?" He looked into the coffee as though trying to discern who exactly it was, then drank.

"Still disgusting," I persisted.

"I don't know," Severine said hesitantly. "I kind of like the idea of having something inside me that was part of Plato."

"That's my girl." My father raised his mug and winked at her.

"Come on, Sev. You want to drink something that someone else already peed out?"

She shrugged shyly, gazing into the fingerbreadth of water left in her glass.

"What it means, Pete, is that we're all intimately connected, like it or not," my father summed up. "We're all made of the same stuff. Everything in the universe is shared. This concept of individuality that we cherish is illusory. We spend all this time in search of others when, really, we *are* others. 'Je est un autre.'"

It would not have felt complete without this flourish of Rimbaud. I tilted my head back and let every last drop of water roll out into my mouth, then put my glass in the sink.

"Feel like a little duet?" my father said to Sev, a command disguised as a question.

She looked at me, smiled resignedly, and said, "Okay, sure," then walked over to my father, who put his free arm around her and guided her toward the sleek black baby grand. Just as they descended the single step into the sunken living room, she turned and shot a quick backward glance at me, as though she were being led to the gallows and wanted one last view of freedom. I refilled my glass, even though I was no longer thirsty, just to have something in my hands. Then came the lift of the clavier cover and the shuffle of tablature pages as they chose the piece, a few quietly exchanged suggestions, and finally the canorous tinkle of keys, something pleasantly light, fuguelike and baroque. At first, I resisted that familiar compulsion to move toward the music, but this broke down after only a few notes, and I soon found myself sitting sulkily on the couch across from them in the adjoining den, gripping my glass like a security blanket as its coolness leached into my palms and I watched my father's strained coordination between each printed and played note versus Severine's sedate and fluently intuitive execution, as though the ivories were extensions of her fingers, as obeisant to the brain's commands as any other part of her.

I could have easily dropped into a recuperative catnap had my mother not seen me there as she walked by on her way to the kitchen. She came in and sat beside me, absorbing the music for a few seconds before leaning over and speaking in a carefully tempered voice, so as not to disturb the recital. I had just taken a sip of my now lukewarm water, tanging my tongue with an unpleasant acidity that wasn't there in my first glass, making me wonder if I really was ingesting something old and rotten.

"What's wrong? You look like you swallowed a bug or something."

"Worse. Dad told me I just drank someone else's urine."

"What? Francis!" she yelled out, purposely using the name my father had long left behind, in order to ensnare his attention. His abrupt stoppage left Severine's contrapuntal line to shine by itself for a few moments before it, too, trailed off.

"Marie, you see that we're playing here."

"What's this about drinking urine?"

My father looked at me with an expression that was equal parts choler and confusion. I boldly held against his gaze for a moment before turning my eyes down into my glass, my spoiled water. By the time I looked back up, he had shaken off both my mother's question and his curdled aspect, found the spot on the sheet music where they'd left off, pointed to it, and counted to three, at which point they both came in as though there had been no interruption. My mother shrugged and smiled and shook her head as if to signal sub rosa that I should pay no mind to my crazy father—*crazy but harmless*, is how she would often stamp him—then tousled my hair and got up to attend to dinner.

So there I sat, still holding my wretched glass of water and luxuriating in a drowsiness that fell just short of sleep proper, as I watched my sister through heavy eyes and struggled with my dampened senses, trying to hear only her notes.

Another key reason I relate well to Don is that, notwithstanding the fact that he is a third-year doctoral candidate in theoretical physics, and in spite of his intellectually incisive and pragmatically lucid take on the world—or perhaps precisely for these reasons—he prizes the profound value of superficiality, recognizes the sweet of its balm balanced against the bitter peril of thinking. We get along swimmingly because we both try to sidestep anything of so-called weight, anything that would seem to be of applied importance. I think we understand each other so well because we unequivocally agree that living is a lost cause and human existence is the bane of the Earth. We agree that even if happiness were possible, we wouldn't want it, because it still wouldn't be sufficient. We both see life as a fruitless effort with only negative outcomes in the long run, but since we find ourselves here, we do our damnedest to piddle away the time with as much undemanding puerility as possible.

Example: sitting on the floor of his room, in front of the TV, he asks me during a commercial break, "How do you feel about lesbians?"

"What do you mean?"

"What do you mean, *what do I mean*? I mean, are you turned on by them?"

He changes the channel.

"Of course. I'm a heterosexual male, aren't I?"

"Naturally," he says, "but I'm obsessed by them," strongly sibilating the last half of *obsessed*.

"Interesting," I remark for the sake of saying something.

"Obsessed," he repeats with the same stressed sibilation, as he changes channels again with his arm held out languidly and the remote dangling from a limp wrist.

"Since when?" Susan asks calmly, sitting cross-legged on his bed, reading his mother's *Elle* magazine. "I don't know this."

"Always, but lately it's been worse. I don't know why. I can't stop thinking about it. At the most random moments I find my head filled with images of two women touching each other, groping, licking, inserting—"

"Yeah," Susan interrupts and holds up a hand. "We get the image."

He turns to his girlfriend. "I haven't told you?"

"You haven't told me," she says, not looking up from the magazine.

"You sure?"

"Yes."

"Because I really think I did."

"You didn't."

"Hm. Maybe I didn't." He sits for a moment in meditative silence. "Regardless, it's gotten to the point that if given a choice between having sex, ho-hum, white-bread sex, or watching two lesbians in action, just watching without any active participation as they feel and fondle and froth each other up, there'd be no question. I don't see how I can even be satisfied with orthodox sex anymore, knowing that somewhere out there, there are two girls going at it. It's such a sublimely beautiful scene, the union of two feminine forms. It almost brings a tear to my eye at the same time that it hardens my dick like granite. Of course, they'd have to be nice hot girlish ones, not all butch and barrel-chested with short, spiky man-hair, because male homosexual sex brings less than nothing to my table."

"This is clearly some kind of subconscious desire to be with two girls yourself," she offers, licking her thumb to facilitate the turning of a stubborn page, still refusing to lift her gaze. "Ever think of that?"

"I have," he says, facing me, though she made the proposal.

"Well forget it." Susan looks up at him. "It's not happening." She goes back to the magazine. "Not with me anyway."

"Even so, that's too facile an explanation, my wanting to be with two girls. And frankly, I don't buy into it. It would destroy the purity." His hands begin to gesticulate in amorphous ways that never really find their form. He returns to the previous channel and lays the remote carefully on the floor in front of him. "See, that's the game I'm hunting: purity. The uncontaminated purity of two females together. There's an unparalleled wholesomeness to this, a kind of unspoiled immaculacy. Do you see what I'm saying? Throw a guy in there and you ruin it. Too much body hair. Too much lustful acquisitiveness. Too much motherfucking testosterone. Do you see what I'm saying?" He is looking at me entreatingly.

"Yes," I tell him, working up a little excitement, for his sake. "Yes, I see what you're saying."

"Good. Good."

The commercial break ends, and so does the conversation.

I would sooner talk about things like this because what I strive for most of all is to maintain a comfortably vacant mind. My prime directive is to keep the mental clutter to a minimum, and to keep Chopin out of my head. Conversation like this is good.

But I wish I could sleep more.

And I wish I liked sports. I think this would be even better for me. I never played sports. I can't even dribble a basketball very well. Holding a baseball bat in my hands just feels wrong. Invariably, I was among the last to be picked for team sports in gym class. Though I am not notably nonathletic or prohibitively uncoordinated, my extreme lack of interest translates into a proportionate lack of skill. Still, I wish I were one of those guys who can spend an entire Sunday on the sofa with a beer in one hand and the remote in the other, steadily switching from one game to the next and shouting passionate profanities at the television when the quarterback throws an interception, munching chips and pretzels and every now and then adjusting the position of the scrotum with quick, manly jerks. I wish I could get all agog when the cleanup hitter wallops one way out into the left-field bleachers or the shooting guard lands a long-range three-pointer, smile with genuine glee and exchange high fives with a buddy when the scrappy little pest scores on a breakaway slap shot. I wish I could be excited about heading down to the schoolyard to play a little one-on-one or toss the pigskin around while making dirty jokes. I wish I were eighteen again at the summer house on Fire Island, swimming through the crepitant surf with Severine while our parents are out shopping for the barbecue, lying on our backs on the blanket, the coruscant droplets of water glittering like jewels on her skin as we dry off in the sun that peeks through the interstices of the clouds, and her legs draped across mine and that laugh that she laughs only with me when she makes fun of my braces and says it's a good thing she doesn't have them because there would be the risk of interlocking and then we'd never come apart, a thought that secretly swelled me with a full-bodied joy I could neither express nor contain, and her pale shoulders smooth and frail, nimble piano fingers small and fragile, and the scent of bayberry and pitch pine and earth and sea salt, the sweet sound of her breathing and the tender turbulence of the wind whooshing through the American beach grass.

And the sound of her breathing.

I wish I were a sportsman.

I remember as if it were an hour ago, her first day of grade school. Although she could already read and write in three languages and play passages of Liszt's scherzos and études though her legs could barely touch the pedals, she was timid to the edge of terror, trying to hide in my shadow as we made our way up those four steep, rubber-coated steps of the big yellow bus to face that sea of strange child faces, unwelcoming, snickering, sniveling, all but slavering like hungry hyenas, the older bullies sizing up potential prey and the younger ones seeking signs of weakness in their even smaller peers, sniffing out the runts of the litter. I was not strong. The hawkish upperclassmen could have pushed me around and stolen my milk money and I would have never fought back, not for myself. But with her tiny hand in mine, clasping tightly as though she'd sink if her grip were lost, I could have been Achilles single-handedly slaying legions of Trojans. If someone looked at her askance, I would have pounced on him, regardless of size or number. And they all realized this in that unnervingly intuitive way children seem to sense things, perhaps because they're closer to their unsullied animal instincts than adults are. Whatever plans they had to intimidate, to tease and taunt, faded as soon as we walked hand in hand down that aisle, one body, indivisible. They turned away and snuck only furtive glances at this pretty little newcomer in her pretty little dress with her soft, flowing blondness and vast brown eyes— what worlds in those eyes—under the aegis of her hypervigilant older brother, a charmed circle of protection that none could penetrate. Though we were the last stop and the bus was close to full, we found a couple of empty seats toward the middle, and I ensconced her guardedly between me and the window. She squeezed my hand and smiled up with sweet relief, and once the bus renewed its jarring passage toward the school, she leaned her head against my shoulder and I watched her watching the neighborhood pass like a reel of film projected against a long, winding screen, and I remember thinking that moments like this, little nothing moments with seemingly no greater significance beyond their unadorned occurrence, these moments are the ones I'll see, if it is true that one's life flashes past the mind's eye in the twinkling before death.

Spencer had exquisite bearing. Near-perfect posture. This sticks in my mind. The guy had first-rate carriage, both sitting and standing. It was impressive. I still see him there in class, tall and poised and athletically built, dressed in layered shades of black and constantly removing his dark tortoise browline frames to squint at the lecturing professor in earnest contemplation. There was certainly pretension galore, but he reinforced this with a refined intelligence and an urbane charm that seemed to justify it, an almost courtly continental civility as companion to his downplayed cosmopolitan sophistication, all of which set him well above the rest of us petty provincials. Even today, when his name rings in my head, that face pops up before me, that great toothy smile, and I feel first a light paralysis, followed by the intense and unilaterally painful frustration of a cluster headache.

When my thoughts are led back to the beginning of the Spencer period and those colorless college days, I am reminded of the importance of classroom topography. He sat a row in front of us, two seats to the right of Severine and three from me, in Existentialism and Modern Art, one of three classes we shared, she and I. It was the first semester of my junior year; she was a sophomore. We went to the same university for two reasons: it is a reputable liberal arts college, and since my father is a tenured professor there, it was completely free.

Spencer's success was due in part to his forgoing the tactic that had brought so many others to ruin: trying to gain access to my sister through me. Most who were interested in Sev were also intimidated by her beauty and brilliance, and since we were always together, I was seen as an easy pathway, the key to a locked door. *Befriend and butter up big brother, convince him of your worth as a suitor, and you're in.* Had they realized how erroneous this calculus was, that if I'd so much as suspected any kind of serious interest, I would have taken measures to smother it at birth, perhaps they would have chosen a more straightforward route. With Spencer, however, the intimidation factor was seen and raised by his stout self-confidence and benign moxie. He was three years older than Severine and one of the few who hunt their game directly, armed with Blarney Stone eloquence and a lively wit that were evident each time he spoke. I have always harbored a deep disdain for those uninhibited, spontaneous souls who speak up so freely in class.

He'd had his eye on her from the beginning. This I knew. I always knew. I would catch him stealing sidelong glances, subtly turning in her direction when there was no practical reason to, flashing a sly smile now and again, which she never returned, even if she had noticed. He was patient, cunning. He took a few weeks to feel out the situation before doing anything. It was not until early October that he decided to occupy the empty seat next to her and eliminate the safe zone, leaning over before class began and speaking in a voice slightly louder than a whisper: "I've been dying to ask you something."

"Ask then," she said, unsurprised, as though she'd been waiting for him to speak to her. "We can't have you die, can we?"

"We all die," I said, and was ignored.

"You have an Italian last name and a French first name. Which one is it?"

"This is what you're dying to ask?"

"What can I say? I'm more interested in the devil in the details than the god of great things."

This is the best he could come up with? I thought.

But she smiled. She smiled and answered him: "Italian by blood. French by books."

"I see," he said, nodding, smirking. "Books are thicker than blood."

She could've stopped it right there. She could've prevented everything with such minimal effort: an aloof grin, a dismissive turn, simple silence.

"Disappointed?" she said.

"Pas du tout."

His response was perfectly pretentious and unimaginative. It reassured me momentarily. If he thought a few feeble French words were enough to get my sister into bed, he was sunk. My fears were groundless. I was almost embarrassed for him. But she smiled again, with no distance or detachment. I could not believe that she smiled again, that she took the bait, wasting time and breath exchanging lines in this lame, flirtatious quid pro quo.

It ended there for the moment, as class commenced, and for the next eighty minutes I simmered and steamed, thinking only of ways to abscond without any further contact. When the time came, I tried to rush us out as though we were already late for an important meeting and couldn't spare a second. I tried to occupy her, but he just wouldn't give up. He re-engaged her, taking the opportunity to formally introduce himself. She responded with her own introductions. The runway had been cleared.

"Where did you learn French?" she asked.

"I'm Québécois."

Québécois? Nobody uses that word. And he's a fucking Canadian. Canadians aren't real people. They're bastardized French. Auxiliary Americans. Does Canada even really exist?

"C'est beau, le Québec."

"Yes," he affirmed, smiling, "yes it is."

No. No it is not.

"Is your father Doctor Niletti?" he asked.

"Yes. That's Dad."

"I took his semiotics course last semester."

"We've been taking that all our lives," Severine said.

He laughed.

She laughed.

They laughed.

"Seriously, it was a good course. Your father's a demanding teacher, but it was worthwhile. Really, I'm not just saying that."

"You think?" I said. "You're not just saying that? And yet, you did just say it."

He didn't answer me.

"You're a philosophy major?" Severine asked him.

Do you care? Do you really want to know this?

"Yes."

"So are we," she rejoined.

"I guess it's not bad having a philosophy professor in the house then?"

"Worse than you can imagine," she said jocosely.

More laughing, more smiles, more desultory chat, more waggish comments and accompanying chuckles, things in common and mutual complaints, all in the space of time between the classroom and the parking lot. In the face of my unheeded prompts to set a faster pace, they sauntered along as though strolling through the park on a sluggish summer Sunday.

"Do you live on campus?" he inquired.

"No, home, with the philosophy professor," she provided.

"In-house PhD? Can't go wrong there."

You already made reference to that.

"And you?"

"I have a place in Brooklyn."

"Oh?"

"Yeah. The Heights. Right by the bridge, steps from the promenade. Great view of the city."

The Heights? Who says this? The Heights?

"You should swing by some time, get off the Island," he recommended.

"Just to be accurate, Brooklyn is part of the Island," I said. "Geographically speaking, of course."

There was a brief lacuna in the conversation.

"Sure. Sounds nice, doesn't it, Peter?"

"Sounds... nice."

"Well, here's my car. Are you far? I could give you a ride."

"No, we're parked right over there," I informed him.

"But thanks."

"Anytime."

"See you Thursday then."

"Yes, Thursday."

"Take care."

"Bye."

"Bye—uh… Peter, was it?"

I'm not answering. I won't answer that.

"Yes. Peter, my brother."

Peter. Why Peter?

"Right. Okay. See you in class."

You cannot be smiling. You cannot be happy to have met him. Are you happy to have met him? Why? Yes, he is… dapper. Okay, he's intelligent enough. It's not a revolutionary coupling of characteristics. Nothing to panic about. Nothing yet. He'll go away, as everything does. Le temps s'en va, le temps s'en va. The semester will go quickly. Talk. To me. Stop thinking about him and say something to me.

"He's a philosophy major," she said.

Anything but that.

… le temps non, mais nous nous en allons…

I cried the first time she went out with him. I lay on my bed with the lights out and wept like a child, like an outcast high school student, a pouty, petulant kid whining over something he can't control. I lay there sobbing shamefully, and I hated it. A few minutes before he arrived, she came into my room, scented with a perfume she had never worn before, or had never worn around me. She sat next to me on the edge of the bed and put her hand on my head, letting it slide to my face to wipe away a tear. I look back at my melodrama with embarrassment now, but I still remember what a special kind of hell it was to hear her rushing around to get dressed and made up, all primmed out for his imminent arrival. Downstairs, Leonard Cohen was singing

"Night Comes On," from time to time my father's voice blending unsuccessfully with the inimitable as he and my mother sat at the kitchen table engaged in one of their epic trilingual Scrabble competitions.

"Stop now. Stop being ridiculous. You're making too much of this. I'm not going to run away with him. It's a date." She tried a bit of tough love.

"A date?"

"A night out. I'll be back. You know I'll be back."

"I don't know anything anymore. And I don't go out. Why do you have to?"

The song ended. I could hear the shuffling of wooden Scrabble tiles and the clinking of glasses.

"Go out with friends, go out with whoever, I don't care. Just not with him."

"He is whoever," she whispered, trying to make her voice calmative, though the words worked against it. "It doesn't matter that it's Spencer. It doesn't matter who it is. Don't say things we both know aren't true."

"Then don't go," I murmured through fractured breath, turning to look at her in the dimness, made up like a porcelain doll. I was almost begging. "We'll tell Dad to say you're sick, that you've got one of your marathon migraines that take days to go away. I'll do it myself. I'll go down and tell him. I'll tell him that you're real sorry but you can't even get out of bed, you can't even put on the light because of the migraine aura. I'll tell him you'll call when you feel better, that we'll see him in class."

"Silly Peter." She smiled and pandered to my infantilism. "My silly Peter."

"You don't really like him, do you?"

"We just met." She paused, looked down at my comforter, and flattened out a wrinkle in its timeworn fabric. "Do something. Anything except lying here. Read. Write, for God's sake." She grabbed my hand and squeezed it supportively, and her eyes grew large with this suggestion, as though her pleading itself would convince me of its merit. "You're always talking about being a writer. Just pick up your notebook and write. I know it's in you."

Empty encouragement. I waited before speaking, to give the impression that I was considering this, though I was quite sure it wasn't in me. Nothing was *in me*. "You can't really like him."

She smiled soberly at the failure of her proposal, patting my hand. "Don't worry. I don't really like him."

How could she like him? How could she like anyone but me?

The doorbell's ring was followed by the scuff of my father's slippered feet approaching the front door and the unmistakable timbre of Spencer's voice, in which I always tried to find something not right, something disingenuous, a touch too feminine, deceivingly insincere. I would have settled for a stutter or two, a mispronounced word or a minor malapropism, a hint of a lisp, a superficial solecism. I could hear him speaking, relaxed, genteel, and congenial, confident yet shaded with the right amount of deference required of a well-groomed young man addressing an elder, specifically an elder on whose daughter he has designs. And my father liked him, a man who does not like many people. I pictured him liking this fetching young fop in his tailored wool sport jacket that I could all but see from my bed, his slicked-back hair, thick and dark as midnight and tastefully glimmering with product, complementing the polished loafers, the modest dash of cologne, the dimpled smile, the debonair gait, the dreamy dark eyes and delightful deportment. I heard laughter, deciphered approval within this laughter. I listened to them talking down-stairs in the foyer, a professor and one of his most promising pupils, directly below my room and the bed where I lay in dry tears while she sat there distracted, already gone.

"How's that paper on Chomsky working for you? I liked where you were going with your outline."

"I did too. But now I'm not so sure. The more I get into it, the more the behaviorist argument gains ground."

"Slippery bunch, Skinner and his ilk. Stick with Chomsky though. He'll see you through."

But Dad... Dad, fils de pute, how the hell can you not realize what's going on? Don't you see that he doesn't give two shits about Chomsky or Skinner, that all he wants is to fuck her, that he wants to deflower your daughter, stick his prick in my sister? Don't you know that's all they want? That's all they ever want.

If I could have just held her there and taken her under the covers and shunned the world outside the room, eschewed all that was exterior; if I could have stripped the world of every-thing that was not she and I, shed all save the essential... If I could have just done that.

"Did you hear that?" I hissed, furious. "He's siding with the behaviorists, for Christ's sake! He can't be trusted!"

She laughed, though I hadn't meant this to be funny, and bowed her head. "You know I have to do this," she said softly, almost imploring. Her eyes always seemed to be on the verge of tears, even when she wasn't. "You have to let me do this."

"I have to let you? To let you?"

She stayed with me for another minute or less, as though fulfilling an inveterate obligation. I could feel her tensing, eager to go. Pulling her hand off mine, she took a deep breath and got up off the bed, relieved of duty.

This for him. All this for him.

"Do what?" I continued. "What do you mean? Do what? Leave me for the night or just leave me?"

She slowly bent into me, her hair cascading onto my face, and pressed her lips to my forehead, resting them there for a moment, just long enough for me to grab her arms and pull her down with me. Which I did not do.

And then she left.

"Don't go," I said, one last time. "Please."

She pushed the hair off her face and walked out of my room without looking back.

She wasn't perfect. I always took it for granted that she was, but now that I think about it, recalling as many unembellished details as possible, it becomes clear that she wasn't. When you got up close, real close, you could see that she had pores. They were minuscule, but you could definitely make them out if you scrutinized, if you knew what to look for, pores like everyone else, sebaceous little apertures marring the marmoreal surface of her skin. They were there. So in the final summation, she wasn't perfect, despite the sad, deep brown eyes and the wealth of sandy hair that on its worst day flowed like the wild wheat fields in Auvers. She was not perfect despite the magnificent melancholic smile that compelled you to look away until you couldn't stand not seeing her, bantam hands that always had a slight chill to them, a voice that spoke only in good-byes.

No, she wasn't perfect. Perhaps if I had realized this sooner, it would have made all the difference.

But enough about her. *There will be time... There will be time to murder and create...* If nothing else, there will be plenty of time to think about her, to try to absolve myself from culpability. For a while I considered going to church, embracing a faith I never had to begin with. I've always been captivated by the concept of confession; you kneel in this austere little box and regurgitate your sins to a sacerdotal stranger, say a few prayers and walk out with a clean slate, tabula rasa. *Go in peace to sin again.* It almost seems fun. I wonder how many Our Fathers a priest would assign should I go to confession and let him in on the deal, every searing stitch of the story. I wonder if he would just say, *Don't waste your time, son. We have a honeymoon suite reserved for you on one of the lower levels, a floor below Paolo and Francesca, but say an extra Hail Mary when you have a spare minute, just to keep in shape. Can't hurt.* However attractive the idea of absolution is, I have never taken it seriously. I couldn't. I can't. My father, despite his strict Old World Roman Catholic upbringing, is an unflinching atheist who formed us rigidly in this tradition. He claims that he did not want to raise his children under the veil of lies that is religion, any religion.

"The real mystery is trying to determine who's more ridiculous, Christians for thinking the messiah came or the Jews for thinking he's still on his way," he would say, as soon as we were old enough to risk extrinsic exposure to such daft dogma and doctrine. "At least Muhammad had enough sense to head to the mountain once he realized the mountain wasn't coming to him. Religions are like brand names. Same thing, different label. Zero nutritional content. Deception, a way for man to comfort himself, to make himself believe that he is not alone in the cosmos, that there is some worthwhile end to his toil and trouble, some goal to all this confusion, that life is not simply an anarchy of atoms and driftless bodies in motion. It is important to remember that illusions, howsoever comforting," (dramatic pause followed by more dramatic climax), "are still illusions. We must understand modern religious traditions as literature, folklore, and myth, and approach them the same way we do the ancient Greek gods and Egyptian deities. With interest, not belief."

Tyrannical dinner-table philosopher. It's nothing for him to say; he had Santa Claus as a child, and the choice to disregard him. We had neither.

My parents tried hard not to play favorites, or at least tried hard to make it seem as though they didn't. It wasn't their fault; they can't be blamed. I would have favored her as well. It was as if I were the faulty first draft, the rough copy replete with errors, while she was the polished and well-edited manuscript ready for publication, a transcendent trophy for the triumph of their finest connubial efforts. Everything I did she could top, almost from birth, and she seemed to make no effort. It just came naturally. As an infant, she seldom cried during the night; I never stopped. She ate anything that was fed her; I was a projectile vomiter and deathly allergic to beets. She learned to walk while I was still mastering my crawl, and she hardly fell during the process. I played a decent alto sax and had bouts of bad acne all through high school; she was a gifted pianist with a Cream of Wheat complexion. It goes on indefinitely. And although it was at times tough for me to always be the silver to her gold, I didn't resent her for it. I became resigned early on to the way things were, was glad and grateful, in a sense, relieved that the spotlight was not on me, because I never had too deep an interest in anything. Her shadow was enough for me.

But beyond these practical talents, there was something else that set her apart, something innate and elemental, a certain peerless grace to her way of being that rarely failed to leave an impression in her wake. The nescient eye might see it as a flair for the dramatic, but there was no artifice or affectation about it, nothing histrionic. It was just her, unselfconsciously nonpareil, Severine being Severine. She didn't try to be more than I could be; she simply was.

She outdid me to the end with her indelible and undirected departure, leaving no means to eclipse her, no leeway for me to fashion a better self. Her exit ensured that she would forever own pride of place in the hearts and minds of those around us. I will always be her unsung older brother, a minor planet, dark and lifeless, to her shimmering sun. And though I am here and she is not, I remain—even to myself, most importantly to myself—only a point of reference, a reminder of something greater that once was. Every time my name comes up, regardless of the circumstances, they will think of that lost, lovely young girl who had everything in the world going for her, a full, far-reaching future ahead of her, and who for some reason, some horrible and unfathomable reason, walked into the ocean one unusually cold spring night.

2

Being and Nothingness

Love, if one could feel it, would be a kind of defiance.

— Carole Maso

My life takes place in a room. I don't work, never really have, never want to. This may sound impractical, even ridiculous, but I have an unassailable fear of working, a deep-seated contempt, a legitimate phobia. I can't stomach the concept.

When I was eighteen, I had a job in a small independent video store that I liked before I became an employee of it. I still remember thinking, on those long-ago Friday nights when I would stop by to rent a DVD, how interesting it would be to work there, surrounded by movies and candy and cool clientele that would be uncommonly thankful for a well-informed film recommendation—the least offensive way of earning a few extra bucks between classes. After the first week the place was ruined. It became tainted with the stench of labor, and I knew I'd never be able to return, not even as a customer. Luckily for me, the shop went out of business only a few weeks after I was hired, crushed by the larger corporate stores that were just coming into vogue back then.

You'd think my parents would give me grief about this: twenty-five years old and I just sit home and do nothing all day, nothing but the basics. I eat and sleep and watch television and go for walks; the consummate sponge. I don't even read much anymore. I'm not interested in discovery. If anything, I reread. After all, Plato did say that we're born with every kind of knowledge we need—*nous*, the timeless and immortal epicenter of our souls—buried deep within the dark and cavernous reservoirs of being, but the spirit forgets it all during metempsychosis, forcing us to relearn everything with each reincarnation, making us re-manufactured psychical matter—and amnesiac at that—thrown into a shiny new suit of flesh that starts on its ruinous road to death the day we're born. It hardly seems worth the effort, the work of a lifetime, to dredge up a past that we are only bound to forget again. And again. And again. But who am I to argue with Plato?

For years I have been waiting, getting up each day with an irksome expectancy, an ever-fainter vestige of youthful hope and instinctual optimism that I never really trusted to begin with. I open my eyes and think that maybe this will be the day, maybe today life will begin, real life, and all that has come before will have been just a warm-up, a preparatory stage with no relevance or significance to this new, authentic life. Then I will be able to forget the past, or make peace with it. Then I can try to live a life outside a room.

But nothing changes. Every day the sense of expectancy grows dimmer. That's the only change. I wonder if it will ever fully dissolve, or at least become so miniscule that its effects will be nullified, like the process of radioactive decay whereby an element steadily diminishes until all that remains is an almost undetectable amount that will not completely dissipate until the host does. I wonder if I can lie low and wait it out. I try to live by the principle that if you act quickly and unthinkingly enough and perform all voluntary functions with a definite degree of mechanical uniformity, like brushing your teeth or washing the dishes, you can preempt thinking, or at least preempt thoughts of any serious kind, thoughts with any gravity—the deadliest kind. If you approach living as nothing more than a repetitive series of mundane utilitarian tasks best executed by rote, you might be spared the worst of it. But it's absence that haunts me, even in my untroubled sleep. It is amazing how quickly the presence of absence steadily diminishes until it, too, fades into something resembling normality, as if nothing is absent at all, as if there had never been anything there in the first place, and so now there is nothing missing, nothing gone, because implicit in absence is an initial presence, and as the remnants of this initial presence erode with time, so does its palpable absence, until all that remains is a wraith, an impression, vague and nebulous, a hot spot where something once was, though you're no longer sure exactly what, as if it were never real, as if it were all some oneiric experience that has itself become blurry and indistinct and elusive.

The transition from then to now is unforgiving. Reminiscence shaves the past paper thin. It wears away the narrative so that I must fight to fatten the memories I am left with.

She preferred Dostoyevsky to Tolstoy but couldn't choose between Proust and Joyce, Sartre and Camus. This I remember.

She loved Leonard Cohen, Lou Reed, and the Rolling Stones but couldn't get into the Beatles, though not for want of effort. She avoided chess because she wasn't as good as she would have liked to be, and she did not enjoy losing. She sometimes found herself engrossed with the simplicity of checkers. She claimed my indolence was contagious, my inertia infective, but she never really caught either. She liked Freud until she came upon Lacan, and then she thought both of them were basically just wrong, though amusingly interesting. She hated television, disliked movie theaters, but appreciated fine filmmaking. She suffered severe hemiplegic migraines that often debilitated her. She liked the ocean but not so much the beach. She liked the sun but not the sand.

She always removed her shoes when entering the house. I imagine she took them off and left them neatly side by side on the shore, like abandoned twin toddlers, before walking into the water.

Her favorite season was autumn, with winter finishing a few steps behind. Spring was tolerable to her until it approached its border with summer, which she found hellish, for the most part. She had a strange fondness for frozen breakfast foods, pancakes in particular, waffles a close second. She adored Munch and Pollock, Giacometti and Cézanne. She always wanted to draw but swore she had no aptitude for it. She did not have a favorite novel. She liked riding her bicycle but was embarrassed to be seen on it. She preferred Beethoven to Mozart, Schubert to Brahms, Schoenberg to Stravinsky. She hated video games. She was never crazy about Don.

She rarely ate pizza. She loved walking aimlessly, especially in shady arboreous parks and along the seashore. She used to whine sometimes. She detested the inconvenience of travel but always wanted to see places. She prized the feel of a brand new book, the scent of an old used one. She had a very discreet and demure little chuckle with those she didn't know well; she didn't realize how endearing it was. She appreciated the catchpenny sentimentality of greeting cards but never sent them. She once said she thought poetry could save the world; she knew how to laugh at herself. She never wore shorts or sneakers and hated baggy jeans. She loved *galette des rois*, Entenmann's iced devil's food cupcakes, and extra chunky peanut butter. She played table tennis but not billiards. She didn't like ice cream. She would jog sporadically, every day for a month or two, then not at all for three. She was against exercise for its own sake, hated stationary bicycles and weight benches, and reserved an especial loathing for treadmills. She liked fall-blooming flowers in spite of herself. She was enamored of burgundy—the color, not the wine—but rarely wore it. She didn't hate sports but had no interest in any particular one. She used marble composition books exclusively for school, leather-bound notebooks for her journals, and refused loose-leaf. She said that every color was somehow a different shade of blue. I was never sure what she meant by this.

She never deviated. She never said she loved me, not in the way I wanted, but she never said she didn't.

I can't complain about my home life. My parents don't hound me about anything and pretty much leave me to my own devices. We see each other at meals and beyond that quite infrequently. Since Severine's death, my father has buried himself in work even more than he used to, coming home from classes and secluding himself in his study, where he is supposedly working on a book, the subject of which he has not yet divulged. Probably some recondite scholarly exposition that none but a scattering of other professors will read, or say they did. My mother, a primary school teacher, has resumed a life relatively similar to the one she had before, this after extensive psychological treatment and accompanying medication. She cooks a lot, and cleans—the house is always immaculate—humming little nonsensical tunes as she flits about the kitchen: children's songs and pop hits from the seventies and eighties. This is a perk for me, as eating comes second only to sleeping on my short list of favorite things to do.

Once in a while she'll ask me to go to the store to pick up some ingredient she forgot on her daily after-school excursions to the supermarket. I think she does this to get me out of the house, out of my room, to give me an airing. Apparently, she believes this healthy for me. She worries. She's a mother, still.

She comes up to my room the other day while I'm lying there on the verge of a twilight nap. The television is on but muted; the low-frequency hum of its electrical resonance relaxes me. My mother is not crying, though it is obvious that she has been. She cries often, and when she realizes that someone has noticed, she turns away and wipes her eyes and constrains a smile to spread across her permanently anguished face, as if to say, *No, no, I haven't been crying. I'm fine, really. See? I'm good*, which mostly serves to intensify the sense of unyielding dolor that radiates from her core. She comes up and sits on the end of the bed. I think about feigning sleep but don't bother translating the thought into effort.

"You have to get out of this room," she says quietly. "Go somewhere, just for the sake of going, just to get out."

I don't say anything.

"It's like a tomb in here. No fresh air, no sunlight. These things have an effect on the body. More than you'd think." She looks to the window as if considering a move to draw the blinds and open it. "I can't force you, but you have to get out." She pauses, turns from me, trying to keep herself composed. "I can't lose another one. I can't go through it again. Losing something that grew inside me, that came out of me… You can't know." It seems like a meek accusation, somewhat condescending, as though her loss is greater than mine, her pain trumps mine. But I know she doesn't mean this. "You have to get out of this room. For me."

I don't say anything. Her brittle composure fissures and threatens all-out collapse. She starts to cry. I'm embarrassed by this, embarrassed for her. Such corny little fripperies, emotions are, such frivolities. And speech, these sounds we make; the second a thought is transformed into speech it loses everything, every iota of authenticity, and I can't take it seriously. It's as though meaningfulness is filtered out somewhere along the way, and what finally makes it to the larynx and through the lips is an absurd combination of tones and timbre, diluted and disrobed, beggarly vocables that are not worth the price of pronunciation; that this is our most effective form of communication speaks volumes.

"Get up and do something, anything, but don't just lie there. You can't keep lying there all day... every day."

"Why not?"

"Do you think she would want you to sit here rotting?"

I glare at her, digesting the possible implications, the unknowable answers to that question.

"Just try," she pleads. "Just make an effort at least."

"Are *you* making an effort?"

She looks down, rubs her cuticle. A tear falls on the back of her hand.

"I read a little before," I tell her, finally. "That's doing something. Something I would think you'd approve of."

I don't know why I want so to hurt her at this moment—hurt her with my reticence, my bullheaded refusal to bond, my inability to release—because if there is anybody I do feel for, even if it is more a sense of pity than anything else, it is my mother, an inferior character like me, overshadowed by personalities and circumstances she deems greater than herself, though she is an intelligent woman, articulate, cultured, a wonderful cook, and still quite beautiful. Her big brown eyes and finespun flaxen hair are integral parts of the physical prototype from which Severine was developed.

"I am getting out. I might go to Don's later." From one room to another.

"Good," she says between tiny inchoate sobs, a vague smile stretching her lips. Though this is not the kind of outing she had in mind, it's better than nothing. "How is Don these days?"

"He's... Don."

"Right. The only guy who leaves his house less than you do." A little recalcitrant laugh tries to rally and break through the hedge of weeping, scarcely starting its revolt before being quashed.

"The world is just one big room."

Watching as she palms her eyes to stanch the tears, though she knows she can't, listening to her sad sniffles and staggering breaths, I give in and place my hand on her shoulder, almost brought to weeping myself. Almost.

"I'm getting out, Mom."

"Good." It's all she can say. She looks at me and seems to want to add something but can't find the words. Either that or she wants me to cry with her, to break down and embrace her and admit—verbally or otherwise, as though my withholding were causing us both great pain—how woefully much I miss Severine, to mingle and meld our loss into a fortified alloy of agony so that we might console each other, we might be there for each other, as a family should. She wants this for herself, and I refuse to give it to her. I will not be generous with my grief. I will not package and parcel out my misery.

Finally, she shifts her gaze and scans the room, taking in the overstocked bookshelves and general sterility of my lair, gives out a moist laugh, wipes an eye.

"This room hasn't changed much since you were little."

Joining in her survey of the surroundings, I picture the typical teenager's room I never had, reeking of pot smoke and sour sneakers and pubescent sweat, walls thumbtacked with posters of ephemeral rock stars and provocative magazine clippings of the sexiest celluloid idol of the moment, maybe some fun-filled photos of good times with good buddies, a school memento or two, a few crippled action figures and nostalgic stuffed animals left over from childhood. I'm thinking of that one time I taped a picture of Metallica above my desk and sat there all afternoon staring at the four surly longhairs in ripped denim and battered leather, preparing my defense for when I would inevitably be questioned as to what on earth had possessed me to put up such an unseemly portrait, and finally ripping it down before anyone saw, tearing it to irreparable shreds as though my identity could have been stolen if it were found and reconstructed.

"I didn't go through many phases," I say. "Most kids do, I think. But I didn't."

"You didn't."

"Neither did she."

"No. She didn't. I sometimes wish you would have. Both of you. Such ideal children. Good little soldiers. Everyone always said how blessed we were to have such good, smart, healthy kids."

"Blessed is the fruit of thy womb." I make a snappy sign of the cross in front of her face.

"You *can* cry, you know. It's allowed. You can mourn."

I bunch my eyebrows in confusion. "Can? As in, physically able to?" Again the urge to injure, to claw at whatever's nearest to me, followed by immediate regret, the claws turning in on myself.

"You can show emotion. There's nothing shameful in being human."

For a second, I think this is my mother lashing back at me, which would be perfectly understandable, if not totally out of character. But no, she means it. And she knows she's on shaky ground.

"Ah. There's the rub. The whole *human* part."

Seemingly spellbound, my mother sits at the foot of the bed, studying my room for what feels like a long time. Then she gets up to leave. When she reaches the door, she asks me if I would like her to shut it.

"Yes, please," I reply.

She wants me to get out of this room and live. But what she fails to see, what nobody can understand, is what this room means to me, even beyond the safety of its space and solace in the familiarity of objects. I often imagine what it would be like to never leave, never, not even for the bathroom, a few steps away, or the kitchen, one flight down. I wonder if I could do without those sporadic sojourns to the grocery store and night walks around the block. I like to hypothesize that life can take place in a room, that an entire lifetime can pass within the same single room, without the occasional visit to the doctor or dentist, evenings in restaurants, movie theaters, and nightclubs, family trips to Disney and adventures in exotic lands. Existence sans frills, a life without weddings and birthdays and anniversaries, a room without windows, no seasons or sun, no backyard swimming pools, Sunday dinners, or playtime in the park, nothing but the unrivaled intimacy of a four-walled world that doesn't bleed or sweat or shed tears, that doesn't bewail lost opportunities and condemned ardor, a world where the dead stay dead and rest in peaceful unremembrance, and time slips silently through days and months and years without notice and without fuss until all its contents are dispersed forever in a single asthmatic breath.

I live on the outskirts of a pullulating metropolis, in the purlieus of the planet, the periphery of the world, in its shadow, its waste, its unwanted overflow, where nothing happens and nothing is expected. Nowhere. So close to everything that you are constantly aware of how far removed it is. There is a certain reassurance in this alienating solitude of a suburban landscape, foreign to city streets and deceptively virulent enough to worm its way into the fabric of everyday life so that you feel it natural to remain irrelevant, preferable to remain dormant. And despite this awesome alleviation of the burden of ambition, they tell me that life is elsewhere.

La vraie vie est absente.

I have to get out of this room, she says. But she has no idea.

There were sixteen years of a relatively normal brother-sister relationship, a close one, yes, very close, but with nothing that would stigmatize it as significantly irregular or aberrant. Perhaps the seed was always there, germinating, waiting for the decisive moment that was to make everything before it seem like a necessary preamble leading up to the inevitable, the natural culmination of a progression—telos. The decisive moment was puberty, a disgusting word for a revolting phase of life. It got us both around the same time. Cut down in the exalted ignorance of youth.

Around thirteen, I discovered masturbation and spent my spare moments in the bathroom with the water running, as if this would throw everyone off, as if no one had any idea why I was in there with such persistent regularity, sometimes every few hours, as if I were the only one who knew about this greatest trick of all and was greedy to keep it to myself. Masturbation was my hebetic asylum, an anchor in the whirlpool of teenage loneliness and perplexity, a way of convincing myself that it was all right to be alone because I really didn't need anyone else. I didn't need a girl. I could take care of things perfectly well by myself. But as often as I would mentally reiterate this mantra and sequester myself in the pursuit of some private pleasure, a few minutes later I would feel lonelier than before.

Severine's moods started swinging drastically during menarche, which only exacerbated things because she was a moody young person to begin with. We both were. We found ourselves clashing, arguing more frequently and about silly, trifling things: her hair dryer plugged in on the bathroom counter, my razor left lying blade up on the sink. She would neglect to keep the curtain inside the shower and drench the floor. I'd leave the toilet seat up and forget to cap the toothpaste. All this bickering brought us even closer, the storm before the calm.

And so what finally happens feels as if it's supposed to, as if there cannot be any other way, and all the confusion dissolves and disappears because she is, after all, a version of me, because she *is*, simply because she is, and this is how it must be. This is authenticity and safety and the only possibility for unity in my father's anarchy of atoms, the reduction of life's complexities to elementary particles.

October. A cool fall night. I am seventeen. A senior in high school. The windows are open and a bracing draft slips through the screen, carrying the fragrance of chrysanthemums, conifers, and burning wood. She steals into my room. It has been a long time. A while ago, she had suddenly stopped coming. I never asked why. But now she comes in, creeping carefully through the unlit passage like a seasoned spy, part of the darkness itself. It is very late but I rouse immediately. She climbs in quietly, as she used to, as if she is afraid of waking me, and slips under the covers. I am lying on my side, facing the wall, my back to her. She pushes herself into me, her body's curves conforming to mine. I remain still. She is crying. I think this is a female thing, a tempestuous raging of hormones that she can't help, like my throbbing. I ask her what's wrong.

"I don't know."

Her hair tickles the back of my neck, and her small chest presses lightly against me. I feel myself harden. How I hate this tormenting and spiteful thing between my legs that feels as though it has been continuously hard since age thirteen. I have never been with a girl, and now my sister is lying next to me in my bed, and I am hard. But there is no awkwardness, nothing that feels as if it shouldn't be exactly as it is. I don't turn around. My eyes are wide open and I lie there. The wind whistles and rattles the window screen. Her sobs are intermittent. I turn, put my arms around her. My stiffened sex touches her leg and waves of sensation respond, vibrate and flow, and finally stabilize. I start to tremble. I tell her everything will be all right. I hate when people say this, hate hearing myself say it, but I can't say anything else, so I say it again. *Shhh. It'll be all right. Shhh.* What will be all right? I brush her hair back. I feel her cold hand on my chest and recoil ever so slightly. She slides her hand slowly down to my stomach, hesitates, slips her fingers under the elastic waistband of my pajama bottoms, kisses me on the chin, the cheek, my mouth. Her face is wet. When she touches me, the sensation is overwhelming. The only parts of my body I can feel are those in direct contact with her flesh. I am immobile, as though I can't breathe, speak, or think. Now her clothes are off. I don't know how they came off, but she is naked, touching me, kissing me, our legs intertwined, the delicate hair between her thighs rubbing against me, her fingernails scraping my skin. And then I am inside her. I do not know how, but I am inside her. And it is the first time I have ever really felt alive.

It doesn't take long. A single tear is wrested from its reservoir, trickles down a cheek, and pools in the crease of my lips.

This is the way the world ends.

Afterward, we lay supine on the bed, keeping even the slightest intimation of movement to a minimum, soaking in the silence broken only by the rustling leaves and the intermittent swish of a car cruising down the block, slowing to a crawl at the stop sign in front of the house, and continuing on its way, each one sounding the same, homogenized, almost soothing. I was nervous, euphoric but unsure, dreading the moment we would have to move, to extricate our entwined figures, trying to grasp exactly how this had changed things and wondering if she was wondering the same thing as she lay static and soundless at my side.

Breaking the trance, the unvoiced ban imposed on movement, I put a timid hand on her moist belly. She remained still for a moment, then laid her hand over mine, and with that one modest gesture, those few inches of transit, brief motion then rest, my worries evaporated. Whatever qualms and misgivings had arisen were instantly dispatched. A holistic heat surged through my being. An unprecedented magnanimity overtook me, suffused with a sense of connectedness with all that I was and was not. My body felt unbearably light, as if I were about to float up off the bed and hover in the space between it and the ceiling, giddy with an overflowing of emotion for everyone and everything around me, my parents sleeping downstairs, my friend Don across the street, my books smiling at me from their glutted shelves, even my father's punishing academic relentlessness. I was indebted to all of it, grateful for who I was because she was there and because this had happened. No, things would not be the same, not ever again. I was found.

We slept.

I woke a few hours later to find her staring stonily at me.

Sev? What are you doing?

She shifted her legs over the side of the bed and sat up, redirected her stare down to her bare feet.

Where are you going?

I don't know.

But it's the middle of the night. Don't go. Stay here.

I wonder what they'd think. I wonder what he'd think.

It doesn't matter.

Of course it does. It always matters. It will never not matter.

I don't care.

Yes, you do.

But not here. Maybe with everyone and everything else and at all other times, but not with us. Not now. Not now and not here.

Yes. Even with us. Even here and now.

Don't worry. This is right. I know it is. You know it is.

She turned to me, arched her lips in a tiny smile, and lay back down.

If you weren't here, Peter, I don't think I could make it.

She hugged me breathlessly, desperately, as though I were the one thing binding her to life.

But I am here. And I always will be. I will never not be here for you. Now go to sleep. The best thing to do is to sleep when you're feeling like this.

Yes. It's the best thing.

It's the only thing.

From my bed I can hear an orchestra of insects, just on the other side of the window. They say this sound is legendary in Provence, but I wouldn't know. I've never been there. It reminds me of those long, lethargic summer nights when we would sit outside on the front porch's teak bench, late, just the sounds of nocturnal nature and the infrequent slamming of a car door from a nearby driveway, a dog's bark, flickering TV radiance in the neighbors' window, neighbors we had mostly never met, people seen from afar going in and out of their house carrying bags of groceries, walking to the end of the driveway to collect the mail, raking leaves, shoveling snow, taking down Christmas lights. We'd listen to the buzzing bugs and watch the windows to make sure nobody was spying from across the street, though even if anyone was awake, it would have been hard to make out much of us in the dark, the house being set a good distance back from the curb. I would be holding a snifter of XO cognac, whose taste and odor repulsed me, just to say that I was drinking cognac, and she would slowly sip her tea, the aroma of lemon washing into me, thickened with August's humidity. Her skin was damp on those nights, damp and fresh, the back of her head in my lap as we watched the stars through holes left in the leaves by gypsy moths. *Europe's most heartfelt and lasting gift*, she called them. Her lips had a trace of sweetness to them, as though thinly glazed with sugar.

I'd tell her she was silly for drinking tea on such a warm night; she'd tell me it was idiotic to drink cognac when I didn't even like it.

"How do you know?" I said in mock seriousness. "Of course I like it. What makes you think I don't like it?" I brought the glass up to my eyes to admire. The brandy's amber glow was mesmeric in the cloudy porch light, but the thought of it touching my tongue and—far worse—blistering my throat on its way to my stomach nauseated me.

"I don't know. Just that every time you drink it that bitter-alcohol frown creeps onto your face. It gives you right up. It looks like you're being forced to drink gasoline. Like Plato with his hemlock." She laughed.

"Why would I drink something I don't like?"

"I don't know. To look more like Sartre? Next you'll be smoking a pipe."

"Sartre is so passé."

"Okay. Derrida then. Also a pipe smoker."

"Did he drink cognac?"

"He must have."

"Why?"

"Because he was French, if nothing else."

"Ah. Of course. Well, in any case, it's an acquired taste." I was still staring fondly at the glass, willing myself to believe I liked it.

"Go ahead, take a sip," she dared.

"No. I will enjoy my cognac at my own pace. It's a slow pleasure. I will not be pressured or rushed." I played along.

"Please, big brother."

"Absolutely not. My pride has been irreparably injured. Je refuse."

"Oh, s'il te plaît. I'll do whatever you want if you just take one sip, one little sip."

"One?"

"Just one. A little one. This much," she illustrated with her thumb and forefinger. "Even if you hate it, one small sip can't be that bad."

"I don't hate it."

"So go ahead."

"Mmm... okay."

I continued to gaze at the glass, trying to convince myself that something so pleasing to the eye could not possibly taste that bad, and as I tipped it back, I held my breath until the last instant, to spare myself the toxic whiff that preceded the liquor's polluting of my mouth's interior. I was anticipating something harsh; this was god-awful. I tried to prevent my features from contorting, but it was impossible.

"There it is again!" She pointed at my face, and her head bobbed in my lap with laughter. "You just can't fight it. You're frowning. Your eyes are tearing. Your nose is crinkling. It's like you're being poisoned. Maybe you can pull it off on someone else, everyone else, but not me. You hate it. Admit it. Just say it. I want to hear you say you're forcing yourself to drink something you hate." She reached out and ran her fingers daintily around the edges of my mouth.

"Yes, well, okay, maybe, but I enjoy hating it. The better things in life require conditioning. Remember Spinoza? 'That which is excellent is as difficult as it is rare.'"

"Uh... yeah. But I somehow doubt he was talking about cognac."

"And besides, I'm only drinking this because absinthe is verboten. Absinthe, of course, would be my first choice." And I'd bend down to kiss her.

I think I was not unhappy once.

And then alone, on the same porch, sitting on the single slate step waiting for Spencer to drop her off, no matter how late it was, often long after my father's curfew—though he didn't seem to care. I brought the issue to his attention when it began to happen more regularly.

"Severine's still not home, Dad," I told him as he was doing some after-hours work in his study. "She's been staying out later and later. You've noticed this, haven't you?"

"Yes," he said after a few suspended seconds, keeping his gaze on the papers in front of him.

"And you don't find it strange, deserving of attention? Maybe a tiny bit alarming?"

"Actually, I think it's about time she found someone nice."

I didn't bring up that, in point of fact, *he* found *her*.

"Ah. Nice. You think he's nice then? I'm sure you don't mean *nice* in its early English usage. Foolish, stupid, senseless."

"Not unless we're speaking thirteenth-century English."

"And because you think he's... *nice*—pleasant, friendly, agreeable—it's okay that she stays out with him until all hours?"

He tilted his head and peered at me professorially from over his glasses.

I continued: "You don't really know him, though, do you? Yet you say he's nice? I'm concerned with this word, because it's had such a murky history in terms of sense development, and I don't want to misconstrue what you mean. What exactly do you mean? What qualities have you seen in him that might justify your calling him *nice*, in whatever way you choose to interpret that word?"

He laid his pencil on the desk and removed his glasses and slipped a flared temple tip into the corner of his mouth, retaining his incorruptible composure. "You're right. You must know him better than I do. Explain. Help me understand why I would not be justified in calling him nice." He removed the temple tip from between his lips and pointed it at me. "Why don't you tell me what qualities you've seen in him that would make him *not* nice? Nice... in the current colloquial." He held his glasses up to the lamplight and inspected the lenses. Then he wiped them with a cloth, checked them again, sprayed them with some liquid lens cleaner, and wiped them one more time.

I couldn't answer. I had nothing to say to my father, who sat there staring at me, upset more for my having disrupted his metaphysical inquests than anything else. I couldn't tell him the truth, why Spencer wasn't nice. I couldn't tell him that it was precisely because I failed to find anything particularly *not* nice about Spencer that the situation was so grave, that my life was being torn in half and the one who was doing it, the bad guy, didn't seem very bad at all.

"You haven't noticed then?"

He craned his neck expectantly and made a minor adjustment to the concavity of his frame's earpiece, double-checked it under the desk lamp, and bent it back the other way. I had to say something.

"Well... uh... for example... just off the top of my head... sometimes, when he speaks... his mouth gets very dry, and you can hear the inner workings of his tongue and gums as he forms words." This is truly one of my pet peeves, so though I'd never actually caught Spencer in the act, it was easy enough to work myself up about it. "It sounds like he's chewing a corn muffin and seriously needs some water to wash it down. It's really kind of foul. It might seem trivial and petty, but it's something. I mean, yes, he speaks well. There's no doubt he's a bright kid. I won't argue with that, but I really find this noise... vexatious."

"Vexatious."

"Yes. Vexatious. Yes. Extremely unsettling. Like you cannot believe. I've met people who do this. It's not totally uncommon. But still, it's exasperating."

"Exasperating."

"Yes. Just like it's exasperating that you're repeating my words."

He looked at me without saying anything.

"So you haven't picked up on this?" I hassled him. "Dry mouth is a clinical condition. There is a reason we have salivary glands."

He twirled his glasses by the stem.

"It can't just be me. I'm sure she's noticed it, being with him as much as she is lately. Pay attention next time. You'll see. I'm not making this up."

"Sartre had a lazy eye, Heidegger was a Nazi, and Socrates was pig-nosed. Should we dismiss them on these bases?"

"Should we just excuse them? Forgive their faults because of their merits?"

He nodded, but not in affirmation. "She'll be home soon," he said, replacing his glasses and guiding his eyes down to the papers on his desk.

"Yes. Sooner or later. I guess it doesn't really matter."

As I'd done before, I returned to my post to wait. This was life at twenty, in my college prime, my halcyon years. I imagined other young bucks at frat parties and dingy off-campus dive bars, bedding freshman coeds in disordered dorm rooms and spending white nights cramming for finals between bouts of beer pong and stoned Twister, and though this lifestyle did not entice me in any way, though I probably would have despised such people if I had actually known any, I envied these lives I envisaged. I envied any life that was not mine.

And on too many nights, my own life consisted of sitting and waiting till Spencer's shiny black midsize SUV rumbled slowly up the driveway. I'd watch him get out, trot around to the other side, and gallantly open the door for her, watch him kiss her chastely on the cheek (a little peck at the outset, during the initial weeks of courting, nothing ungentlemanly, nothing too presumptuous), return to the car, and wait until she reached the front door before tapping the horn once, lightly and quickly, as he pulled out and drove off. The quintessential date cliché.

By this time I'd be drunk on sadness and brimming with anger that would fizzle out as soon as she came near, as soon as she brushed against me or put her hand on my arm. One night as she was coming in, I asked if Spencer ever thought it strange that her brother would wait up for her on the porch, in plain view. She said he'd never mentioned anything about it.

"Maybe he thinks I just sit out here to get some air, or that I have a penchant for watching cars pass, or that I'm keeping an eye on things like some loyal watch dog."

"Maybe."

"Maybe he thinks I enjoy this, that I'm an insomniac and can find nothing better to do than sit here."

"Maybe he doesn't even notice that you're there."

"Or maybe he thinks I still don't trust him, that I don't like him much."

"Or maybe he just doesn't care, or doesn't give it any thought. Or maybe you give it too much." She didn't raise her voice, but it was all hardness.

"Your lipstick is smeared," I told her.

She loosened her scarf around her neck and huffed.

"I'd like it if you didn't wait up for me anymore, or at least if you didn't wait outside."

"What? It bothers you?"

"Yes." Her tone toughened even more. "When I come home and see you sitting outside like an expectant father, it bothers me. It—" She contracted her facial muscles to restrain herself from going further, rested a beat, and continued coolly. "Yes, it bothers me."

"At least it does that then."

She sat behind me, on the bench, while I remained on the step with my back to her. We said nothing for several minutes, adjusting to this new feeling of friction between us, waiting for the acrimony to abate.

A peculiar animal noise emanated from the underbrush along the perimeter of the property.

"We could go away," I said weakly.

"Where? Where could we go?"

"Somewhere. France."

"Huh," she scoffed. "Wouldn't that be just… too obvious?"

"Venice. Rio. Reykjavik."

"It's all been done already."

"Cape Town. Oslo. Antarctica. We could go anywhere. It wouldn't really matter. *Where* is not the question. *Where* is not important."

"No, it wouldn't matter. It wouldn't work."

I turned halfway back and eyed her peripherally. "Why?"

She didn't answer. She was looking past me into the dark street, littered with dead leaves and a few fallen twigs.

"It's cold," I said, turning away from her. There would be an early frost later that morning, and I could already see my breath condense before me.

"Very cold, for fall. It's only going to get colder from here."

"Only fall. And already I miss the spring."

"It'll come back. Eventually."

"You think?"

"It always does."

"No. It just always has."

Nobody really dies around here. Technically they do, but not really. Death should have heft, a certain distinctive gravity, poetic depth. But when someone dies here, even someone you know, it's devoid of reality, as if you were only reading about it in a book or a newspaper, a five-line obituary on some neglected page. There is a distance from death that makes it feel fictional. This place is like a way station, a purgatory; you have to go elsewhere to really die. Dying is not permitted. There's no death here, only evermore massive malls and the great existential quest for a home with the biggest bang for your buck and the highest possible resale value.

Maybe that's why she went to the shore to do it, to get as far away as possible from all the quotidian artificiality, to remove herself from the man-made world before she extracted herself from the world itself, because she wanted death to feel authentic and organic, because she needed her dying to be unobserved, real to herself alone, something that nobody else could be a part of, nobody.

Maybe.

She must have known she'd be back, though, that she'd drift back to shore and end up a caption. She was too smart not to realize that there's as little glory in dying as there is in living.

I remember the headline, page three of Monday's paper:

20-Year-Old Girl Found Drowned Off Shore
Probable Suicide

I see the morose expressions on people's faces as they sit at their breakfast table with the newspaper spread out before them, rejuvenated by two days of relaxation and ready to face a new week, sipping morning coffee and scooping out sugared wedges of grapefruit halves and crunching on buttered toast, a husband and wife reading the account of my sister's death. They shake their heads and say: "Could you pass the cream please?" "Did you read this about that young girl who drowned herself?" "Yes, I heard about that." "Terrible, isn't it?" "A real shame." "So young." "And apparently an accomplished girl. Piano player. Model student." "Too bad." "I wonder why she did it?" "What could've been so bad at that age? Should've been the best time of her life." "Youth is wasted on the young." "Really, what a shame." "And pretty, too." "There's a picture?" "Yes." "That's unusual. Let me see." "Hm. She was a nice-looking kid." "Told you." "Too bad nobody realized she was in trouble sooner. I mean, the parents or something." "That's true. You'd think somebody would've seen the signs." "There are always signs." "Could you pass the cinnamon please?" "Here." "And the wheat germ?" "Let me have the apricot preserves." "That's good stuff, isn't it?" "I prefer blueberry, but it's not bad, this one." "What's the difference between preserves and jelly? Or jelly and jam?" "I don't know." "And marmalade?" "No idea. But we're running low on half and half." "I'll pick some up later."

And then the page turns. There are ads for clearance sales on mattresses and a voucher for a free two-liter bottle of soda with purchase of a large pie at the local pizzeria—dine in only.

"The Dow went back up, thank God. I was really worried for a while." "Yes, it could've been tragic." "Nothing's ever sure in the market." "Not in this market. That's for sure." They kiss, and the husband leaves for work, and the wife rinses the dishes and loads the dishwasher and cleans the crumbs from the toaster and gets the kids ready for school and prepares her grocery list, and that's the end of it. My sister's death is over. Forgotten. A passing sound bite, a few words in a newspaper that is headed for the recycling plant, lost in the pile, fused with pages of movie times and sports scores, advertisements for white sales and ten percent–off coupons for men's business suits.

Death makes a mockery of life, sits patiently in the back row and knows it will get the curtain call no matter what. But life, in turn, cheats death out of its claim to anything more than a moment's seriousness.

There's no dying in the suburbs.

To cap it all, Spencer was an artist. A painter. Classically trained. Art school and everything. Mentored by a draconian Russian formalist at the École Nationale Supérieure des Beaux-Arts in Paris—though he abandoned his studies there to wander

Western Europe with a sketchpad and a Moleskin notebook, teaching English for a spell in Seville and spending a few months meditating at a Buddhist retreat just south of Dijon, eventually trickling down into North Africa and rambling about the upper half of South America before returning to his home continent, where, inspired by his travels and the exposure to such a variety of cultures, he chose to pursue philosophy. While he was no regular on the gallery scene, no big-time player, he was not without talent, and his few shows had met with mild success, or so I was told. And the truth is, I didn't dislike him, much as I tried to. Maybe I hated him. Yes, I'm fairly certain that I hated him, but I really didn't dislike him. I would gladly give up everything to be able to go back and avert his entrance into our lives—this I admit freely—and I place the lion's share of the responsibility for her descent in his hands, whether the evidence supports it or not, but there was nothing particularly dislikable about him. It was what he represented that was abhorrent. What I hated was the concept of Spencer—Spencer in the abstract— much more than the actual person.

The point is, he was an artist. He was an artist, she was an artist, and I was not an artist. And in the light of retrospect, it becomes clear that this did grease the hinge.

It happened shortly after he made his initial approach in the classroom, before they started seeing each other so consistently. It was the first falling rock of the landslide, pivotal to everything that came after.

It had become customary for us to walk to the parking lot together. While less than thrilled with the idea, I was somewhat relieved by the routine constancy of his company, convincing myself that this was as far as it would go: group walks to the car, ambulatory chat, and a little harmless flirtation. His manner was agreeable. He was intelligent, a masterly conversationalist, and the kind of guy that I wouldn't mind knowing under different circumstances — radically different circumstances. So long as things kept within these parameters, everything would be fine. But they didn't. One afternoon, shortly before Halloween, while saying our good-byes and see-you-Thursdays, he put forward, with a soupçon of winning diffidence: "Listen, I paint. I'm a painter. I usually don't tell people this because I haven't sold much, and I'm really... really kind of embarrassed asking — feel free to say no. There's no obligation, of course, and I don't want you to feel uncomfortable about it..."

"Painter?" I said. "Like what? Houses? Interiors? Cars?"

No one was amused.

"I'd really like it if you'd model for me. For a painting, I mean. I'd like you to sit for me."

She refused to look at me, wouldn't even give a glance to gauge my reaction; no cursory search for approval or opposition in my mien. She blushed and, usually so sure and unfaltering in speech, staggered her response. "Uh... yes, of course. I mean, I've never done it before. I really — I've never — I don't know how good a model I'd make. I'm not that good at sitting still, but — "

"Perfect." He stayed her stammering with a hand on her arm. "No buts. You'll be perfect."

He smiled. She looked down. He was the only guy who could make her do this, the only one who could make me feel so far away from her while she was standing next to me. He knew her acceptance was an important early victory, and with me there it was that much more than a simple step toward securing some extracurricular time with my sister. His opening salvo was successful. I had been unconditionally bypassed. Whatever sense of big-brotherly authority I had — or thought I had, or was trying to project—had been summarily negated. I was already being painted out of the tableau, blended blurrily into the backdrop like a diaphanous smear of black ash.

A date was set, and I insisted on coming, warning her that we didn't really know him outside of a closed classroom, and it would be almost reckless if she were to go alone. At first, Sev protested my chaperoning.

"Why do this to yourself? You'll only be bored, sitting there watching paint dry, literally."

I fell back on the ever-reliable, ever-citable Nietzsche for support: "'Against boredom, even the gods struggle in vain.'"

"Pff. You're worse than Dad, throwing around quotes like you're enlightening the world." She looked at me, pseudo-serious, and shook her head. "Or like a spiteful monkey flinging feces."

I won the day, however; she agreed, with some reluctance, and we found ourselves at Spencer's door one brisk and feature-less Friday evening after midterms. He welcomed me warmly with an overly familiar two-handed shake, his left hand lightly clutching the underside of my right forearm to emphasize his pleasure at seeing me, almost as if he assumed I was coming, as if it had been implied in his asking her to do this in the first place. His airy, high-ceilinged second-floor studio was spotlessly clean and well-ordered, with a certain antiseptic quality about it that veered toward the obsessive. I was impressed. It had both a classy contemporary and restrained retro vibe that jibed well with each other. There were a few unframed paintings leaning upright in the corner, presumably his, and several more hanging on the clean white walls: a Chagall reproduction and Schiele's portrait of his sister, along with two others I didn't know. He offered us drinks and apologized for his small apartment's lack of space. Severine remarked that it was cozy and comfortable, with a relaxing aura, whatever that meant. Cringing, I concurred with the original assertion, that it was indeed kind of small. I deplore the word *cozy*.

By the time the stage was set, pleasantries exchanged and requisite small talk out of the way, I was already a little loose, having downed two quick glasses of red wine, which he no doubt had bought expressly for the occasion, and I sat in the corner like a presiding judge, nicely settled in a capacious and cushiony rocking chair whose fleecy umber exterior seemed uncannily congruous to the crooks and planes of my body, actually a bit interested in seeing how this was going to happen and not wholly unreceptive to enjoyment at this juncture. He led her to an off-white bonded leather couch against the wall, instructed her to sit and get comfortable, and prepared his material, setting up the easel several feet from the sofa, equidistant between me and Severine.

"I feel a little stupid," she said with an unsure grin, trying out various cumbersome positions. "Do I look as stupid as I feel?"

"Depends," I said, upbeat. "How stupid do you feel?"

"You look wonderful," Spencer overrode me.

She smiled, which she'd been doing much too often lately, especially in his presence, and it was more than cheap jealousy that so embittered me. I don't like smiles. I don't believe them. They are insincere, contrived expressions of pure idiocy. Smiling people look simpleminded, asinine, and savage, baring their teeth like beasts, peeling back their lips like clowns, ridiculously wrinkling their eyes and dumbly dimpling their cheeks. And she wasn't dumb. There was no reason for her to smile so much.

"Merci, Monsieur."

"Je vous en prie, Mademoiselle," bowing affectedly.

I ground my teeth and swished the wine around in my mouth.

She wore a slinky black crêpe dress that hugged her hips and loosened only slightly at the legs and ended several inches above the knees, with thin spaghetti straps and a scooped front, not too low, just enough, revealing polished shoulders and the smooth upper plane of her chest. He walked slowly backward toward his canvas, studying her as she positioned herself, not quite intently yet, just setting an image in his head, gauging the arrangement of her parts, visualizing the lines of her form. "Help yourself to more wine, Pete," he said without turning, as he continued to examine her. "Or if you're hungry, there are some snacks in the closet. No need to ask. Take whatever you want." I thanked him and helped myself to another glass. His mention of snacks provoked in me a yen for some peanuts or pretzels, maybe a few chunks of cheese—I was thinking a nice smoked Gouda—and crackers with a handful of Black Corinth grapes, but I was too comfortable to consider moving. The wine was improving my humor, and the last thing I felt like doing was lifting myself out of that chair.

As she settled into position, he took in the angles and lighting and installed himself behind the canvas, and all speaking ceased, quite naturally, as if words were no longer welcome, as if there were no place left for speech and any utterance would have been peremptorily sucked into the surrounding vacuum. Everything became coated with a bizarre silence, a silence complicit with the jazzman's trumpet crooning in the background and the almost inaudible scratch of pencil on paper and bristles on canvas, a silence out of which could be woven innumerable inferences and acid allegations, governed by the insinuation of movement, the nuance of guarded glances and slanting, spectral stares. The atmosphere was charged with something we all felt but could not pin down, a kind of concentrated gravity bolting each of us into randomly designated places, like wind-strewn seeds taking root in an untilled field.

She began by sitting upright against the back of the couch, a bit stiffly, somewhat shy and apprehensive, long legs crossed decorously with her snowy calves exposed under the dress, hands resting left over right on her stacked knees, then reversing to right over left. By now, she should have been used to being the center of attention, but she shifted nervously under the light, fidgeting like a restive child struggling to still herself for a year-book snapshot, taking occasional sips from the glass of wine she had been nursing for the last hour, twiddling her fingers, toying absentmindedly with her hair.

I watched him watching her. I drank.

Spencer wore a crisp white button-down with the sleeves neatly rolled at the elbows, flat-front chinos, and oxblood loafers. I mistakenly chose to speak and said, "You're sure that's the right shirt to wear while you're painting, Spence? I don't think paint comes out in the wash. Or maybe the paint-splattered look is what you're going for." He didn't answer. I don't think he liked being called Spence, if he even paid attention to what I said. Neither painter nor model acknowledged my words, as though they hadn't been spoken.

After a while she grew more at ease, noticeably relaxed. She didn't hesitate to shift positions, to cross or uncross her legs, to gather and deftly twist her hair into one long, thick braid that fell apart behind her back, to let her eyes close for a restful suite of seconds or fall naturally on what they would, on the far wall (against which a black-quilted platform bed rested), the wooden floorboards in front of her, the curtained window backlit feebly with streetlight, on Spencer who was painting her, reimagining the eyes that watched him as he essayed to capture every variation of pose and change of position in a drawing, a sketch, to encapsulate her essence in a few figurative lines and a fluid complex of colors. He would instruct her to move a smidgen forward, to turn her head a centimeter to the left or pull her hand back a notch, to lift her chin that crucial quarter of an inch.

With nothing much to do but watch him paint while she sat there, I filled my glass a few more times, the last refill emptying the bottle, which doesn't necessarily mean that I drank so much, considering that both Spencer and Severine had already had a full glass each. Moreover, I don't get drunk from wine, which I have been drinking since I was a kid. What I mean is that my father has had us drinking wine with dinner from the time we were very young, and it is unusual that I feel anything but a mild buzz, a minor mellowing out, a strange, conflicted sense of well-being and paranoia. So I suppose it was a combination of the wine and the gentle jazz, the tedious monotony of his metrical brushstrokes and the soft squeaks of the rocker, that made me drowsy enough to fall asleep. And it was a good sleep, a nice deep red-wine sleep, a sleep that lasts only a few minutes, half an hour at the most, but which seems much longer, and after which you feel thoroughly refreshed.

Before drifting off, I heard Spencer say, "You all right there, Pete? Not too bored?" I responded with one of those hebetudinous grunts that try to summon more than the body can supply and end up sounding inanely effete, and they both chuckled. I remember that she chuckled and dropped her head, and when she raised it she was still laughing, her face regal and rubicund. And I remember how she was sitting as my eyes began to close.

She was leaning with her right elbow on the couch's cushioned back, hand against the side of her tilted head, fingers buried shallowly under a layer of hair with a few fingertips poking out like fleshy, misplaced protrusions. Her left arm lay at rest on her lap, in which she held the half-empty wineglass. One leg was bent limberly under the other so that she was basically sitting on her ankle, with the right shoe removed and her bare foot jutting out from its place beneath the left leg, which dangled drowsily off the sofa's edge. Her lips were closed and slightly arched at the corners, almost a smile but not quite. Something suggestive. Her eyes were wide and alert. Her hair had fallen forward onto her shoulders and chest. I remember this so well because he asked her eagerly to hold this pose as long and as statically as she could, asked her with a kind of suppliant authority, as though they'd stumbled together—artist and muse, maker and mannequin—across a once-in-a-lifetime pose that would have been irretrievably lost if she'd batted an eyelid or twitched a toe. And as my eyes closed, I glanced at his partially painted charcoal sketch—which was excellent—and tried to take the image with me as I went under, as though I could engrave it into my subconscious, will her away from the profane waking world and into the inviolate sanctity of my dreams.

When I awoke, she was facing sideways, with both legs curled up to her chest and her arms wrapped around them, chin resting on the summit of a bent knee. She was naked. Her black dress lay neatly folded over the back of a chair off to the side. I sat there, trying to understand what was happening, my head still hazy from the alcohol and the nap. I couldn't move. My limbs felt both puny and ponderous. It was as though I were being held in place by invisible manacles, somehow stapled into my seat. I couldn't see her face. She was naked. I knew only this.

For a moment, I held out hope that I was dreaming, but only for a moment.

It was a few seconds before Spencer put down his brush and headed haltingly toward her, stopping at intervals to assess her positioning, reminding me of his presence and forcing upon me the full effect of what was going on. My sister was naked and he was painting her. I knew this would happen. I had come to make sure that it didn't, and yet it did. It was almost too predictable to be real. I had failed miserably, tragicomically.

Traversing what seemed a much longer distance than it was, he arrived before her, placed two tender fingertips below her chin, and directed it up off her knee, then took a couple of paces back. But he wasn't quick enough to return to the canvas.

I am not a big guy. I am no brawler and do not consider myself a passionate man, but something extraordinary stirred in me, something strange and wonderful, pellucid and primal, something that impelled me to rise, unquestioning, unafraid, boosted by a breathtaking urgency and obedient to its coercion, determined to act. The wineglass fell from my hand and shattered. The sound of glass smashing against the floor filled all my senses with a kind of engulfing synesthesia, and for a single instant I was freed from thinking, driven by raw animal instinct. I felt the world, felt it shifting in me like a kicking fetus. I moved with involuntary grace, my legs taking me toward my target like a practiced apex predator descending upon his ill-fated prey. I was sailing. Weightless. And then, in an unfortunate flicker of comprehension, I returned to full awareness and realized what I was doing. I was a bird halted in mid-flight, questioning my ability to fly and slowly losing altitude, flapping my wings in desperation and panic as I sank steadily toward the ironfisted earth. This intense, adrenalized fusion of jealousy and rage, hate and hoarded bitterness and whatever else was thrown into the mix, this propellent force that was so unwavering a heartbeat ago, so forceful and feral and unfettered, died out as quickly as it had come, like a match that flares up and is immediately blown out by a passing breeze. I found myself rushing him, a particle set in motion and guided by a single uncompromising charge: collide with Spencer, strike him down. But by the time I got there, whatever fire had fueled my precipitous blast had just as quickly burnt itself out, and I was reduced to myself. I was thinking again, trapped. Ineffectual and impotent.

I stood before him, trying to rekindle the vitality I'd had a second earlier, trying to recall how badly I had wanted to feel my knuckles against his flesh, and how this was the best feeling I'd had in a long time, so pure and directed in its devotion. At this point, Severine was not even involved. I just wanted to hit him. And there, about a foot in front of him, staring stupidly as he cleaned a brush with which to paint my naked sister, I froze.

He smiled at me. He actually smiled at me as if I had hurried up to get a better look at the painting, as if he were saying, *What do you think, Pete?* I did what I do best: I reflected. This was a way out, a chance to avoid taking action. I could simply rub my chin contemplatively and say, *Not bad, but I don't know about this splotch of sepia,* and that would be the end of it; that would explain my sudden rise and approach and abrupt halt. Excuses unnecessary. But I looked at her looking up at us from the couch, sitting naked—her great gleaming eyes, her exquisitely arched back, the silken shine of her shins—and I swung wildly, without thinking, without seeing, without connecting. The guy was right in front of me and I managed to miss him, my rocklike fist disintegrating into an unwieldy quintet of feckless fingers. Maybe I grazed him, tickled his chin, skimmed the edge of his ear, but before I could regain my ground for another assault, I felt his arms encircle my waist. Rattled into sudden sobriety and pumped up way past normal, I successfully pushed him off, stepped back with the quickness and agility of a hungry middle-weight underdog, and swung again, a nice straight right that connected solidly with the broadside of his jaw. He staggered slightly sideways, slightly stunned, probably more from shock than pain, and I paused, lowered my hands—astonished at my own pugilistic prowess—relaxed my defenses long enough for him to come at me again, this time knocking the wind from me and bringing us both to the floor, his superior bulk pinning me down. Still, I pounded his back. I pulled his hair. If I could have bitten him, I would have. I think I was screaming obscenities but don't remember exactly which ones.

Distributing his mass and weight with a skilled wrestler's proficiency, he pinioned my arms with his kneecaps and ground my face into the floor with the flat of his hand, my head turned toward the wall, my cheeks squished between palm and wood. I was completely immobilized. Vanquished. Convinced of my submission, he slowly removed himself from me, first pulling his hands off my face, then sliding his knees from my shoulders. He rose to his full height like a rearing grizzly bear, seeming much taller than he was, standing above me yelling: "I was only changing the angle of her head, that's all! That's all!" His face was bright red, his hair disheveled. I imagined I looked the same. Only much worse.

I got to my feet and moved toward him again, without hesi-tation, this time driven by adrenaline and embarrassment and some weird kind of petrified pride as Severine, naked, stepped in front of me. I stopped short. She was naked. She put her hand on my chest. I felt that I was shaking terribly. It was probably more a severe nervous twitching, a sort of Saint Vitus's dance, that caused my right eyelid to flap fretfully and my upper lip to quiver and my left cheek to jerk, palsylike. I remember hoping this quaking was not as observable as it felt.

"Don't," she said. "Stop this."

I looked at her, standing before me. Her eyes were so wide, and she said nothing more. I had a strong urge to slap her, to smack her hard across the face, a resounding soap opera slap that would leave a flaming brand across her lush white cheek, after which Spencer would spring viciously onto me before I could inflict further damage, subdue the dangerously demented brother, and emerge as the hero of the night. I wouldn't give him the chance.

"Are you fucking insane?" he roared, standing a few feet behind our intermediary.

"She was naked," I said, not necessarily to him, my voice as unstable as my body.

"You're fucking crazy!"

He went to the couch and sat down, chest and shoulders heaving, hands on knees. We were both out of breath. I walked over to the chair where her dress was, picked it up, and pushed it into her hands. I felt him watching me closely, set to pounce at my slightest provocation.

"For Christ's sake, cover yourself," I said.

She slipped it on. He moved toward her cautiously, keeping a prudent distance.

It was at that moment that I knew I was capable of killing somebody, just then as I watched him lean over and ask sensitively if she was all right. I had never before thought about it with any kind of serious premeditation, but I suddenly realized, in a blaze of intuition and a fevered flash of images showing my mind how I would do it, that any person can erase another if the right combination of circumstances presents itself. It's nothing oracular or grandiose. No resplendent revelation. Everybody has the capacity to kill, even if this potential lies forever untapped, bridled *by the better angels of our nature*. We all have a hibernating Raskolnikov somewhere inside, and we each have our own reasons, our own fuses. But there is always a fuse.

Nobody said or did anything for what seemed a longer stretch of time than it actually was, no more than a couple of magnified minutes. What could I do, apologize? Spencer walked to the bed and sat on the edge, smoothing his disorderly hair—which had been soundly mussed up by my tugging—into a semblance of order, a few deracinated strands sticking between his fingers. A viscous streak of saline wetness dripped from my chin down my neck. I don't think he hit me. I must have bitten my lip. I wiped my chin and literally licked my wounds while Severine sat on the couch, gazing at the floor, knees locked as though closely guarding her chastity. I stood there in a paralysis of shame and satisfaction, tasting my blood.

"I'll be waiting outside," I said, after a bunch of seconds. "Come out when you're ready."

She didn't answer. My eyelid continued its twitching, distorting my field of vision like a maladjusted vertical hold, and I wondered if either of them could see this, because it felt like the only physical disturbance of the arrested atmosphere. I turned and walked out of the apartment, through the crackled Kentile hallway and down two flights of linoleum stairs and out of the building, where the November air was prickly and fresh and washed over me like a mountain mistral. It felt inexpressibly good. I sat on the porch steps. It was a long time before she came out.

I am going to be twenty-six soon. My father says, *What I wouldn't do to be your age again,* and shakes his head longingly at the fickle fortune of youth. He tells me that at twenty-five I have the world on a string. This amuses me, makes me think of that Sinatra song, brings to mind an iconic image of the blue-eyed Chairman doffing the brim of his jauntily perched fedora and smiling with a rakish cheerfulness that was and is and likely will be forever foreign to me. I should tell my father that this string of his feels like quickly shredding butcher's twine, but it would make no difference to either one of us what I tell him. I feel old. Old and grizzled. Outworn and obsolescent. The thing is, I have always felt this way. I've never felt young, never felt that youthful effervescence tiding through my gamesome boyish body and carrying me blithely through my salad days. I feel I am at the end of something, after a painfully drawn-out decline, at the end of something that never really had a beginning worth speaking of. When I was younger, I had an unreserved, tacit trust in the future, a catholic confidence that everything would work out, that the end would always justify the means, and the means would without fail lead to the desired end — or to the most beneficial end, even if it wasn't exactly desired. It was just a question of time and patience, Tolstoy's two most powerful warriors. It had to work out. How could it not? That's what the future was there for. Youth is an expectant prologue whose hopes are pinned on a future that must improve upon the past and deliver on the promise of the present. Otherwise, why stick around?

With my father, though, one can have no illusions. *De trop* is his motto, his *cri de guerre.* He says we're all *de trop,* too much, expendable, superfluous, nonessential, a drop in the bucket, a dime a dozen, deadwood. He has been saying this for as long as

I can remember. Father professor, the professor my father. He preaches it in class and at home, and he writes about it in his arcane articles and hefty hermeneutic treatises while he smokes his cigarettes and sups strong coffee and meditates great things. We are all *de trop*, supernumeraries in a soon-to-be deleted scene, each person one too many, painfully contingent.

This is what he says.

Contingent on what, Dad? I asked him, once old enough to understand the definition—if not fully comprehend the encoded connotations—of the term. He answered, smiling beneficently, *Contingent on nothing, and this is what's so fantastic about it.* He says that if everyone is *de trop*, supplementary, dispensable, without any justifiable reason for being, if there is no discernable hint as to why we're here and what happens when we die and what we should be doing in the meantime, then there's nothing to worry about; there's just nothing. *No thing. So don't try so hard.* I asked him, *Why bother then?* and he said, *That's just my point. Don't.*

So I try. I try very hard not to try so hard. I try to not bother. I tell myself that I don't miss anything, that I don't still hear the cadenced sough of her breathing as she slept, the weary sighs of displeasure and the frustrated bang of the fallboard when she was having a bad day at the piano, complaining that the keys were not being friendly, that I don't still see the way her hair would spill sneakily onto her face from behind her ears when she leaned in and lowered her head toward the claviature, and how she would extend her lower lip to puff upwards and blow it out of her eyes, only to have it float back down into place with the next chord, as though defying her to play without looking at the score. I try to convince myself that it doesn't matter that I'll never see her again, because we're all *de trop* anyway, disposable bales of meat and bone, nerves and fluids, tendons and tissue—and, like all matter, *mostly ghostly space*—and that there's not much to lose in the first place, that loss is inherent in life, that life is a succession of losses, it even loses itself in the end, and that this is nothing to weep or wail over; it's just another meaningless morsel of nothing in the greater nothingness.

He says I should revel and rejoice in this nothingness, *mon père le professeur*, that I should be grateful for it.

Grateful, he says.

This is what I try to do. I live alone in a room with the crash of distant waves pounding the walls and the scent of a sister haunting the air, surrounded by the lowery tomes of the Western canon, constantly mocking my resolve.

We never spoke about that night. It was tacitly understood that there was no need to. We both knew that something had been irrevocably vitiated, severed from the source, and though it was bound to happen, this was the night that actuated it. I think even Spencer understood, although he couldn't have known the details.

On several occasions, I came close to telling Don my sacrosanct secret. I wanted to. Don, if anybody. But I feared that doing so would corrupt the purity of it, someway mitigate the almost superstitious sense of fatality that ran through and vivified the whole thing like a spinal cord. Sometimes it's better not to share your pain, because once you do it's no longer yours and yours alone, and because sometimes that's all you have.

I did tell him that my sister was seeing a painter, one night while playing NHL 95 on his Sega Genesis, not so secretly hoping he would suggest an inventive way to rub the painter out of the painting.

"A painter?" he said. "Housepainter?"

"No. Artist painter."

"They still exist? Isn't everything conceptual these days? All video and installation and performance? Pissed-filled jars and shark carcasses in formaldehyde and two-ton piles of Play-Doh and sitting in a chair staring at the audience for ten-hour stints at a time. Stuff like that, no?"

"Maybe. But he's definitely a painter."

"There is no artist anymore, only art. And art is everything and everywhere, which means it's nothing and nowhere."

"I'll tell him that."

"What's his name?"

I held back the payoff, letting it build. "Spencer."

"Ah. Spencer. Of course." He was openly pleased, almost appreciative, as though my answer had exceeded expectations. "A perfect painter's name. I was thinking maybe Giancarlo or Jacques or Pierrot, even William or Marcus, but Spencer will do just fine."

"She's out with him tonight, as a matter of fact. She's with him right now." I thought about what she might be doing with him as I spoke those words.

"Spencer," he repeated. "Does he wear a beret?"

"I haven't seen him in one."

"Mm. Too bad."

"But he speaks French."

"Naturally."

"And he's not bad, as a painter. Not incredibly original, but not too bad. He says he's still finding his style, his own painterly voice."

"He actually said that?" Don turned and lowered his controller, allowing my right wing to slip his defenseman and take an uncontested shovel shot, which was nonetheless swatted off course—rather miraculously—at the last possible instant by the haphazardly raised glove of a slouching goalie. He beamed at his avatar's expertise, then came back on topic. "Oh, fuck me. His own painterly voice?"

"Yes. He actually said that. His words, not mine."

"See, this is one of the reasons I can't put up with artists. This bullshit pretentious artist talk makes my fucking blood boil. I mean, don't get me wrong, philosophers pull that crap too, all that being-in-itself and being-for-itself and being-in-the-world and being-for-others stuff. But I can tolerate that, because it's still somewhat scientific."

"Science was born from and grew out of philosophy."

"Exactly. But then you get these artists trying to find their *painterly voices* and it just… it just fucking burns my ass is what it does. It's goddamn pointless, this *urge to create*. That's another thing I've heard them say, that they've got this unexplainable *urge to create*. They can't help it. They are powerless against this inborn impulse. They are helpless slaves to the muse. How fucking assholic. Another example of how nature's got you by the short hairs. This urge to create is no different from the urge to fuck, just another way of having kids, of furthering yourself, of leaving a piece of you behind for posterity to say, *wow, look what he did while he was here!* It's the same fucking thing, procreation pure and simple."

"Plato said that, about twenty-five hundred years ago."

"Good for him. But I'm saying it here and now, in the king's fucking English. I feel strongly about this. Always have. I'm pro-sex, but anti-art, anti-reproduction."

The second period ended in a stiff tie, two goals apiece, and we cracked our knuckles and stretched our arms and prepared both physically and mentally for the decisive final period.

"He's not ugly," I said in the interim, though I don't think Don was listening. "I mean, he's actually a pretty good-looking guy. I guess I can understand why she likes him. I don't see it lasting, though. It's been a while now. They see each other pretty frequently, but I definitely do not see it lasting. She'll get sick of him. She'll grow out of him. She has to."

"What I'm saying is, they get off on thinking of themselves as rebels, these artists, as agitators of the status quo, but the real rebel is the anti-artist, the anti-creator. Not an *un*creator, not the one who destroys—because creation and destruction are two edges of the same sword—but the one who consciously does nothing, an outlaw to nature, not obeying any of the inclinations she's implanted in him, except the ones he absolutely has to in order to survive: eating, pissing, shitting—"

"Sleeping." I couldn't let this one go unmentioned.

"Yes. And even those compulsory functions he performs begrudgingly."

"I don't think it'll last very long, but she's with him all the time. *All* the time. It's irritating how much she's with him."

"But the true rebel would most assuredly refuse to be an artist in any sense of the word, whether it's a question of having live offspring or painting pictures in his own painterly voice or sculpting birthday-suited women out of wet clay or composing symphonies or shredding solos or whatever." Don bore down on his controller's buttons with the excessive force of his zeal. "The authentic dissident, the bona fide firebrand, would make it his point not to reproduce or take part in this ridiculous drama in any way. He would try to do as little as possible and spite nature by existing on the margins of her schema. Spite, that's the key. Gall. Spleen. Umbrage at existence. An intense ill will toward the natural world and all its malignant maneuverings. The true rebel would waste the life that nature has given him just to spit bong water in her face."

"And he'd be extremely miserable."

"Yes. That goes without saying. But it's the price that has to be paid. And misery is unavoidable anyway. Everyone is miserable. That's just the human condition. We're each and every one of us miserable wretches. But it all comes down to fucking, my friend. Art, music, literature. Beethoven's Ninth, the Mona Lisa, David, Finnegans fucking Wake. Artistic creation is just the overt expression of the sublimated sex drive. It's all about the fuck."

"Freud said that, a little over a century ago."

"Great minds..."

"So, strictly from a scientific perspective, if you're right and this *love* thing is nothing but the instinctual urge to reproduce—"

"Which I am, and it is."

"If it comes down to fucking and nothing more, an animal act, just fucking—"

"A piston in a cylinder."

"Then... if you're castrated, if you cut your testicles off and you're incapable of being aroused, sexually aroused, would you also be incapable of loving?"

His focus remained fixed on the screen, his play unaffected.

"You mean, if you couldn't fuck, could you still love?" he simplified, pausing to take a snap shot from my blue line that went just wide of the net and wincing at the near miss. "First of all, if you want a scientific answer, we're going to have to dispense with any unscientific terms and fictions, love being the main one. You already know how I feel about that farce. As far as severing the balls, that would work of course, but it's easier than that. And less physically painful. It's the skin at the heart of the problem, you know, the body, this… this vile container of mucous and blood and bile and whatever other filthy ingredients." Again that expression on his face, as if he had swallowed something bitter beyond description. "It's really a disgusting thing when you get down to it, and even more disgusting that we're attracted to it. Natural, yes, but still disgusting. Basically, everything natural is gross. Nature is a ghastly mistress. That check was totally illegal, by the way."

"I don't hear anyone but you complaining."

"They have to design better refs in this goddamn game. It's a travesty. You clearly boarded my center."

"If nobody saw it, it didn't happen. But what I'm saying is, disgusting or not, short of cutting off your balls, there's really no choice."

"Leave the question of choice to philosophers. You know what I do when I'm totally fucking frustrated, when I'm as horny as hell is hot and all the whacking off in the world won't help and my willy won't take no for an answer? I conceptualize a smokin' hottie, butt naked, one that would normally spring me like a coked-up jack-in-the-box, and then I picture her pinching a loaf and wiping herself, or picking her nose, or engaging in some other disgusting bodily necessity. I think of protruding nasal hair and purulent cysts and inflamed rashes and ripe, bubbling blackheads and raging yeast infections. Nasty shit like that. I try to picture her insides. The sexiest woman in the world has the same appalling innards as everyone else. You don't even have to go subcutaneous. If you could see the epidermis of a beautiful female breast under a microscope, I guarantee you'd want no part of it, pal o'mine. No fucking part of it." He squinted and massaged the bridge of his nose with a thumb and forefinger. "See, that's what you have to do, reduce the image of female as goddess to female as human, a human like any other, one who suffers from the same horrid biological essentials that everyone else does. Just think about how utterly unattractive humanity is, which is not very hard. It's a simple syllogism. Your father's a philosopher. You must have grown up with this stuff, no? All human bodies are intrinsically disgusting. Women have human bodies. Ergo, women are disgusting. That's it. Case closed. No more to it."

"That solves nothing."

"No, it doesn't *solve* anything, or at least not what you want it to solve. See, the problem is, you're thinking with your dick."

"Which every man with a functioning penis does."

"Of course. Perfectly natural. I'm not blaming or accusing you here. It's *natural*. Fucking nature again, that cunting whore. She made the little head so much stronger than the big one for a reason. You've got to find a way to stop thinking with your dick, and then you really start thinking. But that's a whole other can of worms that we won't get into now."

I checked his forward hard into the boards and sent him ass-backward onto the ice. "Still solves nothing," I said, gloating over my on-screen aggression.

"It's not a question of solving anything. That's why there's heroin."

"And castration."

"And castration."

I came close to telling him right then and there, though I don't know exactly what I was going to tell him.

The third period was winding down with the score tied at three. We both sank into silence and maneuvered our players with sudden-death exigency, my sweaty fingers straining to maintain management of a controller that seemed set on slipping out from between them.

"What the hell, man! You just hacked the fuck out of my left wing!" I yelped, as though I'd suffered the slash myself, while his center drove past my defenses and snuck a quick wrist shot between the legs of my goaltender.

"Hm. Nobody called it." He suppressed a contented smile, though its implication fully commandeered his countenance. "So I guess it didn't happen."

"He's splayed out on the ice like a slaughtered chicken."

"He must have tripped himself up."

One minute remained in the game. I took an embarrassingly wild slap shot from the red line that went way wide. Don fleered as he regained control of the puck and leisurely skated around the edges of the rink, easily avoiding my attempts to steal, as though my players were grating gadflies he had only to turn from to evade completely.

The buzzer sounded and the final score flashed across the center of the rink. I tossed my controller onto the floor in front of me with a bit more force than I'd intended.

"Hey! Easy with that, sore loser. You break it, you buy it."

I picked it up. "Rematch?"

"I think we should go out."

"We never go out." I was almost alarmed at the suggestion.

"I go out. You don't go out."

"Where would we go?" I asked, anxiously fondling my controller as I recalled bygone images of high school weekends at the multiplex or the arcade, which even back then was filled with antiquated video games that no one was quick to waste quarters on, while the one or two updated machines were more expensive and often had a few kids waiting on them. "We can play games and watch movies right here."

"What?" He balked. "Who the fuck said anything about games or movies?"

"Then why go out?"

He hesitated, mouth slightly agape. "To find women, or at least to look at them."

"After all that?"

"You totally missed my thesis then, which means you either weren't listening or didn't understand." He pressed his palms together and softly ground them into each other and spoke with subdued impatience, as though reiterating an already uncomplicated theory in even less complicated language for the benefit of a particularly obtuse student. "Let me rephrase. It's girls... or heroin." He thrust his hands out to either side of himself, as though balancing an imaginary weight in each. "Snatch or scag. Hell dust or the honey pot. Galloping horse or the vertical smile. There's nothing else. Nothing. Everything in between is filler. If all these years of science have taught me anything, it's that a man can only endure life with the help of one of two possible crutches, sex or heroin," balling his open hands into fists, "both of which revolve around orgasm, or around some likeness of the orgasmic experience, something to counterbalance the horrible monotony of the remaining portion of our lives—monotony apart from the momentary bliss of orgasm. So the trick is to find some way to prolong this sense of orgasm, or to get as much of it as often as possible. It's girls or heroin. Smack or sex. Pussy or junk."

His fists remained out there at the end of extended arms. It seemed as though he was waiting for me to say something before lowering them.

"Or suicide."

"Your choice," he said, dropping his arms. "But it is Friday night."

"What does that have to do with suicide?"

"Nothing. But it has a lot to do with girls. The best time to hunt is when the prey is abundant."

"Interesting."

"No. Elementary."

We opted against going out. Instead, we smoked marijuana together for the first time since high school, when we would huddle up between periods in a fetid stall in the boys' bathroom and share a poorly rolled joint, counting our tokes until the warning bell rang. I never liked getting high. Tonight I hated it. Later that night, I walked home with a severe headache and a scorched throat, my eyelids urging me to let them fall. It seemed to take considerably longer than usual to get there, and the neighborhood seemed quieter and darker and more unfamiliar than it ever had. I remember thinking that I was walking through Dante's *dark wood*, and that *I'd found myself in the middle of my life's journey* much earlier than expected. Reaching the house, I was not surprised to find that she was still out somewhere with Spencer at 2 a.m., so I sat down on the porch step as always, reading random shapes into the blank, blue-black sky, and I realized that something had to be done.

I realized, now, that something had to be done.

And a few days later, after I had weighed the pros and cons of numerous courses of action and concluded that there was but one definitive way to settle things, it proved less difficult than anticipated to get what was needed.

3

Only a Living World Can Include Death

And we call it wisdom. It is pain.

— Randall Jarrell

I try to convince myself that I've lost interest in sex, that I don't need it, that it is a base, self-perpetuating desire that leads nowhere, and I am better off without it. I enlist all my powers of self-persuasion and employ every psychological technique and trick at my disposal — including Don's recommendations — in an effort to outwit nature by giving myself a kind of mental cold shower. But none of them work, irrespective of how essentially valid I believe them to be. A fuck would be a good thing once in a while. There's no debating that. I miss the feel of flesh. I miss it terribly. Excruciatingly. As an adolescent, when the incipient stirrings of sexual desire first began to agitate the surface and complicate things, sex seemed like an impossibly far-off fantasy, something you heard about that never really happened outside of magazines and movies, a risqué rumor that may or may not have been true. Other guys had sex. I didn't.

And then I did.

And now I want to unburden myself, to tell somebody. It's painful sometimes, how badly I want to hear myself say it, to discharge the words and feel them resonate in the small space between me and someone else and study the sickened subtleties of reaction when I say that I have lain with my sister, that I have known her from the inside. I want to hear the words and behold their impact. I want everybody to know that for years we fucked regularly, and then she died. She walked into the water. And despite society's near-universal condemnation of such unions as abject perversities, there was nothing unwholesome about ours, nothing wrong with *us*. So the world must be fully apprised of the details: how we sometimes did it several times a day in my little boy's bedroom in our parents' house, on the same shabby single bed in which I've slept since moving out of the crib, while my father was in his downstairs study crafting his sui generis contribution to Western philosophy, and my mother was out on a shopping sortie, always running errands. And even if she was home, if he wasn't writing, it didn't matter. That's what the night was for. The master bedroom was strategically arranged on the first floor so that my father could read peacefully, a safe distance from crying children and ear-splitting teenage music and other aggravating varieties of familial rumpus.

Is this possible? How could no one have noticed? It's a roomy house, easily large enough for four people to get lost in. And the door was locked. Music was playing. We were talking, discussing things, as bright, well-behaved kids do. Hanging out, enjoying each other's company. We were close. No parent would suspect or even dream up such depravity. So we would be found in the same bed in the morning, sleeping or chatting, innocently immersed in the moment. Nothing untoward. It would only be untoward to suspect something untoward about it. We'd share a bed all the time when we were little, no different from scores of other young siblings. Our cuddling was seen as cute then, like puppies nuzzling up next to each other for warmth and security. Now it had become a habit that stuck, a routine that lasted somewhat longer than usual. But with detriment to no one, there was no apparent reason to discourage it. This is something that children do. It's important for siblings to be close. This is a good thing, one less concern for busy parents to fret about.

But before all else, there must be no sweetening, nothing softening or saccharine, only what happened. It is imperative that people realize I had sex with my sister, and it was the only time I really felt alive—when I'd hear the notes suddenly stop and the cover close over the keyboard with a gentle clonk and her steps turn toward my room, when I would feel her figure next to me, her exploratory hands and tongue, her tight, soft stomach and warm, nectarous neck, breasts, nipples, thighs. I want every explicit particular to be known, the inland nations of her body, the glorious geography of her form. But I want to be vulgar, distasteful, unpoetic. I don't want romance. I will not allow the syrup of sentiment to drizzle into the story. Fables are for children, children that we never were. I fucked my sister. The question of love is irrelevant, superfluous, *de trop*. And it must be understood that this is not a confession of guilt. There is no mea culpa here. I would do it again without vacillation, without question. I would give up everything to have it once more, my kingdom for a night, my empire of emptiness for an hour. I want it to be known that I still masturbate to her memory, that I can never disassociate her body from the act, and that because of this, life is impossible now, as dismal and dreadful as the thought of the hollow decades ahead.

All this I want to say, yet I never will. Nobody will know. Despite the railing and raging within, I'll go on and never tell because no one can have this, no one can share in this forbidden knowledge that kindles whatever life is left in me. It is the only thing that is mine alone, and I will keep it here in my hole, my solitary cell, the only place where the world is not too much with me. In my room I will bear witness to the impervious passage of the years and see seasons end from a window and take little comfort from the thought that only a living world can include death.

And yet I still don't want to die.

Something undoubtedly had to be done. Everything that happened supported this conviction, from the moment I saw Spencer approach her, naked on that couch.

Class, for example, had become a supremely disagreeable experience, the three of us aligned so awkwardly in the back row—with Severine squeezed between me and Spencer like an ambivalent arbitrator doing her best to remain impartial, though she was plainly partisan—every Tuesday and Thursday from 11 a.m. to 12:20 p.m., followed by an indigestible lunch at either the cafeteria or an off-campus café, where it was all I could do not to acknowledge how sharply their self-control pierced me, their restraint from exhibiting signs of affection and swapping showy gestures of undergraduate endearment, unlike the couples all over campus holding hands or French-kissing in the commons, promenading about with fingers firmly fixed in the ass pocket of each other's jeans. Spencer and Severine engaged in none of this public display. They were discreet, if only for my sake.

I learned much about Spencer during this time. Besides the two-year difference in age (and the several inches of height he had on me) and the wealth of worldly knowledge garnered from transcontinental travel, he was a clever and captivating raconteur with a rich stock of experience to draw from. Worse, he was an attentive listener, lending a generous ear to those with clearly much less interesting lives to recount. And he never lorded these advantages over me. He didn't have to. A tawdry townie like me was no threat, no ominous obstacle to overcome. Just a brother. A simple suburban brother. But this wasn't the worst of it. The kicker was that I was vulnerable to his charm. Though it stings to admit it, I actually enjoyed his company, the yarns he could spin and the playful panache with which he spun them, his air of laid-back confidence and natty nonchalance that comes only with experiencing the wider world, the world outside a room. Against all odds, I began to like him. Sometimes I would get wrapped up in discussing a new novel or an old movie with him, until I came to my senses and chastised myself for lowering my defenses, for disregarding—however temporarily—our rival positions on the field. He was the enemy. I couldn't allow myself to soften. No quarter would be given.

Like the day he approached me on the Great Lawn, the nexus of campus, a large, impeccably manicured and vibrantly verdant expanse of tall fescue situated between the principal academic halls. During the day, weather permitting, the lawn is filled with students sitting cross-legged in intimate pairs and in larger circles, or tossing a Frisbee or kicking around a grungy hacky sack, studying for exams, lunching or lounging idly in the plush greensward, waiting for their next class. On particularly warm afternoons in late spring or early fall, when everything says summer except the calendar, you might see people tanning themselves in folding deck chairs or beach loungers, shirtless men in shorts and women in bikini tops and Daisy Dukes with foiled reflectors aimed at their faces and frozen water bottles on the ground next to them, thawing rapidly in the merciless sun. I would be there often when I had free time between classes. I used to enjoy lying flat on my back on that soft, springy turf, staring straight up at the sky, or sitting there pretending to read as I watched people pass, catching snippets of conversation and errant glances and sinking into a well of wonderment and envy at the spectacle of young humanity going about its business. Even the odd ones who were just sitting alone doing nothing—to all appearances not very different from me—seemed to have so much more to their lives.

One mild mid-November afternoon, a couple of weeks after I attacked him in his studio, I'm there on the lawn with an open book splayed out facedown before me, leaning lengthwise on a crooked arm and gazing distractedly down the softly sloping grounds, when Spencer comes up to me. There had been little perceptible tension between us since our skirmish in his studio, but nothing had been said about it; no air had been cleared. I'm lying on the Great Lawn with the first volume of Schopenhauer's *Parerga and Paralipomena* open before me (which to this day I have not read past page twenty), and though I'm usually acutely cognizant of people around me, I don't notice him until he's in front of me, suddenly standing right there looking down at me with his hands in his pants pockets as if he had just materialized, in medias res, a dazzling nimbus of sunlight silhouetting him from behind.

"It's nice out here."

I tell him I have issues with the word *nice*, but yes, I agree in spirit.

"Mind if I sit down?" He smiles amiably.

"Of course not." Though of course I would prefer that he didn't. I've never been with him outside of Severine's presence, and it feels oddly indiscreet.

"Schopenhauer, I see," he says, sitting next to me, extending one leg and bending the other under it.

I affirm this and ask if he likes Schopenhauer.

"Not my favorite."

I ask him who is.

"I don't like picking favorites. I've always found it hard to do."

I snuffle and tell him that's nonsense, that everybody has favorites and it shouldn't be hard to choose, because favoritism is a naturally occurring phenomenon, nothing embarrassing at all. Telling yourself you don't have favorites is bad faith. You're bound to like something more than something else, and one thing in particular more than anything else. Or one person.

"Why would I be embarrassed? That's not what I meant by hard," he says, looking at me ironically. "I can't just single out a philosopher like my favorite ice cream flavor. It would kind of devalue the whole thing."

I ask him whom he would choose if he absolutely had to, if everything hypothetically depended on him picking a favorite philosopher, and if he failed to do so, all would be horribly, hopelessly lost. I ask him if he can at least tell me which two or three rise to the top for him. I tell him that's not too much to ask.

He turns his head and deflects my question. "I know you and Severine are close. I know it must be hard to think about her being with someone."

I tell him that he hasn't answered the question, and that *someone* is too inexplicit a pronoun in this context.

"I think it's great that you're close with your little sister," he says, uprooting a few leaves of grass. "I really do."

I ask him why he thinks it's great, and I notice that his dark hair shows salient streaks of lightness when the sun shines on it full force.

"I don't think that needs explaining. You're close to your sister. You get along well with her. Not everybody makes that connection. You're lucky."

I have been in the same position for quite a while and would like to shift, but I resist, feeling this would betray weakness, a sense of surrender. So I stay as I am, uncomfortable, and repeat the word *lucky* with an interrogative intonation.

"Yes, lucky."

I ask him if he has a sister.

"I'm an only child."

I ask him how he would allege to know that it is hard to see one's little sister with someone, considering that he is sisterless himself. What would lead him to believe it would be any more difficult than, say, an overly heavy course load or an intractable problem in symbolic logic?

"I'm just trying to understand, to be understanding," he says, with impressive equanimity. "It's obvious that you're protective. It's obvious that you care. You're being a big brother. All this is good, but you have to understand that it's normal for your sister to go out, to be with someone. To be with a man."

His loftiness annoys me sharply, as does his judicious phrasing. I almost lose my calm but quickly recuperate and ask him if from this I can infer that it would be abnormal for her not to go out, not *to be with a man.*

"Abnormal is a little strong, but yes."

I ask him if he likes Husserl.

"What?" Now he looks annoyed, which pleases me.

I repeat the question.

"I don't dislike him," is his answer.

I tell him I assume from this response that Husserl would not be one of his favorites.

"Not particularly."

I ask what exactly he thinks would make it hard to see my little sister with a man. I ask him to give me specific reasons why I might find this troublesome and implore him not to spare any gory details.

"I came to tell you that I like your sister, Peter," he sums up. "I like her a lot. This isn't some courting procedure. I didn't come here to ask your permission to see Severine. I hope you realize this. Because I'm going to see her either way."

I tell him there's no law against seeing people, that I see people all the time, that I am, in fact, seeing him right here and now.

"I think you're a good guy, despite this wiseass intellectual façade, and because I think you're a good guy, I wanted to tell you that I like your sister. That's all. I didn't come to extend an olive branch or make amends or anything. I just came to tell you that."

I ask him if, in characterizing me as *good*, he means this in Plato's sense of the word. I ask if, in thinking that I am *good*, he somehow associates me with the Platonic ideals of truth, justice, and beauty, because then I would take it as a true compliment.

"Let me tell you something about philosophy. I love it," he says, looking skyward. "The first time I read Descartes in my very first freshman philosophy class, it completely changed me. I love it, but if philosophy cannot be lived, then it is nothing more than mental masturbation. If it cannot be applied to practical situations, it's useless. Don't you think? And I have no time for uselessness. Who does?"

I ask if he is making oblique reference to the oft-quoted line in *Being and Nothingness*, "Man is a useless passion," or if I am drawing lines of relation where indeed there are none.

He shakes his head and smiles cynically. "I like your sister. I came to tell you that, and I hope you're all right with it. But if you're not, then you're not."

I tell him that I have always had an aversion to the word *practical*, and though I don't wholly disagree with what he's saying about philosophy, I caution him not to undervalue practical uselessness, or the practicality of the useless. I ask if he would like me to ask him if his intentions are noble, if he will *do right by her*.

"I really hoped you'd be okay with this. I think we could get along, you and I.

I don't say anything.

"You know what Schopenhauer says about reading," he says, rising and brushing grass and specks of dirt from his beige corduroy pants. "Too much is polluting. You lose the ability to think for yourself, to feel for yourself, to feel in general. You forget how to live, and since that's the real object of philosophy... well, you see where I'm going. Kind of counterproductive, isn't it?"

I tell him that he is dead wrong and refer to Cicero's much celebrated statement that "to study philosophy is nothing but to prepare one's self to die." And further, that Schopenhauer didn't invest life with great value to begin with, that he regarded life largely as a burden, a brief, burning, onerous interlude between the peacefulness of nonexistence before birth and after death.

"Yes," he says, nodding contemplatively and glancing up over my head. "I don't completely disagree. But no one reads much Cicero anymore. Or ornery old Arthur."

After a brief breathing space—during which we just look at each other like confused combatants unsure of who holds the high ground—he turns to leave, lifting a hand behind him as he starts off.

"But at least he's dead," I yell after him.

"What?" He stops momentarily but keeps his back to me.

"Nobody may read much of Schopenhauer anymore, but at least he's finished with the enervating interlude of life. That's more than we can say."

He remains still for a couple of seconds, dips his chin a bit, and walks away.

Before long, the couplet "Severine and Spencer" began to seem natural. I was acclimating to the situation as to cold ocean water that is almost unbearable at first but soon feels tolerable, then decently comfortable, then just the right temperature. The more they were together, the more it seemed as though they should be together. Even their names got on well, the syllables singing in silky consonance; like storybook characters destined to be remembered as an enduring dyad, Spencer and Severine harmonized in ways Severine and Peter never did. She would go out without my knowing, not surreptitiously, not because she felt it necessary to covertly slip out under my radar, but rather the inverse: it was a nonissue; she felt no need to mention it to me, to even say good-bye.

But why was it so hard to talk to her, to say anything to her, to look at her? How could it have suddenly become as though I didn't know the person I was seeing? She would come home tired and content—it was insufferable to see her this content—and go upstairs to bed, and I'd follow at her feet like a neglected pup. At first she'd say, *No, not tonight, not tonight,* a solicitous refusal, and I'd say, *Okay,* because I still had some lingering pride and a dwindling reserve of hope. But desperation soon set in, and I told her I couldn't leave unless she did something—could she please do *something*? I just needed her to touch me, and so she did. She did only what was necessary, the meager minimum, and then I left.

One night, very late, I came into her room. She hadn't been out with Spencer, but I hadn't talked with her the entire evening. This was not very unusual anymore. She was in bed, reading a tattered old hardback whose title had long faded from the cover. She stopped and smiled at me over the book, almost as she used to. Was I deceiving myself in finding a gladdened glint in her eyes when she saw me dithering at the doorsill like a skittish child, torn between fight and flight? She looked so pretty, her face freshly scrubbed and creamed for the night, so cherubically clean and warmly aromatic. It was the olfactory influences, ultimately, that resolved my indecision, that led me in to lie next to her, and it was perfect. Then she spoke. If only she hadn't.

"You smell like pot," she stated flatly.

"Are you sure it's me?" I rebounded, knowing full well the unwashed shirt I was wearing was the same one I had on in Don's inadequately ventilated marijuana den the night before.

"You've been smoking."

"You know I don't smoke."

She turned a page. I leaned in close to her, shut my eyes, and inhaled.

"Do you need me to take care of you?" she said, business-like, slipping a heavily notated index card between the pages and slapping the book closed before laying it faceup on her stomach and looking at the wall across the room.

"What?"

"Is that why you came in?"

"What?"

"It's not a trick question. Do you want me to?"

She reached over and put her hand on my sex and began to stroke it mechanically over my pants.

"Yes," I said, "that's why I came in."

Unzipping my fly and working her fingers under the waistband of my briefs while I lay motionless, my eyelids drawn tightly down, she continued with her hand in the same sorry mechanical manner—almost grudgingly—before finishing with her mouth in an equally unenthused—albeit effectual—fashion. It was a poor, perfunctory performance, but it did the job. Then she got up, washed in the hall bathroom, and returned to her reading. I lay there. She read for a while longer—maybe fifteen minutes—and we said nothing. Finally, she put her book on the nightstand, snapped off the bedside lamp, and turned onto her side, her back toward me. This is what it had come to.

"I'm going to sleep," she said, her words moving away from me.

I didn't say anything. I didn't move.

"You know you can't stay here."

It was true. She'd been in my bed since we were kids, but we never slept together in hers. It was something we just didn't do, something that didn't feel right, for whatever reason.

"Let me sleep here with you tonight."

"I'm very tired."

"So sleep. That's what you do when you're tired. Just sleep, and let me stay here."

"I can't," she said, repositioning her head on the pillow.

We lay on our backs in the deadening darkness. It pained me to be this close to her without touching her.

"Why?" I said.

"Because I'm tired. I told you." Her voice was muffled by the pillow, but the sense of nuisance in it was rich and resonant.

"That's not what I was asking. Why? Why is this happening now, after all these years?"

She didn't answer straightaway, and I thought she might have fallen asleep. I was about to shake her angrily when she finally spoke, her tone tired and tense, as though my badgering was depriving her of the pleasures of sleep.

"You knew it had to, eventually. I knew. You knew, didn't you? It had to end, even if neither of us wanted it to. Maybe it's my fault. Maybe it shouldn't have started."

I tried to make myself ignore that last sentence, to delude myself into believing I hadn't heard it, or better yet, that it hadn't been said. She quickly disabused me.

"We made a mistake, and we have to deal with it."

"But why this way? Why so suddenly?" I asked.

She closed her eyes and shook her head with her lips pressed tightly together and the skin on her chin cockling like crinkled paper. "That's not relevant. You'd rather we were weaned off it like addicts, with occasional doses of methadone to make it more palatable, less painful?"

"That's how you see this, all this, as an addiction? A curse? Something bad? Something that never should have happened?"

"What did you think? What kind of future did you see? Kids? A house with a two-car garage? Holiday dinners? PTA? Really. Tell me. Where did you think it would end?" She seemed to be riled up enough to turn, but she didn't.

"I didn't think it would end. Did you? All this time you knew there was an expiration date? Were you counting down in your head? Were you hoping it would come sooner rather than later?"

"No. No, of course not. But did you really think this could be forever?" And now, finally, she turned to face me, the tip of her nose grazing mine, those big dark eyes seeming to glow like blazing obsidian in the circumambient gloom.

"You know what I think now?" I spoke in a leaden whisper, with a weight that sank my words back into my mind. *I think I don't want to think anymore. I think everything I have ever thought has been thought already, recycled uncountable times, thought and rethought until not a single salvageable shred of constructive mental stimulation is left in my head, only the ideational detritus of a lifetime of longing. That's what I think, if you really want to know.* But I did not say that. I said, "I think we should stop talking about this."

Silence. The plumbing squealed and the house crepitated. More silence. The wind whipped against the window, rattling it in its frame. Houses make so many mysterious sounds, all kinds of curious rasps and secretive squawks, cawing and cackling like some ignored pet petitioning for attention.

"The semester went quickly," I said, and though I can't stand when people say things like this, complaining that time passes too fast or too slowly according to their mercurial moods, I find myself a repeat offender.

"They all do."

"Are you ashamed? Is that it?"

"No."

"So why? Why did you crawl into bed with me then? Later, I mean, after we were little? Why start something if you know it has to end?"

"Everything ends."

"Not good enough."

"We did what we did because we were scared and lonely and had no one else, nothing but each other."

"Still not good enough. And even so, what's different now?"

"We were two scared and lonely kids, but we're not kids anymore, even if we are still scared and lonely. I'm not ashamed to admit being scared. I can't help being scared. I don't think that will ever change. And loneliness is just the way it is. You have to accept being alone because there's no other choice. But then you get older... and... You just get older."

"So now that you've grown used to your fear, accepted your loneliness without shame, now you've grown out of me. Is that it?"

"That's not everything."

I felt tears welling behind my eyes and held my breath to keep them at bay, which caused my cheeks to slowly billow out like a threatened puffer. In the past, I wouldn't have minded her seeing me in tears, but I did now.

She reached out and placed her hand over my eyes like a blindfold. "It's not because of Spencer. I like him, but he's not the reason."

I exhaled, having successfully beaten back all but one little wandering teardrop, which spilled out onto her palm. "What *is* the reason then?"

She removed her hand from my face. "There is no reason. There's never a reason. Not really. It just seems like there should be. What else have we learned from Dad, if not that? We only frustrate ourselves by searching for reasons that aren't there. What do you want to hear, that I've fallen in love with Spencer? Would that make it easier?"

My eyes shut against the dark and I lay as still as possible, concentrating on the warm weight of her palm against my heart and the feathery touch of her fingertips resting delicately on my sternum.

"Have you?"

"I think you should find a girl," she said.

"Have you?"

"No."

I cupped her hand in mine and slowly sloughed it off me.

"It's okay," I said, not knowing what I meant by this.

"Are you sure?" Her hand approached and resettled, and again I withdrew it.

"And me? Where do I stand?"

She pulled up my zipper, her thumbnail grazing my stomach. "That's up to you."

"What a stupid thing to say. A really stupid thing to say."

"It can't be what you want. It just can't *be* anymore." She was trying to speak softly, but her voice seemed to carry beyond her intentions.

A thump came overhead. The ceiling creaked, followed by the soft skittering of a squirrel's paws across the roof, fading out toward my room on the other side of the house.

"How can you talk about it like this, in such a cold way? So analytically. I don't know how you do it. So calm and clinical." I was trying to sound so myself.

"Because that's how we have to talk about it. And that's how we have to deal with it."

"Don't you feel bad at all? If I saw you cry, shed a tear, show some sign of remorse, some compunction or compassion, maybe that would help, maybe. It seems like you don't even feel bad at all. Like you miss nothing, like there was nothing worth missing. Like it was all—"

"That's not true. It's not..." She cut her momentum and stopped before her voice rose above a certain threshold, then restarted with a kind of phlegmatic mournfulness, as though speaking of a recently departed loved one who had long been suffering from a terminal disease, and whose decease — while sorrowful — was anything but unanticipated. "It's not true. But you can't resurrect what's dead."

The terrible finality of the word and the way she pronounced it, with both gentleness and iron resolution, plunged me to a depth theretofore unimaginable. My mind seemed to stop processing for an indeterminate passage of time that might have been seconds or minutes, and it felt as though my body had seized up like a malfunctioning machine with a sudden, fatal glitch. She killed me. There is no other way to say it. I felt worse than dead. I felt inanimate, nonextant, nothing more than the pulverized remnants of a ruined seashell lying wasted on the shoreline, waiting for the tide to wash me away.

"I think this is a phase, all this." I swallowed hard as I said this, and nodded intensely, almost violently, the side of my face chafing against the pillow. "I think in time you'll see what was meant to be," I told her.

"How can you use those words, *meant to be*? You know you don't believe that."

She was right. I didn't believe it. But I meant it, somehow. I was embarrassed that the words had passed through my mouth, but at least they were honest.

"We have to put distance between us, at least a little, at least for now," she said, and brushed my hair back.

"It's already there, this distance. You've put it there."

"I think you should find a girl."

"I heard you the first time."

"Do you want me to, again?" She took my chin lightly between her thumb and forefinger and directed my face into hers.

"No."

"Are you sure?"

"Yes."

"I could, if you want."

"I said no. It's okay."

She released my chin and turned around, pulling her knees up and enfolding herself inward like a snail, making sure no part of her touched me. "I'm going to sleep then. I don't want to talk about this anymore. Not now."

I rolled over onto my back and stared up through the dark at the stark white ceiling. "You didn't love me, then." This was neither question nor statement but an ambiguous amalgam of both.

She said nothing.

"If you didn't love me, then why?" I tried again.

"Because we had to."

"I still have to."

"You'll find a way, Peter. It will be all right."

I hate when people say it will be all right.

"Okay," I said, not getting up. "I'll find a way."

Several extended seconds of unblemished stillness passed. Before I got to the door, I heard the mattress groan as she shifted and settled in. The antique beech grandfather clock ticked loudly in the downstairs hall, but otherwise the house was eerily silent, horror-movie hushed. The situation, as it was, could not have gone on. I knew it was over, that my sister was lost to me, that the wreckage of my torpedoed love could neither be dredged nor salvaged, and that things would never be the same. I knew this but couldn't accept it. I wouldn't sink without a struggle, without bloodying my hands as I dragged another down with me. Something had to give, and I knew I had to quickly capitalize on whatever vestiges of motivation were left.

Lou is my cousin, the eldest son of my eldest uncle, the one serving the sentence for racketeering. I don't have much contact with him, as we have little in common aside from the fact that our fathers are brothers, which is about all they have in common themselves; whatever genes we share do not amount to much else. Happily, our extended family gets together only on major holidays, so contact is limited to these occasions, when I'm duty-bound to manufacture conversation and affect an air of interest, to pretend that I'm genuinely glad to see them and eager to hear about what's happened in their lives since Christmas or Easter or the last birthday, communion, or funeral. But since Lou has gone into his father's profession, there was no doubt that he was the one to reach out to. He was surprised when I phoned and asked to see him—I had never called him before—and after I explained that it was not a matter to be dealt with over the phone, he told me to come down to his club in Bay Ridge, a few blocks from the Verrazano Bridge, a kind of insular ethnic enclave you wouldn't think existed anymore, little changed by time, though gentrification and intrusion from fresher immigrant groups threaten on all sides save the Narrows. So the next night, a foggy Friday in late November, while Severine was out with Spencer and my parents were at some year-end departmental shindig whose invitation I declined, I trekked into Brooklyn to ask my cousin for a gun.

Each time I see Lou he looks disproportionately older and heavier, though he never fails to tell me how he is watching what he eats and cutting back on the booze and just about ready to join that gym he has been talking about joining for years. At thirty-eight, he is already as bald as he will probably get, and his raven eyes seem to be perpetually underscored by sooty half-circles that might or might not signify a lack of sleep but that either way make his sockets seem like empty, inky hollows. The club, of which I had always heard them speak at family get-togethers but had never been to, is a sort of private bar, fronted by a wide tinted window stenciled in matte gold with the words, SAVARONELLA BROS. SOCIAL CLUB, in large and elongated lettering; and beneath in big bold black: PRIVATE. Inside is a narrow railroad suite that seems to extend indefinitely as you proceed through, the front room, which has a bar and some cocktail tables (and which is the only room with a window), leading to a more intimate space with a large round mahogany table in the center and a great ornate chandelier hanging from the ceiling (which lends a rusted lambency to everything below), and that to a third, even smaller room (conspicuously devoid of furnishings, just bare russet walls and a dark red shag carpet in the middle of an unfinished wood floor), at the end of which is a closed door.

I was welcomed warmly by Lou, who introduced me to the guys—a rough dozen sport-coated men sitting around with drinks in their hands and cigars or cigarettes dangling from their lips—as his little cousin from Long Island, the professor's kid, the bookworm, and offered me a glass of white wine, which I accepted. He was wearing a maroon silk dress shirt with the top three buttons undone, an unconstructed navy blazer, and tan slacks. He appeared glad to see me; and to the rest of the men I seemed to be an amusing novelty, for in a sense I was one of them, by blood and heritage, by name and outward appearance, and yet in another, more material and significant sense, I was entirely alien, of an altogether different universe, a sheltered suburbanite trespassing into the heart of a shadowy and age-old urban tradition.

After five minutes of painfully platitudinous conversation, Lou ushered me through the smoky rooms and opened the door at the end to reveal, rather anticlimactically, a simple and staid office with a few small gold-framed landscape paintings on the walls and a meticulously neat and unassuming birch desk. We sat down, Lou behind his desk in a high-back, button-tufted black executive chair, and I across from him in a plain gray steel folding chair that brought to mind grammar school band class. He clicked on a brushed nickel pharmacy lamp that spotlighted the surface of the desk and only cast more shadow onto his face, then pulled two cigarettes from a crumpled pack of Camels and held one out for me. I don't smoke. I abhor cigarettes. They make me physically ill. But I accepted it.

"So how's your parents, good?"

"Fine," I said. "Everybody's fine."

"And Sevy, what's she up to these days?"

"Same thing. School. You know. School. Classes."

He nodded as though he expected more and would have been offended if I didn't elaborate.

"School," I said, my attention diverted momentarily by the shiny red bulbous nose in the portrait of a sad clown on the wall behind Lou's head, which I was only just now noticing.

"Right, right." He squinted as he sucked in and exhaled.

"And you?" I puffed on my cigarette, careful not to swallow the smoke.

"Same old routine. No complaints, except this fuckin ulcer I got." He laid his hand on his stomach. "People still bustin my balls to no end, but you know, that's the business. This is what you sign up for. If I wanted some horseshit no-pressure job, I woulda become a mail carrier. Or a motherfuckin disgraziato street sweeper like that idiot uncle of ours."

"I'm glad I came down, Lou. I've always wanted to see the club. I'm always hearing about it." I took a sweeping look around the room, puffed again on my cigarette, and suppressed a cough. Besides the desk and its chairs there was nothing. The dull, drowsy, patternless wallpaper was numbing. I wasn't even sure what color it was. Maybe a dark brown or a muddled red.

"What's on your mind, Petey? What drags you out here? Seeing you down here's kind of like seeing a tropical flower in the desert."

I pushed myself past the instinct to delay. He was a man who would respect directness. Cagey small talk would get me nowhere.

"I need a gun, Lou."

"A gun?" He leaned forward while saying this as if he had possibly misheard me, and an amused grin slid onto his face. "A gun. You need a gun." His inflection was more declarative than interrogative, his reaction not unexpected, nor unjustified, nor unprepared for.

"I'm going hunting with some friends. I bought a beauty of a rifle from the sporting goods store, a 12-gauge, real nice, but I need a handgun to go with it. For close quarters. I don't know, they're telling me that I need one. Close quarters, they say. What do I know about hunting?" I chuckled and threw up my hands.

"Hunting?" he echoed, reclining.

"Yes, hunting."

"Hunting—where, hunting?"

"Upstate."

"Where upstate?"

"I don't know. North. Upstate."

"It's a big state."

"Bigger than some countries." I wasn't sure if this was factual, but it sounded as though it should be.

"And he doesn't know about this, your father?"

"I don't think he'd go for the idea. I'm a little embarrassed, but I figured you could help me out here. The other guys just asked their fathers, but you know mine."

"Yeah. I do," he scoffed.

A point in my favor.

"I've never come to you for anything before. I figured you could help me out here maybe."

"And you figured I would give you this thing, just like that? This is how you figured?"

We sat motionless and silent for a few prolonged seconds. I was trying to think of something to say, something humorous or explanatory, but mainly I just regretted coming. Lou's face was flushed. A vein in his forehead pulsated.

"What, you got girl problems?"

"No." I laughed this off as though nothing could be further from the truth.

"You seem like you got something wrong here, and at your age it's usually a female at the bottom of it." He leaned in. His tone and expression grew sympathetic. "I've seen guys fucked up by a broad like nobody's business. Madone. I know about girl problems. They're the worst. Ninety-nine percent of the time it's a broad causing the problem. It's a goddamn shame we need them and that fuckin hairy patch between their legs."

"I don't have girl problems, Lou," I said quietly.

"That may be the problem." He lowered his gaze and pointed at me. "Every time I see you I ask about the girls, and I get the same answer. A clean-cut young guy, not bad-looking.

Some brains. I mean, what's going on here?" He raised his arms—palms up—and looked from side to side. "You should be bangin a different one every week, like there's no tomorrow." He pumped his right fist a few times. "Minga, when I was your age..." He laughed and waggled his hand in front of him as though he'd punched a wall and was shaking off the pain. "I think you're not aggressive enough, is what I think." He stopped for a moment and stared fiercely at me as though wanting to jump out of his skin and inhabit my body and achieve everything I couldn't achieve with it, for my own sake. "When's the last time you been laid?"

"I don't have girl problems."

"No?" Lou cocked his head. "I think you do." He seemed delighted by this deduction, smiling grandly and tapping out the words on his desk with a spunky finger. "I think you do."

"I didn't come here for psychoanalysis."

"Come on, when's the last time?" he whispered. "Everybody's got dry spells. No embarrassment. It's me and you here. We sweep for bugs every day. Nothing said in this room leaves this room."

I put off responding for a good five seconds. "I'm going hunting. If you can't help me, it's no big deal."

"I didn't say that. I just don't like bullshit."

His tone and visage suddenly turned curt and cold. He paused and slowly rose, pushing himself out of the chair, and went toward the front rooms. "Stay here," he ordered, without turning.

What was I doing here? I wanted to smack myself in the head, not in a slapstick comedic way but hard and heavy, really give myself a shot to the temple. I wanted it to hurt, to make my brain joggle around my skull a bit. But Lou came back quickly and sat down again before I could raise a hand against myself.

"Hunting, huh?" he said.

"I was invited."

"They said you need a handgun... for close quarters?"

"That's what they told me. I've never gone hunting before."

"So this is what *you're* telling *me*? Close quarters? Like if the fuckin deer comes at you with a knife or something?"

I nodded and gulped and struggled to keep from blinking excessively. I was pleading the Fifth.

"I'm no professor," he said, "but I am not stupid."

"No, of course you're not stupid. Nobody's saying you're stupid. The word *stupid* was never even spoken, until you said it right now."

He didn't lift his eyes from me, and I tried hard to keep mine on him, to match his slit-eyed, somewhat sinister gaze with my own, because I knew that if I withdrew, there would be no question that I was lying. There was probably little question in his mind anyway; I've always had a poor poker face, and Lou was far more adept at reading people, as his trade required.

"What are you hunting?" he asked.

"Deer. What else?"

"Ever eat deer?"

"No. Have you?"

"No. I hear it's tough."

"Yes. And gamey."

"Chewy. Hard to digest. Gives you agita." He rubbed his stomach. "They call it venison, but it's deer."

"I know. Like how they call pig pork and cow beef. But they still call chicken chicken."

"Go figure."

"Yep." I nodded, pursed my lips, and nervously kneaded my quadriceps. "Yep."

He leaned halfway over his desk, still holding me in his rigorous regard, put his hand inside his sport jacket, withdrew a pistol, placed it on the table in front of him, and slowly slid it toward me until an inch of its handle hung over the edge. Then he sank back again.

"It's not easy to whack somebody, Pete. And I don't think it's you. Frankly, I don't think you got it in you."

There was no need to dissemble shock at his suggestion. My first reaction was denial, a natural gut reaction to the unnaturalness of the thought of me whacking somebody, and to the grim ridiculousness of the euphemism itself: to *whack* somebody. I almost heard myself say, *Are you kidding me?* but I realized it was too late. My cousin, in fact, is not stupid. In most matters, especially those germane to his work, he is quite shrewd. But I couldn't tell him the truth, even if he knew, even if he knew that I knew that he knew. I looked away, forced out a phony laugh, and dismissed the notion as sheer bosh.

"I've never even hit anyone, Lou. I've never even been in a schoolyard scuffle. You think I'm going to shoot someone? Me? I can't even imagine pointing it at someone." In trying to sound convincing I only seemed patently pathetic.

"Pick it up," he said.

"I mean, I'll probably have enough trouble shooting the deer. I probably won't even fire a shot. To think that I would—"

"Pick up the gun," he repeated sternly.

"What? Why?"

I picked it up.

"Point it at me, and don't ask why. Point it here," he tapped the center of his forehead. "Right here."

Slowly, I raised the gun to eye level and held it straight at my cousin's head, right hand cradling the grip and left supporting my wrist, a thin layer of perspiration coating my palms. He just sat there for a few seconds, looking directly at me as if the gun weren't aimed point-blank between his eyeballs. He didn't bat a lash. It was heavier than I would have imagined—yet so sleek and streamlined—and after a while my arms began to tremble, but I held it as commanded.

"Good," he said. "Put it down."

I dropped it on the table and pulled away fast, as though it were an accursed object that I was relieved to have out of my grasp. He leaned back again. His fingers grazed audibly over a bristled cheek as he rocked slowly in the chair, finally taking his eyes off me and focusing on the pistol.

"Nice-looking piece, ain't it?"

"Yes," I answered, thinking about how much I wanted not to be there.

"You're a smart kid. That's why I'm doing this. Whatever you do, be smart about it, got it? I'm giving you this thing here, but that's it. That's where it ends. What you do with it you do by yourself. I wash my hands, you hear me?" He seemed slightly sad, as though regretting in advance what I was going to do.

"I'm going hunting, Lou. I'm just—"

"I don't wanna know any more," he interrupted, putting his palms up defensively and shutting his eyes. "I wash my hands. You hear what I'm telling you?" He rubbed his hands together as if under a faucet, then shook them dry. "Hai capito?"

I nodded and looked down broodingly, then looked up at him.

"Ho capito."

He reached over, picked up the gun, and slid the cartridge out from the bottom of the handle. "This is the magazine. The bullets are in here. And don't give me that fuckin look like you know it all! What do you know about a gun, ah?" He paused irritably as if waiting for a response, though he knew none was coming. "Look. You slide it in like this, and you give it a little shove like this," jamming the clip in with the base of his palm. "Then you take off the safety—make sure you do that if you want the bullets to come out—you pull the top back like this, and bang, you do what you gotta do." He pulled out the clip again and laid the gun down. "And lemme tell you something. You still wanna shoot something at close range, you make sure you look it in the eyes when you do it."

It was, in fact, a *nice-looking* gun.

"It's only for close quarters. I probably won't even have to use it."

"Listen to me." He leaned over and pointed at his face with his ringed pinky and forefinger, speaking through gritted teeth. "In the eyes."

That was it. He wrapped the gun in a clean yellow rag that he took from a desk drawer and gave it to me like a present. I cached it in my backpack next to the unread Schopenhauer and a mostly empty notebook I kept to jot down random thoughts and ideas. Then we walked two blocks down to a restaurant where the staff treated us like resident royalty and the other patrons regarded us as rock stars, and everything that had transpired in that dim little room seemed forgotten, as if it had never happened. We ate and drank and laughed over linguini and lobster, steak pizzaiola and shrimp oreganata, and though I have never had any kind of real relationship with my cousin, we enjoyed each other's company that night more than ever, knowing we could not go much further than this and savoring the moment all the more so for it. He was pleased that I had come to him and happy that he could help me, because I had never before shown any interest in cultivating a friendship, which is not to say that he or I wanted to start then, only that it was better than nothing. Blood, after all, counts for something.

So now I had a gun. And I liked having it. I liked knowing that I had it. Maybe just having it would be enough. Maybe I would never have to use it. I liked looking at it and feeling it, unfolding the yellow cloth to admire the polished black metal and wipe down its surfaces to a streakless sheen before gingerly rewrapping it with the tender concern of a fresh, first-time father swaddling his infant son, comforted by the idea that if I were again taken by that irresistible urge that had propelled me into action, I could go out and make things happen, bring pain down upon those deemed deserving. At a moment's notice, I could meet that urge with the means to satisfy it. I liked the feel of a firearm in my hand, the grip's grain rough and ragged against my fingers. I put the barrel in my mouth once, not out of any suicidal impulse, only to get the barest, briefest sense of what it might feel like to be a hairsbreadth from oblivion, standing at the edge of a cliff looking down, wondering how long the fall would take and if I'd feel anything when I hit the ground. I thought it would be something special to feel the cold steel barrel on my tongue, pressing against the wall of my throat, tingling my teeth. But it wasn't.

I didn't yet know what to do with the gun, but I knew the key was to envision the scene, to rehearse it over and over like a well-made play until my lines belonged to me, until I owned the act and could play the role without thinking, until I could *be* the part without playing it. If I could see it happening, picture myself doing it, then it could be done, whatever it was.

Yes, it could be done.

4

A Season in Hell

He, not God, could by that means cast himself and his sister both into hell, where he could guard her forever and keep her forevermore intact amid the eternal fires.

— William Faulkner

I never told her how afraid I am, how afraid I always was. I never told her that everything I do is couched in fear, poisoned by doubt, cowardice and shame, and shadowed by a crippling uncertainty that hobbles my every effort and hampers my every thought, how the most negligible actions and nugatory undertakings inspire me with a debilitating dread that binds me to the bed as though it were the only haven from the humdrum horror that is everywhere. I never told her, but that is what it comes down to: fear. Fear and trembling. Angst and apprehension. I am still so afraid. A life of such unqualified inconsequence, such nothingness, fills me with terror. Pure, untapped terror.

And looking back, reviewing the ruins of the past from the enlightened present, I still can't answer the questions, like how we became strangers, how, after such an eternal span, we suddenly became brother and sister. Out of some kind of casual courtesy, she would ask me about my day, what I had done, where I had gone (as though I went places), things she never used to ask, things she had no right or reason to ask and no real desire to know. Her vapid interest was poorly feigned and painfully patronizing. I seethed at her happiness, her unrestrained, unreasonable, unacceptable contentment, which I felt as a deeply personal affront, so inimical to my own welfare. I never tried to hide that. She should have at least respected my openness.

Even now I become flustered when I recall her demeanor during that phase.

There was that time when, home after a long night out with him, she came into my room before going to bed, while I was lying there trying futilely to absorb what I was reading. I had long since stopped waiting for her. I was striving to give up, to give in, but her unexpected appearance in the doorway momentarily obliterated all that had gone amiss—until she revealed the circumstances of her call, her visit to the condemned man, and it all came undone; the perceived panacea proved to be only a more lethal poison. She and Spencer were going to a play on Friday, off-off-Broadway. Some avant-garde basement theater in the East Village. Friends of his were in the production, and some of these friends were girls, she mentioned, less than subtly. I was welcome to join.

"I have plans Friday," I said, barely looking up from the page, desperately anchoring my eyes to the unread words.

"Do you?"

Of course not.

"And I don't like plays. When have you known me to go to plays? I like to read them, not see them. The best plays remain unperformed. They are unperformable." I didn't believe that, but at the time it seemed just the thing to say.

She pulled the door three-quarters closed and came to sit next to me, lightly pushing the book down and away from my face.

"I'd really like you to come. It would make me happy if you came," she said, and lowered her gaze to her twiddling hands, as if my refusal had troubled her.

"It would? You're telling me it would make you happy if I joined you, you and Spencer? You would honestly like me to come with you? This is what you would want? This is what it would take to make you happy?"

"Yes. And again you're making this into something. You're not even trying to make it easier, Peter. I'm doing all I can."

"Oh yes. That much is certain. And it seems easy enough for you. Everything's always been easy for you."

She moved to leave and I grabbed her hard, held her in place. She looked down quizzically at where my hand clamped her arm. I had never been forceful with her, never laid any but the most adoring of hands on her. Moving only her eyeballs, the rest of her body remaining as unresponsively still as a carved ice statue, she gave me this look—surprise, shock, maybe a dollop of distaste. Not fear, not yet.

"Can you guess what would make me happy, at least for the moment?" I quizzed. "Can you?"

"I didn't come for that." Her eyes turned away.

"What's the difference?"

"No, not now."

The present is just an unbroken string of nows.

"Why not?"

"They're still up, walking around down there. I can hear them."

This had never been a problem. She knew my parents would not come up. Their life was downstairs, the distance to the sun.

"Besides…" she added. Her countenance was of boredom and mild annoyance. She had just washed off her makeup, and her skin gleamed with stripped-down smoothness. The gun was a few steps away under a pile of folded T-shirts in a dresser drawer. I felt it as a living thing, its pulsing presence calling to me from its burrow.

"You can't expect me to stop just like that, at least at the physical level," I said, my fingers loosening enough to rub the soft skin on the inside of her forearm. "It's unnatural to ask someone to stop like that."

"Unnatural?" she snickered, seizing the opportunity to wrest her arm from my grasp.

"You can't expect me to stop wanting so suddenly. You can't take away everything at once and leave me nothing."

"How then?"

With a bang, not a whimper. A big fucking bang. My hand felt suddenly empty without the gun in it, somehow incomplete.

"I want to know if you've slept with him yet."

"You'd rather it be gradual? Drawn out? You'd prefer we make this as slow and painful as possible? Would you rather we jiggle the tip of the spear around in the wound before removing it?" She paused and looked up, smiling, then shook her head and sniggered. "What am I asking? Of course you would."

"I want to know. I just want to know some things, like if you've gone down on him. Or vice versa."

She didn't answer. She just quietly smirked.

"Have you slept with him?"

She turned to me, wild-eyed and fierce. "Yes."

"Does he know? Have you told him about us?"

"He knows you're my brother."

"And that's all?"

"That's all there is to know."

Artfully, her hand settled on my thigh, edging toward the center. She was suddenly all softness and serenity, the thorns of a moment ago dissolved into tenderness. I wasn't buying it. The gun was loaded, lying in the drawer under my clothes.

"What are you doing?" she asked as I got up.

"Shutting the door."

I saw it in abrupt cinematic images. Twin shots. A pair of bullets. One to her face, that cruel, flawless face, the other through the roof of my mouth and straight into the temporal lobe. It could be done in seconds, the eradication of our past, the extinguishment of our present, and the aborting of our future, complete annihilation of all our thoughts and feelings and memories, leaving no record of our having ever been anything other than ordinary brother and sister. Or damaged, deranged brother and poor, victimized sister. Seconds from now it could be done, two reverberating reports, two gaping, bloody holes, and no one would be wise to our history. It would be beautifully crystallized, so perfectly preserved in cryptic completion. Hurriedly, as though any additional delay would mollify the purpose that was hardening in my head, I threw off the covers, bounded out of bed, scampered across the floor, pulled the door shut and locked it, my book falling facedown on the floor in the process.

"I think I'm starting to hate you," I said, standing across the room with my back to the door and my hands crossed behind me as though concealing something. But this could never be. It rang untrue even as it came out of my mouth, and she knew it.

"Come here." She opened her arms to me, but I held fast.

"I can never forgive you."

"You don't have to," she said soothingly.

It could be over in seconds.

"Come here," she said.

Seven seconds. Seven years or seventy. Sartre was right. There's no difference once the illusion of eternity has been lost.

I stood there, estimating five short steps to either the bed or the gun. But if I had done it, if I had taken those solemn steps toward the dresser, she could not have made her grand exit; she could not have walked into the water. And so I went to her, and she stayed with me one last time, and after it was done and she lay asleep, I watched and watched her, measuring her breath, drinking in her sleeping scent, studying the part of her lips and the soft, anodyne angles and delicate midnight sheen of her face, fragile fingers arched limply beside her head on the pillow, and like a revelation that had always been there below the surface, recessed and overlooked but ever-present, ever-potent, I understood that I could never stop wanting her, and that nothing real or imagined, nothing promised or pledged, nothing in this world or any other could ever satisfy or substitute for this want.

The day after this conversation, I learned that Spencer was coming over for dinner. My initial reaction was something akin to nausea, an unremitting sense of defeat and dire hopelessness that I tried unconvincingly to pass off as indifference because I knew it was too late to change anything. Severine informed me of the invitation a few days in advance, adding that she would fully understand if I didn't want to be there, that she wouldn't be upset if I'd rather not attend. I told her I wouldn't hear of it. She cut to the chase and said she thought it would be better if I weren't there, that she would prefer I make a conciliatory excuse and absent myself from the occasion. I assumed an inflated air of offense and said I wouldn't think of missing such an event. She tensed her jaw, pressed her upper lip hard upon the lower, and dropped the argument.

My mother, who had suggested the soirée in the first place, was unabashedly excited about our guest, due in part to the novelty of the occasion—we seldom had company—as well as to her desire to learn about Spencer firsthand, this heralded young man with whom her daughter had been spending so much time, her first real boyfriend. My father had had him in class, so my mother was the family member least acquainted with my sister's beau, a deficiency she was eager to remedy. She had met him only in passing as he waited for Severine in the hallway, had talked to him only briefly on the phone when he called. Here was her chance to discover more of the man himself.

It was the Wednesday of the week before Thanksgiving. My mother had spent the afternoon in the kitchen preparing a menu of Caesar salad, tortellini soup, filet mignon, sautéed asparagus, stewed spinach, and lemon meringue pie for dessert.

"It's so rare that we have a guest," she justified, as I sat at the kitchen table drinking a tall, cold glass of chocolate milk and nibbling a Twinkie and watching her aproned form move from fridge to stove to pantry to counter to oven with the effortless artistry of a cooking show host. "I want to make sure everything is as close to perfect as possible. You know how we feel about perfection in this house." She glanced up cunningly from her cutting board without breaking the rhythm of her dicing. "And besides, I'm dying to meet him."

"What are you talking about?" I said. "You've met him at least twice already."

"Which amounts to less than ten minutes. I think I should get to know him a bit better, my daughter's first boyfriend." She smiled saucily with these last words, as though they tickled her tongue.

To me they were pure gall and wormwood. I stared glumly into the creamy entrails of my Twinkie, having suddenly lost all craving for it. "And you think a family dinner will reveal his soul or something? Bring the skeletons out of his closet?"

She popped a destemmed mushroom cap into her mouth and raised her eyebrows. "You never know. Food and drink have been known to bring out a bone or two."

The Santoku's Granton edge blade bounced rapidly up and down against the bamboo board as she sliced the shallots with uncanny accuracy, and though I would never have wanted to see her carve off a finger, a tiny punitive slash would not have been altogether unappreciated. My voiceless prayers were left unanswered as my father came around the corner.

"Don't get your hopes up. People are generally much less interesting after you've spent some time with them."

I smiled into my chocolate milk and took an especially delicious sip, only to have it leave a sour aftertaste when my father couldn't refrain from adding, as he began rinsing vegetables: "He's a bright kid, though. Right near the top of the class. Writes well too. Might have a real future in academia."

How could I have been expected to leave it at that?

"If you call that a future," I remarked. "Those who can't do..."

"... don't do anything," my father finished, keeping his eyes on the sink. "And I haven't seen *you* do much this semester, son."

"Unless moping counts," my mother piled on.

"It's something."

134

They seemed to be willing to leave the sparring at a stalemate, but I couldn't let it go.

"So you're fond of him?" I don't know why the word *fond* came out, except that I had overcompensated in my attempt to sound natural and conversationally matter of fact, masking my discomfort with the subject by ingurgitating what remained of my Twinkie and washing it down with a savory slug of milk.

"Chocolate milk?" He winced as though I were a dog he'd caught drinking from the toilet. "What are you, five?"

I put my glass down and stared at it. "It's nonfat. With plenty of calcium and vitamins A and D. Nourishes the body *and* the brain."

He halted washing to concentrate on staring at me, then quickly rebooted, backtracking to my question. "As much as I'm *fond* of anyone, I guess." He pat-dried some lettuce leaves, then addressed my mother as he laid them out beside her to be torn into bite-size bits. "But as you said, it's her first boyfriend." That phrase again! He casually moved on from washing to peeling, methodically rubbing a paring blade down the length of a Kirby cucumber in remarkably even strokes. "No reason to think he'll be her last."

I wasn't sure if this was pulling the knife out or sticking it further in, so I just took one last long swig and left the room with what little remained of my milk and one certainty in my mind: I would not spoil the dinner they were working so hard on. I was even going to enjoy it. I was prepared.

Spencer arrived four minutes early, by my watch, the jingle of the doorbell humming through the house like the buzz of a bark beetle boring through a pine tree, rallying three of us from different points in the house to the front door. Out of some kind of undeclared deference, my father and I stood back so Severine could answer it. The guest of honor entered with a sunlit smile, a genial greeting and a solid handshake for the men, and a kiss on the cheek for my sister and my mother, who pulled herself out of the kitchen just long enough for an abbreviated reception before shuffling back in to make sure the pie didn't overcook.

Self-assured as always, but not cocky, never showing a chink in his well-bred armor, our gracious guest presented us with a bottle of the recently released Beaujolais Nouveau and a box of Leonidas cocoa-dusted Belgian dark chocolate truffles, as well as a small mixed bouquet for my mother. He looked suave as ever, tieless in a properly pressed deep burgundy shirt and a fitted black blazer over dark, sandblasted jeans, clean-shaven, faintly cologned and subtly pomaded. I watched and admired as he chatted comfortably with my father, and I realized that what made him more handsome was the fact that his handsomeness was not picture-perfect, his features not fine or surpassingly symmetrical, neither roughly masculine nor remarkably unique, a bony little bubble on the high bridge of his nose and a few misaligned teeth marring the bottom row, his stubble-free skin displaying several shallow pockmarks above a high left cheek-bone and some minor razor irritation on the side of the chin, even a small, scabbed-over cut whose incrustation I could only hope might break and bleed sometime between appetizers and dessert. Pleased as I was at first blush to notice these defects, it is just these kinds of erotic imperfections that can often make the object of desire even more desirable.

I had to start immediately, establish a firm position from the beginning with some simple, safe, disarming chitchat, and I had to be believable; I had to believe myself to convincingly incarnate the role. Craft and patience were required, slowness and tact vital. It was my turn to play the artist. I approached him, excusing myself for interrupting, and asked pleasantly if he would like an apéritif. Then I made four Kir Royals, heavy on the champagne, and we proceeded into the living room, where trays of baked brie en croute, chèvre-stuffed dates with candied almonds, and prosciutto-wrapped melon balls were arrayed on the black bamboo coffee table, so prettily arranged they seemed more like centerpieces than hors d'œuvres. Conversation flowed smoothly, without a hitch, and by the time supper was served, Severine was visibly relaxed, her earlier uneasiness allayed by my natural and affable behavior, which betrayed no insincerity or hint of hostility. I had successfully settled our nerves.

Apropos of dinner itself, everyone seemed to have a festive time. My father was characteristically reserved and not terribly interested in the whole thing, though he remained a paragon of politesse and flawlessly fulfilled the duties required of his rank as head of the household. He chimed in when the conversation swung around to books or academics, but he understood that this occasion was primarily for my mother's sake. She, showing a concerned maternal instinct, proceeded in subtle, noninvasive ways to garner information about Spencer's background and family, starting with the general and moving toward the specific, never probing beyond the boundaries of propriety. The good-natured interviewee gladly offered responses to her questioning. It was like a game: she took as much pleasure in fishing the stuff out of him as he did in seeing it meet with her gratified smiles and nods of assent. She would take advantage of a brief lull in the conversation to say something such as: "So, Spencer, how long have you lived in Brooklyn?"

"Since I came to the States, almost two years ago. I'd prefer the city, of course, but Manhattan rents are out of my league for the moment."

"Brooklyn's a city in itself," she proudly defended her hometown, even though she had no family or connections left in the borough. "I spent the first thirteen years of my life there. I don't go back much, but I'd still take a Junior's strawberry cheesecake and Grimaldi's pepperoni pie over anything they have across the river."

Spencer laughed pleasantly and tilted his head in a diplomatically concessionary way that somewhat reminded me of Ronald Reagan. "I'm kind of partial to John's, on Bleecker, but when it comes to food, I always try to keep an open mind and an impartial palate."

"A truly enlightened soul," I commentated, slipping into sarcasm for an unguarded second.

My mother laughed charmingly and picked up her thread, circumventing the tasteless toxin I had injected.

"My husband is from Downtown Manhattan," she volunteered, laying her hand on my father's shoulder, his cue to kick into the conversation.

"We were all dying to get out. Some of us literally dying." He followed the prompt. "Now all you young people are willing to pay exorbitant rents to live in the same tiny tenements we dreamed of escaping. They were cramped and crumbling back then, forty years ago. I can only imagine what kind of shape they're in now. It amazes me."

"The romance of city life," Severine said.

"Sure. The romance of rats and roaches." I couldn't help myself. "Not to mention the human vermin."

They all looked at me. Severine glared threateningly, but that was it. I focused on my food and controlled myself from there on in. My mother sailed in again to patch up the tear.

"Have your parents come down here? What do they think of New York?"

"They love it. To visit, of course. But they have no intention of ever leaving Montreal."

"I don't blame them. It's beautiful up there. Do you visit them often?"

"Between semesters, and sometimes on the odd weekend when I miss speaking French."

I was burning to point out that, strictly speaking, Canadian French and *real* French are two drastically different animals, but I managed to control myself. "You could always come here for that," I said with an Academy Award–winning grin.

"That's nice to know." He raised his glass to me and then downed it.

We soon had the guy's life laid out on the table, and by dessert everyone was so sated with food, wine, and conversation that we fell deep into a collective torpor, the animated talk of a few minutes earlier giving way to enervated exchanges like the following:

"The pie is excellent, Mom."

"Yes it is, Mrs. Niletti."

"Good, I'm glad you like it. Last time I overcooked it a bit."

"Not this time." This was my contribution.

"No, it's not overcooked at all." A spirited second from Spencer.

"Good."

"Yes, it really is very good."

"More coffee?"

"I'll have some."

"No, thank you, I'm fine."

"None for me. I'll never sleep if I have any more caffeine."

This was the closest to awkward that the evening had come so far. Having nothing left to say, we sat around and exchanged achingly trivial looks until I finally suggested that we three move to the basement to relax for a while before Spencer embarked on the long trip home. Everyone enthusiastically agreed, especially my father, anxious to get this over with. Spencer of course offered to help with the dishes, and my mother of course declined, explaining with an appreciative smile that she didn't often get to play hostess and wanted to make the most of it.

On our way out of the dining room, while he was thanking my parents and telling them how wonderful everything had been and how it was an especially nice thing for him because, as a single man living alone, he usually dines out or makes something quick and, frankly, not very good, Severine squeezed my arm lightly, took me aside—just out of sight—and placed a soft, careful kiss on my cheek. She leaned into me, her lips lightly glancing my lobe, whispered, *Thank you,* so close that I could feel her warm, moist breath on my ear, and dotingly stroked the back of my head. This I was not ready for. I knew my performance had been good, and I was betting on my ability to persuade her that I had at last come around. Aside from a couple of slight snags, it had gone exactly as planned, but this was not supposed to be part of it. For the past several weeks she had shown me nothing but increasing callousness alternating with irascibility, as if my presence was a bother at best, my very existence vexing. All that moderated enmity had fueled my resolve, and now, just when everything was coming together, just when the fateful moment was at hand, this happens. A little contact, the brush of her lips against my face, two willowy words whispered into my ear, and I feel conviction siphon out, disperse, and vaporize around me. I consider the luster of her smile as she squeezes my arm, her brightness and buoyancy as we make our way down the basement stairs, and I nearly wish it were enough to see her like this, illumined in a way I'd never quite seen her before. For a moment, I wish that I were able to accept or at least live with the knowledge that this was a brightness for another sky, not mine. I wish I were able to be her brother. But I know I cannot.

The basement is very comfortable and, though spanning the same dimensions as the first floor, quite cozy. It is spacious and sparsely furnished—the entire square footage occupied by an old couch, a rhomboidal glass coffee table, a barely watchable nineteen-inch television, a disused Olympic weight bench set, and a warped Ping-Pong table—and nicely finished in light gray carpeting and diagonal cedar wall panels slanting down from popcorn ceiling to floor. Though only a single story down, it feels like a completely separate and isolated space with little connection to the upper levels. I've always liked being below ground; once the door closes and you descend the split stairway, the basement seems securely sealed off, secluded and safe from the outside and upstairs, like some clandestine chthonian bunker or enshrouded subterranean shelter set aside for those in the know.

We sat on the faded orange couch, which my parents had transferred from the den when they refurnished, and talked and drank our digestifs, three bright young things discussing art and film, literature and philosophy, college kid colloquy peppered with gossip and pop culture quips and silly sitcom references. Severine seemed happy, very happy, critically close to giddy at moments, relieved to see her brother so easy and untroubled around her inamorato, laughing and joking and actively participating in the convivial confab and actually appearing to enjoy himself without pretense. My mother came down to say a final goodnight to Spencer and to bring a bowl of pretzel nuggets and kettle chips. She was taking her position as *lady of the manor* more seriously than I'd ever seen, and her outstanding efforts had no doubt contributed the most to the success of the evening, which seemed as if it would finish as auspiciously as it had begun.

It was at the height of merriment, in the midst of a communal laugh, in fact, that I deemed the moment favorable, reached into a narrow crevice between the couch pillows, and pulled out the pistol. Wearing the remainder of a smile from a previous moment's mirth, I held the weapon in front of me as if displayed on a platter, slowly and carefully enunciating the words I had prepared for the moment, which had perfectly presented itself. "I picked this up the other day," I said, as though showing off a hard-won medal, my eyes resting easefully on the firearm as I tilted it one way and then another, exposing it at different angles to render the full of its glory to my audience.

I had invested much in this simple phrase, coupled with the presentation of the gun, my pièce de résistance. Her reaction was crucial, bound to fall on one side or the other of the razor-thin border between fear and mockery. Had she laughed it off from the beginning, had they simply dismissed me and my gun as frivolous, as nothing more than moronic, preposterous posturing, I probably would have laughed it off as well and gone on drinking, relieved that I didn't have to go through with it. Then maybe I would say something stupid, maybe not, and Spencer would go home safely, and Severine would kiss me again before bed and thank me a second time, very softly and sweetly and sincerely, and I might ask her to come in, and she would look down and smile somberly and deny me my wish as though I were a headstrong child who should have known better than to ask in the first place, and I would sit up in the dark, waiting for the miracle, and that would be that.

But it wasn't.

Expression vanished from Severine's face; the illusion was broken. She realized the entire night had been a scandalous lie, and for perhaps the first time in her life, if only for an instant, she was afraid of me, or so I like to believe. I drew sustenance from their startled silence. I was emboldened by their dumbfounded disquietude. I continued.

"It's a nine millimeter." (I'm still not exactly sure what that means.) "Nice-looking piece, no?" I paraphrased Lou and turned the gun sideways, gangsta style. The words felt foreign on my tongue. My voice wavered a bit, but I think I was the only one to perceive it. Spencer's expression had something nervous to it, a pinch of panic, as well as a challenge, a provocation, a dare.

He leaned toward the table, glanced over a few pretzel nuggets and picked a winner, then sat back, slid it slowly into his mouth and slowly crunched, waiting to completely swallow before speaking. "Interesting choice of words. I never thought of guns as particularly nice-looking. Where did you get it?" he asked, licking a speck of salt off his finger.

"Interesting choice of questions, but not the most important thing."

"Why, then?" he said.

"Ah. Now, that's more to the point."

I reached over and picked up my glass, calmly took a sip of sherry, replaced it on the coaster, and leaned back, all without uncrossing my legs.

"I don't know. Maybe it's just an extension of my childhood, when I always wanted a BB gun and my father wouldn't let me have one. You remember that, Sev, don't you, how he would never let me have one? I was a careful and responsible kid. He really refused to bend. I never understood why he was so stubborn about it."

"Maybe he was afraid you'd shoot your eye out." Spencer grabbed a chip. "We've all seen *A Christmas Story*, haven't we?" Then he ate the chip.

"Ha," I said without laughing.

"I never understood why you wanted one." Severine fixed her eyes on me intently, sardonic.

"Good question. Probably just because I wasn't allowed to have one. Forbidden fruit and all that." I paused. "So I borrowed one of Don's and Dad found it, remember? And then he called Don's parents. I couldn't believe he actually called them."

"Who's Don?"

I found it strange that he would ask this; Don's identity didn't seem to be the crux of the story.

"A friend of his," Severine answered.

"A *close* friend of mine," I augmented, finishing my wine and holding up the glass in my left hand so that the high-hat lighting shot through it prismatically. "You've never cared all that much for Don, have you?" I made this sound inquisitorial, as though suspecting her guilty of a crime she should have long since confessed to.

She tossed her hair back flippantly and turned away. "I've never thought enough of him to care either way."

That sounded about right. It always seemed to me that she carried an unexpressed contempt for my best friend, a sort of clement disapproval of our camaraderie that she curbed herself from voicing because she knew how I valued him and would have never endangered such a rare commodity.

"Regardless, we used to hunt pigeons together in Don's backyard. I loved shooting them but always felt pretty bad after, watching them fall from the tree and hit a few branches on the way down and finally smash on the ground and writhe around a bit before dying. Maybe that was part of the game. I didn't feel as bad shooting crows, though. Watching the crows die didn't really bother me at all. I always felt they deserved it, for some reason."

"Guns were never my thing," Spencer said. "I find them so very white trash. Kind of like bowling, you know."

"Bowling is a perfectly fine pastime. What's your gripe with bowling?" I snickered, looking at Severine as though this were confirmation that something was seriously off with Spencer. Who doesn't like bowling? What's not to like?"

"There's nothing wrong with bowling, in itself. I enjoy knocking down a few pins from time to time. It just seems to me that the guys who have guns are the guys who sit around and spit tobacco into soda cans and beat their wives and berate their kids and go bowling with other guys like themselves, drinking cheap beer and burping for fun." He paused and focused on my eyes. "Guns have no class."

"Oh, that is so cliché, Spencer," I chided him. "And that whole tirade is pretty elitist."

"So be it." He ducked his head defiantly. "Ainsi, soit-il."

"I suppose you're more of a polo or archery man. Perhaps a little croquet or equestrian. No common old American yellow mustard for you, only Grey Poupon."

"What I'm saying is, guns have no place in civilized discourse."

"Civilized discourse?" I stammered out a laugh and looked at Severine with connivance. "Is this guy for real?" Then back to

Spencer. "I'm surprised to hear you say something like that. Sounds like you picked it up from an after-school special. An anti-firearm commercial campaign or something. Are you going to tell me next that guns don't kill people, people kill people?" I waved the gun in front of me with a casual, sweeping gesture. "I'm surprised and, frankly, more than a little disappointed, even somewhat skeptical about your whole weltanschauung."

"You couldn't just say *world view*?" She tried to slap me down, but I ignored her censure. "I mean, you don't even speak German."

Spencer kept to his game. "Diderot said that 'skepticism is the first step toward truth.' Philosophy, your love, was born of such thoughts and feelings. Maybe you should thank me, Peter."

"My love? Do you want to hear about my love?" I tapped the gun's chassis against my chest. "Should I tell you about *my* love?" I almost relinquished my position. I almost ceded control.

"Peter," Severine said with stolid gravity, as if the inflection of her voice could quell me. "Stop." Then she modified her tone with a touch of imploring. "Please stop. This is childish."

"Ah, that gives me a good idea!" I perked up. "How about a story about our carefree, idyllic childhood? What do you say, Spencer?"

"Now *that* I would like to hear."

"Where'd you get it, Peter?" she interjected incongruously into the repartee.

"Spencer already asked me that, not ten minutes ago."

"But now I'm asking you. And you never answered."

"I would prefer not to answer. I am a man of preferences, like Bartleby. Besides, why are you so concerned? You can't think I would *do* anything with this. What would I do, shoot somebody? You, Spencer?" I waved the gun around with perfect nonchalance, first in the direction of the boyfriend, the barrel a few feet from his forehead — "No flinching," I said — then toward Severine. "You, Sis?" Finally, I turned it on myself and pressed the muzzle to my temple. "Me? Do you really think I would shoot myself?" I felt the suction of the gun's metal mouth against my head and imagined the eager bullet lying in wait in the chamber, inches from my brain.

Basking in authority, in the rigid reticence I engendered, I leaned back against the worn, ragged cushions of the old threadbare couch and rested the gun in my lap, hand wrapped loosely around its grip, finger caressing trigger. Now was my time. I had endured more than a month of corrosive frustration and waded through one demoralizing dinner, and finally my crowning moment was here. I had earned this. I had created it, framed the scene with a director's eye, anticipated possible variations and prepared for potentially derailing permutations. It was flowing. All was on track.

But my glory faded as quickly as it had arrived.

"If you do," she said with a bemused stare in the direction of the table, "if you do decide to shoot yourself..." looking up at me severely, "please make sure it's through the mouth and not the side of the head, like so many sad suicide failures you hear about. If you're going to do something, do it right. Especially if it's going to be the last thing you do."

"Yes," Spencer picked up before I could process the sting. "Otherwise you risk brain damage or blindness, or even lifelong defacement, literally. Not to mention extreme embarrassment."

Then she laughed. She let out a single self-satisfied giggle, banefully budging the weight that had kept the room balanced in my favor, and the first fatal fractures began to appear in the delicate structure I had orchestrated. I don't think she realized that it was this laugh, even more than the remark, that was so searing, this horrible, scornful simper. With this laugh it became clear, and in its echo I fully grasped what I had only told myself but had not yet been brought to believe, that there was no pale chance she would ever again be mine; that she never had been mine. Whatever remaining pinhole of light that had persisted in my mind to this point was engulfed in that bleary, black-hole laugh.

And him, he wasn't afraid. The bastard still wasn't afraid. After a few minutes of edgy concern, he stuck with his original evaluation: I was still just an artless older brother from the bland backwater, innocuous and despairingly jejune, all show, no bite, and not even much bark. There was never anything to fear. It was all a farcical false alarm.

I said nothing during the long seconds their laughter took to fade out, and remained silent for the longer seconds afterward. But the decision had been made, and there would be no reneging. A bullet had to go somewhere. Anger and pain were the only scraps left to feed on; I had to make use of them. From dejection and defeat I would cull the courage to carry on and will myself forward into battle.

"I guess this qualifies as an uncomfortable silence," Spencer spoke into the mute denseness, "except... I don't know about you guys, but I find it kind of comfortable." He laughed, leaned back luxuriously, and draped his arms on the upper edge of the sofa, the right extended over Severine's shoulder.

"My brother cultivates uncomfortable and embarrassing situations. I suspect he actually likes them." She snuggled up close to Spencer. "Once, when we were little, he asked during Christmas dinner, just after the ham was laid on the table, where Vachina was. Apparently, he had heard some of the older kids talking about it in school and thought it was a small country in Southeast Asia." She turned bitter eyes on me. "You remember that? Ever find Vachina on a map?"

I didn't answer. Spencer didn't laugh. He looked down. I think he finally felt the tragedy. I think he pitied me. Maybe he always had.

But she wasn't done mortifying me. "I think it might be somewhere between Cambodia and Laos, but geography was never my thing. Maybe it's farther down by Indonesia. If you ever do locate Vachina, Peter, please let me know."

The hurt was so pervasive and immeasurable that I scarcely felt it. I half-smiled into the empty bowl of my wineglass, placed it gently on the table, and commenced the opening rites.

"'Because I do not hope to turn again, because I do not hope, because I do not hope to turn...'"

"Oh Christ, what are you saying now, Peter?" she said. "You're always quoting somebody. It's so tediously pretentious and melodramatic and just... just plain pointless. Don't you have anything original to say?"

I would not be swayed.

"'Because these wings are no longer wings to fly... but merely vans to beat the air...'"

"A little after-dinner Eliot." Spencer said excitedly. "Good choice. Maybe a bit démodé at the moment, but he'll come back eventually. These things work in cycles."

"It's the most overquoted poem in the English language," she carped.

"True. But not that part," Spencer qualified.

She leaned toward me, smiling, malevolent, vulgar, vicious, teeth like fangs, crossed thighs spying out from under skirt, a slice of cleavage centered below bitter eyes glassy with worry, drink, rage, and—unless it was merely a watered-down reflection of my own shoddy state—a scintilla of sadness. "Those who don't know how to use their guns should keep them holstered," she spat, like a serpent spewing venom. "You need experience to be a good shot, and if you're not good, then really, what's the point?" Her face was menacing and mocking, her eyes insidious. If I weren't already past the point where I could feel anything, I believe she would have frightened me.

"'The air which is now thoroughly small and dry…'"

"Ça suffit! Arrête ton cinéma!"

I had to do it right then. No more delay. Another instant and all would be lost. Act with blinders—block everything from mind—raise gun—pull trigger—now—before thoughts flood and fuddle my brain and the engine of instinct seizes up. Block—raise—squeeze. Do it!

But do what? Shoot her? No. That was never part of it. Were I to kill myself right after, the seconds in between would be too long. But he had to go. That much was certain. And it didn't matter that he was Spencer. He was nameless and faceless, just someone that could not *be*, so long as I *was*. It didn't matter that in the world's eyes he had done nothing wrong, surely nothing to merit the wrath of a sick, fiendishly obsessed brother. I was ready to take the fall, prepared to be blackened. I didn't care about the repercussions and vicious rumors that would forever be fastened to me and to her and to the family, so long as there was no *he*, no *him*. There could never again be a *he*. I didn't care that she would never be mine, that for killing him she would hate me more than she knew how to hate. I didn't care, so long as *he* didn't exist. I could tolerate life without her only if there were no other. This was my one nonnegotiable condition.

"So can we move on now?" she said, leaning back, her hostile expression relaxing. My ruminative state must have lasted longer than I thought. "C'est fini, ton drame?"

"Yes. It is finished."

Briny globules of sweat grew out of my forehead, overflowing pores, dribbling down the valleys of my eye sockets and the sides of my nose, gathering at the ridge of my mouth. The gun was still resting in my lap. I closed my eyes and saw the steps—grip—raise—steady—aim—squeeze. Deliverance required but a centimeter of movement, the smallest expenditure of energy, just enough to lift the few pounds of pistol and press my forefinger against its trigger. Just this, and the course of our history would be reset.

And he still wasn't afraid.

"Since we're quoting, Peter, and you have a gun in your hand, I'll throw one into the mix." He cleared his throat and straightened himself up on the edge of the couch. "'Murder is always a mistake. One should never do anything one cannot talk about after dinner.' Good one, no? Appropriate." He laughed and looked from me to my sister, then fell back next to her.

"That's not Eliot, is it?" she asked.

"No, Wilde."

Murder. It stuck in my head like a spike, penetrating the haze of alcohol and drowning out their frisky palaver. The word had not come into mind until now. Extermination, perhaps. Manslaughter, maybe. Murder, not by a long shot. I had never thought of myself as a prospective murderer. It was coequally frightening and tantalizing and repulsive. I had to soften the edges, make it familiar and palatable, enforce my resolution by winnowing away the connotations of the word so I could live with its defining me. It was not a question of justification—this I already had—but of dignity and faith. I had to distinguish the act, infuse it with literary and intellectual motives, elevate it to the ether of poetry, the firmament of philosophy. If murder it was, *murder most foul*, then it would be homicide of the uppermost order, refined to a degree where the act was more lyrical than bloodthirsty; art, not slaughter. Raskolnikov. Meursault. And Humbert. Humbert above all. Holy Humbert, my idol and icon, my hero and mentor, the Virgil to my Dante.

The bullet was begging to go somewhere.

He was speaking to me.

"Peter... Pete..."

"Yes."

"I was talking to you."

"You know Chekhov's most famous dictum, right?" I said, hunching forward and quickly rocking back. "Something like, if a gun appears in the first chapter, it absolutely has to go off by the second or third."

Obviously, I had no choice.

And then his mouth opens. He blinks and inhales in preparation to reply. It's not so much that time seems to slow as that I feel outside it, mentally outpacing the actual course of events, my brain attuned to a slightly faster tempo, as though I can see what's happening before it happens. With a smooth upward gesture, I raise my gun, *my* gun, and it feels unreal—I can't believe I'm doing this, I can't believe I'm holding a gun, I can't believe it is actually happening—but so right, so true. I tense my fingers and look at my sister, whose eyes are now fiercely transfixed on the axle of my motions. Spencer abruptly arrests his speech as I angle the barrel toward the ceiling just above him and my finger starts in slow retrograde, the hard steel trigger yielding in faint increments to the applied pressure, and I lower the gun so that the barrel is parallel to the floor, aimed at my man, and he stares wide-eyed and wildly and tightens his jaw and grips the couch pillows behind him as if already shot, hollowed out by Brother Peter's bullets, and my sister sits there, her incredulous features steadily fusing into an impromptu grimace of stupefaction and total terror, lower jaw dropping as though she's going to speak or shriek or cry out for help that cannot possibly arrive in time, but nothing comes out, and she looks from the gun to me, and I see in a flicker of light reflecting off the glass table before me, I see in this little vaporous flash, like that evoked by the flavor of a tea-soaked madeleine, the ghostlike image of a sullen, sad-eyed little girl in a loose white lace nightgown, looking up at me.

My free left hand rises and smothers the barrel and pulls it in toward me as the deadly decisive force is brought to bear on the trigger, which suddenly snaps back and slackens, and what I can only describe as a freakish crackle of thunder inside my head that sets my ears ringing like an amplified tuning fork surmounts everything, even the lancing pain in my palm, and when the screaming wanes, my eyelids flutter up and I see little viscid gobbets of red dotting the glass table, and I look at Severine, my beautiful sister, my beautiful sister Severine, who is holding her face in her hands, also sprinkled in red, saying my name in low, breathless tones.

Spent gunpowder burns my nostrils. In a rapturous daze, watching her moist face fall through a swirling, slender helix of smoke, my eyes close, and I let myself tilt backward until my head sinks into cushion.

5

Noli Me Tangere

Let me look at the foulness and ugliness of my body.
Let me see myself as an ulcerous sore running with
every horrible and disgusting poison.

— Saint Ignatius of Loyola

One should be proud of one's scars. An unscarred body be-
speaks an unlived life. I view my cicatrix as a mark of battle, the
memento of a noble wound won on the field of combat. I am not
ashamed of this hole in my hand, regardless of its origination. I
am not in the least embarrassed or remorseful, repentant or
guilt-ridden. Neither the hole nor the scene associated with it
causes me much grief upon reflection. In fact, there's not even a
hole anymore, but a small fibroid patch of roughness, a quarter-
sized, crater-like scarification on the palm and outer portion of
my left hand that you wouldn't notice unless your attention was
somehow drawn there. The wound was through and through:
the bullet entered and exited my flesh without interference and
is still lodged somewhere in the basement wall. The extreme
close range carved out a clean, well-defined cavity—singed a bit
about the edges like a piece of seared meat—that has healed
well, leaving only a minor physical souvenir of that night.

As I slipped into a state of semiconsciousness, I looked
down at my juddering hand, palm-up at the end of my arm, and

caught a glimpse of the orange couch showing through the small round hole, from which blood soon began to flow more and more profusely until the entire lower half of the hand was bathed in thick, glistening crimson. It seemed as though nobody moved for many minutes, but it was actually only a matter of seconds before I heard the basement door open and my parents' voices wafting down, followed by hurried footfalls and my mother's gasps and cries as she rushed over, grabbed me by my shoulders and looked from one of us to the other, crying frantically, "What happened? My God! What happened?"

The rest was procedural. I recall it chiefly in vivid broken images and addled freeze-frames. Many words were spoken in several different voices, but I could not apprehend any of them. A towel was wrapped around my hand to stanch the bleeding—I don't remember who tended to the wrapping, but it was nice and tight, a linty beige bath towel that quickly reddened with wet—until the paramedics arrived and whisked me away to the hospital, where they patched me up and kept me overnight for observation, more for the mild shock than for the ugly but not very serious wound. I regained nearly full use of my hand not long after. By some stroke of fortune, the bullet sailed between the third and fourth metacarpals, shaving both but fracturing neither, leaving every ligament and articulation intact, the only significant noncosmetic damage being done to the palmar metacarpal arteries, causing an aching stiffness and slight restriction of finger manipulation. But humiliation was the real injury. I had shot myself in the hand. There were no mitigating factors, no clever excuses to explain it away.

Later, after I had been worked on and drugged up with painkillers, I was allowed visitors. My father, seated comfortably against the wall, leg over leg in a wide, blue-cushioned vinyl chair, held me in his gaze as though I were a familiar specimen whose unexpectedly queer behavior had led him to question this familiarity. The first words out of his mouth were: "Where did you get the gun?" This was the question on everyone's mind.

I was lying on my back, propped up by two blue pillows. He interrogated me with such studied seriousness that I felt like laughing it off without reservation but found myself strangely unable to articulate expression, my features frozen into calcified neutrality. I glanced down at my bandaged hand, elevated by its own pillow—also blue, like most everything else in the room— and raised it an inch or so off its perch. He was looking at me as though I had no choice but to answer, so I answered with my own question.

"Why didn't you name me Pierre? Why?" The authentic underlying anguish, mixed with the comical surface of the sentence and my dour, hammy delivery, had a destabilizing effect on the room.

"What?" He squinched his eyes, unsure what to make of this, or if I even knew what I was saying.

"Or Pietro? Petrus? Even Cephas would've done. Anything but Peter." The vocalization of my name seemed to have emitted a sour stream of saliva into my mouth. "It might've helped."

The truth was, he went on to inform me, bypassing my comments like so much ridiculous rambling, I could have been charged for possession and even reckless endangerment had he not told the doctor it was his own licensed weapon that had been unintentionally discharged while I was moving it, and had the obliging doctor decided to push the issue and follow the law that requires hospitals to report all gunshot wounds, which—thanks to my father's formidable powers of persuasion—he did not. "Not yet at least," my father cautioned. I told him that was nice of them. That I greatly appreciated their consideration. He said there was enough alcohol in my blood to classify me as legally intoxicated, which was the only semblance of a defense I had. I told him I supposed that was good.

I wouldn't tell him where I got the gun; I wasn't about to sell out my source.

"I'm not going to ask you what you were thinking. I'm not going to ask you what you were trying to do."

"Ask Severine."

"Some questions are beyond answering."

"Did you ask her?"

"She says you were acting irrationally, like a crazed child. She says you were someone she didn't know last night."

"*I* was someone *she* didn't know?"

"And then you shot yourself in the hand."

"Again, I had been drinking."

He gripped the round wooden arms of his chair, pulled his torso forward, and annunciated with amplified clarity: "You shot yourself in the hand." He leaned back.

I heard the muted laughter of orderlies rolling a crash cart through the hushed hallway, rising to crescendo as they passed the door and trundled it away.

"Did Spencer go home?" I asked.

He paused before answering, cleared his throat, rubbed his eyes.

"She says she was scared, your sister. Truly frightened. You just pulled out this handgun you planted as though you had something planned, as though you had some kind of misguided mission." He wrapped his large left hand over his right fist and squeezed, cracking a few knuckles.

"Do I seem like the mission-oriented kind of guy?"

He reversed the placement of his hands and popped the row of knuckles on his left, one by one, slowly. "She says you're troubled, that you're clinically depressed, and she blames me for not seeing it. She claims I don't want to see it. What should I have seen?"

I looked up at the institutionally white ceiling tiles, my eyes running from the smoke detector to the sprinkler to the lighting panel shining dull radiance down on my father. "I don't believe in depression. It's too easy an explanation."

"For what?"

"For everything."

Pause.

"Be that as it may, she thinks you have problems."

"Who doesn't?"

"Serious problems. And I'm not convinced she's wrong."

"Is she here?"

He paused again, reflectively this time, as though appraising the question, or his answer. "No."

I swallowed my hurt and smiled soberly through the disappointment. Part of me knew—and was glad—she wasn't here; another part expected her to be worrying in the waiting room, next in line to see me. "Everyone's problems are serious. The world is just one big fucking serious problem. If it weren't, we wouldn't need philosophy, would we?"

"If we didn't need philosophy, then we'd really have problems."

I was in no mood for intellectual jousting, however much it typically titillated me. "I'd like to rest now. I'd like to get a little sleep, as long as I have to stay here tonight."

"You realize there are consequences to actions."

"'For every action, there is an equal and opposite reaction.'"

"You shot yourself in the hand."

"You keep telling me what I've done as if I don't know!" I yelled, then turned my head toward the wall, keeping him in my periphery.

He stroked his stubbled chin with a thumb, the forefinger of his left hand languidly tapping the flattened tip of the chair's arm. "Do you, though? Do you know what you've done?"

My father wields his words, even the simplest, in a way that invests an artful profundity in the most seemingly clear-cut and desultory statements, making you wonder if anything he says can be taken at face value. It is a trait I possess as well, to a lesser degree, especially when engaged in conversation with him. At times, I hear myself speaking with his voice, not just with the words he would use but with the very modulations and mannerisms that animate his vocality, and it infuriates me, makes me want to tear out my vocal cords.

"There are even consequences for what I didn't do," I said. "There are always consequences, corollaries to every action, however minor. There's no escaping causality."

"That doesn't mean we have to be enslaved by it."

"Doesn't it, though? Aren't we all slaves to the dilemma of determinism? Chattel on the chopping block of history?"

"Only if we choose to be. 'Freedom is what you do with what's been done to you.'"

I laughed. Becoming embroiled in conversation with him is like being hustled by a low-profile chess master who anticipates your moves well in advance and knows exactly how to counter and control, making you think you have the advantage until it's too late and you realize he had you checkmated within the first few moves. Nevertheless, I kept playing.

"Nobody *chooses to be*. I didn't choose to be what I am."

"No," he said sympathetically, as though acknowledging the burden of my being and accepting a degree of responsibility for it. "You can't choose *what* you are, but you can choose *who* you are."

"Semantics," I sneered.

"No," he countered, raising a finger. "Ontology. Ethics."

I stopped speaking. I laid down my king.

His upper lip rippled as he ran his tongue along the top row of teeth. My father rarely leaked evidence of bewilderment and strove at all times to conceal his agitation. Now he looked downright disturbed. He was feeling me out, bedeviled by the idea that his son, whom he had shaped and molded from the loftiest ideals of Western thought, had brought up in a progressively principled, high-minded humanistic environment, might have attempted something so imbalanced, so stormily out of sync with the great golden mean. This is what worried him most, not the possible threat I was to myself and others.

"Your mother wants to see you."

"Ah." I nodded.

"How does it feel?" he finally came out with halfheartedly, as an afterthought.

I hadn't thought much about my maimed hand until then, but it immediately began to throb, though still somewhat numb from the anesthesia.

"It hurts." I lifted the swathed limb for display.

He shifted in the chair, switching the position of his crossed legs.

"Ask me," I said.

He didn't answer. His eyes narrowed while the rest of him remained thoroughly unresponsive. He surely sensed something off about my offer, detected a ruse of some sort lurking behind my apparent openness.

"Ask me," I repeated.

"Tell me." He spoke these words supersoftly and raised up his chin in a kind of ecumenical gesture, as though inviting me to freely and joyfully unbosom myself to a nonjudgmental, all-forgiving auditor.

I wanted to. I wanted to tell him everything from the very beginning. They had given me plenty of painkillers, and I was aching and weak and beyond exhaustion. I wanted to dump it all on him, all the sublime and sordid minutiae of this thing of ours. I wanted to lash out at him, to scream at him and unload it all, to say it and be done with it. But to a father, not a professor.

I told him what he wanted to hear, what he needed to hear. And I spoke it with convincing candor. I served up an impregnably simple situation that was guileless and absurd enough to be believable.

"I was drunk. I was fooling around. The gun went off."

Elbows on armrests, he brought his hands together at his chest and crisscrossed his fingers, steepling the forefingers and pressing their conjoined tips against his philtrum as he pondered my statement.

"I didn't mean to shoot myself in the hand. I had the gun hidden there so nobody would find it. We hardly ever use that couch. Then we happened to go into the basement. I was just messing around and got carried away in the moment. I never meant to fire. Before I even realized it, the gun just went off."

"It just… went off?" He opened his hands like a blossoming flower.

I looked down contritely. "That's what happened."

Vague fragments of gratification appeared on his face, the foreshadowing of a slim smile that never came to be. I was outplaying the chess master, or he was letting himself be played. It didn't really matter either way.

He waited, probably debating whether or not he wanted to pull the loose ends of my story. "But why have a gun in the first place?"

"Because I wanted one. Just because I wanted one. I don't know why."

"You wanted the gun... because you wanted it?" He threw this harebrained tautology back at me to see if it would stick, giving me a last chance to change my statement before family history accepted it into the archives, apocryphal or not.

"Who knows why we want what we want? We're all slaves to the dilemma of desire. I wanted a gun. I don't want one anymore."

He remained there a few minutes, silently assimilating my version of what went down with Severine's account and his own suspicions and suppositions, then told me I would be coming home the next day. Normally, they would have sent someone in to question me in a case such as this—if not a police officer then at least an in-house investigator, just to cover their legal bases—but my father had assured the doctor that it was best left to him, and that if he felt it necessary, he would call for intervention. The doctor had conceded him this too. My father's arguments are difficult to defy. I asked him what he would tell the good doctor now.

"That it was an accident," he said, rising to go.

"She's really not here, Severine?"

"No, she's not here."

"Did she even come to the hospital?"

"She did not," he said flatly.

"Where is she? Is she with him?"

He was standing before the door with his back to me. He held the handle a second before turning it. "Get some rest. I'll send your mother in. We'll pick you up tomorrow afternoon."

Letting the heavy blue door slowly squeak closed behind him, he walked off into the hall, where I heard him exchange a few incomprehensible words with my attending nurse. A minute later my mother entered, bedraggled and tear-stained, and she stayed with me for a long time.

Things changed after the shooting incident. My mother treaded lightly around me, treating me like a delicate and difficult child whose care called for extreme patience and exacting attention. She struggled hard to toe the line between ministering to my needs and giving me the required space. She would cook my favorite dinners—chicken Kiev and lasagna—and bring home handpicked bakery treats for dessert—Linzer tortes, red velvet cake, frosted nut-free brownies. I would come upstairs to find my room tidied, my fresh laundry folded and neatly stacked atop my dresser. But she stopped short of intrusiveness. She knew that, despite her instinctual maternal desire to assuage my suffering at any cost, even to the extent of self-sacrifice, there was only so much she could do; the unseen demons plaguing me were beyond her reach and immune to the weapons in her motherly arsenal. My father regarded me with a mixture of disappointment and revitalized interest, as if there had suddenly appeared this curious new aspect of me that demanded further analysis. I would feel his weighty stare on me like a tangible shadow, which would linger a few seconds even after I lifted my eyes to meet it. And Severine went out of her way to avoid any extended contact with me. There was nothing subtle about how she ostracized me from her life as though my company were a contagion. She wasn't hostile or mean—she didn't make a show of her resentment—but she did little to disguise her disgust and went so far as to sacrifice convenience in order to evade me whenever possible. For example, despite the compatibility of our class schedules and the fact that we had customarily gone to school together, she would now ride with my father, though his timetable did not always coincide with hers; she'd go to school a few hours earlier than necessary rather than get in the car with me. Regardless of how early she was, she would breeze into the room right on time, just as the pre-class chatter was dissolving and the professor was making last-minute addenda to his lesson plan, and leave abruptly when finished, as if she had a standing appointment that she couldn't afford to be late for. But at least she was there. Otherwise, I almost never saw her. A chasm had opened between us. We were tectonic plates shifting away from each other, and I had no idea how to bridge the gulf. Rushing to get ready in the morning, she would greet me with a shallow, standoffish smile and barely look in my direction, as though we were marginally acquainted guests sharing a common bathroom in a fusty foreign pension, as though she were extending an off-handed, amicable courtesy out of conventional civility, while she would have clearly preferred it if our paths never intersected. Two nights a week she would eat dinner home, three at the most (I was home every night, naturally), and her conversation was spiritless and superficial. She wasn't really there. It was as if she blamed my parents as well, for being unwitting accomplices or active enablers or at least abiding eyewitnesses guilty of gross negligence, partially responsible for my lunatic behavior, and perhaps responsible in the greater sense for making us who we were. I don't know where she spent the rest of her time. She couldn't always have been with Spencer, but I never asked.

I began to feel toward myself the antipathy she exuded. In the mirror I saw a repugnant and unrecognizable monstrosity, a hideous, unlovable creature, whereas in the past I had always been satisfied with my looks, which I'd considered a rougher, darker, masculine analogue to Severine's rarefied beauty. Now I saw only ugliness. I felt only shame at my existence. I didn't want to see or be seen. I wanted to be invisible. She had made me hate myself.

My parents initially hinted at the benefits of therapy. Then they suggested I see an analyst friend that my father knew from grad school, a lauded expert in Gestalt therapy and an *all-around upright guy*, in addition to being a gifted clinician. Finally, when it became obvious that I wasn't even pecking at the bait, they outright asked me to go, asked me in a way that seemed more requisition than request. I wondered if this was one of the consequences my father had alluded to in the hospital. "You just don't seem yourself," my mother said, sitting in the den shortly after my overnight hospital stay, a bright orange fire crackling in the inglenook hearth, a late Beethoven string quartet playing in surround sound. "And we feel helpless about it. Maybe someone on the outside can do something, see something that we can't, offer a fresh perspective. At least try it, for us. For all of us. We just want to see you happy."

I wondered if I had ever seemed happy to them.

"We're all affected by this, Peter," she went on, gingerly taking my hand—dressed in medical gauze—in hers. "And we're always here for you. Never think you're alone."

165

The fire sputtered and threw tiny yellow and blue sparks into the air. I told them how surprised I was to hear that, since we all knew that aloneness is the fundamental state of being in the world, as my father had always taught. Staring at the hypnotic flames tickling the charred brick walls of the fireplace and leaping up into the chimney, I told them I didn't want to go. I wouldn't go. I told them that I thought I was suffering from an acute case of seasonal affective disorder due to a premature and exceptionally cold and unpleasant outbreak of winter weather, and that this would pass, as all things do.

They exchanged conspiratorial looks of thwarted concern and wasted effort.

"Spring is a long time off," my father offered.

"And even then, there's no guarantee."

"The semester ends soon. Maybe you should get away for a while," my mother suggested.

"Maybe."

"Sure, why not? A different environment could do some good. A change from the outside might work its way in," my father seconded, trying to sound cheery but coming off false and somewhat discomposing; lighthearted optimism was just not something he could pull off, and when he tried, it usually had the exact opposite effect of what was intended.

I remember thinking that my parents were operating with remarkable calm and tact, conducting themselves with almost superhuman temperance, considering that their son had recently blown a hole in his hand.

"Someplace warm," my mother elaborated, taken in by her own suggestions. "Beaches, palm trees, margaritas. Sun and sand and clear blue sea. People in warm, sunny climates have a much lower rate of depression."

The D-word again. A rebarbative image invaded my mind: hooting hordes of spring breakers littered across some otherwise paradisiacal panorama with coolers of Budweiser and brown bottles of suntan lotion strewn in the sand around their lounge chairs, blasting the worst music imaginable at extreme volumes and fist-pumping and high-fiving and chest-bumping every time a buxom bikinied sophomore passes with so much as an inadvertent, sunglass-obscured glance in their direction. If they had to dwell on a D-word, I told my parents, I would much prefer they humor me with *despair*.

"If it is a case of the winter blues, some natural vitamin D might be just what you need," my mother persisted, sounding almost convinced.

Another D-word.

"Sartre said human life is born on the far side of despair," my father said, lapsing back into his conversational comfort zone. "But he never said it had to end there."

For a second, I was nonplussed at the atypical hopefulness of this, coming from my father, but I quickly recovered. "He also never said what was on the near side."

"We could go somewhere together, the three of us," my mother said carefully, tilting her head.

"Yes. I think that's a good idea. I haven't been away in a while," I said.

My mother looked relieved and mildly invigorated, as though her next move would be to telephone the travel agent and research all-inclusive deals to the Bahamas.

I hadn't given much thought to the gun—I hadn't thought about it at all, oddly—but just then wondered what had become of it. I didn't dare ask, though my father had likely solicited the aid of his elder brother in finding a convenient way to make the evidence disappear. I imagined what Lou might say if he found out what had really happened: *What the fuck's the matter with you?*—accompanied by a stiff smack on the side of the head. It would have been the most straightforward question put to me.

We decided that it would be best for all to keep the truth of the matter under wraps, the details confined to our immediate family and, of necessity, Spencer. When someone asked me why I had a bandage around my hand, I would reply reflexively that I had been careless in cutting a bagel and had nearly bisected my palm, a credible story that would elicit vicarious grimaces and sympathetic sighs. *It's not half as bad as it sounds,* was my token rejoinder. As with the studio incident, the shooting was never mentioned between me and my sister. Nor did I ever find out if Spencer had divulged any of the story, but I doubt it. I didn't see much of him after the semester ended. During those last few weeks, the most I remember him saying to me was: *How's the hand?*—with cold cordiality and a dab of derision. I was a little disconcerted that he exhibited no symptoms of anxiety or panic in my presence, after my having pointed a loaded gun at him over a nightcap.

The situation was now at its worst: my desperate actions had only succeeded in driving her further from me and closer to him, and this time things would never again be as they were. I didn't know her. She wasn't vicious or vindictive or noticeably chilly. She didn't randomly reprimand me or treat me like some kind of afflicted reprobate (though that was how I felt). She was simply faraway and foreign, and there seemed to be nothing I could do or say to bring her back.

There was always recourse to drastic measures. I could try to execute correctly what I had botched the first time—though at this point I had little confidence in my ability to do anything right—but I didn't feel the same inciting desperation. I had lost that rabid compulsion to redress the egregious wrong that had polluted our lives and dominated my existence over the past few months. I was still far from acceptance or acquiescence, but I did not feel the obdurate urge to act. Winter recess brought with it an unforeseen calmness of spirit, a welcome resignation that I think was in some way related to my hand. The numbness had begun, the preliminary stages of the permanent retreat into my room.

The holidays came and went quietly, and I did not go away for winter break. We didn't even celebrate the feast days with family; my mother apologetically excused us on account of my father's unusual busyness that semester and my own unwonted illness, some kind of protracted flu or lingering chest cold that made it mutually advisable to keep me inside and safely away from others. Spencer went north to visit his parents in Montreal, during which time Severine was around the house more than usual, still doing a noteworthy job of keeping out of my way. For Christmas she gave me a nicely packaged two-volume set of Robert Musil's *The Man Without Qualities*. I didn't buy any presents that year. Neither did I return to classes the next semester, a decision reluctantly encouraged by my father at the behest of my mother, who argued that some time off might be therapeutic. There was no rush. School would be there when I was good and ready to return. This is also when I started to spend even more time with Don. He knew the truth about the shooting—or knew at least that my wound was self-inflicted—and I think he was slowly gleaning the greater truth. I was hoping that one day he would just come out and tell me that he knew, that he had known all along, and that he just saw it as natural; uncommon, against the grain, but perfectly natural, knowing Severine and me as he did. Or rather, just knowing me as he did. I would not have been surprised. Not with Don. But I couldn't reveal it, even if he did suspect something. He had to discover it for himself. It had to come out organically.

Don and Susan had been a couple for over a year, and he was always happy to get together with me so long as they had already gotten sex out of the way, which was generally the first thing they did when she came over, and which they assumedly repeated after I left, considering Don's carnal appetite. Sometimes the three of us went out. We would go to a movie or a pool hall, sip root beer floats at the faux-fifties ice cream parlor or share a baker's dozen donuts at the all-night sweet shop, but most of the time we would go to the diner where Susan's brother worked, a cheap and cheerless Hopperesque joint that was never really crowded, even during prime dining hours. It was never quite empty, either, always host to a few mopey stragglers even in those wee, woebegone hours of the morning when everyone with someone to be with is home with that someone. We would plant ourselves and loiter over dry Danish and stale coffee and oversweetened hot cocoa until our bodies ached from sitting too long and our minds went as flat as the watery fountain soda they served, and though it was nothing terribly exciting, I look back on those nights yearningly, with the kind of nipping nostalgia reserved for moments that seemed anything but memorable at the time, that seemed utterly forgettable while they were being lived, but later feel like precious lost time you'd relish to revive. In that entirely unremarkable place, sitting in that moth-eaten corner booth overlooking the crumbling asphalt and pitchy potholes of the surrounding parking lot, in that drab roadside diner that always seemed so depressing and desolate, where anything you ordered tasted the same and you would not be surprised to find a fingernail in your burger or pull an unwashed hair from the guts of your muffin, I felt safe and at home. It was a not-so-clean, not-so-well-lighted place, but in some odd, inexplicable way, I felt that I belonged there. It was one of the few places in which I've never felt *de trop.*

But there is something more about this transient period of ataraxia, something that initially bolstered me and eventually contributed to my sharp descent, which I neither applaud nor regret. It was the time of my first experiences with a prostitute.

6

Tender Is the Night

Man can do what he wants, but he cannot want
what he wants.

— Arthur Schopenhauer

It happened out of the blue on an otherwise unexceptional
Wednesday night. We left the diner earlier than usual, around
1:30 a.m., and came back to Don's house for a quick smoking
session before Susan went home. Recently promoted to Junior
Employee Relations Specialist in the human resources department of the local headquarters of a nationwide auto insurance
company, Susan now had to punch the clock bright and early
instead of midafternoon, and as her new supervisor was a noted
stickler for promptness, she had to dutifully bow out of our
nighttime revelry, at least until settling into her new schedule.
Don's grad courses were in the evening, so he lived primarily by
night, like me. We both feared that it would be the death of us to
someday have jobs requiring any kind of regular morning hours.
Plus, work—actual labor—was as anathema to Don as it is to me.
He frequently talked about being a professional student, racking
up a slew of advanced degrees until his parents finally tightened
the purse strings and/or he exhausted all possible scholarships,
research grants, and teaching fellowships. It was a frightening
dead-end eventuality, getting a job, but he had successfully

avoided it this long, and there seemed to be no plausible threat on the horizon. His parents put no pressure on him to pitch in with the bills—in fact, they surely afforded him some kind of stipend or allowance, as mine always have—and granted him unrestricted reign over the realm of his room. They believed strongly in education and were in no rush to see their son move out, so Don had it made for the foreseeable future. Susan, however, had been running the rat race since she had graduated from high school and had every intention of advancing as far as possible within her present company, which was all well and good as far as Don was concerned. "By the time my parents have had it with me," he would aver, "Susan will have a nice cushy executive position that can support us both. Family insurance, a big fat pension. I'm all for women in the workplace. Shit, I'm even for kids, cripples, and animals in the workplace, as long as *I* don't have to be there."

Waiting in his room as he walked her to the car, I peeked out the window and saw them standing in a floodlit halo cast by the driveway lights overhanging the open garage door, engaged in a deep, drawn-out kiss. I stopped watching before they were done and began flipping through various late-night talk shows, home shopping networks, and infomercials for celebrity psychics and miracle cures for male pattern baldness. Don came back in shortly and sat on the edge of the bed, staring at an undisclosed point in space just above the carpet, either pregnant with thought or just stultifyingly high. The screeching of tires echoed from somewhere not too far away and not too close. A night bird hooted.

"I like having a girlfriend," he said, somewhat penitently, after a few seconds of reflection, his eyes still focused on the point. "I like knowing she's there. I mean, I need to know she's there." He stopped talking for a minute or two. "The problem... The problem is not that I'm not attracted to her, because I am. I'm still very attracted to her, maybe even more so than before. Sex with Susan is about as good as it gets. I love her body. I still fantasize about it when she's not around. Sometimes, when I don't see her for a few days, I miss it tremendously. It's plain painful how much I miss it."

"*It* meaning her body or sex?"

"Both. They're kind of coterminous for me." He held up his forefingers and faced them about six inches apart, like opposing poles of an electrical circuit. "So it's not that I really need another woman, per se, because there's not a hell of a lot of variation to the female body, when it comes down to brass tacks. A breast's a breast. A hole's a hole."

"'There is only one woman in the world. One woman, with many faces.' Nikos Kazantzakis."

He looked at me leerily. "Who's that? The grouchy Greek who owns the diner?"

"Uh... yes."

He leered a little longer, slightly spaced out, then broke his gaze and turned toward the darkened window, which reflected both of us in its frame like a washed-out old photograph. "Well, regardless, the problem, I know now, is that I need lots of sex. That's it. I need it more often than I'd thought. I mean, we all need sex—we're all sexual beings—but when I don't get as much as I require, my mind clouds up. I find my thinking processes hindered. I'm just not fully functional unless I'm having sex as often as possible. And I hate not functioning at full capacity."

"I never function at full capacity. Or maybe my capacity is just much lower than most."

He massaged his temples with four fingertips on each side, thumbs circling under mandible. "And the sad fact is, Susan's not always around. Especially with this new work schedule of hers. It's a simple question of supply and demand."

"Someone's got to work. Better her than you."

"By all means, yes. But there's still this issue of availability."

"You're almost always available."

"Precisely."

I switched channels. A commercial came on for a three-disc collection of hit songs from the eighties, introduced by a generically pretty, middle-aged blonde with big, sparkling white teeth and an outrageously outmoded body wave.

"I guess that's not unusual," I said.

"No, I guess not. Wait. Which part?"

"Wanting sex so much. We all do."

"Fuck *wanting*. I'm talking about an urgent *need* here," he emphasized, his voice crisping and his features crinkling as though my misapprehension was seriously insulting and more intentional than I was leading on. "Burning necessity. Not *want*. I'm talking about an exigency of the most extreme kind."

I went through four or five channels before settling on the last half of an *All in the Family* episode.

"But like, right now, for example," he said, "I really feel like I need sex, post-fucking-haste, like I just have to have it. I'm all on edge. I feel myself getting seriously out of whack. I can't even enjoy Archie Bunker, who usually has an exceedingly sedative influence on me."

"Me too." I smiled hazily. "I love his breezy bigotry."

"Masturbation would only stave it off for an hour or two, tops, or maybe even make it worse. And those other techniques I talked about, they don't do much. I need to fuck. It's worse than ever, this drive. I've never felt such a compelling need to fuck so often. Maybe it's the stress of school, my orals, my dissertation, pressure to publish. But I don't take all that stuff too seriously. If theoretical physics has anything practical to teach you, it's not to take anything too seriously."

"It's all de trop."

"What?"

"Never mind."

"Whatever. I thought the sweet leaf would dull it, but no, I just keep getting these irresistible urges. Jesus, it's like I'm going through puberty again."

"You should've said something earlier. I would've left you and Susan alone."

"Nah. We fucked before, and she was too tired for a repeat performance. Weed tuckers her out, you know, and she doesn't *need* sex like I do. I don't think she even likes it that much."

We watched the end of *All in the Family*. As soon as the credits began to roll, Don spoke again.

"So, to be honest, what I've been doing lately—what I've been doing is having hookers."

His words were swift and perfunctory, as if he couldn't wait to get them out, and then he fixed his eyes on me, gauging my reaction, something he rarely seemed concerned with.

"Where do you go, the city?" The image of a slovenly old crack whore with carious tawny teeth and a bruised leathery face layered gaudily with ill-applied makeup, wearing a tatty white faux-fur jacket over a soiled black bra, red leather short shorts, and knee-high pleather boots, entered my brain. I pictured Don and me approaching her on some seedy side street in the shadow of the Manhattan Bridge, haggling over the cost of a blow job, Don angling for some sort of two-for-one special.

"I don't *go* anywhere. I call an escort service. I order, they deliver. Like Chinese food or pizza."

"I didn't realize you could do that."

"You've lived a sheltered life, my friend."

"What about your parents?"

He crimpled his brow and tapered his eyes dubiously, lips knit into a tight frown. "How long have you known my parents? How many times a day do I smoke up in my room with one or both of them roaming freely around the house and the sweet smell of cannabis wafting out from under my door?"

I wasn't planning on giving an answer until it became clear he was waiting for one. "Very long. Many."

"Then why ask dumb questions, Pete? Why waste your breath? You don't have an unlimited supply. They're just happy to have their only son home with them instead of away at some expensive upstate school in some shitty little shared apartment in some shitty little cow-fuck college town. They have me. What more could they ask for?" He spread his arms out in proud self-presentation. "As for me, I have my pot, my girl, my friend," pointing at me, "and my freedom. What more can *I* ask for? If I want a little snatch on the sly, I lock the door, I ask her politely not to make too much noise, and that's it. My folks never stray from their room past twelve, and if they do, they wouldn't come in *here*." He stressed *here* as though it denoted a no-fly zone he'd negotiated with his parents, and he seemed moderately miffed that I hadn't immediately grasped this.

I knew how things were in his house, of course. For years I had been a witness and a party to his parents' often staggering leniency, but despite the parallel universe in my own household, it has always astounded me to learn of what goes on in other people's homes without their knowledge.

"Do you know what you're getting when you call? Do you have any idea what they look like? Can you pick them out?" The concept of having a woman dropped at your doorstep for the express purpose of having intercourse was fascinating.

"You can browse the selection online, but they're never as good when they show up. Those pics are all photoshopped and shit. And half the time it's not even the same girl. I usually just ask on the phone what they have, choose one that sounds good, and hope for the best."

"Sounds like a gamble."

"Nothing's ever as good as you hope. As long as you don't expect much you'll be all right. That goes for life in general, by the way. No charge for that little wad of wisdom."

Attention shifted back to the television as M*A*S*H* came on, and until the next commercial we sat and watched quietly, though it was never one of my preferred shows. Then Don said, "I'm going to make that call. How about it? You in?"

Expecting the question and hopeful it was soon to come, I assented automatically, with a noncommittal nod to conceal my excitement, an excitement composed mostly of morbid curiosity and a keen desire not to go home yet. There was as well the thrill of illicitness and novelty, and this particular novelty involved (ostensibly) uncomplicated sex, which did spice the sauce a bit, but it also gave me pause. Before another word could be spoken, Don dialed up a company called Warm and Willing Escorts, based in the adjacent town. It wasn't until I heard him making arrangements on the phone that I began to second-guess the decision, and part of me was hoping he wouldn't go through with it, or that nobody would be available, or that the service was about to be raided by the local police and the board of health and immediately shuttered. As it happened, the girl he would have preferred was booked up until 5 a.m., and since his parents generally got up between 6:30 and 7, that was cutting it a little too close, even for their extreme brand of laissez-faire parenting. So we had to settle for an untried Tibetan named Lhamu (5'6", 120 lbs., 34-28-34, black eyes, waist-length black hair, golden complexion, per the description he received over the phone), who would be here shortly.

"What are the chances you're ever going to fuck a Tibetan chick again?" he reasoned, in all seriousness. "Tibet. Dalai Lama land. Himalayan muff, man. That's exotic shit. And she comes highly recommended by the management. They even offered a guaranteed replacement if we're not satisfied. There's really nothing to lose." He laughed giddily and his voice rose half an octave. "She'll be here in twenty minutes."

We waited outside, since the doorbell would have woken Don's parents. It was a frigid night, and the driveway was checkered with icebound patches of tightly packed snow left over from a storm a few days earlier, mucky with the stains of car exhaust and tire treads. It had been a stormy season. Don was visibly excited, constantly rubbing his hands and blowing on them for warmth, arguing astringently for the legalization and governmental regulation of prostitution, an argument I'd often heard him similarly lay out for marijuana. Within minutes of the promised arrival time, a two-door midnight blue Lincoln with tinted windows rolled to a slow halt in front of the house, one tire crawling up the curb and bouncing softly down on the street as the driver straightened out. Don waved. Ten seconds later, a squat feminine form emerged from the front passenger side and leaned over to say something to the chauffer before closing the door, then advanced warily up the drive. Holding her puffy ivory down coat closed tight in front, she took short, quick steps with stumpy legs that protruded from under the cumbrous coat like black-stockinged tree trunks. The clicking of her heels seemed remarkably loud against the silence of the neighborhood at that time of night, and steady as a metronome. Her face slowly came into view as she approached, flashing a professional salacious smile when she saw both of us staring at her like famished foxes waiting for a rabbit to hop within range before pouncing.

"She's not bad from here," Don whispered, squinting into the near darkness, just before she entered hearing range. Though I couldn't make out the details of her body with the coat on, she was passably pretty and seemed to match the description fairly well, but as she got closer, it became apparent that her hair was nowhere near her waist and her height barely broke the five-foot mark. When the floodlights from above the garage hit her flush, I noticed that her face was cratered here and there with pock-marks and caked with makeup, the excessive rouge and garish red lipstick creating a clownish effect that was more silly—and slightly sinister—than sexy. Still, it wasn't horrible. As Don had pointed out, so long as you don't expect too much... *A hole's a hole.*

"Well, hello," Don delivered in an awkwardly artificial bari-tone, grinning at her like a devious teenager with all manner of machinations and misdeeds already running through his head.

"Well, hello back," she said with a slight, indistinguishable accent, looking from Don to me. "I'm Jackie."

We introduced ourselves and shook hands like executives at the beginning of an important board meeting.

"I thought your name was Lhamu," Don said suspiciously.

She laughed. "I wouldn't even know how to spell that."

Then came the communal lull, a cooperative and respectful silence in preparation for what was about to happen. I tried to get a good full look at her without being too conspicuous, though there was neither need nor reason for discretion. I am going to have sex with this girl, I thought, this girl whom I've never seen before and will probably never see again. She is a whore who has lain with countless others, but she's also a girl, a human female like any other, and I am going to share the most intimate human experience with her, she with me, we who know nothing of each other, who will always know nothing of each other, except this, this thing that I've shared with only one other, only with *Her*, who can be placed beside no one else. So how can I do this now, this same act? How can I do it not with Her but with her?

My thoughts were brusquely stifled as Don sounded off: "Shall we go inside and get to know each other better instead of standing here freezing our nuts and bolts off?"

"Sure," Jackie said, "but first we get business out of the way, yes?"

That was the easy part. As agreed upon over the phone, we had the money ready: $350 for the full servicing of two gentlemen in an hour-long session. Don ended up getting his two-man discount, as the normal charge would have been $200 apiece. I think the markdown enhanced his enthusiasm. We handed her the cash. She counted it, consulted her watch and said, "Okay, we start the hour from when we go in," and waved at the car.

Don insisted that I go first, predicting that I'd be nervous and would need some extra time to *get my piston pumping*—a surprisingly generous consideration in light of his evident eagerness—but I declined. I admitted that I was nervous, but what I needed was to relax for a few minutes, to sit down and unwind and let the quickening anticipation level out a bit.

"Fine," he said, "but don't have any liquor or anything. It'll soften you up. And don't think too much about it either. That'll do the opposite and you'll blow your load in a second flat. Keep your hands away from your dick and just..." looking around for a way for me to safely occupy myself, "watch TV. But nothing too serious. The Weather Channel or C-SPAN or something. There's a delicate balance to be maintained here. I'll be down in a half hour, done or not." Had he taken the whole hour, I would not have protested. I wanted to stall as long as possible. "Here. Eat this." He grabbed a banana from the fruit bowl on the chef's island and tossed it onto the table in front of me. "Potassium is good sex-prep."

Don handed me the remote and led Jackie up to his room while I waited downstairs in the kitchen with a glass of iced tea and the phallic fruit—which I had absolutely no appetite for—recreating the images of her I had gleaned from those few minutes outside, leafing through them like mental photographs, trying to make myself susceptible to arousal. I labored to visualize her body under that bloated coat, but there was another in the way, always another at the fore. Severine would probably be home by now, in bed, sleeping. I thought to myself that I would never be able to get it up, that I would just let her keep the cash because she had come and I didn't want any problems with the guy waiting outside in the Lincoln. I just couldn't do this. I wanted to be home in my room. I unpeeled the banana and brought it close to my mouth but found its cloying pungency so nauseating that I had to leave my seat and dispose of it in the undersink trash bin and wash away the lingering offensive scent with some more iced tea.

As recommended, I turned on the Weather Channel and watched the local, regional, and national five-day forecasts. Twenty minutes later, just as the international meteorological outlook was about to air, I heard the door open, and then Don came down, zippering his fly and buckling his belt. He leaned against the refrigerator door and looked at me across the kitchen, distracted and a little deflated. He sniffed and crossed his arms and asked, "What's the weather going to be like?"

"Cold."

He nodded. "She's not bad. A little thick around the middle and in the ass. I wouldn't want to fuck her on a continuous basis, but man alive, can she suck a good dick. Too good! So good that I shot before I could stick it in her."

"Oh."

"Yep. She gets some real powerful suction going, that one. I feel a little gypped, to be honest, but like I said, it was really a hell of a blow job, and that's nothing to sneeze at. Maybe not worth a buck seventy-five, but far from the worst way to waste a half hour. And anyway, it's probably good to have a few extra minutes your first time." He took a glass from the cabinet above the sink and poured himself some iced tea, leaned back against the counter, and drank it in one gulp. I just sat there. "Well hurry up, man. Clock's ticking." He tapped the face of his watch. "And every tick is money spent."

I rose from my seat. Now I was just standing there afraid, actually fearful of ascending those stygian stairs as though some kind of pain or punishment awaited me, a via dolorosa that could only end badly. Don refilled his glass and looked at me, losing patience with my mystifying procrastination and motioning fervently in the direction of the stairwell, which suddenly seemed so lurid and foreboding. On the count of three I would go, like pulling off a Band-Aid, trek up there and do what had to be done, or something like it. Once the process was started there could be no turning back. I would count to three, but I needed a few more seconds to prepare, just a couple more moments of reprieve to exorcise all thoughts from my mind before hopping onto the stage for this unrehearsed performance.

So I continue to stand there, watching my friend watch me, watching him finish his second glass of iced tea, crush the empty carton with one hand as though demonstrating a feat of strength, raise his arms in wonder and say, "Hey man, I got my money's worth. Sort of. But you're paying for this time. I suggest you make haste while the night is relatively young." Then I begin the countdown. On three, I turn around without saying anything and mount the stairs, dreamlike, dazed, disembodied, and when I open the door to Don's dim and stuffy room, Jackie is there on the bed with the covers drawn up just below her breasts, smiling dully at me through painted Asian eyes, and I stop a few feet from the bed, and since I'm nervous I don't look at her eyes but at her breasts. I focus on her breasts, and they're nice breasts, full and round and milk-white, topped with perfect little pink nubby nipples that are staring back at me, and she notices where I'm looking and tweaks both of these nipples with thumb and fore-finger and smiles so that her eyes become even narrower and her cheeks dimple in a way that should have been cuter, and she says, "Your friend was a little bit too excited. You have more time now," releasing her right nipple and patting the bed. I walk over.

"You should take off your clothes first, no?" She giggles, and it embarrasses me, angers me slightly. "Don't be nervous," she says.

"Me? Ha, I'm not nervous." Swift denial. The worst form of admission.

I unhurriedly unbutton my light blue pinpoint Oxford shirt and slip out of it arm by arm and sling it over the back of Don's computer chair, and then I loosen my belt, undo my zipper, let my jeans drop and step out of them leg by leg and carefully pick them up and fold them and lay them on the seat of the same chair. "I'm not nervous," I repeat. But I feel ridiculous, standing there beside my friend's bed in white briefs that look like diapers and stretched tube socks that droop at the calf. I feel naked, as though I've never been this naked, and I don't want to do this. I don't want her to touch me and I don't want to touch her, but I have to see this through, so I try to get myself to want to. I tell myself that they all had whores, all the great ones: Flaubert, Van Gogh, Henry Miller, Chopin, all baptized in the brothels of Paris.

But this is not Paris.

I climb onto the bed and sit next to her as she pulls the sheets off and crawls out and makes her way to her knees and puts her hand on my chest and pushes me slowly backward and reaches down and pulls off my briefs almost roughly and flings them somewhere into the room. Small rolls of flesh bunch up at her stomach as she sits up and produces a condom from under the sheets like a magic trick. I am almost surprised at how hard I am. "Just lay back," she says, and I check myself from correcting her grammar. "I take over from here." She leans over and runs her tongue down my chest—her tongue is warm and pasty—past my abdomen, slips the condom on with both hands, unrolls it, and locks her mouth on my penis, enveloping it to the base. I think about Don's comment as the suction rapidly increases in evenly graduated increments, as though her mouth were some sort of automated pneumatic device. After a few minutes she

185

stops, peers up at me and—grabbing my penis with her right hand and stroking it just enough to keep it going—says, "Are you ready? Do you want to fuck me now, or should I keep going with this for a while?"

I consider the options. "You can stop that, I guess."

"You mean you're ready for a fuck?"

She seems endearingly sincere in her uncertainty, and also a little pathetic, kneeling there with my penis in one hand as she looks up at me and asks if I want to fuck her, if I am ready for her vagina to receive my dick. I feel a pang of sympathy and a touch of guilt.

"Yes. I'm ready."

She smiles approvingly, slides up and straddles me, lifting herself as she directs my penis into her and smoothly drops down onto it with effortless efficiency. This is the first time I am inside a girl who is not my sister, and it does not feel good. It does not feel right. I close my eyes but it doesn't help. It's still her, not Her. She leans over and her pendulous breasts dangle above my face, brushing against me, nipples skimming my nose, and I perceive the distinct odor of perfume and cigarette smoke, sweat, saliva, and other men.

Severine's skin sometimes smelled like baby powder, which she liked to apply after showering.

Jackie begins to moan softly. I wonder if this is part of the job, if she thinks this is seductive. She moans and says that she likes my cock inside her, *my huge hard cock deep inside her*. I want to appreciate her efforts to sound convincing, and the feeling is becoming so intense that it really shouldn't matter what she does or does not say, but I think that I would like to smack her across the face just for using the word *cock*, just because I don't like the way it sounds coming out of her mouth. I would like to smack her first and then finish up, but it is too late, and she must sense it because she whines, "Are you ready baby? Are you ready?" as she gyrates savagely on top of me, digging her acrylic nails into the flesh of my chest and throwing her head back in well-acted ecstasy, and I would like so much not to come, not to want to come, just to smack her, but I can't hold back and I feel the condom filling up and she is grinding so fast and hard that it hurts my pelvis until finally she slows and lets my penis pump out its contents into the rubber as my body seizes and shudders and at last loosens and lies there like a newly made corpse.

She says, "Okay? Done?" still moving on top of me, her hands anchored tightly to my chest. "Are you done?" she repeats louder.

"Yes. I'm done."

She remains on top of me for a few seconds, swaying in a sluggish circular motion and pulling her hair up in back of her head, surveying the prints and posters on Don's walls, ranging from a framed reproduction of a shot from the Hubble Space Telescope—the deepest photo ever taken into the universe—to a dog-eared magazine cutout of Testament left up from the thrash days of the late eighties, to an old poster of the once-famous porn star Traci Lords standing under a dew-dappled palm tree in a red string bikini with her eyes half-closed and her arms arched languorously back behind her head. I want to shove this woman off me. I am appalled by the fact that my penis is still inside her, that her flesh is still in contact with mine, and I am disgusted with myself for having come. After taking in the room around her, she looks at me, taps my chest, and says, "Good? Okay?"

I wait about five seconds. "Yes."

"Good." She taps me again and dismounts, rolls over to the other side of the bed and sits on the edge, reaches down to the floor for her clothes. In the middle of her back there is a fiery, pissed-off pimple that I hadn't seen before, glowering back at me as I watch her. There is nothing left of whatever attraction I had felt, which was, at its strongest, only the attraction of sex itself, having little to do with Jackie. What's left is revulsion, an omni-directional, all-encompassing odium. I look down at my watch and realize that the entire operation has taken only twenty-five minutes. We have fifteen minutes left. I'm not sure how these things work, if we could get a refund for unused time, if maybe Don could come up and use the remaining minutes—but it's too late anyway. Her panties are on and she is hooking her bra.

"That was… nice," I offered.

Why did I say this? Of all words. It had been horrible, filthy, frightening. A humiliating and degrading experience.

"Good," she replied, half turning toward me so that I could see her smile in profile, her front teeth overbiting the lower lip. She hummed pleasantly and slid her legs into dark stockings.

"I mean… it was nice."

She looked up at me momentarily, then back down at her bra, adjusting its cups. "Twice as nice."

I manufactured a laugh. "Do you work every night?"

"Depends. Sometimes I'll have a few customers in one night and have other nights off. Sometimes I work every night. It's not exactly a job with regular hours."

"I see." I had to keep talking to her, to keep her talking to me, to prevent her from leaving. I didn't know why, but I knew I had to keep her there. "I hate regular hours. I'm not much on jobs either."

One of her eyebrows rose higher than the other. She took a deep breath and smirked. "Lucky you."

She stood up and slipped into a tight lavender spandex skirt, sucking in to pull up the waistband that last inch below the navel and smooth out its creases. There was a thin, faded red scar running vertically down her lower abdomen. I wondered how she'd gotten it, if she'd had a Cesarean or been in some kind of accident. Maybe a disturbed and disgruntled john sliced her with a box cutter before she could scream out or call her driver to rush in and rescue her. I imagined this hulking bruiser of a bodyguard going to work on the guy so that he'd never again damage company property. Hazards of the job. I was tempted to show her my own fresh scar, fingering its scabrous surface as I stared at her mark.

"You're very pretty." The words just seemed to have come out of me, uninvited.

She smiled as she put on her body-hugging black tube top, which left much of her stomach uncovered and accentuated the little scarred paunch she carried around. She wasn't very pretty.

"Are you really from Tibet?"

"What?"

"The agency told us you were from Tibet."

She laughed. "I'm Chinese, by way of Flushing, Queens. I guess Tibet's a little more exotic."

"China's pretty exotic. Cantonese or Mandarin?"

"Mandarin."

"Oh."

"Why? Do you speak Chinese?"

"No."

"That makes two of us."

"I like Chinese food though."

"That makes one of us."

Who doesn't like Chinese food? I thought but didn't say.

She was fully clothed now, and I had run out of things to say, but I definitely preferred her with her clothes off. She brushed her hair and drew a stick of spearmint gum from her purse, unwrapped it, and slipped it into her mouth, then offered me one. I declined. She began to chew, snapping obnoxiously and looking around to make sure she hadn't forgotten anything. I felt a desperate need to fill the space between us with words, however meaningless, but my mind was an empty well.

"What do you do?" She saved me with her question.

"Me? I'm a student." How banal. "But I also write. I mean, I'm a writer but also a student. For now. I mean... I like to write, but I'm a student. Now. I'm taking a leave of absence, though. To concentrate on my writing."

"Oh," she said in a lilt. "What do you write?"

Oceans of emptiness. Reams of nothingness.

"Fiction. I'm working on a novel."

She clearly was not impressed, but she went on. There was time to kill and she would rightly give us the hour we had paid for. Better to while away the minutes with a little paltry prattle than to risk my asking her for a speedy second-time-around.

"What's it about?"

"What is what about?" I had already forgotten my creative falsehood and honestly had no idea what she was talking about.

Irked at my idiocy, she jutted her neck forward and let her mouth hang open and scowled. "Your novel? What's it about?"

"Yes, my novel, yes." I clasped my hands and rubbed them studiously. "It's, uh, postmodern stuff. Post-postmodern, really. You know, not really about anything, and yet at the same time about everything. Lots of irony. But sincere irony."

She pouted, perplexed, then suddenly lit up with spontaneous comprehension and extended a long wine-red fingernail.
"Oh. Like *Seinfeld*?"

I didn't know how to answer, so I compressed my lips and
nodded evasively. "How about you? Do you do anything else
besides… this? As far as work goes, I mean."

"Sure," she snickered, "I do brain surgery on the side."

My laugh was only partially fraudulent, as it was the closest
she'd come to wit all night. She seemed to be gearing up for a
more serious response when a cell phone sounded from within
her purse, the ringtone a primitive electronic version of the Spice
Girls' "Wannabe." She answered it—"Yeah, I'll be down in a
sec."—hung up, and showed me her phone's lit screen to prove
the time. "Hour's up," she said with a well-forged expression of
regret, as though she were breaking my heart against her will.

"Le temps s'en va," I said, and immediately wanted to stop
the words before they reached her ears.

"What?"

"Nothing. Nothing. I know the hour's up."

I led her to the door and stopped before opening it. "I'd like
to make another appointment."

"You'll have to call the agency." Again with regret, a tad
less persuasive this time. "It's my own rule. I always go through
them."

"We couldn't just set something up privately, like between
you and me?"

She hesitated, seemed to consider overriding policy for a
hot second, but ultimately stood firm. "No. I don't do that."

"Okay. Fair enough. But what about tomorrow? I'd like to
make an appointment for tomorrow night, at my house. I live

right across the street. Do you know offhand if you have any openings for tomorrow night?"

Zipping up her enormous coat, she tells me that she should have some open spaces tomorrow night, unless the agency has booked her up in the time she's been here, which is unlikely. Then she moves hastily to the door.

"Rushing off to another appointment?" I ask smilingly.

She doesn't answer. I say thank you, but she is already in the hall and on her way downstairs.

I trail down behind her at a respectful distance. Don opens the garage without so much as a nod good-bye or a mannerly appreciative smile, and when I start to walk out with her, he grabs my arm and hisses into my ear, "What are you doing?"

"It's like an ice rink out there."

"You do not walk a whore to the car. You don't escort an escort. It's not the fucking prom, man."

I blush and stay inside with him and watch Jackie trot out of the garage, carefully navigating her way over the glacial pavement and down to the car waiting in the street at the foot of the driveway.

"I was just looking out for you. She slips and falls and breaks an arm or something and you've got a lawsuit on your hands."

Don knits his brows. "I'll take my chances. And besides, we have homeowner's insurance. An umbrella policy." He presses a button on the wall and waits for the garage door to completely descend before we go back inside, where the tangy aroma of warming food permeates the kitchen and draws us toward it like starving dingoes to carrion. "Leftovers." He opens the oven and sticks a mitted hand inside to remove the contents. "I get hungry after fucking, you know, but not usually so much after a blow job." He offers me some penne and broccoli that he scoops out of an aluminum pan.

I tell him I'm not hungry, but he serves me a full helping anyway, and we sit across from each other at the butcher block table. I'm waiting for him to ask about my Jackie experience, but he just starts forking his pasta and after a few avid mouthfuls tells me that, despite her formidable fellating skills, he wasn't thrilled with her blasé attitude and mediocre looks, that he is not going to use her services again, and that he has half a mind to call up and demand that promised replacement.

"Like I said, the girl knows how to take a dick in her mouth—I'll give her that—but no dicksucking is worth that kind of cash, no matter how good it is. Except maybe if it was from Madonna. I know she's getting a little long in the tooth, but I've had a thing for her since I was a kid. That broad could be eighty-fucking-five years old and I'd still let her polish my pole. She was the first one I ever jerked off to, you know."

Head bent over dish, he looks at me as though he's just laid some seriously hallowed wisdom on me and expects a commensurate reaction.

"I think I did know that."

"Yep. I almost wore out the tape rewinding and replaying that *Lucky Star* video. They say you never forget your first. Who was yours?"

"Uh… Traci Lords, maybe." I honestly don't remember my first masturbatory fantasy, but Don's poster is still fresh in my mind, and the prime of Miss Traci Lords fits the time frame, so I go with her. It actually may be true.

"Mmm." He smiles lasciviously and winks at me before sliding a forkful of broccoli into his mouth and speaking through his mastication. "Nice choice. Very nice. Movie or magazine?"

He reaches back and grabs the remote from the counter to power up the TV, which happily distracts him from my failure to answer. An anchor on an early morning news show is talking about a young Long Island college girl who had gone missing over a week ago.

"You know her real name is Nora?" he says.

"Why would the police release a fake name? And how the hell do you know that anyway?"

"Not the dead girl, you nitwit. Traci Lords. Her real name is Nora. Nora Kuzma." He trills the *r* and pronounces her last name with an exaggerated Eastern European accent, elongating its syllables so that it seems unalluringly exotic, like a homely babushka. "It's a lot less whackworthy than Traci Lords, I'll tell you that."

The case has been well publicized. Her unclothed body was discovered last night in a small neighborhood park not very far from where she lived—and not much farther from where we are presently sitting—in a dense bracken just off a well-trodden dirt trail that runs from one end of the grounds to the other. She had been beaten with a blunt instrument—most likely a baseball bat or a baton of some sort, as wood splinters were found embedded in her flesh—raped, stabbed repeatedly, and raped again, once dead. (How they know she was raped after death is beyond my ken, and part of me suspects the media of sexing up the grue-some details.) There were incisions all over her body from head to toe, believed to be both ante- and postmortem, the result of a very sharp, straightedged blade. The police have no suspects or leads. There were no witnesses. She was last seen walking out of her house early in the evening to fetch the mail, hoping a pair of shoes she ordered online had arrived. When she didn't return, her mother went out to check on her. The mail was still in the box, but there was no sign of her daughter, until the disfigured remains were later found in the park.

"Not even safe to get your damn mail anymore. Ghoulish fucking world we live in," Don says with his mouth full, shaking his head and ravenously attacking what's left of his food. He is chewing loudly and vulgarly, which is unlike him. It annoys me. "But I guess different people have different turn-ons. Let him who is without sin…"

In the top left corner of the screen is a photo of the girl, probably from a high school yearbook, peering out as the male talking head somberly relates her fate. She is smiling, happy and hopeful. Shiny helixes of bright blonde hair spiral down the sides of her face and out of the frame. Then the picture fills the screen. She is wearing a small gold puffed heart on a thin gold chain that undulates softly over her collarbone and disappears behind her neck. I find myself wondering if this necklace was found on the body. It doesn't seem as though robbery was much on the perpetrator's mind, though murderers do tend to cherish keepsakes of their kills, at least in police procedurals.

"They'll find the guy. You can't get away with shit these days," Don says confidently, finished with his meal. He leans back and pats his stomach, then loosens his belt and unbuttons his pants. "Fuck. I ate that way too fast. That's my problem, whether it's sex or eating. I just don't know how to pace myself. Never have."

He changes the channel before the story is over, jumping from another news broadcast—in which a celebrity chef is being interviewed fawningly about his new low-carb cookbook—to the end of an old episode of *Cheers*.

"Man, I must've seen this one ten times," he says.

"Me too." I am looking at the uneaten food on my plate, the bloody pasta and macerated broccoli sprouts.

He lays the remote on the table and we quietly watch the rest of the show.

By the time I left Don's house, there were glints of gray light streaking the sky, hinting at a bright, icy day to come, as if the sun's rays were themselves frosted. On the walk home, I thought about what had just taken place, and I figured that in some way I had been a virgin before it. Not technically, of course, but the fact would forever remain that my first sexual experience away from my sister had been with a prostitute; my first real-world fuck was a discounted whore. Severine was with Spencer, I with a whore.

I needed more of a buffer between what had just happened and my return home, so I sat on the porch step for a few minutes until the gelidity became nearly intolerable, benumbing my buttocks and starting in on my legs so that I had to stand and shiver in place for a minute before surrendering myself to the warm, dark silence of the sleeping house. I wanted to shower but was too worn out in every way, and my room was so close now. At the top of the stairs I stopped. I felt as though there had to be an excuse to open her door, telling myself it was to see if she was home, although she rarely stayed out as late as I did with Don. I would just stick my face in until I could make out the shape of her body beneath the covers and detect her breathing in the overpowering silence of the house at 5 on a freezing winter morning. That's all. Just to make sure she was there. I pressed my ear to her door and heard nothing but the amplified scrape of my own cartilage against wood. With movement so laborious and slow that it didn't seem like movement at all, I turned the knob until I felt the latch bolt retract completely, pushed the door a few inches forward, heard nothing, pushed a few more centimeters, and peeked in, but it was still too dark to see. I had to know she was there. Ninety-nine percent certainty would not suffice. After standing a few distended moments with only my head hanging in past the lock stile, I opened the door just enough to slip inside, then closed it just as painstakingly, losing patience toward the end and letting the bolt click against the strike plate before easing into the groove. A bird chirped loudly, not far from the window. Two quick, shrill peeps. I crept over to the bed on the balls of my feet and reached out timidly for her form. Sitting down, I placed my hand lightly on her hips and hovered over her as she lay on her side. Her body could barely be felt beneath the sheet and two blankets. My hand settled more comfortably and began to move in small concentric strokes. Her voice broke out unexpectedly, quiet and firm. It seemed to come from elsewhere in the room.

"You're so shy, still so timid. Almost bashful." She laughed, lampooning me. "How could you be, after all this? I can feel you planning your move so far ahead, speculating, wondering if it's going to work. It's like I can hear you asking yourself if you should do it, weighing your options."

"My options," I said.

"Did you go out tonight?"

"I met a girl. Like you said I should."

The hallway was slowly brightening. Some early sunlight leaked into the room through the clefts between door and frame, but the closed shades and drawn curtains prevented the bulk of it from entering directly.

"Where?"

"With Don."

"Where?"

I moved up against her from behind, nesting myself in the calming contours of her shape and wrapping an arm around her and slowly squeezing as though attempting to extrude the space between us and blend our bodies into one. A toasty heaviness came over me. My eyelids grew leaden. Her hair tickled my face as I breathed in its scent of shampoo and slumber and let a few honeyed strands slip between my lips.

"I met her with Don."

"I didn't realize females moved in Don's circle, besides that girlfriend of his. But that's good. However it happens is good. What's her name?"

"That girlfriend of his? Susan."

"No. The girl you met."

For an instant, I couldn't remember her name. I could not recall a single thing about her. Had it actually happened?

"Jackie. Jacqueline," I said drowsily.

I laid my head beside hers on the pillow, gathered her hair off the back of her neck and touched the supple, sleep-warm skin there with my lips. She remained still.

"Jacqueline. Is she French?"

"No."

As if living in the best of all possible dreams, I swung my arm back around her and pulled the covers down, dragged two fingers along the velvety flank of her unclad leg and slid my hand up under the front of her camisole, softly sweeping my fingertips across her sylphlike stomach and circumscribing an areola. She remained still.

"Everybody will be getting up soon," she warned.

"Not me. I don't think I'll be getting up at all today, as a matter of fact."

"When was the last time you saw daylight?"

"Daylight's overrated. Daylight depresses me. 'I 'gin to be aweary of the sun.'"

She reached up and stayed my probing hand with hers.

"Your hands are cold," she said, squeezing my fingers.

"It's cold out." I freed my hand to cup her breast.

"Pretty name, Jacqueline."

"Yes it is." I fondled her nipple with my forefinger. "She's a prostitute."

Why did I say it? Why did I have to tell her? In her presence my defenses were depleted. I was effectively and affectively disarmed. There was a pitiless drive to bare all to her—always this exigency—but she never backed me into a corner or forced a confession, as though she knew when I was withholding, felt it in her bones when I was lying, and knew as well that I would eventually unravel on my own. She reduced me to nothing, and I was always willing, happy, and grateful to be reduced.

"Still, it's a pretty name," she said in a tired whisper.

"She's a whore."

"I heard you. I understood."

"That's all you have to say?"

She paused.

"Was it enjoyable?"

I paused.

"It was sex."

"So you enjoyed it."

A sudden rage reared up in me. I grabbed her arm and violently twisted her around, pressing my face against hers, my lips to hers. She pulled back and pushed me away.

"I don't think I can take this much longer," I said, holding fast to her arms. "I can't keep up this front. I can't even cry. I feel like I want to but can't. You're not *you* anymore. I don't know who you are. I'm trying to hate you. I'm trying so hard to hate you. If you felt even an infinitesimal degree of what I feel, if you realized only the smallest fraction of what you're doing to me, you would hate yourself. There wouldn't be enough regret in the world to deal with the self-loathing you'd feel. If you, the you I used to know, *my* you, if you realized what you're doing, how you're killing me, you would... you wouldn't be able to live with yourself."

The things you say when angry.

"How can you do this? How can you let this happen when you started it? How can you...?" I gripped her face, turned it toward me forcibly and kissed her hard, then pushed her back, still holding her expressionless face in my hands. "Come away with me. That's the only way it can work, the only solution. Please. We'll go someplace far away, very far, someplace where we don't speak a word of the language and it'll be just us and nobody can even talk to us, nobody will be able to say a word to us. Please. I know it sounds ridiculous, but I'm dead serious. I've never been more serious. Or desperate. Please. Nobody but us. Please don't say no. Please come with me."

I was holding her face so tight my hands ached, but she did not try to free herself. She just looked at me coldly and spoke through my grip.

"Solution? To what? It's only a problem because you made it one. You've created this tragedy. You're trying to hold on to something that's already gone and has been gone for a while now. A ghost. That's the tragedy. You're too smart to make that mistake. 'You can't step into the same river twice.'"

"Please don't say that. Not that. Not now. No philosophy! No more fucking philosophy!" I squeezed and shook her, but

200

still she made no attempt to disengage her head from between my hands.

"You're hurting me," was all she said, with quiet grimness.

"No. You're the one who's doing the hurting." I released her. "If you don't come back to me, I don't know what I'll do."

"Look at what you've done already." Her eyes inflated with anger, but her voice held at its inflexible level. "Look at yourself. If you keep on the way you are, I *will* go away. Without you. Maybe not with Spencer but definitely without you. You want an answer, a solution? There it is."

I regained composure.

"Just say it. Just say the words and then I'll let you go. I'll free you. Just let me hear them and you can go wherever you want, and I won't try to stop you. I've never heard you say them. Say them now, just once, and that will be it."

She put her hand on my cheek.

"You're my brother."

She knew how to make the poison work.

"You're my brother, Peter. My brother."

Now it was she who held my face. I cried, finally. A tear or two.

"And him? Do you love him?" I said, beaten.

"I don't."

It didn't help. Not how I thought it would.

Unspeaking, we lay there face to face as the room lightened around us. I was overwhelmed with fatigue and failure, routed by the night's events, but I couldn't stay. I didn't want to move, but I couldn't stay there. Her body was touching mine, her ankle crossed over my shin, arms interlaced, maybe for the last time, I thought. She reached over and grazed my lips with two fingers. There was only one place to go. I pushed her face from me, disentangled my limbs, rose, and walked down the hall, where my room awaited.

When I woke the next day around 4:30 p.m., an Edith Piaf song was playing somewhere in the house. At first, I thought the warbly, lachrymose singing was the accompaniment to a dream I was waking from. Before getting out of bed, I called Warm and Willing Escorts to request Jackie for the evening, explaining that I had used her services the previous night and had mentioned I would be calling. The woman on the other end, who had a raspy, chain-smoker's voice and called me honey, said that she knew nothing about it, but Jackie had two hours open between 10 p.m. and 12 a.m. and another between 3 and 4 a.m. I chose the later slot.

I felt unclean, as though I still had her pungent, prostitute's smell on me, but I didn't want to shower. I wanted to eat. I like to think that my modus vivendi conforms to that of a beast in the wild that doesn't move unless it absolutely has to, a creature that sleeps and lolls around most of the time and summons the strength to rise only when threatened or hungry or otherwise obliged in some biologically exigent way to lug itself from its sacral sloth. Animals don't seem to suffer boredom. They seem perfectly satisfied with the bare essentials of life and understand in whatever instinctual way that boredom is the state of nature, and that to try to overcome it is to invite unwarranted hardship and heartache. Hobbes was wrong, or at least not completely right: it is not a war of all against all; it's self against self.

Downstairs in the kitchen, my parents and Severine were seated at the table for a late-afternoon snack. There were cold cuts and two types of cheese and a sliced baguette laid out in an attractive pattern, with the meat folded around the cheese and the bread bounding it all in cute little pieces of edible fencing. Each family member was examining something: Severine, a few pages of sheet music; my father, the *New York Review of Books*; my mother, a teacher's union magazine. I found the daunting domesticity of the scene unsettling and was inclined to retreat straight back upstairs.

"Good morning," my father said as I entered, breaking a piece of bread and taking no pains to soften his sarcasm.

"I got in late," I explained groggily, heading toward my seat.

My mother rose, kissed me on the cheek, and went to the cabinet to get a plate for me.

"I'm not hungry," I told her, knowing she would set me a place anyway and I would eat. I was actually very hungry. "I can't eat as soon as I get up. I need time to generate an appetite."

"If you keep going to bed and getting up later and later, you might eventually come around full circle and return to a somewhat normal schedule," my father suggested.

"That's an interesting conjecture," I said. "But normal is so uninteresting."

My mother put some slices of prosciutto and salami and a few small squares of ricotta salata and provolone on my plate, along with a rounded end of the loaf of bread—my favorite— which she always saved for me. She brought a wineglass and made to fill it, but I stopped her and said I'd prefer a Coke.

"Do we have any?" Severine seemed flummoxed by the possibility.

"Since when do you drink that… stuff?" My father fluffed his paper. "Have you seen what it does to paint? Next thing you'll be asking for is a stick of beef jerky and a can of Bud."

"It is the king of beers." I wrapped an extra slice of salami around the provolone, squeezed it between a folded chunk of bread and stuffed it in my mouth, and when I finished chewing said, "If we were European, do you think we would live like an American family?"

He took off his glasses and rubbed both eyes.

"I would hope not," was his indifferent response.

It was 5:13, according to the oven clock, and the nighttime was already fully formed. My mother came back with an ice-filled glass and a warm can of Coke, which she placed before me.

"You're in luck. I get a craving for soda every once in a while. You can have some of my stash."

"In thirty years of marriage, I've never seen you take a sip of soda," my father said, aghast, looking from her to the can, from the can to her, from her to me, as it changed hands. The can made a loud hissing sound when I opened it; soda fizzed over ice cubes and foamed to the rim of the glass, stopping just before overflow and retreating back down with quiet popping.

"Well, I guess we all have our secrets," she said, picking up my glass before I could taste it and drinking a bit, then placing it back down in front of me. "So who's this girl?" She turned to me and smiled with pleasant mischievousness.

"Which girl?"

"Is there more than one?" my father chimed in, leaving his periodical.

"This girl you met," my mother pressed onward.

I looked at Severine.

"A girl," I said.

"She has a name, I presume," my mother intoned with exaggerated curiosity, pleased at the prospect.

"Don't we all?" I drank some soda, giving the suspense room to expand. "Jacqueline."

"Pretty name," my mother said, thumbing the pages of her magazine. She couldn't keep that smile off her face, and it was starting to bug me. "French?"

"Of course," I answered without a stutter.

"Where did you meet her?"

"With Don."

"I knew he'd be good for something one of these days," my father quipped. "Though I'm a little suspect about the pedigree of woman one would meet with Don."

Severine smirked. "Don't be. She's a professional."

I glared at her sideways and spoke before anyone could pry into my girl's profession. "She might come over tonight, as a matter of fact." At last my sister looked at me. "But she works in the evening, so she wouldn't come until late. You'll probably be asleep. You'll meet her another time."

"What does she do?" my mother asked.

"Yes. Do tell." Severine dipped her head and peered up at me inquisitively. "What is it that she does, exactly?"

"She works in the evening."

They were on tenterhooks, waiting for me to fill them in. I forked some more food and looked down into my plate as I ate. Then I finished my Coke and said, "What?"

"Is she a student?" my mother asked.

"Who?"

"Jacqueline."

"Any more soda around?'"

"You've got to be kidding me." My father was openly perturbed by this request.

"It's not like I'm asking for a vial of crack."

"They found that girl," Severine said, maybe in an attempt to rescue me, maybe just because she was sick of talking about Jackie. "That girl from around here that was missing."

"I know," I said. "It's all over the news."

"She was raped and murdered." My mother shook her head and cast down her eyes.

"Then raped again," I added eagerly.

"They said her head was almost completely turned around, facing backward," Severine said.

"Like in *The Exorcist*," I commented. "Probably the boyfriend."

"Why do you say that?" my mother asked.

"It usually is. Crime of passion."

"You hear a thing like this and you start to think maybe those Christian crazies are right." My father picked up his paper again. "Maybe it's high time for the Rapture."

"Amen." I crossed myself with a hunk of bread in my hand, then tore a nice mouthful out of it.

As we finished eating, the tree-mounted patio light blew out and plunged the backyard into a darkness so impenetrable that the bay window became a broad black mirror that reflected the familial scene in a way that made the simulacrum somehow more real than what actually was, as though we—mother, father, sister, and brother sitting around a clean white table, the same oblong slab of textured Formica that we've had since before I was old enough to remember—were a reflection of the reflection, whose primary source was untraceable.

"Spencer is coming over tonight too," Severine announced.

I shook the melting ice around in my glass, staring into it.

"Maybe we can all go bowling," I said.

"We'll probably go out." She laid her fork and knife parallel to each other across her cleared plate.

"Bowling *is* out. I thought you liked bowling. I like bowling. Who doesn't like bowling?"

"There's an article in here about Heidegger and Hannah Arendt that might interest you," my father informed us, pointing down at the paper in front of him. "They would have made quite the postwar philosophical power couple if he hadn't fallen for Hitler instead."

"Maybe it was the moustache," I said.

"I read it." Severine turned casually toward me. "An affair between two intellectuals is bound to end badly. Doomed from the start."

"Aren't they all, though?" I met her offhandedness with some of my own, slurping up the last of the syrupy carbonation.

"I'm finished, if you want it." He slid the article over to me. I took it with no intention of reading it.

"I'm going back upstairs for a few hours," I responded, then rose and just stood there clumsily. "I didn't sleep well last night. If I don't come down, please wake me for dinner."

"I hope you're enjoying your dreams," my mother said, half joking, half concerned.

I found this a peculiar thing to say. "What?"

"You miss so much of the day. I hope you're at least getting something out of your sleep."

"I get sleep out of my sleep. I stopped dreaming a while ago. It only gets in the way."

"I'll wake you for dinner," she said.

"Wouldn't miss it."

"Read that article," my father counseled.

"Wouldn't miss that either."

I went upstairs to bed. A few minutes later, as I was about to drift off, just on the verge of that prized moment of unreality when one is poised between provinces, the door sliced open and Severine stood there, filling the gap.

"You can't be sleeping again already," she said.

"You underestimate me."

"She's not really coming here, is she?"

"She is. Tonight. It's all arranged."

"Are you sick? You're bringing a prostitute here, to our house?"

"Am I sick, she asks."

She was silent.

"Why does it bother you, because I'm with a prostitute or because I'm with a prostitute in our house?"

"It doesn't bother me."

She stood directly underneath the lintel and said nothing.

"Either come in or go out. I can't sleep with you standing there."

She didn't come in. I turned around and slept.

At 11 that night, my eyes opened to the sound of ice pellets battering the roof and window. I lay there and listened, picturing the shingles frosted with crystal, the streets slickened with rime. I hadn't woken for dinner. My mother had apparently tried to call me several times from downstairs and had finally come into the room to rouse me, but it was no use; I wouldn't move. I got out of bed around 12, weary and drugged with a surfeit of sleep. The house, midnight silent and winter dark, still smelled of fried eggplant and tomato sauce. Severine's room was empty. They had gone out to a hip new café or an edgy art film or a jazz club, well-cultured young couple that they were. I still hadn't showered, still didn't want to, but thought I probably should, before Jackie arrived. Whore or not, hygiene and some degree of etiquette still applied. That left three hours to clean up, eat, and prepare.

By 2 a.m., all I had accomplished was some aimless ambling about the house, some indiscriminate web surfing, and the rapt viewing of back-to-back episodes of *Taxi*. I still hadn't taken a shower, and I decided that I wouldn't. I just washed my face and wet down my hair, put on some clean clothes and underwear, and shaved, because whiskers annoy me. Then the jitters kicked in, about half an hour before Jackie was due to arrive. Normally, I would lie in bed to allay this, but I couldn't risk falling asleep and having her ring the doorbell, so I sat downstairs on the sofa and turned on the television and watched a few minutes of the rebroadcasted primetime nightly news, which was just getting to an extended piece with new information on the grisly slaying of the Long Island college girl—namely, an anonymous eyewitness who might have seen her talking to someone by the mailbox in a dark green four-door sedan (possibly a Honda or Toyota), and a detail leaked by an unnamed source close to the investigation suggesting that she had been flogged and sodomized with a fencepost, which was found in a dumpster a block away, coated with blood and fluids and some potentially usable fingerprints.

I hadn't spent much time in the den lately. In years past, we used to watch videos there, the four of us together on that old orange couch that has long since been relegated to the basement. My parents would doze and wake several times before retiring to their bedroom, leaving me and my sister to channel-hop well after the video had finished. I was always the last to go, primed at night when everyone else was ready to end the day. Severine would eventually drop off as well, her head falling lightly onto my shoulder and the rest of her nestled snugly—puppylike—between me and the couch. A mawkish little scene, one that I would give a lifetime to have back.

My reverie was broken by the turning of a key, the clang of a lock, and suppressed voices. I turned off the television and slipped below the edge of the couch's back as though preparing an ambush. She was home. They were home. The kitchen light went on and tarnished the darkness. Soft, unshoed footfalls came quietly across the tile.

"Maybe he went out." Spencer proposed.

"He said she was coming over late tonight. He said it was all set up. Isn't there some kind of 24-hour cancellation policy or something?"

He laughed. "It's not an appointment with the shrink, Sev. They can't bill his insurance."

She laughed. "I don't know. Maybe they took a credit card number or something. Business is business."

"The oldest of them."

Their voices were enlivened and pert. She had told him about my impending guest and they were sharing a laugh over it. I was now a punch line. What else had she told him?

"He can't have her in his room," she said. "I mean, I don't think he'd take her to his room."

"Where else would they... transact business? The kitchen table."

"No, but... his bedroom?

I felt as though I could hear Spencer shrug. They laughed quietly, kissed audibly, the sound of suctioning saliva reaching me as I entered the kitchen and stood there silently while they finished their foreplay.

"No, not in his bedroom," I said, startling them. "We'll go in the basement to ensure privacy. She should be here shortly. Hello, sister."

"What are you doing in the dark?"

"Nothing, of course. Hey, Spencer, how are things?"

As always, he was both meticulously and unsystematically well put-together, in shabby-chic jeans torn at one knee and an oversized black and yellow striped crewneck sweater topping a faded gray T-shirt, his hair stylishly windblown, scarf carefully draped carelessly around his neck. And the glasses, of course. I was bored by this now, the impeccable *sprezzatura* of his fashion sense. Wasn't she?

"Not bad," he replied. "You're looking well. It's good to see you, Peter."

"Am I?" I laughed. "Is it?"

His persistent cordiality was galling. I was not looking well. I had just seen myself in the mirror, and I was looking markedly unwell. My face was an irritated shade of crimson from shaving, my neck was coated with cuts and razor burn, and my hair—already losing its wavy, youthful thickness, with my hairline taking the first manifest strides toward inexorable retreat—was too long and out of shape and greasy. When I had gone a few weeks without a trim, it began to look wispy and insubstantial, aging my appearance by several years. Every afternoon upon waking, I would rue the loss of a few more strands lying listless on my pillow, taken from my head without struggle as I slept.

I didn't ask about their evening out. She took his distressed leather jacket and hung it in the hall closet, tucking his scarf into the sleeve.

"She told you who I'm waiting for, I guess?" I looked from one to the other.

"Yes. It didn't seem like such a secret, if that's what you're insinuating," he defended her.

"No sir. Nothing secret about it. No such thing as a brother-sister confidentiality privilege. Probably for the best. If there were fewer secrets in the world, maybe things would improve. We should all be completely honest and open about every little thing, every object concealed in our baggage, every insignificant bone of the skeletons cloistered in our closets. Privacy is such an odd, outdated notion in this wonderfully interconnected age of ours. We should all cultivate our own little gardens only to let everyone trample our lawns." I was out of breath, or I would have gone on.

Spencer's grin was gratuitous and blatantly patronizing. "It's nothing to be embarrassed about, Peter," he said evenly.

"I'm not embarrassed." I tried to mimic the pacific levelness of his tone. "Do I seem embarrassed to you? The only reason prostitution is stigmatized is because America the beautiful is still so pathetically puritanical, and beyond that, the only reason it's against the law is that the government is not making money off it. By the way, it's cheaper for two, you know, and you're here anyway... I mean, I'm sure she would accommodate you if you'd like. She's nothing if not accommodating."

Before he could react, I stunted him further. "Oh, don't get flustered, Spencer. You're blushing. I'm clearly kidding." I was outnumbered, like a cast-out child on the playground, but I had the shock of my impertinence working for me. "I know you're well taken care of. Both of you. Only the best for my sister. And whoever she picks gets the best in return, needless to say."

They exchanged knowing glances, the kind that adults give each other in the presence of misbehaving children who aren't worth the effort to chastise. They were mindful of the moody infant's volatility.

"What've you been doing tonight?" asked Severine, sitting in my mother's chair at the kitchen table and coiling her hair up into a loose bun. She suddenly looked drained.

"Oh, I think you know the answer to that. What could I be doing?"

"I never see you around campus anymore," Spencer interposed with poorly put-on disappointment.

"I'm rarely there."

"Leave of absence?" As if he didn't know.

"Kind of. A bit of convalescence also. Remember?" I raised my palm.

"Will it disturb you much if we watch TV up here while you're...?" Severine asked.

"You never watch television anymore. You used to call it *that demonic machine. The idiot box*. You used to say it makes you stupid, numbs the brain, anaesthetizes you."

"It does," Spencer chimed in. "You might as well be sleeping if you're going to watch TV. Both activities are about equally productive."

"Don't disparage sleep," I said earnestly. "Sleep is always there for me when nothing else is. Even you might find you'll need it one day."

He puckered his lips and nodded. "Sounds a bit heavy-handed, but—"

"We have a film," Severine said defensively. "That's what we're going to watch."

"Is it foreign?" I asked.

"No."

"Then it's a *movie*, not a film. In America we make *movies*. What *movie* are you going to watch?"

Spencer held up the DVD—*Rosemary's Baby*—which he seemed to have produced from out of nowhere.

"Interesting."

"Where will you be?"

"I told you. In the basement."

"Is she really coming?"

"She's really coming."

I couldn't figure out why she was so concerned.

"Will it bother you if I sit inside and watch with you while I wait?" I asked.

"Not at all," Spencer answered for her too, stepping over to my sister and placing his arm gently around her shoulder, one of the only times I had ever seen him display affection so overtly. Severine seemed surprised and uncomfortable, as if she didn't know where to look. I was not seized by jealousy at all; on the contrary, the amateur move gratified me with its uncharacteristic boldness. It almost seemed insecure.

The oven clock stared out at me: 2:57.

"Ah." I braced up. "I guess I won't be sitting with you after all. I have to go outside. She'll be here any minute, and I can't keep her waiting."

"Not when you're paying for every minute," Severine said as I started to go.

I had no time to parry her thrust, so I absorbed the blow and moved on.

I went out through the garage, leaving them in the kitchen. The long, dark Lincoln was already there, idling patiently by the sidewalk with its tinted windows and shining silver hubcaps, engine purring and softly smoking in the frozen mist. I walked carefully down to the center of the driveway, dotted from top to bottom with solar-powered perimeter lamps that burned with subdued brilliance through the ossified layers of icy encasement. I stopped and waved. Same routine: the passenger door opened, the girl got out. Merengue music blared briefly as the driver lowered his window and beckoned Jackie back to the car. They exchanged a few words, and she approached with tiny, cautious steps, keeping her eyes on the ground.

"You should do something about this driveway," she said as she got close.

"If you stick to the middle you're all right. It's the edges that are dicey."

"Someone slips and gets hurt they'll sue your ass off. Wouldn't be pretty."

"We have homeowner's insurance. Umbrella policy."

She looked unkempt tonight, a few frizzed strands of hair standing shaggily out of place from the rest of her thick black mane. Only an aura of jaded cynicism animated her tired bearing. I had no desire to be with her. I never did.

"Do you remember me?" I asked.

"It was only last night."

"I know, but I figured you see a lot of clients."

"There are only so many hours in a day. Dan, right?"

"No. Don was the other guy. I'm Peter."

"Oh yeah, Peter."

As before, I paid her on the spot, then escorted her in past my parents' wing as quietly and unobtrusively as possible, though her heels echoed through the foyer and left slushy scuff marks on the clean white kitchen tile. I deliberated asking her to remove her shoes before entering—they were going to come off soon anyway—but it seemed like a tacky request, even for the situation. We stopped in front of the den, where Spencer and Severine were sitting next to each other, the TV not yet on and their heads conspicuously turned away as though they hadn't heard us enter, which—unless they were sleeping, comatose, or dead—was virtually impossible.

"This is Jacqueline," I announced, standing at the entrance to the room with my girl.

They turned.

"Hello," he said, rising, smiling. "Spencer. Nice to meet you." Ever the gentleman.

"Jackie," she pronounced shyly, pulling together the front of her puffy coat. I was intrigued by her timidity.

Severine was staring from her place on the couch.

"Don't just sit there looking stupid, Severine," I said. "Say hello to the lady."

"Hello," she said, frowning frigidly at me.

I felt triumphant. I wasn't sure why, or what I was trying to accomplish, but it seemed at the moment like some sort of small victory, which was the most I had to hope for at this point.

"This is my sister, Severine, and her…" I couldn't bring myself to say *boyfriend*. "Spencer."

Jackie looked at me and nodded as we stood there next to each other, Spencer still on his feet on the other side of the couch, smiling awkwardly, until all our attention was brought to the canned laughter that blasted out from the television Severine had just turned on.

"Lower that," I commanded. "People are sleeping."

"Who's sleeping?" Jackie asked.

"My parents. Right down the hall." I smiled, pointing in the direction of their room. "Don't worry, it's far enough away, and they're sound sleepers."

"I don't think she's worried," Severine said, silencing the televised hilarity as she switched inputs and started up the DVD player. "Are you worried, Jackie?"

"Not if you're not," she said to me, then leaned over and whispered in my ear, "You're paying for this time, you know."

"Everyone keeps telling me that," I spoke up into the room. "I'm well aware of what I'm paying for."

"It doesn't matter to me what we do. I get paid by the hour, so whenever you want to get to business..."

I didn't care. This *was* business, as far as I was concerned, and I was happy to be paying for it. But we couldn't just stand there.

"Well, I'll let you watch your movie then," I said. "I'll be downstairs if you need me."

"Good night." Spencer was still graciously standing.

Jackie nodded at him.

"Yes, it is," I said, smiling at Severine.

On the floor of the basement I had spread out an old floral-patterned saffron duvet and a flimsy black blanket, both of which had been languishing in storage for years, waiting for overnight guests we never had. They reeked of mildew, even after some refreshing spritzes of upholstery deodorizer and a few hours' airing out. Despite the pleasant finishing and overall atmosphere of contained comfort, it is always several degrees cooler and often dank down there when the dehumidifier fills and no one empties the bucket. I turned on the lights and walked over to the quilted coverlet, pulled out a frazzled folded edge and smoothened some uneven patches. Jackie stepped out of her shoes and took off her coat to reveal the exact same ensemble as the night before, and she was even less attractive in it now. The rank absurdity of the situation struck home as she slowly bared herself to me: I was in the basement of my family's house with a subpar hooker while my parents slept and my sister and her boyfriend watched a movie one floor up. I was delving deep into pathetic realms that I never could have foreseen, but none of this bothered or embarrassed me. I was insensate. I sat down on the couch and impassively watched her remove her clothes with the same interest I would have invested in watching a sitcom rerun I'd seen several times over.

"You'll have to take off your clothes too, to do this right, re-member?" she said, as she stripped down to her bra and panties, all professional tonight. Last night's piecemeal disrobing must have been for first-time clients. Or maybe she'd just had a bad night at work and was in no mood for ritual. So I followed suit, and we went through the motions as routinely as participants in a played-out performance piece whose aggregate success is de-pendent upon the exact execution of carefully choreographed individual actions. I undressed, lay down on the blanket, and let her suck my penis for some time before entering her, hearing garbled fragments of film dialogue directly above us and feet traipsing into the kitchen to get a drink or a late-night nosh from the pantry. Jackie didn't bother to moan or talk dirty or show any signs of enjoyment this time. She jounced on top of me and bounced off my body like a resentful kid bitterly whittling away at some dull-as-dishwater chore her parents had assigned her as punishment. It was done in less than half an hour.

"You want to do it again? You still have some time," she offered, while I was already wilting inside her.

I was surprised she asked; one time around seemed enough of an ordeal for her. Maybe she figured it was better to pass the leftover minutes riding me than having to talk.

"No. I don't think so. Not yet anyway."

"Well if you do, you've got to decide quick. There's not *that* much time."

Even if I'd wanted to, I couldn't have. My penis was in no shape for an encore.

She slipped off me, and we sat naked on the blanket, the cold of the underlying cement starting to seep through. She took a cigarette and a lighter from her bag, lit the cigarette and pulled some smoke into her mouth, held it awhile before sucking it into her lungs, exhaled, removed the cigarette from between her lips, and then asked if she could smoke in the room. When I said yes, she offered me one, which I took and lit from hers. I puffed on the thing without inhaling, but the rancid smack of smoldering tobacco in my mouth was already enough to sicken me.

"Would I be offending you if I asked your age?" I said through a cough.

She took a long drag.

"Nope."

"How old are you?"

Smoke blew out her nose.

"Just because I'm not offended doesn't mean you should ask."

"Oh. Sorry."

She laughed. "Thirty-one."

"You look younger. I mean, thirty-one is by no means old, but you look twenty-five, twenty-six, max. You almost look younger than I do."

"I know. Asians always look younger. It's our skin."

She did look younger, but it wasn't her skin that gave the impression of youth. She checked the time on her cell phone and puffed her cigarette. Smoke enveloped her face like a mushroom cloud, and a fine flake of ash fell onto the blanket on her lap. I quickly rose, still in the buff, and rushed to the bathroom to fill a disposable paper cup with water to serve as a makeshift ashtray. She told me to take off the condom while I was in there, warning that my cock could suffocate if I left one on too long. It sounded ludicrous, but I figured this might be something a working girl would know. Pulling that slick and slimy piece of rubber from my body, I mulled over her half-baked caveat and considered how much more painless life would be if my member were to asphyxiate, or if by some providential stroke I woke up dickless, free, with no memory of my former oppressor and its despotic control over me. It is such an ugly, odious organ, sagging sadly between my thighs like a shriveled old inverted mushroom. I stood in front of the mirror with the cigarette drooping stupidly from the corner of my mouth and pulled my sticky, flaccid penis taut and imagined what it would be like to hack it off, testicles and all, to slice the despicable thing from my body and toss the bloody refuse into the wastebasket along with the semen-filled condom, then bag it all up and dump it in the trash can and drag it out to the curb with the rest of the family's garbage. I opened the medicine cabinet and withdrew a pair of grooming scissors, the kind used for errant nose hairs and wayward eyebrows, spread the blades and slid them gently around my manhood. The cold metal felt good. Would it change everything, this quick flash of steel and skin? How much blood would there be? Could I die from this? I saw myself passing out on the hard bathroom tile with my severed dick in my hand as I slowly bled out, and while I didn't have much self-respect left, even I would not want my corpse to be found in that condition. I dropped the scissors, urinated, and left the bathroom.

"I was thinking that I'd like to see you again… outside of these circumstances," I said, after a minute or so of silence, back on the comforter. "Would there be any possibility of that?"

"What do you mean?" she said, incredulous. "You mean, like, you want to go on a date?" She sneered slyly.

The word *date* always rang strange to me. I had—I have—never been on a proper date.

"Yes."

Her grin widened and was joined by a short laugh.

"Like… to a restaurant or something? The movies? A little miniature golf maybe?"

"I would prefer bowling or billiards, but the specifics don't really matter," I said dejectedly.

"But we already fucked."

I nodded. "We did."

"And besides, I don't go out with clients. I never mix business with my personal life. It's very important that I keep those separate, you know."

"Wise."

"But we can fuck again, real quick," she consoled. "There's still ten minutes left."

"No. I don't think I'm ready."

"I could blow you if you want."

She seemed eager to make reparations for turning down the date.

"Sounds nice, but I think I'll pass. Unless you'd reconsider my proposal."

She squinted and crinkled her forehead. "So you're saying that you would want me to blow you now if I agreed to go on a date with you another day?"

"Yes, that's right."

She chortled. "I guess no blow job then."

"I guess not," I said, as though she were crazy for giving up such a grand opportunity and would soon regret her foolishness.

She asked if I was sure, absolutely sure, then walked over to the couch to collect her clothes, humming as she separated her bra from her shirt (it sounded like Bon Jovi's "Wanted Dead or Alive," but I couldn't be sure and didn't want to ask) and her fishnet stockings from her skirt. I sat in my underwear, studying the fag end of my cigarette. I watched her snap on her demi bra and slip into her stockings and was suddenly taken by a strong, stirring impulse to slap her. I felt defiled and sad, rejected and sappy, and what I wanted more than anything at that moment was to hit her. I put on my pants and shirt, dowsed the butt of my cigarette in the cup, and walked up to her.

"I'd like you to leave now," I said.

"Yeah, that's the plan. That's why I'm getting dressed."

"Please hurry." I said this with exaggerated politeness to compensate for the ire fermenting inside.

"I said I'm getting dressed." She raised her voice and stared at me with fuming eyes that only increased my desire to hurt her. "What, you got somewhere to go? You have another girl coming that you're gonna ask out?" She pulled her tight elastic shirt over her head.

"No, I just want you to leave. Now. Please leave. I'm asking you nicely."

"Christ. I come here on business when I didn't even want to because you were so fucking weird and creepy last night, and then you ask me on a date. A date, for God's sake! I try to be nice and let you down easy, and now you pull this. Believe me, I'm not looking to stay here any longer than I have to."

"Weird? Weird how? How am I weird?" I came up close and scrutinized her face as though trying to see into the enigma of her soul. "And what kind of creepy are we talking here? Serial killer creepy? Ghost story creepy? Monster-in-the-closet creepy? What exactly is the make and model of my type of weird and creepy? Surely not pedophile creepy?"

"Like that. See." She abruptly wiggled into her skirt and clipped back her hair with a big red bow-tie barrette. "Just the way you are. Fucking freaks me out," she added, looking away from me and shaking her head as she checked to make sure she was completely dressed.

"But what exactly do you mean? You say someone's weird, you should delineate this. You just don't say someone's weird without having reasons, without giving an example, without saying what you mean. That's just not fair. What did I do that makes you think I'm weird?" There was a drib of belligerence in my voice, and I was precariously close to her, but she showed no trepidation.

"I don't know." She wrung her hands, frustrated, searching in vain for the elusive answer. "It's just... how you act. The things you say and how you say them. Normal human beings don't talk like you."

"Normal human beings?"

She rolled her eyes, roughly rubbed her broad, flat nose as though wanting to grind the thing into her face, and sucked in her stomach as she cinched a shiny red patent leather belt—the only accessory that she had not been wearing the night before—tight around her waist.

"Forget it, all right? You're not weird. You're normal, just like everyone else. You're just right. There's nothing weird about you. Forget I even said anything," she barked, shaking her head and raising a dismissive palm. "You're A-okay, okay?" She made a circle of her thumb and forefinger.

I took a moment to tame the urge to respond hostilely and spoke with a softness that belied my budding indignation. "Okay. But how can I forget what you just said? You said I'm weird and creepy and unlike normal human beings. What is it about the way I act or talk or am, exactly, that freaks you out? Please give me a concrete example. Please." I joined my hands in prayer.

She ignored me.

"Just one. Just one quick little illustration."

She ignored me some more.

"Just one teeny instance of my creepy weirdness or weird creepiness and I swear you'll never hear from me again."

"Oh, I am never going to hear from you again, that's for sure. Consider my number lost."

I let her finish buckling her belt—which contracted her waist a couple of inches—and waited until she turned up toward me, pulled back my arm, and smashed my palm against her cheek, my right hand hitting her left cheek hard, my eyes closing at that idyllic instant of impact. My hand stung. I was trembling all over. It was a stupendous sensation, so radically relieving and startlingly cathartic, like the endorphin release and well-earned fatigue after a good workout (or so I've heard, not being a fitness buff myself). She let out a truncated shriek. Her head wrenched sideways with the blow and remained there for a moment in apparent disbelief. She exhaled heavily and looked at me, her eyes wide and her lower jaw hanging open. Teeming with self-congratulation, I relaxed my arms and let them fall to my sides. She turned, her mouth motionlessly agape as if she had something to say but the words were wedged in her throat.

A gunshot from the television upstairs. A whish of wind. Icicles falling to the ground from the eaves.

"You're batshit crazy," she said at length, slow and calmly, flattening her hand against her reddened face and taking a few chary steps backward. "You're not weird, you're fucking crazy." Hands all atremble, she nervously took her cell phone from her pocketbook and dialed a programmed number, keeping her eyes on me throughout. I knew she was calling the big goon in the Lincoln, but I wasn't afraid. I knew he was prepared to deal with problems that arise with the girls, issues of these kinds and worse, but I wasn't afraid. "Javier, I'm coming out," was all she said, as though nothing had happened apart from what was supposed to have happened, and she hung up, folded the phone, and put it back in her purse. "I could have you busted up for this," she said in a quivering voice. "I could have you busted up real good."

"I could have you arrested," I responded immediately, smiling weirdly and creepily.

"You're a fucking bastard. An insane fucking bastard."

The scarlet patch on her cheek—already expanding and deepening—was like a target begging my hand to strike. I had to restrain myself from smacking her again.

"Please leave now," I said. "If you would have left when I asked you to, this wouldn't have happened. We could have avoided this. You have no one to blame but yourself."

She might have been on the verge of tears. I wondered if she'd ever been slapped before. Her rough-hewn streetwalker persona had been hammered down to that of a scared little schoolgirl finding herself in over her head. But she kept her hackles up. She wouldn't simply surrender.

"Don't you take a fucking step near me," she said, backing toward the stairs. "I can let myself out. You stay the *fuck* away from me."

She stressed *fuck* so hard I thought she would have bitten into her bottom lip. I let her start up the stairs before I followed, keeping a couple of feet between us. Her unease was positively intoxicating.

"I'm just going to unlock the door and open the garage so you can leave," I told her at the top of the stairs, showing her my open and unthreatening hands.

She hurried through the foyer and past the den and just about jogged across the kitchen, not stopping to look back when she reached the door, and fumbled a second or two with the locks before telling me to open the fucking thing and let her out. As she walked out, she turned and called me a fucking bastard again, and I watched her dash down the driveway to the car, one foot losing ground momentarily on a strip of ice. Any second, I expected a muscle-bound, goateed guy with a lot of gaudy gold jewelry festooning his bulky person to bound out of the driver's side with a blackjack or tire iron or a chipped black snub-nosed pistol, but the Lincoln just revved its engine and cruised slowly up the block and away.

My stomach was knotted. It was 3:54 a.m. She had beaten me out of six minutes I'd paid for. I closed the garage door and went back inside, poured some orange juice into a plastic cup, and took the rest of the eggplant my mother had left me from the fridge to the table without bothering to heat it. The movie was still playing in the den. I walked in and saw Spencer sitting up and Severine asleep, her head resting on his shoulder. I stood there watching them for a few seconds before he turned and looked at me without saying anything. Then Severine's eyes

226

opened and her head rose from his shoulder. She rubbed her face sleepily and looked at me as well.

Silence.

"Enjoying the movie?" I said.

Spencer replied, "I've seen it before."

"Haven't we all?"

Silence. Mia Farrow spoke with John Cassavetes.

"I'm going upstairs," I declared. "To sleep." Then I stood there for another few moments.

Spencer paused the movie to say goodnight. Severine restarted it, turned back toward the screen, and replaced her head on his shoulder. I left the unstirred eggplant on the kitchen table and clambered up the stairs to my room, where I lay on my bed in the dark, wide awake and restless, agitated, waiting for the television to turn off and for him to go home, for her to come upstairs. Crossing my arms on the pillow behind my head, I thought about the slap, revisiting the split second my hand made contact with Jackie's skin, the momentary unburdening, the transitory freedom, the brief bliss of spontaneous violence. I took pleasure in the hope that she would always remember that slap, and the hand that had given it to her, the face to which the hand belongs. But other than that, most of the pleasure I had reaped was already fading.

It was a while before Spencer left, well past 5 a.m., shortly after the movie ended. I heard her open the refrigerator and put back the platter of eggplant I had left out. Then the house went dark, and I heard her fatigued footsteps as she trudged up the stairs. My heartbeat accelerated, as in times past, but the steps did not approach my room in a hasty, childlike shuffle, as they used to. She did not slink through the darkness and make her way stealthily to my bed, as she so often used to; it seemed an eternity since she'd done so. I waited for her to finish in the bathroom and listened for the faint click of her night-table lamp, the squeaking of the bedsprings as she settled in, and finally, noiselessness.

I tried to repel the impulse to go to her, to be next to her, but everything was so quiet and dark and dreamily stagnant—almost otherworldly—and the threat of morning was still a while away. I pulled the covers off, slid my pinned-and-needled legs out one by one, and skulked toward her room, freezing at every creak of the floorboards and more than once considering a full pullback, so that the space of a dozen steps seemed to take as much time to traverse as the trip to Don's. As usual, her door was left open a crack. I pushed it just enough to slide in, reached her bed, and sat down slowly, very slowly, sitting still and letting my eyes adjust to the dark—her room was always darker than the hallway—until I could make out enough simple shapes and indistinct images to orient myself.

"You stink," she spoke into her pillow. "Your body actually smells. Do you realize that? And you look horrible. Disgusting. I can't believe you've let yourself fall so far. It's like you've... transformed."

"Into what?"

She kept quiet. I remained in a sitting position.

"I did it for you," I murmured. "Everything I do is for you. I know you know that. Even tonight. Even that was for you."

I felt a light perspiration break out over my forehead and upper lip. I put my hand on her shoulder. She withdrew harshly.

"Don't touch me."

A toilet flushed somewhere in the house; water hissed through piping.

"Because of her?"

"Who?"

"Because of the whore?"

She snorted scornfully. "Because I don't want you near me ever again. You are truly sick. I mean it. You are sick, Peter. You are a sick man."

"'I am a spiteful man. I am an unpleasant man. I think my liver is diseased.'" I channeled the Underground Man. She did not appreciate it. "We're all sick."

"Not like you."

"Then help me." My voice crackled. I nearly broke down. I reached out to touch her again but stopped myself halfway. "Please help me."

"It's far too late for me to help you, but you do need help. Maybe someone else can do it, but I can't."

The pipes cleared and the house regained its silence.

"You can't or you won't?"

"It's not a choice, Peter. You don't want help. That's the problem. You want to sit around and burn in your own little private hell and blame everyone except yourself and not lift a finger to help yourself. What you don't want is help."

A car alarm rang out, probably from a neighbor's driveway, someone getting a jump start on the wicked rush-hour commute into the city. Its stridency lasted only a few seconds before the two-note chirrup of an electronic key fob silenced it.

"Then to hell with you too," I said quietly, my voice maintaining a becalmed balance that was totally at odds with what was happening inside me. "I just hope one day you know what it's like to suffer like I'm suffering now. And I hope it's sooner rather than later. And I hope..."

I could hardly make her out in the predawn dark, just the adumbration of her profile against the pillow and the ethereal curvature of her blanketed body rising in bas-relief from the bed like a half-finished sculpture, her hands cupped and resting side by side before her face. She was so beautiful. She was still so damn beautiful. I pushed myself up off the bed.

"Don't worry. I won't come near you again."

I waited several solid seconds. Then I left the room without looking back.

7

The Sickness Unto Death

A free man thinks of nothing less than death.

— Baruch Spinoza

There was nothing left of daylight when I woke. The sleet must have temporarily knocked out the electricity at some point earlier on, and as a result my bedside clock flashed 12:00 a.m. I had no idea what time it was, only that it was well into evening and I didn't want to get up. I couldn't get up. The house was quiet, so queerly quiet that it felt as if time had finally ceased to matter, as if existence had slowed to a crawl and would soon stop altogether. I probably lay there for over an hour, trying vainly to return to sleep. Then I called Don and told him that I had to get out, and not just to the diner. I had to go someplace where my mind would be occupied, someplace where there were women. There had to be women. "Oh, I am *so* feeling that," he said, excited by my proposition, especially since Susan was at an office party and would not be coming over. He suggested a club that some of his postgraduate peers had been talking up all semester. "It apparently has a pretty favorable female-to-male ratio, which means something like three or four guys to every girl, rather than six or seven."

"I like those odds."

"My lab buddies can't shut the fuck up about this place. It's supposedly a pretty hot club. I'll pick you up at eleven."

"First of all, I'm having trouble with the fact that I just heard you say the words *pretty hot club*. And second, can we take the word of guys who spend their days in lonely labs studying string theory and playing with gluons and leptons and all kinds of other words that I have no clue what they mean?"

"First of all, the lab is *not* a lonely place. You haven't seen a party until you've seen particle physicists throw down after a long, hard semester. And second, I resent your tone."

I wasn't sure how serious he was about either point, so I just said, "Oh."

"Okay then. I'll pick you up at eleven. And for god's sake, please look presentable."

"When do I not?"

I was already waiting outside when he arrived, ten minutes early. On the way to the club, I told him about my encounter with Jackie.

"Good." He nodded his endorsement. "I can't believe you asked out a hooker, especially that one, but I think everybody could use a nice smack once in a while, just to keep them in line." He smiled, amused at the thought. "Maybe that's why things have gotten so out of control. Girls are not getting the slaps they need. It's hard to get away with it nowadays. A little smack in the face is abuse."

"A little love tap on the ass is harassment."

"You lay a finger on anyone today and they haul your ass off to prison. You did good." He smiled approvingly. "You did her a favor. But you're lucky her pimp didn't come in and beat the living shit out of you."

"That's what she said."

"I've never hit Susan. To be honest, though, she's never been out of hand. She hasn't asked for a shot yet. That said, if the situation called for it, I don't think I would hesitate. And I think she'd understand that I would be doing it for our conjoint good, as a couple." He gazed thoughtfully through the windshield at the road ahead. "Have you ever hit your sister?"

"What?" I was taken unaware.

"Have you ever hit Severine?"

"Why would you ask that? I mean—no, I've never hit her, but why ask me that?"

"I don't know. I was just thinking about it. Being an only child, I never had to worry about fighting with siblings, but I've heard that these things can sometimes get pretty over the top, so I was just wondering if you ever had to slap her around a little bit. Especially a kid sister. Nothing too harsh, you know, just a light smack when she needed it."

"No. We never fought like that. Not like that."

"I didn't think so. Severine doesn't seem like a pain in the ass. Maybe you're the one who needed an occasional slap," he opined, his serious expression unchanged. "Yes, I definitely think a good old whack across the face would do you some good from time to time."

I looked at him suspiciously. Was he hinting at something, implying that he knew more than he let on? He returned my glance briefly, inscrutably, then put his eyes back on the road.

"Still, like I said, everybody could probably benefit from a nice solid sock in the face now and then." He made a fist and mimed a punch. "We should never underestimate the efficacy and indispensability of physical violence. It's gotten a bad rap in this soft modern world we live in, but we shouldn't forget where we come from."

"Long Island? It's not a very violent place."

"No, jackass. Where we all come from. Evolutionarily. The jungle. We're apes. Violent apes. Violent by nature. We didn't evolve in classrooms and comfy suburban houses. Our reptile brains will always be subject to the laws of the jungle, not the mall. That violence is in us." He gritted his teeth, removed both hands from the wheel, and pumped his fists. His foot fell fast and heavy on the gas pedal, and the engine responded in kind, suddenly speeding the car to a good twenty-five miles per hour—and counting—over the limit. I considered mentioning what kind of fine a ticket for such a violation would entail and how many points would be dumped onto his license, but I wasn't sure myself. "And that inborn, instinctive violence can't be expunged. It can never be fully exorcised, try as we might to do so."

"You can take the ape out of the jungle…"

"Voilà." He nodded, and his right eyebrow climbed a half inch up his forehead. "And this whole fucking world is one big fucking jungle. So let your inner ape shine, is what I'm saying."

He returned his hands to the wheel and slowed down significantly. I turned on the CD player and some depressive indie rock singer started in, lamenting a lost love in murky monotone over folksy, fingerpicked guitars.

"Nah," Don snapped his fingers and ejected the disc. He reached over and pulled another one from the glove box and slipped it in. It spun for couple of seconds before some brutal, down-tuned death metal blared from the speakers. "Now that's the soundtrack to this modern motherfucking jungle of ours." He cranked up the volume, banged his head a few times, let out a rasping roar that blended nicely with the low, guttural growl of the vocals, and tapped a forefinger fiercely against the wheel in perfect syncopation with the blasting snare drum.

It felt as though we were flying, but according to the speedometer we were back down to within fifteen miles per hour of the limit. I leaned my head back, closed my eyes, and abandoned myself to the modern violence of hurtling over highway asphalt in two tons of motorized steel and radial rubber, whizzing past timberland and towers and godforsaken undeveloped lots and congested clumps of residential developments, at speeds that blurred it all into a single stretched streak of undifferentiated landscape.

Cornered between a kosher deli and a stationery store in a strip mall just off the parkway, Waxe looks nothing like what you would expect from a nightclub, even with bright blue neon letters sprawled above the black-windowed storefront and a vertiginous strobe flashing red and green and blinding white from above the metal door. It looks more like one of those all-purpose discount centers that proudly advertise every inventoried item as costing ninety-nine cents or less, before tax. I had never been there, but it was fairly popular among savvy suburban twenty-somethings, and I had often seen flyers for Waxe's *Wet and Wild Wednesdays* and *Too Sexy Saturdays* tacked onto corkboards in the student commons. There was a line to get in and a twelve-dollar cover. Don had cut a coupon from the newspaper, allowing us free entrance before midnight, and they also gave us a hand stamp for half-price well drinks and three-dollar domestic beer until 1 a.m. As we walked in he told me to loosen up: "You look like you got a hot poker stuck up your ass. Chill out. Relax. You have to at least make it seem like you have confidence. Pussy's no pushover. Pussy can smell a pussy." He leaned over and sniffed me.

These places hold few surprises. I'd been to similar clubs two or three times before, but what I experience upon entering one defies depiction and always hits me harder than I'm ready to be hit, regardless of how prepared I think I am to walk into that loud, overcrowded and overheated room and see flesh flaunted everywhere, hopped-up, aggressively horny males and nubile female forms tossing themselves about in a frenzy, like maenads at a backyard Bacchanalia, fragrant with perfume and sweat and smoke, drinking, moving, touching, laughing, scanning the field for potential mates, flashing teeth and legs and long enameled fingernails and seductively shaded eyelids and plump, painted lips. There's an inexpressible sensation that comes over me when I enter this atmosphere, a kind of uncontainable excitement and animal determination and irrepressible exuberance and horror, absolute horror, at the tyranny of instinct. The call of the flesh. And there is no defense. There's just no way to tamp down this discomfiting hodgepodge of emotions.

It was inhumanly hot and hazardously overfull—probably illegally so—and as I squeezed through the tight cracks between people, I could feel their sweat rubbing onto me. I immediately regretted my desire to come here. We ordered a couple of Long Island iced teas and established our places at the edge of the dance floor, with a full view of its spectacle. I watched the mass of bodies writhe and wriggle to the bass-driven electro house that seemed to shake the entire edifice. The well-heeled clientele was strikingly homogenous, predominantly white and between eighteen and twenty-five, maybe a few in their late twenties and on the verge of aging out the scene. In the middle of this swarming mob of unbridled, unsupervised youth, which was

236

fueled by furious hormones and sustained by cigarettes, pot, and beer—the separate scents of these substances coalescing into a wretchedly unified miasma that sickened me—I was gripped by an acute sense of isolation, total and ineluctable solitude, and it felt as though I had never been so alone, as though the solitude had permanently attached itself to me and would never leave. I wondered what Severine was doing at that moment, at that very moment. My immense animosity toward her swelled and surged and peaked again. She was the reason I was here, in this place.

J'ai une peur affreuse de retrouver ma solitude.

But there were girls. Plenty of them. That was what we were here for. Girls and liquor. Low-cut tops and tight, short skirts, bursting cleavage and meaty thighs and diamond calves and exposed, pierced navels. I wanted to fuck them all, every single one of them with their compact bodies in full bloom, and knowing I would very likely come away empty-handed deeply disgruntled me. I drank and surveyed the herd, the fertile flesh farm, and my frustration bubbled. I had been eyeing a brunette on the floor, attracted more to the way she moved—undulating her hips and sashaying sultrily in a manner that had something of both the sensuality of a Turkish belly dancer and the practiced prettiness of a contemporary ballerina—than to the way she looked. She was far from a beauty. At twenty or so years old, her chief attribute was youth itself, her firm, flexible skin and girlish vigor, and in a few years her already less-than-perfect ass would be warping and widening, and her bubbly C-cup breasts, now bouncing so jovially in her little purple halter top, would begin their inevitable descent. Still, she was, at least for the immediate present, eminently fuckable, gyrating on the floor, swinging her haunches and wildly tossing her long, burnished black hair—her stand-out feature—whipping it around like a sorceress in heat as she flailed her arms and thrashed about in the crowd. She was a bundle of pep that had not stopped moving since I first saw her. Don noticed my interest and pushed me to approach, to dance up to her, to make my move.

"Go ahead, man. Go get her. She's waiting for a guy like you."

"Like me?"

"Look at these mooks." He gestured at the men around us. "She's not going to do better than you tonight."

It was completely ridiculous encouragement, but I appreciated the effort. I decided to wait until she stopped dancing, studying her for two more sadistically awful songs until she heaved her shoulders, fanned her face with a hand, and headed over to the bar, alone, where she daintily wiped her forehead with a napkin while her friends continued to frolic around the floor. She was separated from the herd. Now was the time to attack. I had to go. I couldn't. My mind was urging me on but my body was holding back, or vice versa. I couldn't be sure. I felt like a Beckett character trapped in some absurdly insignificant existential quandary: *I can't go on, I'll go on.*

"You have to go now," Don said, his elbow jabbing me sharply in the ribs.

I must. I can't. I won't. I have to. I want to but I don't want to want to.

"Don't be a fucking baby," he admonished. "Go. Don't think. Thinking is your enemy." He poked my forehead with a finger. "Thinking does not exist in this dojo! Just go. Go. Go."

I began to sway coolly in her direction, which is as close to dancing as I get, and my drink splashed onto me as I wove gracelessly through the mad crush of clubbers. The nearer I got, the less attractive she became, the camouflaging distance and dimness losing their erstwhile effectiveness. When I finally leaned against the bar next to her, I kept my eyes trained on the graduated shelves of liquor bottles in front of me, as if I hadn't made the journey over there just for her, as if I had come for a drink, of course, and she happened to be there; clubs and bars were designed for just such fortuitous circumstances. Out of the corner of my eye, I saw her turn and look at me, size me up in a glance, and then turn back to the dance floor. She knew what was coming, and she knew immediately how she would handle the situation. Women seem to have a heightened instinctive sensitivity when it comes to detecting the approach of predators, like gazelles who feel the presence of the lion crouching in the bush, even before they see it. The game was over before it began. It usually is.

Her toned arms and bare shoulders were glossy with sweat. Her cottony cleavage rose and fell like an organic entity unto itself. I leaned over and spoke.

"Hello."

No response or reaction.

"Hello," I repeated, louder.

"What?" she said. The noise level was high, but I had no doubt that she had heard me.

"Hi."

"Oh. Hi."

"Would you like something?"

"Like what?"

"A drink?"

"Already have one." She displayed her half-filled glass and an unconvincing semi-smile, then looked out at the floor.

I guzzled the remainder of my cocktail and ordered myself a beer.

"I see. I'm Peter, by the way."

"What?"

"Peter. That's my name. Peter," I said, loud enough for the couple on the other side of her to hear. They both looked over. The guy said something into his companion's ear and they both laughed. "As in... like... Saint Peter." It was the only reference that came to mind on such short notice.

"Ah."

"Or Peter the Great." Peter Rabbit, Peter Falk, Pete Rose, or Peter Pumpkin-eater. The associative string was really unspooling now. "What's your name?"

"Me?"

"You're the only one I'm talking to."

"Vicki," she replied, stone-faced, staring at the same three-tiered liquor shelf I'd been observing moments ago.

I put out my hand and she shook it, her fingers floppy as wet noodles in my grasp, palms soft and small and moist. She was nodding her head to the music, so I did the same, though I couldn't imagine anything more offensive to my ears. I could smell her perfume, something citrus. Her skin looked nice up close, hale and rosy.

"Is that short for Victoria?" I slurped the foam on top of my beer.

"What?"

"Is Vicki short for Victoria?"

"No."

"No?"

"No."

I tried to think of what else it could be short for but came up blank.

"It's just Vicki then?"

"Just Vicki."

"I see. Mine's just Peter." Peter Abelard, Peter Parker, and of course, Peter Pan. "Or Pete."

We both looked straight ahead. I considered making some crafty comment about the plethora of bottles, or the rows of glasses of various shapes and sizes, or the waxy patina of the bar itself, but I couldn't think of a witty way to frame such a remark. A new song started playing, and though it sounded no different from the one that had just ended, it elicited a deafening chorus of approval from the flock, which began to move insistently now, drawing into itself more strays from the sidelines. Vicki began rocking her upper body to the music, leaning back with both elbows on the bar and slowly swinging her hips. My right shoulder momentarily touched hers. Her jeans were stretched taut as cellophane around her bottom half, and her blouse was cut low. Her stomach was flat and smooth. A gold ring through her navel was attached to a slim silver chain encircling her waist, which she would occasionally fiddle with. I began to sway again, in response to her movement.

"I guess you like this song," I said.

She shot a brief look of ridicule and annoyance at me, but I forced myself to forge ahead.

"Would you like to dance?" I offered.

"Um, not really, no." Another half-smile, less convincing.

I sipped my stout and then raised it in her direction. "Sure you don't want a drink?"

"I still already have one," she said with a derisive lilt, lifting her glass again, this time minus the half-smile.

With disguised difficulty, I drank down my bitter beer and ordered a gin and tonic. The bartender, a tall platinum blonde in a black bustier and black leather pants, with black serpentine tribal tattoos slithering up and down her brachia and spiked black leather gauntlets running halfway up her forearms—she looked way too heavy metal for this place—smiled mockingly as she handed me the glass. I turned again to Vicki, but she pre-empted me with a look of complete disgust, as if she knew I was about to speak and sincerely hoped I would reconsider. Nothing came out. I was sweating profusely. I watched a droplet splash into my glass.

"That's a nice outfit," I said. "It looks really... nice on you."

She nodded.

"How about the next song?" I said, abandoning all dignity to desperation. "Do you want to dance to the next song? It should be a good one."

"Why?"

"Uh... they're all good ones. Don't you like the music?"

She rolled her eyes and huffed, pushed herself off the bar, glowered vaguely in my direction as though I were a misty ap-parition that she couldn't really focus on, and said, "Look..." just as two of her friends came over with glaring smiles, flanking her enthusiastically. The first one, a chunky but pretty blonde whose noisome nasality revealed that she could come from no other place in the world but Long Island, said, "Vicki, there you are! Like, what are you doing just standing there? We, like, just met these awesome guys. Come on!" The other—also blonde, tall and slender and by far the most attractive of the three—said, with almost identical intonation, "Yeah, and they're, like, traders. Come on, they're buying drinks."

"Why would you want to drink with traitors?" I joked. "And they're not even traitors. They're *like* traitors"

The first blonde turned around and looked at me as though I was misplaced or seriously misinformed and was perpetrating

242

a pernicious malfeasance by talking to her friend, as if I should have known better. But she quickly turned away. I was not her problem. I was not a problem at all. I was a fly to be shooed, nothing more. They had only to walk away and I would vanish and crawl back under the rock from which I came. Vicki finished her drink in one draft, put her glass on the bar, adjusted her top, and took off with the blondes. I watched them cross the room and melt into the throng. I felt sick. Physically sick. There was a hand on my shoulder. Don was next to me. He had heard most of the exchange.

"Fuck her, man. I fucking despise catty cunts like that."

Through sheer force of will, I finished my gin and tonic and ordered another.

"The hell with her. It's noxious bitches like her that justify rape," he went on. "Plus, she was a fifteen-footer. Once you get within fifteen feet of her you realize she's not hot at all. Sure, her body was banging, but her face was a five at best. A four without makeup. You wouldn't want to wake up sober next to that. But at least you made the effort." He patted me on the back. "I'm proud of you."

Eventually, Vicki and her group came back into view. I kept my eye on her the rest of the night, as I poured more and more alcohol into my body and felt more and more vitriol for everything happening around me. She danced with her girlfriends most of the time. They formed a kind of protective circle, and whenever some hapless guy essayed to dance his way in, they would cruelly humor him awhile, make him think that maybe he had a chance, and eventually dance away, excluding him without his realizing it until he found himself wholly edged out of the enchanted orbit. At the end of the night, I saw Vicki on my way to the bathroom. She was making out with a guy in a dark corner, one of the traders, perhaps. The night's prizewinner. The one in a million. The fittest survivor. His broad back was to me, and I saw her face as she kissed him, her eyes closed and her hand clasping the back of his head, her French-manicured nails enmeshed in his hair.

In the bathroom I pissed all over myself.

For the rest of the night, I stood against the bar and watched. I watched them all, their svelte young bodies twisting and turning and flopping everywhere, wriggling and writhing and contorting themselves into all kinds of unnatural positions as they teased and tortured the drooling boys eyeballing them from the fringes of the floor. I watched Don dance with a few of them. He is an excellent dancer with a natural sense of rhythm. He says it's in his Sicilian blood. After a few songs, he brought one back to the bar for a drink, introduced her as Sally, and tried to get me into the conversation, but I was too downtrodden to be interested and too drunk to be coherent, so I just smiled and nodded and ordered another drink, I'm not sure what kind. He leaned close to her and laughed at what she said and gently touched her arm as he recounted a humorous story or asked her a question. She was pretty but had crooked teeth, shapely but minute-breasted. It was getting late. Only the injured remained, the undesirable excess, the *de trop*. Don got her number anyway and repeated his best-loved aphorism: "A hole's a hole. Never know when this number might come in handy on a dark and stormy Tuesday night."

I watched Vicki leave arm in arm with the guy she had been kissing by the bathroom. I still couldn't make out his face, just that he was tall and well-built and wearing a blue and white striped button-down hanging over jeans with a pleat pressed into their sides.

"Who the fuck irons jeans?" I said.

"I think the gays do."

"I hate them, Don."

"I didn't know you were homophobic."

"No. I think I hate women," I told him, as exiting dancers filtered off the floor. The lights brightened and flickered, signaling last call. Closing time was near, and the thinned pack voiced its chagrin with a collective jeer. "I hate them. I don't think I've ever really hated anything like I hate them. I don't think I ever realized how deeply I could hate until now. It's like I want to hurt them, like I would get pleasure from seeing them hurt."

He looked at me clinically. "Yes. I understand. And I do sympathize." He put his hand over mine on the bar. "Actually, I think resentment is a better choice of words. But let's put some perspective on it. It's the young ones who deserve the full force of whatever ill will we're talking about here. Young, attractive ones from eighteen to thirty-five, give or take a couple years. The ones at the height of their natural beauty and youthful sexual allure and nubility, when they can afford to be hyperselective and reject at will with full immunity, when they can browse and examine and sample for however long they choose and then just discard the specimen if it turns out to be unsatisfactory." He wagged an admonitory finger. "These are the ones that are most dangerous. These are the ones to hate, if hate you must. They know the power they have. That's the worst part. That's what's so damn devastating. They know what they're capable of by just dressing a certain way, moving a certain way, talking and acting a certain way. They know what they are capable of just by being what they are. Not *who* they are, *what* they are."

I drank. He went on. He always goes on.

"I guess they're not to blame for the way things are, though, for the rituals of attraction and the mating system that excludes some with such cold-blooded insistence. They didn't ask for that moist, hairy patch that we'd do anything to penetrate."

"And I didn't ask for this thing either." I grabbed my crotch a bit too hard. "I didn't ask to want to stick my dick in them. I don't want to want them. But I want them more than anything, and I hate the fact that I want them. I hate that they know I want them and there's nothing to do about it. I wish so much that I didn't want them. That's all. That's what I want, not to want them. I don't want this wanting."

He cocked an eye and nodded and rapped his knuckles on the bar. "They reject with heartless impunity at this age, simply because they can. Look at that one." He pointed to a petite blonde rhythmlessly wiggling her lithe little body in the middle of the floor, commanding attention from a group of guys that surrounded her like predators in wait. She was wearing the equivalent of a bra—lacy and mustard—and leopard print tights that accentuated every undulation, her cleavage glistening with perspiration and her firm belly twisting in agonizing flow. "She knows exactly what she's doing, little fucking minx that she is. She's totally aware that she's frustrating the fuck out of those guys, and she loves every last second of it. She just can't help herself, the hussy, can't get enough of it."

It was late, and the remaining females were few, the males desperate. I went to the bathroom for my first bout of vomiting. When I returned, there was practically no one left, save the blonde and her salivating circle of male admirers. Don pointed her out again.

"Fuck it. Let her do it. Let her have her fleeting moments in the sun. They won't last long. Life will see to that. She'll have her years of youthful beauty, a few more days of early middle-age elegance, if she's lucky, and then it'll be over, so let her bask in her glory while she still can. Once they pass a certain age, it's all downhill for them. The hips broaden and the flesh loosens and everything starts to sag. Once they've been humbled a bit by life, crapped out a couple of kids, once they've lost that irresistible power of attraction that they wield like a cat-o'-nine-tails to lash those judged unworthy of their beauty, then they're not so bad, not nearly as dangerous. Then the seats of power change. The worm turns. Our wine gets finer, theirs turns to vinegar. You just have to wait it out."

"'Les belles années passent vite.'"

"What?"

"Nothing."

The lights came on fully now, exposing the sticky squalor of the dance floor, coated with spilled beer and crushed cigarette butts and wet shreds of cocktail napkins and various other substances that it was better not to think about. The blonde barmaid in the black bustier told us that she was closing out the register and we had to leave.

"Gotcha. We're just going to finish our drinks," Don said.

She put on a moue, dropped a filthy wet rag onto the bar, and proceeded to wipe it down with hard, masculine strokes. The rag touched my elbow, which was leaning on the bar, and I pulled it away in disgust.

"You see I'm trying to clean the bar here," she grumbled. "Could you move please?"

"Could you ask me nicely?" I bit back, rubbing the sullied spot on my arm. "My elbow is a lot cleaner than that rag. The bar is probably cleaner than that thing."

"What the fuck? What are you guys still doing here, any-way? Can't you see there's no one left?"

I hadn't noticed, but the only other patrons, another couple of guys, were exiting as she spoke. The place was empty, except for the bartender and us.

"No more girls. Time to go home and beat the meat, boys," she said bitchily, miming masturbation with her multi-ringed right hand. "Palmela and Handrea are waiting for you."

I leaned on the bar, turned slightly in her direction, and mumbled something that even I couldn't really make out in my current state of inebriation.

"Excuse me. Are you talking to me?"

Don stepped in. "He said you're very beautiful."

She pulled her head back doubtingly. "Yeah, well, whatever he said, you guys have to leave. Like, now?"

"Oh. Are you, like, asking us or, like, telling us?" I said, wobbling against the bar.

"Get the fuck out of here, you dumb-ass drunk."

"Cunt," I muttered, a little louder and more clearly than my initial mumble, though it was still mostly indiscernible above the thumping music that continued to play at a much higher volume than necessary. A mean-looking behemoth of a bouncer with a shiny bald head came over and asked if there was a problem, probably hoping there was one. Don grabbed my arm and pulled me from the bar.

"No problem. We're just leaving," he said.

"Putain salope de merde," I bellowed.

"Get him out of here," the bouncer ordered.

"I will—I am—he's just a little drunk—we're going—"

"If you have something to say, say it so I can hear it," the bartender cut in calmly, engaging me with a fierce feline glare, as

248

though she was ready to jump over the bar and take a swing at me herself. "If you have any balls."

I looked at the bouncer. Another one came over to join him, just as bald and mean-looking but black and even bigger than the first. I looked at the bartender, her perky breasts—speckled with glitter—sparkling brilliantly in the light, upper torso bound in skimpy, close-fitting leather, bouncy blonde hair floating thickly around her irate face, and I mused that there had been a disproportionate number of blondes that night.

"That's what I thought," she said, turning back to the task of running her rag over the bar. "Little gutless wiseass. You're all the same. No balls. And you wonder why you go home with nothing but your dinky little dick in your hands."

I ripped myself away from Don and leaned toward her ferociously. I wanted to fuck her and to break her taunting face, to smash it down onto the bar with a two-fisted overhead strike. This time I enunciated the words at full volume and in plain English, with precision and clarity, so there could be no mistaking them. "I said you are a fucking useless bitch. A worthless wench. A two-dollar twat. A dirty dishrag whore. And a dumb fucking putrid cunt." I paused perfectly. "That's what I said." I was pleased with my delivery and impressed with myself that I was able to get it all out without stumbling over my words. It wasn't easy.

Nobody moved or spoke. She was surely expecting something vulgar, a lewd come-on line or juvenile sexist comment, perhaps even an obliquely misogynistic insult, but not this. This stopped her in her tracks. My declaration immobilized everyone, like a stun gun. But it wasn't enough. There were more to be done. I had not yet begun to fight.

I lunged at her before she could react, snatched a handful of that long, brassy blonde hair, and pulled her head toward me over the bar. I gnashed my teeth so hard I thought the top row would snap off into my throat. She screamed and grabbed at my hands, but before I could do any more I felt another hand on me, not Don's, a large, claw-like mitt with thick, steel-strong fingers that wrapped almost completely around my biceps. Despite the pressure on my arm that was quickly becoming pain, I kept my eyes on the bartender, her hair in my hand as her head bowed to the force of my wrenching. Her hands took hold of her hair near the base of her scalp, and we engaged in a clumsy tug of war, fighting tooth and nail for possession. She was quite strong and determined, but I had the higher ground and would not release that hair, like a pit bull with its jaws clamped down on a steak bone. I pulled hard, reached around and secured my grip with the other hand. I would not be satisfied unless I yanked it out, until a good-sized portion of that blondeness was extirpated and scattered on the floor. But a sharp blow on the back of my head forced it down, then another, then a fist on my back that sent my diaphragm into spasms. Unable to breathe, I went down, a foot in my ribs, and rolled up into a ball, covering myself, my arms taking the brunt of more heels and soles.

"You little shit," a deep voice said, as I was dragged toward the entrance and pushed out the door onto the pavement and kicked again. "I see your fucking face again I'll smash it in, you fucking little prick." I looked up and saw the bald bouncer—the white one—standing above me, face flushed and snarling like a rabid Doberman, foamy spittle forming on his lower lip. He kicked me one more time for good measure and wiped his mouth with the back of his hand. Don was next to him, keeping his distance from both me and the enraged man until it seemed relatively safe to intervene. Then he inched over and hovered hesitantly between me and my attacker, speaking calmly and deferentially.

"We're sorry. It's all right, man. He just drank too much. He's sorry. It's all right. We just want to get out of here and go home."

No, it's not all right, Don, I thought I was saying. It's not all right, because they're all fucking whore bitches. You said it yourself, they deserve the hatred, and my life is ruined because of them, because of one of them. I have no life anymore because of her, and I can't live with that. I can't live without my life.

But I was not actually saying this. I was on my back on the concrete, coughing and wheezing. I turned my head, threw up, and wiped my mouth with the collar of my shirt. A trickle of blood danced down my lip. I couldn't feel much at the moment and wondered how damaged my body would be when the shock wore off.

"Little piece of shit wants to drink like a man and act like a tough guy and can't hold his fucking liquor." I heard the voice and strained to look up. The bouncer loomed above me, his beefy nostrils dilating and contracting, two deep black holes in a pulpy mass of pink. "Don't you fucking look at me, you little prick. Keep those eyes on the fucking floor," he growled and started toward me again, pointing, his forefinger guiding like a mast.

Then I felt another foot that was distinctly different, sharper than the others but less forceful. It was the bad-tempered blonde bartender, jabbing me three times in my side with the spiked toe of her shoe. "Look at him. He's fucking pathetic." She shook her head at me and delivered one last kick.

I looked up again, and now the black bouncer made toward me, champing at the bit for his turn to pummel the piñata, but she took his arm. "That's enough. If we fuck him up any more it'll be trouble for us and the club. Just leave him there and let's go inside."

"What? I want this fucker to suffer." He seized me by the back of my leather jacket and started to tow me up like a canine mother lifting her pup by the scruff.

"Don't waste any more energy on this fucking creep. Let him lie out here and freeze."

It would have taken almost no effort for him to pull away from her and pound me into pomace, but he didn't. "You're lucky, you little bastard," he said. "Lucky. And you too." He turned to Don. "I should whip your skinny white ass just for being with him."

Heedful of the warning, Don held up his palms and took a slow step backward. "I don't fight, man. I can't abide violence. I'm a pacifist." He took another step back." And I'm Sicilian, so I'm not totally white, either."

The bouncers went back toward the door, turned to me one last time, reentered the club with the bartender, and slammed the door behind them. I was battered and bloodied and bruised, but there was still no pain. It didn't feel as though I was the one they were beating; it didn't feel as though I was the one who had chatted up Vicki and assaulted the bartender, who had imbibed so excessively and was already paying the price for it. I sat up without a problem. It was a clear, starry night, and the frosty air refreshed my febrile face.

"Shit, man! What the hell is wrong with you?" Don bent down close but didn't touch me, as though afraid contact would worsen my wounds. "I'm not going to tell you how stupid that was. You'll realize it on your own tomorrow." He put his hand lightly on the back of my head. "You all right?"

I didn't reply.

"If that bouncer didn't already clobber you, I'd give you a couple of uppercuts myself." He came up closer and scanned my face. "You're bleeding a little."

I touched the blood on my lip. I didn't remember taking any blows to the face, so I must have scraped it on the ground during the melee. Astoundingly, I emerged from the drubbing more or less uninjured, the most serious of my wounds a nasty little abrasion on the elbow, from being thrown onto the cement, and a few bruised ribs that I would feel in the morning. My face was untouched except for the bloody lip. Nothing was broken or cut. All my parts seemed to be in working order.

"That could have been a lot worse," Don said gravely.

I looked up at him, nodded, and smiled woozily. I felt as though I could have leaned over and curled up and gone to sleep right there on the cold hard concrete. "I'm fine. Let's go."

I remained sitting for another two minutes or so, cleared my head, and got to my feet without a problem.

The drive home was a blurred, nauseous montage of bland highway roadside, deserted residential streets, and incandescent commercial thoroughfares lined with gargantuan supermarkets, diners, gourmet delis, and ancient tobacco shops. Dilapidated railroad stations and joyless neighborhood dive bars and forlorn fast-food restaurants next to posh boutiques and upscale nail salons. And malls. Innumerable malls. Multistoried, monstrous malls. A whole world of them. I watched these things breeze by the passenger window and thought about how dismal it all is. Why do they build such doleful places? Why do they perpetuate the bleakness with such tenacity? I leaned my head against the cold glass and shut my eyes. All this is me. This is where I come from and where I belong. This is what I am. I felt like crying but lacked the initiative.

"More snow tomorrow. Perfect, " Don said, commenting on the weather report.

I hadn't been listening.

"What?"

"Another six to eight inches. Man, after these past few mild winters I thought we'd never see anything more than flurries. Global warming and shit."

Mais où sont les neiges d'antan?

"You sure you're okay? Maybe we should get you checked out."

"What do you mean? Why wouldn't I be okay?"

"Uh... because you just got your clock cleaned by a couple of big angry bouncers and a bitchy barmaid. You might have a concussion or some kind of internal damage."

Internal damage.

"I'm fine."

We passed Walt Whitman's birthplace, a split-level farm-house enclosed by a freshly painted white fence. Whitman was born on Long Island, not far from my house. He was born *here*. America's poet was born right here where I was born, and he lived part of his life on this same strip of land on which I've lived all of mine. The *Good Gray Poet*, badass bard of democracy and nature and life, wild, savage, beautiful life, has been duly commemorated, his legacy fitly preserved, immortalized in a singularly suburban way. Across the road from his birthplace—a well-maintained and largely ignored historic site protected from demolition by both the state and federal governments—is the

Walt Whitman Mall, an enormous shopping shrine frequented by almost all denizens of his beloved homeland. His poetry may not live on through the masses, but for most Long Islanders who find themselves here well after the poet walked these grounds, his name will always be associated with the God of Retail, as long as the mall stands.

Good-bye — and hail! my Fancy.

"Last chance to drop by the emergency room," Don offered, as we approached the exit for the hospital. "You never know — you might go to bed feeling okay and wake up dead."

I let him slow down but didn't speak until we were well past the ramp.

"I'll be fine."

"You want to kill some time at the diner?"

"I just want to get home. I'll be fine."

Don dropped me off at the foot of my driveway apron, nearly hitting the mailbox as he stopped short and slid on a patch of black ice. I was drunk and he was nicely buzzed, but there was no gaiety, no inebriated laughter or fooling around: a worthless drunkenness. We hadn't exchanged any words of note since leaving the club, not until he unlocked the doors from his side, after seeing how much trouble I was having manually, and inquired again after my condition: "You sure you're all right?"

I was half in, half out of the car, just looking at him. His face was distorted and rancorous — I almost had to turn away — his swarthy complexion blanched and drawn, and I knew I looked worse. I was trying to determine if I loved him, loved him as my one and only true friend, the brother I should have had, or if I despised him, if I hated him as much as I hated myself. I wasn't sure. All I knew was that I wanted to tell him it was crap, all this

talk of scorning women and denying love, of blaming and hurting and hating, all this animus and bile, because even if love
doesn't exist, even if the concept is fatuous and illusory and
maddeningly manipulative, even if we spend lifetimes in vain
searching for it, love is all we can hope for, and once that hope is
gone, there is nothing else, and then the emptiness becomes truly
unbearable. It wasn't just drunken reverie. I was compos mentis,
thinking more clearly than I had in a while, and if I could have
spoken, I would have told him that he had been wrong all along.
We want to be loved, madly and heedlessly. We love because we
want to be loved. *The rest is silence.*

"Remember, don't lie down. Keep your head elevated. And
try to rest your brain. Don't read or watch TV or anything. And
most important, don't go to sleep for a few hours."

"What do you want me to do then?"

"Just sit. Or stand. Better if you stand. Or walk around the
house or something."

"I can do that."

"Good. You'll be all right," he continued. "Only the good
die young, so I think you got a long life ahead of you. And don't
let them get to you, son. They're all bitches. Harpies and harlots.
Just remember that. Every one of them. It's not you, it's them.
You weren't wrong. You just picked the absolute wrong time
and worst place to let it out. They're all fucking bitches."

With some effort, I managed a smile, pushed myself out of
the car, shut the door, and leaned back inside through the open
window.

"When you finally do go to sleep, take some aspirin before
your head hits the pillow. Tomorrow will be too late."

*Il est trop tard, maintenant, il sera toujours trop tard. Heureuse-
ment!*

I remained there, leaning on the squishy weather strip. My eyes began to close and I caught my chin dipping downward.

"Hey, hey!" Don yelled and slapped the wheel. "What did I just say? No sleeping. Come on. Get back in and let's get you some coffee."

"No." I straightened up. "I'll have some inside. Promise."

"If I find out you went to sleep too soon and woke up in a fucking coma, I'm going to shake you the fuck out of it just to beat that ass."

I laughed. "Go home. It's freezing out here."

"All right. But seriously, you take care of yourself. At least tonight."

"You're my friend, Don," I stammered.

"And you're *my* friend, Petey." he rejoined with a titter, catering to my intoxication.

"I love you."

"I... uh... love you back, Petey."

"We all just—" leaning back and throwing up my hands, only to fall forward against the car, "want to be loved." I stared, waiting for him to acknowledge my unburdened honesty.

"True," he said, nodding, looking around, stretching his arms forward over the wheel. "True. Question is," turning back to me and thrusting his head turtle-like toward the window, "by whom?"

My mouth opened and some kind of guttural sound came out, a clipped, raspy wheeze that stopped short of a gasp, but I was aware of no thoughts behind it. My heart sped up and my breath suspended of its own will, but before I could process this last statement, before I could determine if he was alluding to the great mystery at the heart of my existence or had simply stumbled upon it unwittingly, a mere verbal coincidence and nothing more, I pushed myself up and tottered backward, compelled to get away from the car at all cost, waved a limp, unsteady hand, and wrestled the word *bye* out of my mouth.

"Don't forget," he yelled out. "It's them. All bitches. All fucking bitches. They're just receptacles for sperm. They're not worth the aggravation. Not worth losing sleep over."

I leaned against a tree and followed the taillights down the street and into his driveway, then I turned and hunched over and vomited on the low shrubbery around the mailbox, kneeling on the crystallized grass, which felt as cold and unforgivingly hard as the pavement outside the club. Whatever meaning, if any, lay behind Don's words, I hadn't the energy to contemplate. Whether he had discovered the arcanum of my life or had only inadvertently scratched at its surface didn't make a difference anymore. All I wanted was to get inside, and the house seemed very far away. I knew I couldn't make it without throwing up again, so I sat there for a few minutes before plunging a finger down my throat. The sound of retching broke sharply against silence, a brief dissonance swallowed up in the early auroral hush. I sat shivering on the ground and looked around at the neatly rowed houses staring down at me like dispassionate sentinels, vomit congealing on the front of my coat.

My watch read 4:43 a.m. No proof of life. No movement.

Suburban quietude is a uniquely redoubtable phenomenon, as far removed from urban ruckus as it is from rural tranquility, somewhere in the muddy middle. Serenity has nothing to do with it. Peace and calm do not apply. On a frozen winter night, the neighborhood is like a fossilized forest, a *valley of dry bones,* a vestigial reminder of all that could have been. Lives are passed here trying to forget not what was lost in youth, but what was never found.

I rolled onto my back and lay flat. The sky was clear and stippled with stars. There was no wind, just cold.

My eyes opened. It was still dark, maybe darker. I turned my head toward the street and saw a fire-engine-red minivan rolling slowly down the block and stopping briefly in front of each house. I found this odd and a bit worrisome—maybe someone was casing the neighborhood—until I realized it was the newspaper delivery person firing his morning missiles out of the driver's side window. A bagged paper was lying a few inches from my face, which must have been what woke me, though I didn't remember hearing anything. My watch read 4:48.

My fingers and ears seared with cold and my feet were numb, but I felt a little better, my head a little clearer. The light above the garage glowed bright like a homing beacon, its beam sprinkling out over the jeweled blacktop. The house did not seem as far anymore. I could make it.

I recalled the image of Don sitting behind the wheel mouthing, *All bitches. All fucking bitches.* He had no doubt taken a few hits from the bong before bed; he always used to say that he could never fall asleep drunk unless he was high as well.

My watch read 4:51. The sky showed no signs of lightening. It was tar-black with flecks of burning blue starlight branded into its façade.

In one strained motion I pushed onto my knees and stood, knowing it would be harder to rise gradually. I anticipated the dizziness, but this did little to allay its effects, and I walked slowly and carefully up the ice-coated driveway, halting every few steps to secure my balance. It took some time to get to the garage. I arrived without falling, fished my keys from my coat pocket, and worked them into the hole. Again the absolute quiet was brutally shattered, the raucous mechanics of the garage door screeching like a flayed animal. I thought the whole neighborhood would have been able to hear it. I looked around for any inkling of life, but there was nothing, of course. The silence seemed denser when the screeching stopped.

Nothing. No thing.

I opened the door and entered, punched in the alarm code, got it right on the second attempt but didn't take the trouble to reset it, kicked off my freezing, sodden shoes, and dropped my grimy jacket on the mudroom floor without bothering to brush it off. I was sick in the kitchen sink and washed my face with cold water. Then I went upstairs.

When I come into her room she wakes, tells me to stop at the door, says she can hear me trying to contain my breathing. She asks me why I am breathing so loudly.

"Because I'm out of breath."

I lurch over to the bed on feet too heavy to lift completely off the ground and drop myself down where her legs are. She pulls them in away from me and sits up, pushes herself back so she is propped against the frame. Strands of golden hair fall about her face in pastel waves.

"Don't come near me. Don't touch me. I told you not to come near me."

It's that voice again, that harsh, alien tone, that stranger's voice.

"You smell like puke. Get out."

She is right. It's a fearsome fetor, a lecherous, guttersnipe's effluvium. I am respiring heavily, panting like a dying animal, and my clothes are spotted with dried vomit.

"But it's so cold. It's so cold outside," I plead.

"Get out," she repeats vehemently.

"Why are you doing this? I'll go. Just tell me why you're doing this to me? I don't deserve it. I've done nothing but—"

A tear rolls down my cheek. My cut lip prickles. There is a pain in my chest, my ribs are on fire, and my queasy stomach is drowning in beer and gin. It is dark, and I don't know how she knows I'm crying, because the tears are falling silently, but she softens for an instant and touches me without disdain for the first time in what feels like forever. She wipes the milk-warm saltwater from under one eye. She thaws.

"Why?"

We are lying on our sides in the dark, facing each other, eyes level with eyes.

"Because there is no more," she says without flinching.

"No more what?"

"Just no more"

"I don't know what that means. I have no idea what that means. I don't think you do either."

"It doesn't matter."

More tears come down. She reaches a hesitant hand around me and settles it on my back.

"It's over. It's gone. And what's gone doesn't come back." She retracts her hand. She stops touching me. "It's time to move on, time for both of us to move on," she whispers, her face so close to mine I can feel the weight of her words ramming into me.

"I don't know what that means either."

I kiss her cheek. She pulls away slowly, inoffensively. I stay still for a second, two, three, four, then lean in toward her and kiss the other cheek, then her throat.

"No," she says lightly. "No."

"But it's so cold outside."

It is painful to have her so near and not touching me. The heat of her body—still slack and languid with sleep—flows into my chilled flesh, and I slip my hand behind her neck and under her hair and pull her to me, determined but not forceful. I take her face in my hands and my lips meet hers, hot and moist, laced with a light lamina of perspiration. I kiss her on the mouth, hard on the mouth. Her nose is cold but the rest of her is warm and soft, so amazingly and unbearably soft. She pulls away, pushing at my shoulders.

"It's only me," I reassure her. "Don't worry, it's only me."

I grip her shoulders and push slowly and steadily against increasing resistance and crawl on top of her, pin her arms flat to the mattress, move up and take hold of her wrists, slide them out beside her head, my penis rubbing against her through my wet trousers. She squirms, gasps, but I take no notice and have little trouble subduing her. I look down at her, immobile, captive, and tighten my grip to combat spasms of struggling. She could easily scream, wake my parents, break the brutish silence, but she does not. Her efforts to free herself are not convincing.

"Don't Peter," is all she says. "Don't do this," quietly, breathless.

"Shhh. Shhh."

Now she is genuinely trying to get away, lunging her body upward and sideways, thrashing like a hooked fish—still without sound, our movements seeming coordinated and rehearsed, like a campy scene in a stylized silent film—but the more she struggles, the more I do. I can't stop myself, can't let her go. I slide her wrists up over her head and hold them with one hand while the other moves under her shirt and around her small waist, and I push up her shirt and bury my face in her stomach,

262

sweet-smelling velvet skin. Freeing her hands, she grabs my hair and pulls back. This hurts, but I do not care and will not let it interfere.

"No. Don't go," I say, re-taming her with ease and delicacy, caressing her breasts, trying to find her mouth with mine, but she turns her head from side to side, skillfully eluding my kisses, spurning my tenderness, so I press my weight against her to keep her in place, my chest fixed to hers, belly to belly, and I reach down and pull her panties to her knees, my hand probing her nether regions, stroking the downy coarseness and pliant lips. Her gasps become louder, so I force my mouth on hers, my tongue inside. I rip the button from my pants and pull apart the zippered flaps.

My penis is touching her unclothed thigh. I refasten her wrists to the bed.

"Please."

She is sobbing. The tussling slows and then stops.

"But I love you," I say.

Skin so white and clear it shines like ivory in the inviolable darkness.

Amor, ch'a nullo amato amar perdona.

I enter.

I never realized how dark her room could get, darker even than mine. It was hard to believe that the sun would be up soon. Maybe it wouldn't. I lay on my banged-up back and looked up at the ceiling, though I couldn't see it clearly, imagining a cosmic panorama of twinkling little stars beyond the blackness, paling against the slowly brightening sky. My body was starting to stiffen and swell from the beating. I had gotten some blood on her pillows and sheets.

"Do you remember that Halloween at the pumpkin farm?" I said. "I was around ten, I think."

"..."

"Do you remember?"

"I remember."

"I was a vampire and you were a witch."

"You were a vampire every year."

"Remember how I cried because I dropped my pumpkin, my perfect pumpkin that I searched so hard for? I scoured every square foot of that patch, and I'd never seen a pumpkin so round and full and flawless. I was so happy, really happy and proud that I found it. It slipped right through my hands and split open, and I remember looking down like I couldn't believe what had just happened, just looking down in shock and horror, and then I started to cry. I was always crying about something, wasn't I? And then you started to cry. And Mom took a picture of us both, standing side by side in tears, you with your pumpkin in one piece and me with mine on the floor in a broken heap of slimy orange guts. My shoes were all covered with seeds and pulp. I wonder if she still has it, that photo. I'd like to see it."

"Why?" Her voice was low and tinged with trembling.

I didn't know why.

I took her withered hand, turned, and laid my head on her breast; her heart beat loud and steady in my ear. My eyes closed and I thought of that summer my parents sent me to day camp. Severine was too young, and I didn't ask to go, but my mother was swayed by the advice of neighbors, most of whose children were shipped a few hours north to some sylvan sleepaway, a thinly veiled excuse for unburdening themselves of parenting for a couple of months, though they would contend that being away from home and out from under parental supervision fostered independence and strengthened invaluable social skills. That first day, as I tied the laces of my brand new high-tops and put a package of chocolate chip cookies in my camp bag, Severine turned her large round eyes up at my mother—she was in her footed white pajamas with little embroidered pink hearts—and asked where Peter was going, and my mother told her that Peter was going to play and have fun with the other kids for a while. My sister looked puzzled and sad, but she repressed any incentive to voice her reservations. The concept of my going away to have fun had spooked her into stricken silence, as if she knew that were she to say or do anything to prevent me from going, she ran the risk of being shanghaied herself. So she bottled her fear and corked her frustration and stood there holding my mother's hand, and I cried myself sick as I waited at the bus stop across the street, watching them wave to me from the front door. It took all the restraint my seven-year-old soul could muster not to run back into their arms. I felt betrayed and abandoned. I did not want to pal around and play half-court hoops and eat tepid tinfoil lunches with the other kids; I didn't want to go on day trips or overnight cookouts or sit sardined on sweat-drenched bus seats, shooting spitballs out of plastic straws. Peer-bonding games of tetherball and tennis held no interest for me. I needed neither swimming skills nor archery lessons nor arts and crafts assistance, and I had no wish to *make new friends*, as my mother said to coax me into enjoying the experience: "You need to get out and be with people your own age. Don't you want to be with other kids like you?"

Like me?

On the bus, I couldn't stop crying and immediately became the butt of my fine fellow campers' contumely. My humiliation climaxed when my unstrung stomach gave way and I threw up all over the back seat. The ensuing uproar was so riotous that the driver pulled over and came back to see what all this kiddie commotion was, only to find me in the center of an incantatory ring of gawking campers, bawling so hysterically that she was afraid I was going to choke or have a seizure. I remember that she was a big, comforting woman with short black hair and glasses, and that she smelled like potato chips. She sat with me and put her arm around me and told me to calm down and breathe, while those *other kids my age* stood around and gaped and guffawed. After several minutes of friable collectedness, I burst out again, tearfully begging to be taken back. The exasperated driver finally gave in, radioed dispatch, turned the bus around and brought me home, where Severine waited, nose to the screen door, hailing my homecoming with an exultant smile and dewy eyes. I had been plucked from the precipice of demise and returned to her intact. My parents called the camp and got ninety percent of their money back. Summer camp was never mentioned again.

I couldn't bear to be separated from her, even in our own house, even during those two hours twice a week she spent with her piano teacher, the innocuous Mr. Ling, that sweet, five-foot nothing Taiwanese who had the privilege of placing her faultless fingers on the keys and arching her lissome little back when it fell out of position, of sitting beside her on that padded black bench—raised high to accommodate their diminutive statures— and feeling the vibrations of her movements and the mellifluous sway of her body as she played. She knew I was standing just on the other side of the wall, listening to every dulcet tone, every word of instruction and praise, critique and commendation. Right after the lesson, as soon as he left, I would plop myself on the sofa and listen to her run through the newly learned pieces until she tired and came over to sit next to me. We'd tune in to an episode of *Diff'rent Strokes* or *Silver Spoons* and talk over the commercials. Her fingertips would sometimes absentmindedly tap out on my arm or leg the piece she'd been practicing, and I'd feel the depth of each note on my skin; I could almost hear the melody through the nerve endings. Occasionally, my father, just home from class or after a long session in his study, would come in while my mother was preparing dinner and ask Severine what she had learned that day, ask me what I had done at school. He'd inevitably shake his head at the declining value of the American educational system, then fall asleep with his mouth slipping open a crack—*just enough to let the flies in*, my mother would say—and his glasses dropping down his nose, and we'd giggle at this, waiting to see if he'd wake before they fell off altogether. Sometimes we'd nap, too, there on the couch together. I was always keen on napping. There was a time when she was as well.

6:55 a.m. Light infiltrates my eyelids. I look up. She is awake and unmoved. I lift my head. There is some blood on her from my lip, daubed across her chest and lips and neck. I lick my finger and rub the redness clean, her flesh malleable to my touch. I lie back beside her.

Footsteps echo through the downstairs hallway. I am in that lovely limbo between sleep and waking, so I think it might be a dream, this noise, until the refrigerator opens, and then a glass or plate or mug is taken from a cabinet and placed on the table. This should be an alarm, a signal to return to my room, but I don't move. I replace my head on her breast, rising and falling with her even breath. This is where I want to be, nowhere but here, her nipple touching my cheek and my bent leg resting across her midsection.

Back to limbo.

Footsteps coming up the stairs. At this time on a Saturday morning? There are no early risers in my family. I check the clock: 7:23. It is daylight but still dark in here. She seems to be sleeping, but I know she is not. I run my finger lightly over her face in a line from her forehead down her nose and lips and chin and back up around her cheekbones, like a blind man sketching features in his mind. Her eyes open briefly, close suddenly.

The footsteps stop at the top of the stairs. My father is at the door in his dark blue terrycloth bathrobe and navy pajama pants, peeping through the crack. I know it is hard for him to make out what's inside because it's a good deal brighter in the hall, but he sees something. I hold my breath. The door opens a little more in slow, measured increments, light creeping in with each push. He looks at me. I look at him. Standing there with his hands lost in the robe's deep front pockets and his legs hidden behind the door, he seems to be studying the situation and taking mental notes, drinking in the scene as though it were a still life whose every prop and positioning holds secret significance. I can't take my eyes from his image lit up in front of me, his thick black glasses and chiseled features, the square, clean-shaven chin and dusky pigmentation that he passed on to me, wiry ringlets of gray sprouting from his chest and a mass of gunmetal gracing his head, which flops about sloppily in the morning before he combs it back, nearing sixty years old with hair twice as thick as mine, hair that I never had, that he never passed on to me. He stands there looking, his expression neutral, neither consenting nor reproachful, and I know he knows. I know he's known for years, and this makes him different. This changes something, deeply, dynamically.

He slowly pulls the door back to where it had been until all that is left of him is an obscured slice of blue between door and jamb. I hear him retrace his steps down the stairs and open and close the door to his own bedroom, and then nothing.

I pull the covers over my shoulders.

"That was Dad," I say, after a while.

I know she is not asleep.

"Dad was here," I repeat.

"..."

"Say something. I want to hear your voice."

"..."

"You haven't played in a long time. I miss it, hearing you play the piano. Why haven't you? It's a shame to let your talent go to waste. If I had a fraction of what you have, I'd—"

"I'm not with him anymore."

I can't process this immediately. The words mean more than I am able to take in right now.

"Spencer and I, we're not together."

I check myself from reacting too quickly.

"Did you know?" she follows up. She is not looking at me while she speaks—she is looking straight up.

"No. How could I? Since when?"

"The other night, the night we watched the movie. The night you had your... guest."

I should be happy, but I am not. The only thing I can think of to say is, *I'm sorry*, but I am not. It's a Pyrrhic victory, but still a victory.

"What happened?"

"Does it matter?"

"I don't know. Is it definitive, this break?"

"People don't stay together. Or if they do, it's out of fear. Or weakness. Usually both."

She draws a deep intake of air and my head rises with her expanding lungs, then sinks back in as she exhales.

"You're so stupidly stubborn. So selfish and thickheaded," she says.

I consider my rebuttal.

"Everybody's selfish. That's the nature of having a self, the way of the world. We're all just caretakers looking after our selves."

She smiles and closes her eyes as though amused at finding herself amused at the same joke she's been hearing for years. "You're always ready with a response. Some creative excuse. And you're never, ever to blame. You're the victim all the time, the innocent, wronged victim. The maligned and misunderstood good guy. Even now. Especially now." Her hand falls on my head on her breast, fingers sifting through my hair, nails lightly scratching my scalp. "You're the hero of your own story."

"Aren't we all?"

"It's always been about you. No one but you. You and only you."

"No. That's not true. It's always been only about you. You and me. Only you and me."

"You and your selfish solipsism. You think, therefore you are, and nobody else counts because you can never really know what they think or even *that* they think and therefore never truly be sure that they *are*, so they don't matter, right? Because you can't really be sure that they even exist. Only *you* matter. Others are only objects for your subjectivity. Isn't that what it says in your bible? Nobody else is in pain, or if they are it's insignificant.

Nobody has suffered like you have. Poor boy. Poor Peter. Poor sweet suffering Peter."

I close my eyes and let my mouth drift open, let my tongue slide sideways out of it and slither along her chest and down the slope of her trunk.

"That's not it. It's like Dad has always said. He's right. He's always been right, but in a different way from how we imagined. Existence is contingent. It's weak-kneed and worm-eaten and could fly off at any second. But we all have our own individual contingencies." My speech sounds bizarre because part of my mouth is pressed against her stomach. "And you are mine. You're my contingency." *I can't exist without you*, is what I mean to say in the simplest of terms, unclouded by philosophical bullshit, straight and clear and honest for once, just plain honest. She speaks before I can.

"I should hate you for what you've done. For all that you've done."

She doesn't hate me, I suspect, but what she feels extends far beyond her words.

Le silence éternel de ces espaces infinis m'effraie.

My hand searches her face, wet with a fresh tear. I wait for others to join it, but there is just this one solitary tear streaming down her cheek.

"I love you," is all I can say.

"No, you don't," she retorts instantly, her voice faraway and easy with regret. "You think, therefore you are. That's all."

"I want to live. I want so badly to live, but I can't. I don't know how."

I grab her hand and clench her fingers in mine and pat the back of my head lightly, then harder, pounding my head with the heel of her palm, hard enough to make me dizzier than the hangover already has, enough to hurt. I hit myself twice, three times. My eyes tear up. My nasal sinus congests. She makes no effort to halt the hammering or to add to it. I plant my face deep between her breasts, squeezing her fist tighter, and hit myself once more, my knuckles stinging, head throbbing, tears coursing out and making a wet mess of both of us. I stop and hold myself still, pressed up against her, smothering my face in her stomach.

The clock reads 8:38 when she pulls her hand out of mine and nudges me softly, slides from under me, pulls up her panties and sits on the edge of the bed, sits there for some seconds, sits there a few more seconds, rises, and walks to the bathroom.

I lie in her bed without her. Alone.

8

Transformation

There is but one truly serious philosophical
problem, and that is suicide.

— Albert Camus

Severine wasn't the first. Suicide runs in my family. We're
prone more to heart attacks than cancer. There's been a stroke or
two, even some fatal pulmonary emboli, but suicide is what
catches your attention. Suicide distinguishes death for us. I can
cite three examples off the top of my head, and there have probably been more back down the line. One of my maternal cousins
jumped from the sixteenth story of a Brooklyn high-rise the day
after her twenty-second birthday and died instantly, staining the
sidewalk and almost killing a passing pedestrian in the process.
A great aunt took a mouthful of downers and drowned herself in
the bathtub, though some in my family still speak of this as a
tragic accident. The one that hit closest to home for me was my
grandfather. At the age of eighty-three, partially blind and
stricken with a fairly advanced case of Alzheimer's, he came to
live with us against his will, forced to leave the tumbledown
Lower East Side apartment on Mott and Hester where he had
spent most of his life, raised his children in four small rooms,
and saw emphysema torture and slowly consume his wife of
fifty-five years. As if he wasn't decomposing quickly enough, as

if the natural course of things wouldn't have finished him off within another few years, the doctors and my parents concluded that it would be better for him to leave the combustion of the city and come out to the suburbs, where he could rot in tranquility among his loved ones. And so he came. There wasn't much he could do about it.

My grandfather was not depressed. Depressed is not a term that applies to his generation. He had always talked about his hard immigrant's life with a pitch of pride and pleasure, as if he would not have had it any other way, as if his reward had been in the very difficulties he'd faced. Now there were no more workaday worries or financial hardships, but he faced a strange new difficulty, one that no amount of dogged determination or nose-to-the-grindstone grit could overcome. Retired and wifeless, superannuated and directionless and probably sensing his own obsolescence, he found himself for the first time in his life with nothing to do and, worse, no reason or desire to do anything. Still, I wouldn't say my grandfather was depressed. This is not the word I would choose.

One sunny summer morning, we rose to find his room empty, the house alarm deactivated, and the front door ajar. He had been told the four-digit code in case of emergency, but how he remembered it bordered on the miraculous; how he managed to accurately compose this sequence of numbers (if you entered the incorrect code more than three times the alarm would sound) was something that would have pushed the limits of plausibility, if it hadn't actually happened. I remember my first thought: He's dead. He must be dead. I don't know why I thought this. There's no way I could've suspected what had happened. And yet this is what I said to myself: He's dead.

274

We searched the backyard, walked around the block, checked the basement in case he had somehow found his way down there without being able to find his way back up, rang the neighbors' doorbell to see if he'd mistakenly come to their house after an early morning stroll—maybe he thought he'd saunter over to the local *latticeria* for a fresh hunk of mozzarella, or go to see his old friend Pasquale on Mulberry Street, who had left the neighborhood twenty years ago and died ten years after that—drove around the development, and finally called the police. I was wrong. He wasn't dead. He had taken himself to the overpass of the highway (up the block from my house) at around 8:30 a.m., the pinnacle of rush hour, when wearied commuters crowd the road like an angry herd galloping into the city, and jumped—or more likely walked—off the ledge into oncoming traffic. But the fall didn't kill him. The drop itself just broke a few bones. He landed between vehicles, so most of the damage was done by the car(s) that ran him over before he rolled off onto the shoulder. The ejection of a body into rush-hour traffic caused a multivehicle crash—a domino effect of cars and trucks, buses and vans, stopping short and slamming into each other—and a few motorists were injured as well, though not as seriously as my grandfather, who was ambulanced to the ICU in extremely critical condition, comatose.

He never regained consciousness, died the same night. We were all at the hospital, but neither my sister nor I was allowed to see him. I was eleven at the time, she ten. He must have looked pretty bad. All we were told was that Grandpa had had an accident, a very serious accident, and he might not be able to come home with us. Severine and I stayed in the waiting room for hours, playing cards and watching a tiny ceiling-mounted television that was too far away to see and turned down too low to hear. My mother and father took turns updating us, bringing back sweet and salty snacks from the cafeteria and assuring us we'd be going home soon. Finally, my father came out and called my mother in and told us to stay there and not to move. We hadn't moved all night.

"He must be dead now," I said to Severine, who was sitting quietly in her seat and swinging her legs back and forth. They didn't reach the ground. She was always petite, and I remember those chairs being particularly high.

"Do you think they'll tell us?" she asked, looking up at me as though I had all the answers.

"Maybe not right away."

"They should tell us."

"They will. Probably later, when we get home."

A lady sitting several chairs over turned around and gave us an annoyed look. Severine's swinging was vibrating the row of connected seats. I told her to stop. She blushed.

"I wish we could see him," she said.

"He might not be conscious. He wouldn't even know we're there."

"Not for him." She rubbed her thumbnails together and turned away as if mildly ashamed at her motives, speaking more to herself than to me. "For us. So we'd know what it's like to die."

"I don't think watching someone die would help much." Though I was morbidly intrigued by the idea.

"Maybe not. But it would probably be the closest you could get."

Looking down at her knees, she paused, swung her legs again unconsciously, then realized she was doing it and stopped. She seemed sincerely regretful. Not about the leg-swinging but about missing the opportunity to be near death, even if it wasn't her own, to be in the same room with someone whose life was leaving him, as it was leaving him.

I wasn't very close to my grandfather, so I can't say that I was greatly affected by his death, but I remember my amazement at his resoluteness and efficacy, marveling that this sick, world-weary senior could plan and pull off such an elaborate suicide, that he could manage to get out of the house undetected (especially since my father was always keeping close tabs on him), walk up the street alone, stand on the ledge as the traffic zipped by below, and not lose the nerve to fling himself into the howling crush of fast-moving steel and grinding tires, knowing that this would be his closing act, choosing this to be his final enterprise. And beyond the logistics, I wonder if he considered the possibility that this would be what was most remembered of him, at least by me, that despite his eight decades plus of life and all the stories I'd heard about the excitement and austerity of the immigrant experience in New York—the tales of my father's youth, when my grandfather was a stern yet affectionate paterfamilias, respected and feared, loyal to a fault to both friends and family and not an enemy you'd want to have—that even though his life was full of actions and decisions that touched so many others, roads taken and not taken that shaped the lives of his descendants right down to his grandchildren, right down to me, that in spite of this, the thing that always comes to mind when I think about him, no matter the context, is that he ended up a broken old man who consciously decided to terminate his life by throwing himself onto the roadway.

The last act is defining. Everything that precedes it ends up seeming ancillary, an extended preface that doesn't amount to anything once the book is finished. Death completes us, and death that is courted or willed transforms a life retroactively, defines it in a way that passive death does not, overwrites the anterior narrative so that the deed itself, the taking of one's own life, eclipses the very history of that life. This is one of the lures of suicide: control, or at least the illusion of it. The right to write your own ticket out.

I used to extol self-slaughter and venerate those who had the will to forsake all possibility of amelioration on what comes down to a hunch, a wager—conscious or not—that nothing in death can be as evil or atrocious as what one is currently living through; the terror of the unknown can't hold a candle to the pain of the present. But I lost this respect. Suicide no longer holds any allure for me, and I hold little esteem for suicides. I do hope, however, that life passes quickly.

9

Ocean Beach

What we cannot speak about we must pass over in silence.

— Ludwig Wittgenstein

Entropy, in thermodynamics, is the steady and inevitable deterioration of a closed or isolated system due to the increasing and irreversible degradation of usable energy within that system. It is the movement in nature from order to disorder, the evolution—or devolution—of matter toward a permanent state of inert uniformity, of thermodynamic equilibrium or heat death, which is what all matter aspires to; the terminus of the universe. *Things fall apart*, in defiance of our best efforts. *The centre cannot hold*.

For the forty days and nights between the last time that I lay with her and the night she killed herself, Severine was in the house almost all the time, going to class and coming straight home, as if from an exhausting job that she was working at only to pay the bills. She had changed completely. She would sometimes spend whole days indoors, lazing about in varying stages of dishabille and the doldrums, uninterestedly leafing through my father's scholarly journals and putting them down a few minutes later in favor of a sunset nap. My mother ascribed this general despondency to the breakup—anyone would. A broken heart does not heal overnight, especially one's first. My father knew that things were not so simple, but why complicate them even more? Entropy would take care of that on its own.

But my mother was happy, in a way. The four of us were once again a unit, as in the old days. We watched films in the family room and talked books at the table. We ate together and were all safely in the house at night when she and my father locked up and went to bed. I would watch her smile again at the dinner table and look at both of her children and quickly divert her gaze when she saw me notice, as though self-conscious about her satisfaction in light of Severine's suffering, which she was powerless to lessen. It was good to see her like this. Brief as this period was, life was beginning to resemble more and more that which it had been for so long.

I, too, was reasonably content. My initial skepticism and suspicion that Severine and Spencer might get back together faded, due partly to the surface state of things and partly to my own desperation: I wanted so badly to believe it was true, that the lost past had been regained and even enriched, made *strong at the broken places.* We had only to let a little time pass and things would fall back into order, like chessmen restored to place after a taxing match. Out of chaos we would regain the cosmos. Only afterward did I see what a tenuous thread was holding everything together.

Spencer was in fact erased from the page so swiftly and conclusively that it soon seemed he had never been there, his whole presence a vaguely remembered piece of a once vivid dream. And if she was pining for him, it would pass. I was not worried.

Severine and I interacted little. I spoke to her in flavorless platitudes, sheepishly, and didn't go near her room, especially at night. I knew she needed time, and I was willing to be patient, so long as it was only a question of time. She reverted to her taciturn child-self, but more deeply now, girdled by an uneasy and powerful zone of silence that fended off entry like a rampart. When any of us got close to that perilous region where words were impossible—that minefield of muteness—we too refrained from speaking; we too felt the frailty of language, its inability to communicate anything of real importance. Her scarce smiles were understated and pensive again. Her voice lost the robust ebullience it had garnered over the last months and returned to its former temperate tone, privately plangent, but only to the ear that knew how to hear it. She was my sister, Severine, once more. She rediscovered the piano, lulling me to sleep on dreary, nameless afternoons. Sometimes I would find her there on the bench with her hands folded on her lap, staring solemnly at a sheaf of sheet music on the rack as though hearing the notes in her head while she hummed quietly along to the melody playing only for her. Or she'd sit alone in the living room, swimming in the oversize leather recliner with a book—which she often was not reading—cradled in her lap.

Days washed away in routine. A welcome complacency overtook me, and I stifled anything that told me otherwise, discounted any innuendo that the center could not hold, despite the troubling intuition that the sister who was returned to me was somehow not the same one, that I had truly lost her. I buried this feeling and paved it with layers of denial and rationalization. I simply would not accept that her vacant and sorrowful stares were anything more than the lingering but ultimately short-term aftereffects of an illness, somewhat serious but far from life-threatening. I chalked up her remoteness and lassitude to the healing process, which would eventually seal whatever cracks remained and make us whole again. This was the way it would be, now and forever, if by the strength of my will alone. She was there. The rest would fall into place.

Et tout le reste est littérature.

Right under my nose, however, entropy was afoot. Particles were advancing unalterably toward disorder and degeneration. The plot was already in motion toward its end, and I would learn that the descent into hell is steeper when the promise of salvation seems to be in view.

Winter's harshness dragged on into early April, with only brief bluffs at breaking here and there, followed by another bout of snow and ice and unseasonably cold temperatures. It was Thursday. She appeared in my room just after dusk. I was reading in bed and, oddly, didn't hear her come in, so I wasn't sure how long she'd been standing there by the time I looked up over my book to find her framed by the doorway in a long white nightgown, like the despondent specter of a jilted bride. It was unduly early to be wearing nightclothes, but she had done this a lot lately, changing as soon as she came home from school—even if it was only midafternoon—and remaining in her sleepwear through the evening and into the following morning. It was nothing unusual to me; I have been known to spend days at a stretch in pajamas.

"What are you reading?" she asked quietly, as though loath to disturb me.

I lifted the book, the Musil she had given me.

"Ah."

"Is something wrong?" I said, of all things.

"What could be wrong?"

Televised voices reached us from downstairs, news anchors and on-scene reporters. There'd been a game-changing break in the case of the murdered college girl. Based on suspicious and contradictory statements made when initially interviewed by the police, the middle-aged son of a longtime neighbor had been brought in for questioning and confessed to her abduction, rape, and murder. He was now in custody. No motive had as yet been provided, but the authorities seemed confident that he was their man. Some neighbors expressed shock at the arrest, claiming that the alleged perpetrator was a quiet and shy but polite and respectful person who had lived among them his entire life and had never exhibited any kind of deviant or dangerous behavior. Others, however, didn't seem so sure about his character, and claimed to have long suspected some sort of latent turpitude belying his distantly quiescent exterior. The murdered girl's family was unavailable for comment, and the police were asking the press and the public to accord them privacy during this time of anguish and bereavement.

Severine continued to stand motionless in the center of my room, her hair washed but uncombed, still damp from her bath and clumping like fine gold thread. She looked awkward and inelegant, as I had never seen her look before. Her nightgown fell loosely over her slight frame, which had become slighter over the last few weeks, and her bare feet were in the new beige leather slippers my mother had bought her earlier in the week. She smelled of lemon-scented shampoo and perfumed soap, and there might have been a tiny crust of dried toothpaste in the crook of her mouth.

"There's nothing wrong." She looked up into the corner of the wall as though her eye had been caught by a spider dangling down a string of webbing. "But I'm pregnant."

She continued to stare at—*into* or *through* seemed more apt—the wall. I waited for the sound waves to settle and blend in with the room's aura of reticence.

"How do you know this?"

She smiled without showing teeth, still facing the wall.

"Are you sure?" I persisted foolishly, fishing for something to say.

"Yes." She nodded and blinked, keeping her lids down for an extra fraction of a second before lifting them and finally meeting my eyes with hers. "Of some things."

I didn't ask whose seed it was, though this was the question that flew to the forefront of my mind. I asked in lieu, "What should we do?"

"What's to be done?"

"I mean, there are choices to make, options."

That word again. *Options.*

"We can't not choose, isn't that it?" she said. "Not choosing is itself a choice, isn't that what you mean?"

I was sitting up, back braced against three pillows, book on lap, fingers fiddling with the frayed upper trim of my blanket.

"Just say what you mean, Peter. And mean what you say."

She was with child. This did not unhinge or repulse me, didn't make me rueful or even upset. I was calm, if not a little thrown. Shocked, yes. Dumbstruck, very much so. But almost immediately, a gush of raw and unchecked emotion upswelled in me, a burgeoning joy at the pictures that passed through my brain: I saw her in dowdy maternity dresses with a swollen belly and a haggard, pregnant face, a keep-away sign to male predators; I saw her bent over the toilet bowl in the early morning and bingeing late at night, dead with the fatigue of extra weight and desperate for midday naps. The child didn't matter. I wasn't thinking about the baby. I didn't care about it apart from it being something that would enduringly bind her to me, something, at last, that was sure to keep us together indefinitely. With each second the vision grew more foolproof. I had cuckolded the cuckolder. The kid would be conveniently credited to Spencer, *her first real boyfriend* — Spencer, who would want nothing to do with it, or with her, who had fled the scene and was not coming back and was not worth tracking down, who would take the fall for committing the betrayal that would embitter her toward men for years to come. As for me, I would sacrifice my future for my abandoned sister and her bastard. I would save her and at last play the hero. I had to. It was the role of a lifetime.

"I'll take care of you," I said, eyes welling.

"How do you mean?"

"You and the baby. I'll be there. Always."

"That's not the issue." She rubbed an eyebrow, confused by either the words themselves or what they meant. "Hm. I just…" nibbling her lower lip, still rubbing. "I just wanted to let you know. I thought you should know."

Everything told me to spring from the bed and grab her shoulders — and do what? Say what? I'm sorry, I love you, I need you? I wasn't sorry, and it was too late for any of that. I couldn't have stopped her. Nothing I could have said or done would have made a modicum of difference. She had done it already. She was gone in all but body. There before me, speaking in a voice I will never stop hearing, a voice at once so firm and frangible, so serenely decided and racked with affliction too great to evince, was my sister's shade. Severine was already dead.

"I thought… you should know," she reinforced, staring at the tips of her slippers. "These are a little stiff."

"They're new. They'll break in."

"I don't want the baby. I definitely don't want it. About that there's no question."

"We can arrange that."

"I don't want to arrange it." A shard of acerbity stabbed out of the stilled surface of her voice.

"Sev, just—"

"I don't want anything. I don't want to be taken care of. It's okay. I just want to not have to worry about anyone or anything anymore. I don't want to have to worry about myself. Everything is all right. Everything will work out. Things have a way of working themselves out on their own."

She smiled as though she truly believed this.

"Sev..." I had nothing to say.

"It's good not to want. It's liberating. I don't want you to worry. It's all de trop anyway. I'm not worried. So you shouldn't be."

Unceremoniously, she made to leave, her nightdress trailing behind like a bridal gown.

"Wait," I said.

She stopped but did not turn around.

"Don't go."

How many times in my life had I said these words to her? *Don't go.* Again I attempted to rally the strength and will to get up, but it was futile. It is so hard to leave that bed.

"You say you want to live but that you don't know how." Her body seemed to rotate around, as on an axis. Her eyes were unfocused, looking past me, past everything. "Neither do I. You've seen to that."

It didn't hurt. I didn't care. The reality is that I didn't care if she loved me, because my love for her was selfish and acquisitive, controlling and covetous, greedy and grasping, the truest, most honest kind. Love in its purest manifestation. I could live without her loving me so long as I possessed her, solely and completely. So long as she let me love and be near her, it didn't matter if that love was requited. I had enough for both of us. If I had her in body, her soul and spirit would eventually follow.

She remained, so still.

"Don't go," I mumbled hoarsely, one more time.

I couldn't stop her.

Not moving from my bed, not even changing positions, I lay thinking, reassuring myself that it didn't matter what she said or didn't say; the situation was long past words. A couple of hours passed, and I finally got up and went to her room to tell her again that I would take care of her in perpetuum, and maybe add that bulletproof bromide: *Everything will be okay.* I could ask for nothing more, want nothing more than to be there for her, always and forever, and now was my chance to prove it. But she wasn't there, nor was the car we shared, which was unusual but explainable. Maybe she had gone for a drive to clear her mind. Or maybe she had gone to Spencer's and they were reconciling right now. *The horror! The horror!* This thought contaminated my psyche and gained more credence as time wore on—as negative ones tend to do—and I took great pains to keep the image of them sweetly spooning in his quaint little Brooklyn bachelor pad from demolishing my mindset. There was always something to spoil my good mood. I went back to bed and did my best to downplay this worst-case scenario, as I waited for her one more time, and surprisingly, the more I thought about it, the less concerned I was. Even if she had gone to him, what could come of it? They would spend one last night together, and in the sobering light of morning, he'd realize that it wasn't worth upending his life over suburban Severine and her unplanned pregnancy. I ended up falling asleep early, well before 2 a.m., and passed a newborn's night of sweet, dreamless sleep.

The next day when I awoke, minutes before noon, I did not linger in bed as usual. I checked her room—empty—and went downstairs. My mother was in the kitchen washing a chicken for dinner, holding the dead thing up by its legs and rinsing out its excavated bowels with cheap whiskey. She commented with a wry smile that I was up early and asked what the occasion was.

"What day is it?" I said.

"Friday."

"That's the occasion."

She smirked and shook the excess liquid from her chicken and dropped the carcass onto a bamboo cutting board on the counter. "Works for me. Let there be more Fridays then."

"Where's Severine?"

"I haven't seen her. Maybe she had to go to school early."

I had a bowl of corn flakes with banana slices, then went upstairs, then came back down to watch my mother dissever the chicken. For once in my life I couldn't sleep. I was now sure she had gone to him. Just when things were going well, she went to him. I could imagine nothing worse. What could be worse?

There were times growing up when I thought we would always be children. Envisioning adulthood was as thorny and fraught with dread as realizing that one must die, as impossible as conceptualizing the bare facticity of one's own expiry; a world without her was inconceivable, like nonbeing, negative space, the eternal existence of God. But now it seems there never could have been any other way. I have never thought of myself as a fatalist, but it seems now as if she has always been dead.

In the winter, Severine wore a flowing red hooded coat that looked like a cape—her *famous red raincoat*, she called it, after the Leonard Cohen song, "Famous Blue Raincoat"—and a chunky black woolen scarf that was so long she would wrap it several times around her neck and still have some slack hanging down her back. She had matching black gloves and boots and a black felt cloche hat with a stiff stingy brim and a narrow burgundy band of silk circling the base of its crown, which she wore low, almost over her eyes. I used to tell her she looked like Little Red Riding Hood, and that with the hat on she was a danger to herself and others on the road because she couldn't see. She hated when I said that. About Little Red Riding Hood, not the road.

I found out my sister was dead when my mother answered the phone that afternoon. I watched as she listened and dropped the receiver and fell to her knees and tried to cry, to scream, to force something out of her incapacitated throat, which would emit nothing for the good part of a minute, watched her face twist and contort and go from deathlike sallow to deep red in the space of a few seconds that seemed eons, heard that harrowing howl I had never heard come from a human being before and have never heard since. Sitting at the kitchen table with my glass of milk and a half-eaten cupcake, I watched as my father rushed in from his study with that pallid look of pure, unmasked panic on his usually so unflappable face to find my mother on the floor bleating convulsively like a lamb at the slaughter, incapable of repeating what she had just been told until he lost his own self-possession and shook it out of her, then froze perfectly in place, froze as though a gunshot or stabbing had sent his body into a temporary state of suspension before it processed the injury, and when the fact finally registered, he put his palm to his forehead, ground his palm into his forehead as though attempting to rub out the thought, to dispel the image of his dead daughter, and fell forward into my mother and their helpless embrace, almost filmic as they struggled to bear the brutal weight of their loss and shoulder as one the piercing pain that held them together as though speared, along with the sudden, unsought insight—only just developing and not yet wholly coherent—that something binding them together had been irreparably broken, something their union had created and brought into the world had been ripped out of the world forever, scrubbed from the earth, along with the forced appreciation of finitude, not as conveyed in fiction or philosophy, poetry or song, not in name or notion, thought or words or concept but for real, up close and real for once, all too real. Not the idea of death but death itself, palpable, unavoidable, ubiquitous death, *unvanquished and unyielding.*

My father held his wife, not bothering to try to calm her as she moaned between uncontrollable spasms of tears and rocked in his arms like a mental patient in a straightjacket: *She's dead. She's drowned. Dead. She's dead. She's dead. She's dead. Oh God. Oh God she's dead. She's dead. She's dead. She's...* And when she could not stabilize her breathing long enough to sustain speech, she put one hand over her open mouth and squeezed, then covered that hand with the other as if she wanted to permanently seal it. But the same words kept coming, and none other. *She's dead. She's dead...*

I sat at the table and watched. Particles froze. Existence broke off. I knew then that childhood was untrue.

No, I did not stop her. I wasn't there as she stood alone on the shore in the dark and the cold and stared at that roiling, boundless black mass before her, the faceless void. I didn't feel the mist and the moist breeze, smelling of salt and kelp and sea slime, the miniscule drops of ocean that dotted her face. I did not sit down next to her and pull in my knees at the edge of the shore where the water crept up in timid rivulets to bathe her bare feet, the fringe of the sprawling ocean reduced to a sorry, shimmering transparency as it dissolved noiselessly into the sand. I did not hear—no one heard—the rustle of her clothing as she rose and brushed the sand off her bottom and took a tentative step forward to test the water, to warm to its welcome, half a foot dipped in, a shiver, an ankle immersed. I did not grab the hem of her gown from the seawater and pull her back, did not take her shoulders and turn her around and lead her back, back into life.

I did not get to wave good-bye and watch her form recede into night.

And the nightgown again, the hem of the nightgown floating up until it becomes saturated and blends with the black, the initial shock of the frigid saltwater inching up her legs to her waist, her arms outstretched, fingers skirting the surface of the water, tracing lines in the sea. The smooth sand and rough, rocky bottom. The foamy white crests. The lulling drone of the surf.

All aquiver now. In up to her chest, swaying with the waves, a formless pull from under, not yet strong enough to overcome, still time to walk out and return to shore, to me. She hesitates, unacclimated to the water, shivering steadily. Ocean at her breasts, her clothes hang heavy with wet about her shoulders while her lower half is weightless. The impassioned whispers of the sea thunder through her eardrums, calling her back to the primeval source, honoring her origins. But she is not listening.

She is not thinking of things like this. She is not thinking of me. I am not on that shore with her.

Now the ocean tickles her chin, confident and playful, sure of success. Her hair floats carefree, trailing her steadfast advance in tangled clumps and swampy strands that lunge backward toward dry land. She does not look back. She stands on her toes to keep her mouth above water, arches her head back, closes her lips and transfers all respiratory responsibility to her nose, the water pushing at the edges of her mouth with implacable insistence. She slips under, holds her breath, shuts her eyes, *and all the world drops dead*; here, everything is silent and still, blissfully tranquil, insentient and invisible, a hypnotic netherworld where things are both exactly and nothing as they seem, and where this seems somehow right, whole and harmonious and seamlessly synchronous. Bubbles of exhalation escape her nose and squeeze out of the corners of her mouth, surging slapdash to the surface and puncturing its placidity. The ripples relax and level out again, conform to the rhythm of the tide and disguise her entry. Then it comes, the salty influx. Patient, it comes in subtle bursts, breaking the seal of her lips to let her sip, to test its flavor. Then she opens her mouth and it charges in, filling her airy crevices. She can only just resist the urge to resurface, can barely beat back the instinct to breathe. It takes adamantine resolve and a steeled singularity of purpose to walk forward until her feet lift off the bottom and the tide assumes control, accepts her burden. The dauntless current coos and convinces her, reassures her with its sweeping strength, tells her not to worry—it will take care of everything. A few seconds of frantic reflexive paddling before commanding herself to desist: *Stop this childishness. Quit it now.* Saltwater flooding her lungs; trying to cough it up, but air is losing its battle, the last of it chased out by water and escaping in a few final fleeing bubbles that break promptly on contact with the surface. Not pain but pressure, an unbelievable, irresistible force pushing from inside. Next the brain. The water infiltrates her head and submerges the circuitry, the pressure finally subsides, her consciousness muddles and ebbs, her limbs become one with the undulations of the sea, her deluged body loses its buoyancy and begins to descend. The heart is still pumping, but it's only a matter of minutes now, seconds. The brief excitement is over. She has come back to the ocean. Entropy has done its work, moving particles toward inert uniformity.

Back on the shore, all is quiet and calm, as though nothing has happened. Her footsteps are already being washed away, and soon there will be no natural trace of where she walked on the beach that night, then nothing at all, until the ocean spits her out again, keeping the vital part of her for itself.

But I wasn't there, finally. I wasn't even there to ask her why. *Why*. The weakest word in the language.

I was not there.

My sister's body was found shortly before noon by a jogger who has a home on the beach, about a twenty-minute walk from our house. She and her lawyer husband live in the city and are rarely at the shore in the winter or spring, but their yearly trip to the Bahamas had been cancelled because he was in the middle of an important high-profile case, so they elected instead to go out to the beach for a few days for an early springtide retreat. I know their house, a stately stone construction with French doors and large picture windows and an inordinately high and imposing crow-stepped gable facing the street. I used to see it when I would go for long bike rides as a kid, valiantly straying outside the immediate neighborhood *to explore strange new worlds* and get a glimpse of otherness. It looks more like an old baronial manor house transported in toto from some European country estate.

We do not know exactly where Severine entered the ocean, on which stretch of sand she took her last strides. She didn't drive there—we found the car just up the street, on a side road near the overpass that my grandfather jumped from—so it had to be within walking distance. There are several possibilities, including the public beach and a smattering of privately owned subdivisions of the coastline. I do not believe my sister would have walked through someone's property, so I'm guessing it was the community beach, which we hardly ever frequented. We were never big beachgoers; I was ardently against getting wet, and she had little tolerance for the feeling of sand in her shoes, but this is where I imagine she did it. I see her standing barefoot on that solitary strand in the dead of night, buffeted by the strong sea breeze and squinting against sprays of water and gusting grains of sand, and I imagine she took a long valedictory look at the world behind her before walking slowly and with unswerving purport into the welcoming water.

The beach is pretty deserted from fall to late spring. If that woman hadn't been jogging, if she and her husband had flown to the Caribbean as planned, Severine might have been lying there dead much longer.

She was wearing the red coat, her *famous red raincoat*, over her nightgown when she was found, with her waterlogged wallet and ID in the pocket. Her feet were bare, hands gloved. The hat was not recovered. She didn't wear the scarf; that we found on the floor of her room, where it must have fallen off unnoticed as she left, because it would have been categorically unlike her to leave things in disarray, even if she hadn't planned on coming back. According to the report, her body was found at low tide, several yards from the water, prostrate on the shore. Her eyes were open, hair snarled and full of sand, stuck with seaweed and salt and all sorts of shoreline debris. The coroner's office turned the coat and gloves over to the police, who—having no need of them for the investigation, which was quickly closed—returned them to my parents. Suicide was the conclusion. Deliberate death by drowning. No trace of drugs or alcohol in her body, no sign of foul play. A clean suicide. Case closed. Next.

Curiously, the medical examiner's report mentions nothing of her pregnancy. I don't know if they failed to detect it or if she in fact wasn't pregnant, if she lied to me, or if she misread the home pregnancy test, which itself may have been unreliable. I know only what she told me, and I know only that she's dead, and anything and everything else is secondary.

News like this travels fast in a neighborhood like mine. Sickness, death, divorce, infidelity, foreclosure, and bankruptcy are among the most valued coins of gossip. The untimely death of a young girl, a presumed suicide no less, right here in the neighborhood, someone they had known for years, whom they had watched grow from pretty little girl to beautiful young woman, is gold, ample fodder for a juicy bourgeois chinwag on the phone, quick conversations at the market, and downtime natter at the gym between spinning and Pilates. Don already knew when I called him that night.

"Severine's dead," I said, right after his hello.

"I wasn't sure when to call."

"She walked into the water."

I could hear his girlfriend's voice in the background, asking him to pass her the phone after. I was relieved that Don didn't say, *I'm sorry*. At a loss for words—which was rare, and would have been an interesting and somewhat amusing phenomenon, under different circumstances—he seemed stuck between not knowing what to say and being wary of remaining silent. He started to speak and cut himself off with an uptight clearing of the throat and a guttural gasp before anything intelligible could be uttered.

"You have company," I said.

"Just Susan."

"She drowned herself, you know."

"I know she drowned."

"I'm trying to imagine the strength of will you need to drown yourself. It can't be easy." It couldn't have been easy for Don either, on the other end of the line, but I didn't care; I wasn't really speaking to him. "I'm trying to imagine myself doing it, and I don't think I could. It's a strength that I don't have, that I could never have. Imagine holding yourself under until you're out far enough and the undertow takes over and saltwater pours in through your nose and mouth and inundates your body. Can you imagine it?" Now I pushed him, for a change. "I mean, can you imagine yourself doing it?"

"I can't."

"No. You can't. Neither can I." I pulled the handset away from my ear and considered hanging up, not out of anger or frustration or sadness, just because I suddenly wanted to stop talking. I watched the timer's digital display accumulate seven seconds before recommencing. "Once the tide takes you it's probably pretty easy though. That probably does most of the work. Of course, by then it's too late to turn back. You're in. Like it or not, you're in. Even if it's quick, it can't be pleasant."

"No. It can't be."

Susan asked him again if she could speak with me. Don probably knew I didn't want that.

"Did you know she did it herself?"

What a dumb thing to say, a stupid question to ask. As though she'd gone for a midnight swim in forty-degree water and things had somehow gone horribly awry.

Don paused before answering. "I just know she was found on the beach."

"Well, she did it herself."

The line was silent.

"Do you want to come over?" Don asked.

"No. I'm going to stay in tonight."

"I can come there if you want."

"No. I'm going to stay in alone. But thanks. The wake's Monday. I wanted to tell you that."

"I know. And, look… whatever you need… I mean it."

It was hard to find anything to say. I sympathized with his discomfort.

"I know," I said.

We hung up. I didn't know what to do or how to react. The house was the same as last night, the same sounds and smells and sights, the same walls and rooms and furniture, but now she was dead, so its sameness was completely different. I felt this but didn't fully absorb its import, how the things around me would be so radically altered by her absence. Her chair at the kitchen table was there, but she was dead, so it was no longer *her* chair; her clothes were now just clothes; in the bathroom her perfume still hung in the air like the lingering sweetness of wilted flowers that have just been removed from the vase and thrown away, her toothbrush in its holder and her comb in the cabinet, loose strings of her hair — what last night was her hair — roped around its bristles. On the way to my room, I passed hers but didn't go in. The door was almost fully closed. I stopped in front of it, then continued on to bed. Last night she was standing in my room. The room hadn't changed. Nothing else had changed. But now she was dead, so it was a different room altogether. Now she would always be dead, and the room would always be different. Dead as dreams. Unceremonious, uncelebrated, finished. Dead.

On my unmade bed was the black pajama top that I had worn for the last week and forgotten to bring downstairs so my mother could wash it; she had told me she was doing darks. I decided I would wear it again tonight. I closed the door to shut out the light, regretting that I couldn't blot out that bright yellow sliver between the bottom rail and the floor, though I wasn't planning to sleep. I would go to Don's house later, when Susan was gone, while my mother was in bed, drugged up and trying to sleep, my father next to her attempting to postpone his own tidal wave of grief by tending to his wife.

I leaned on my pillows and waited. I waited for the darkness at my back, which had been there all the while, biding its time and anticipating this moment, to rush forward and wrap around me like a python.

I never found out why Severine and Spencer broke up. As she said, it doesn't much matter, but I would have liked to know. It was so sudden and unexplained. I spoke to him one last time at the wake.

Open casket viewings are gruesome and medieval, with the corpse lying comfortably on display in its satin-lined coffin, all prim and proper and made up like a macabre marionette while the mourners and admirers line up to kneel before it and gawk at its deadness and offer unstated thanks that it's not yet their time, as they pretend to pray and ponder the loss and whisper their final good-byes. But there had to be one, for the sake of the family and tradition. And since there was no way to be sure that she had intentionally taken her own life, no note or other explicit evidence—besides the medical examiner's statement, which held no brief in the house of God—that she had died outside a state of grace, we were allowed to have the memorial mass in a Roman Catholic church, and Severine was permitted all the pomp and circumstance of the Sacrament of Christian Burial in consecrated ground. So long as the theoretical possibility existed that this was nothing more than some terrible and tragic accident, the church was willing to turn the other way and—for a nominal *donation*, since we were not regular parishioners—afford us its hospitality.

I was standing with Don in the back of the funeral parlor. We weren't talking, just standing there watching everybody mill about without knowing exactly how to act, the men shaking their heads in sad incomprehension while the women wiped discreet little tears from the corners of their eyes and dabbed their running mascara with crumpled tissues. Spencer approached me from behind, tapped my arm lightly, and said, "How are you?"

How am I?

"I am," I said. "How are you?"

He pursed his brow as though thinking over the right way to answer this.

"I'm… here," he replied in a lowered voice.

"Yes." I nodded. "Yes."

He looked at Don, who looked back. I did not introduce them.

"I'll be going home next semester, back to Canada. I'm transferring to Laval."

"Oh." I almost left it at that. "Why?"

"Many reasons." He paused. At the front of the room, my father and my cousin Lou exchanged bear hugs and back pats and kisses on cheeks. I hadn't seen Lou since he gave me the gun, and I didn't want to see him now. When he looked over at me, I turned away and pretended not to notice.

"I've decided to specialize in French philosophy," Spencer continued. "It seems fitting to study it in the language it was written in."

"It does."

"And then, well, I never liked New York much anyway. I came because it's always seemed the place to be, because it's supposed to be the center of the world. And it probably is, but even so, I don't want to be here. Sometimes it's better to be off-center. And besides, now..."

"I never liked New York too much either, but I don't think anywhere else will be different. It's all under the same sun."

"Maybe. But home is home."

"Yes. For better or worse."

He sidled up close to me but not too close, as though some law of propriety called for a certain distance to be kept at times like these.

"You know, we had stopped seeing each other for a while before... not long before..."

I let him stew a few seconds before presenting my rejoinder. "I know."

"She broke up with me. She's the one who ended it."

As though this was supposed to offer me some comfort and/or satisfaction. Which it did.

"I know."

I didn't know, and I was suddenly worried that he might think her suicide was a result of their breaking up. At the same time, I didn't want to completely absolve him of any guilt he might be feeling. It was a delicate balance to maintain.

"Don't worry," I told him. "She was over it. Well over it. She knew there was no real future for you two."

His look was comprised of pain and puzzlement and maybe a bit of relief. He might have been about to say something, but his mouth opened only to close a moment later, letting out nothing but silence. Then an aunt of mine came over, one of the many old and grizzled little Italian ladies in long black dresses and black lace mourning veils. Spencer and I held each other's eyes while she leaned in and squeezed my face between her shaky, blue-veined hands and kissed both my cheeks and my forehead. He stepped back and held his hands together at his waist, remained in that reverent position for a minute or so, then turned, nodded solemnly, and walked away, walked straight out of the room without a backward glance. I was strangely saddened by this. Contrary to what I would have expected, watching him leave only added more depth to the emptiness that had already made its home in me. I knew it was the last time I would see him, and I somehow wished it weren't. Another part of her was lost forever as I followed his exit from that dark, densely packed room into the bright spring sun.

My aunt told me sorrowfully what a wonderful child my sister was, how beautiful she looked, and that she was happy now, happy and beyond harm in heaven, and she stayed with me for a while inquiring about my own life before rejoining the other aunts and uncles and cousins and old family acquaintances who had come to pay their respects. I wanted to ask her if she was senile or stupid, or if she just thought it the proper thing to say, because my sister only looked dead, neither beautiful nor happy but dead, very dead, her face drawn and thickly overlaid with makeup to hide the ravages of saltwater on her immaculate skin, her formerly abundant hair dry and straw-thin and filled in with extensions, eyelids and lips sewn shut with stitching that you could see if you looked closely. I looked closely. I examined her exanimate hands and muted-red manicured nails, mascaraed eyelashes that would never again flutter over eyes that would never see or cry again, would never meet mine again, eyes once so vivid and vibrant with melancholy now still and lifeless, closed forever—or *for infinity*—defunct and done for, extinct, reduced to vitreous globes prey to putrefaction, maggots and bacteria, dirt and poetry.

She looked dead, that's all. Not beautiful or happy or safe or anything else but dead. She was just dead, lying dead in the casket.

But I didn't say this to my aunt. I took her hand between my own two and said it was good to see her, so good of her to have come, and kissed her and was glad when she walked away. Soon after that I left. I'd had enough condolences from family members who meant nothing to me. Or to her. It seemed almost like a party in the poorest of taste, everyone getting together to see the deceased one last time before the big post-wake lunch in the event room of a local restaurant, most of us not having seen each other for years and not planning to see each other until the next wake or wedding, christening or confirmation, which hopefully would not be soon. I couldn't take any more. Don and I went back to his house and played NHL 95.

There was no eulogy, thankfully. My father requested that the priest say nothing extraneous to the rite, just the necessary prayers and sprinkling of holy water and the dropping of fresh flowers on the casket before she was lowered into the ground and covered with dirt. So no one got up in front of the respectfully hushed crowd to talk about her rare talent and loveliness and who she was; no one rose to the altar's podium to praise her extraordinary uniqueness or lament the loss of such priceless potential, nor could they have, because no one really knew her. My sister. Long lost sister Severine, dead, drowned, doomed and destroyed, sorry sister, broken, buried and beatified, sad, sad sister. This is my oration, my elegy to you, my private little farewell, my last indulgence: I am sorry, Severine, so sorry. I am heartily sorry that I could not stop myself from loving you, my sickness unto death. I am sorry with all my shattered soul that it was not this love alone that drove you into the sea, but if things had been different... They would not have been different. And *were it not that I have bad dreams*, I would prefer it this way, would *count myself a king of infinite space* because you are no less mine now than then, and you will always be so, enshrined and encapsulated in littoral death. And from the filmy window of my hermetic bedroom world, everything beyond the glass seems tranquil and good and sometimes beautiful—even inviting, though I know better—a subdued and senseless pantomime that repeats in recurring cycles, season after season, year after year, until the last syllable of my own recorded time, when all will be razed in ruin, all will be washed away, and nothing will be worth a single spilled tear or a peal of mad laughter, a longing sigh, a sober look back over time that has erased itself.

Two days after her suicide, I received an envelope in the mail with no return address. Inside were six sheets of quadrille ruled journal paper folded into sharp, even thirds, inscribed in black ink in her precise hand, torn from her diary, dated the day before her last. She always loved writing letters, the longer and more flowery the better. She always said that one of the telltale signs of a deteriorating civilization is the decline in epistolary communication. I don't know how she had the fortitude at such a time, but it's fitting that this is among the final things she did. And it's good that a scrap of her story finds a home in mine.

I considered going to the shore to read them, trying to guess where she took those final steps and sitting there on the sand, to make some elegiac gesture out of it. But in the end, I decided it was more appropriate to read them in bed, in my room, where I belong. Sometimes I think I penned the words myself—I can hear myself in them—sealed them up and mailed them off and somehow blocked out doing all this so that the sacred sensation of receiving and reading them would be undiminished. But no. The words could only be hers. Even if they're only mine now:

> In a way, Peter was never my brother. Or maybe it was I who wasn't a sister. We don't always fit so conveniently into the roles the universe doles out for us, and fate doesn't take kindly to switching halfway through the production, like a ruthless stage director who refuses to tolerate even the slightest divagation from his script. The price of a part in the play is unflagging adherence to character at all times, a kind of cultish loyalty to his vision. Absolute surrender. And there is no offstage.
>
> It would be too easy to say we weren't meant to be brother and sister. Nobody's meant to be anything. But to say what happened between us happened despite our genetic bond, that we fell in love even

though we were siblings, would make it sound like a mutation, an aberration. Something that should not have been. Which of course most people would believe. An abomination even. I didn't love Peter because he was my brother; I loved him because he was Peter. And wasn't Eve of the same flesh as Adam, cut from the identical swatch of heavenly cloth? Wasn't the rib taken from him and used to kindle her creation a constant reminder of their more than physical attachment, their inherent oneness? Especially to her, knowing a piece of him was always deep inside her, hidden from the outside but from which she herself could never hide, lest she lie to herself. (Though Eve was certainly quite capable of lying.) Surely they shared more than some DNA and common chromosomes, and yet God didn't seem to mind their naked frolicking through that pleasure garden, didn't seem to care about how they explored (almost) every delight within it, including each other. He watched over with fatherly approval and let them do as they would without interference until they disobeyed, until they did precisely what he told them not to without having been told why. Do what I say because I say it! Never mind the reasons! Overbearing, pompous patriarch. What did he know about living with someone else inside him?

Big brother. How I adored the sound of that childish little phrase, slightly goofy sounding, that little alliterative couplet that used to so warm me up when I heard it. I loved saying it. I have a big brother. No, it's okay, my big brother's waiting for me. No, not today. I can't come out after school, I'm studying with my big brother. I remember the first time I was old enough to notice him noticing the other boys noticing me, and how I felt. Funny. Flattered not by the attention the pimpled, hormone-driven teens lavished on my fresh, still-forming breasts—surprising even me under the soft cotton filigree of my summer dress—but by how my brother bristled like a wolf, a young alpha male in training, set on edge by approaching rogues from another pack, how he took offense for me, and how that made me feel safe and wanted, full and whole, pampered and protected. And they would see us together and look away in spite of themselves, almost embarrassed, as though they knew ours was a closed circuit they couldn't break, a shielded unit they couldn't penetrate. I didn't need anyone else, because I had him. Why go out looking for something that you've always had to begin with? And so I clung to him as I had since before I can remember, and I never wanted to let go because I knew, somehow, I knew that if I did let him go, if I did push him away, everything would fall apart like an unbalanced chemical reaction, the electrons streaming away from one molecule and attaching to the other, priming the mixture to explode. And once that happens, it can't be reversed. You can't unexplode something. I made the decision to dive in, and you can't change course midair. It's sink or swim at that point.

Of course, I knew we shouldn't have been doing what we did, from a practical perspective. Of course there was no choice but to end it, regardless of what was to come in its wake. I did what had to be done. I don't think it's possible to ever stop loving someone, and I surely do not mean this in an inspirational, movie-of-the-week kind of way, because I don't believe there's even a standardized working definition of the word love that would allow us to talk about it in measured and quantifiable ways, as we would a pound of flour or a cup of sugar. But if there is something real to this thing we call love, then it would never completely go away, because nothing ever completely goes away. Once something is, it can never truly not be. Scientists are still detecting radiation from the Big Bang, almost fourteen billion years ago. As youngsters, my father had us memorize the laws of thermodynamics, putting particular emphasis on the law of conservation of energy, which states that energy cannot be created or destroyed, but can only be redistributed or changed from one form to another. And so if everything in the known universe is somehow part and parcel of this preexistent and everlasting energy, and love exists in this universe, then love can never be destroyed. How it changes form, I suppose, is something that even the physicists can't get at.

I never felt alone with Peter. Even at those tiresome extended family dinners, the cringeworthy Christmases, the never-ending Easters and tedious Thanksgivings. The way we'd sit next to each other at those long, loud tables full of ridiculous relatives passing plates of meteoric meatballs and painfully stuffed manicotti, knocking knees in secret complicity even as we kept up appearances for the clan, wondering how we could possibly have come from the same gene pool as these Brooklyn barbarians with their crude street speech and comical gesturing, their stubborn, old-world simplicity and infuriating ignorance of anything immediately outside their proximate sphere of awareness. Peter used to say that if we tied everyone's hands down there'd be no communication whatsoever. It was such a relief to get home and be rid of them, to be where we belonged, where we fit. But just because we fit there doesn't mean we liked it. It was only right when we were alone together. With each other. It was after these family gatherings that I was most acutely aware that it wasn't because Peter was my brother that I loved him. My father presented us with Platonic paradoxes early on, and the one that always tickled me most was about love. Is the beloved object loved because it is loveable, or is it loveable because it is loved? Does loving someone make him worthy of love—does the very act of loving create its own justification?—or is there some inherent, internal quality that invites that love, that merits it, that calls it forth like a magnet, as a siren lures a sailor to his ecstatic, welcome death? I loved Peter because I did. We found ourselves in love with each other.

And so when I think of what to say about it now that the walls of the fortress are tumbling all around, its ruined rock façade piled in jagged heaps and leaving me only the smallest room to move, to breathe, to be; when I consider where I am and wonder what detour could have been taken along the way to avoid this juncture, I ask myself if I would have taken that detour, knowing it could have saved me—us. If I could take that impossible leap into the past, would I undo it all, right from the beginning? I ask this all the time, and the answer is always the same.

The final page was blank. There was nothing but a pinpoint of black ink in the upper left corner, as if she had started to write something else—maybe something directly to me—and then thought better of it.

When I finished reading, I held the pages for a long time. Then I refolded them, put them back in their envelope, stuffed the envelope into a manila folder, and buried the folder under a thick stack of old term papers and other miscellany at the bottom of a cluttered drawer I seldom use. I haven't looked at them since. But I know they're there.

10

Afterlife

One must choose in life between boredom and suffering.

— Madame de Staël

I have a dog now, a little poodle crossbreed that my mother found during a late March cold snap, cowering in the corner of the supermarket parking lot with no collar or ID tags, looking lost and dirty and pitifully alone. She alerted the manager, some announcements were made, but nobody called to claim him. She said he seemed tired, hungry, and frightened, so she brought him home and we've had him ever since. As my father doesn't like pets, the dog stays in my room most of the time. He, too, is a staunch proponent of inactivity, spending long days doing nothing at the foot of my bed and only making the necessary journey downstairs for water and meals and the occasional game of fetch with his squeaky toy in the shape of a small red rubber shoe, which I lob the length of the kitchen so he can hustle over to it and leisurely trot back with the thing pinned between his fangs. Apart from his two daily walks—tended to in the daytime by my parents, while I naturally take the nocturnal shift—and some alfresco playtime, he spends the larger part of his life indoors and shows a clear preference for my room, probably because I am always there, though this fact is not the decisive point for him; I'm just someone. A living body. Which is fine with me. I like having him near. I like to feel him resting next to me at the foot of the bed, his furry warmth pressed against my legs.

There is no way to be precise, but the vet estimated my dog to be ten years old, about seventy in dog years, though I never bought into the whole conversion formula. He is small, so he could live fifteen years or more, even twenty, though this would be exceptional. I often watch him, just watch him as he sleeps, stretches, or ambles around the house and the backyard, always completely absorbed in what he is doing, so marvelously lost in the moment and brightly oblivious to the fact that his existence is in uninterrupted movement toward its own end. I observe him sleeping next to me, not very far from death, obscenely close to it in geologic terms, and I am moved by the thought that he has no idea that one day he won't wake at the foot of my bed and crawl up to lick my face. His lower brain and canine instincts might clue him in on some level, but he has no clearly apprehended idea of what's to come, of what end awaits him, no conscious conception of what has already started. The most he under-stands, perhaps, is that it's becoming increasingly difficult for him to do things he used to be able to do so effortlessly only a couple of years ago, like racing up and down the stairs, hopping on and off my bed at whim, chasing squirrels and rabbits, or even fetching his toy. And when it happens, after a long and grueling descent or a short and quick one, he'll just *be* no more, and he will not question or begrudge the process, he will not struggle against it or go to great lengths to delay it, and he will not rage against the result. I envy him.

I think my sister would have liked him. We never had a pet growing up.

In my room there is a clock radio that displays the time in radiant red digits, large, boxy, threatening numerals. Sometimes, while lying in bed, I stare at it, watching the numbers transform into each other through the lighting up and darkening of one or more bars of the seven-segment LCD display, and I try to guess exactly when it's going to happen—that instantaneous change from one minute to the next—not by counting down but by anticipating the transition, feeling the interval work to a peak and expire as 3:36 turns instantly into 3:37. Seconds become tangible atomistic units in perpetual motion that I can all but hear as they occupy the room, fading in and out of existence after a fugitive cameo, appearing just long enough to make their exit before I have the chance to recognize them. I can spend substantial time watching the clock, lying inert as slow-moving minutes pass into unhasty hours. I doze off and wake up and everything in the room is exactly the same. There are no detectable footprints of change, nothing that would indicate now instead of then, except the digits. They reassure me. They let me know, with merciful indifference, that time has passed.

It has become an addiction: the more I sleep, the more I want to; the more I am awake, the less I want to be. I must stop this, I tell myself. I must stop all this sleeping and do something. One must do something. Life is *doing*. Things have to be done. But I've already devoted so much time to *not* doing, dedicated everything to my nihility project, watched the years dwindle and depart with nothing to show for their passing, that it would be disloyal to the memory of those dead days if I were to abandon them now and make a halfhearted attempt at doing, at being, after all that has been buried.

But lately, I've been out more than usual. I go for drives, middle-of-the-night tours through the wilds of suburbia, never straying too far from home, from my room. Initially, I would ride through neighboring developments, imagining all kinds of nocturnal activities taking place behind the few lighted windows, but I soon established an itinerary of sorts, making my rounds at several 24-hour places, the only ones that display signs of life after midnight: the donut shop, where I'll have a jumbo black coffee and a frosted cruller with sprinkles; the convenience store, browsing through magazines and endless rows of candy bars and power drinks. Sometimes I go to the supermarket, my favorite late-night stop. I love it there. I rarely buy anything, just walk around the aisles, the blindingly bright aisles with their hard white hospital flooring and insipid fluorescence and illusion of cleanliness. Most of the time there are no customers, just me and a single cashier and some bored-looking guys stocking the shelves, but every so often there is another shopper: a night worker, a nurse, a security guard, everyone eyeing each other with surreptitious suspicion.

I return with a strong sense of accomplishment, a funny feeling of consummation or fulfillment of some indefinite duties, especially when I arrive home as slivers of daylight splinter the dark, as if I have done something admirable and brave just by making it through one more night. Frank Sinatra said: "Basically, I'm for anything that gets you through the night, be it prayer, tranquilizers or a bottle of Jack Daniels." I don't know how I know that, but I'm glad he said it.

Recently, however, I found myself jaded by my regular haunts. Just making it through the night was becoming problematic, and neither prayer nor tranquilizers nor whiskey was going to cut it. I don't think it's indicative of anything other than a nagging need for a respite from routine that I stopped in a strip club one night, or that it's anything more than a desire for the tiniest tremor of sexual stimulation that I've been going there on a fairly regular basis ever since. It's less than a fifteen-minute drive from my house, a gloomy, run-down structure on a worse-for-wear industrial strip of a multilane turnpike, a sort of large, freestanding shack with no windows and no name, just a big white billboard, planted in the grass near the street, that reads: GIRLS! GIRLS! GIRLS! over the silhouette of a reclining naked woman. The club has been there for ages without having undergone any recognizable alterations, and as various businesses and buildings around it come down and go up anew, renovate and update and expand, this one remains exactly as it has been for as far back as my memory goes. Its changelessness is comforting. Don and I had always talked about going, but it was just one of those things that's fun to theorize about; neither of us had any desire to actually spend time or money there. This nameless venue lies smack on the route to the supermarket, and after passing the place uncountable times throughout the years, I finally succumbed to temptation and stopped in about six months ago, on a windy and wet autumn Tuesday just before last call.

The strippers there like me well enough. Though my tipping habits are far from exorbitant, I am well-mannered and mellow, quiet and respectful, and manifestly unthreatening. I don't talk too much and I don't try to touch them where I'm not supposed to. They squirm around on my lap for a song and I pay them for the pleasure, and I don't expect them to have any deeper feelings for me than they would for an ATM. I don't probe into their lives; I don't inquire about their day jobs and daydreams, and I don't ask about their husbands or lovers or their little children that are home sleeping as they bare their breasts and shake their asses for cash. I don't ask what they want from life, because whatever they do outside the club doesn't mean squat to me, and they know this, and they appreciate it. Sometimes they tell me about themselves. Sometimes they want to talk—as a rule, it's strictly a one-way conversation, and they rarely want to hear about anyone else—volunteering unsolicited information that I pretend to take interest in, though they really don't care whether I do or not; they view me, by and large, as little more than a cordial captive audience. Maybe I am a good listener after all. Even the bartenders are well disposed toward me. They sometimes offer me an early buyback on my second glass of watered-down, overpriced gin and tonic or six-dollar bottle of spring water. I've become something of a regular. I've never been a regular anywhere.

I usually don't get to the bar much before 1 a.m., when the after-work crowd of boisterous businessmen is long gone and only *the faithful* remain, those you see night after night on the same stools with the same drinks, slipping soggy singles under the G-strings of the same girls, who bend over to kiss them on the lips and wiggle tits in their faces and thank them by their first names. I am, by a considerable margin, the youngest of the faithful. Most of them are men in their early forties to fifties, married or divorced, probably with a kid or more and a blue-collar job and a commuter car they've driven here from the train station. I nod at them in greeting, in simple recognition of our shared presence, but that's all. I don't talk or socialize. I don't fit easily into any mold of the prototypal regular. I wonder if they wonder about me, though I don't wonder about them.

Typically, I stay until closing time, when the music is turned off and the house lights go bright and only the most faithful of the faithful remain. Then I go home and masturbate, have a snack, and try to fall asleep by sunrise, sometimes watching the earliest broadcast of the morning news, ending my day to the anchors' bright-eyed banter and lively reporting of overnight events, traffic and weather, the latest trends, the juiciest gossip, and the most necessary new gadgets.

Svetlana dances the late shift (8 p.m. to 4 a.m.) on Sundays, Mondays, and Wednesdays; she prefers to front-load her week. It happens that those are the nights I usually drop in, as I try to avoid the weekends, when drunken frat boys and other vociferous groups of the young and testosterone-driven inundate the place and transform it from a low-key den of sleaze to a rowdy sexual circus. Svetlana emigrated to America from Moscow a little over a year ago, left her family in Brighton Beach, and has been here on Long Island only a few months. She has long straight blonde hair, light creamy skin, and cold coal-black eyes. She is not beautiful, but she is a girl. Her skin is soft and always smells nice, and when she sits on my lap and wiggles, I am never disappointed.

When work is slow, Svetlana sometimes relaxes and has a drink with me, which is allowed and even encouraged between sets, since I'm the one buying. These conversations generally end in the back room with a lap dance, an extra-long one, which the owners would frown upon if they knew. I don't like her rough Russian accent—it is just about as harsh and unappealing as any oral emanation a human being can produce—and her voice is a little low and masculine for my taste, and what she has to say is usually dull and poorly articulated, but it is nice to have a girl next to me from time to time, talking, even if I am paying for the privilege.

One insufferably slow Tuesday, just past 3 a.m., Svetlana asked me why I was there so often. She caught me by surprise in her unabashedly frank Eastern Bloc manner. She usually talks exclusively about herself.

"Because I like it here," I answered.

"Because of the girls?"

"That has something to do with it."

"You don't have girl of your own then?" She sucked on a cigarette and squinted so tightly her eyes all but closed.

"No," I said. "I have a dog though. A little black one."

She didn't laugh. "A dog? Like, pet dog?" Her pronunciation sounded more like *thug*.

"Yes. He's a good thug." I adopted her cacoepy, which was fun, especially because she had no clue I was doing it. "A very cute and loyal thug."

"No girl but thug."

"Why? You don't like thugs?"

"No. I like cat. Thugs are dirty. Cats, they clean themselves."

"Cats lick themselves. They don't take showers."

"Neither do I. I take bath."

"At least you don't lick yourself." I laughed to tone down the mordancy.

She stared at me, threaded eyebrows arched in confusion or anger or frustration—I wasn't sure which—and probably a little boredom. But there was nothing much else to do, and I kept the drinks coming, so she stayed.

"I used to have a sister."

"Used to?"

"Yes. Used to. Not anymore."

"Why not?"

"She went away."

"Went away where?"

"The Atlantic."

This time it was definitely confusion.

"The Atlantic Ocean," I clarified.

"Ocean? I don't understand?"

"That's okay. Nobody really does."

"Sister and thug, but no girl then," was her summation. "This is why you are always here." Her consternation gave way to pride at having reached this conclusion, and she raised her chin and nodded knowingly.

We both stared at our drinks for a while. There were only three other guys at the bar: one old drunk in a grubby greige flasher's raincoat buttoned from neck to knees, whose head bobbed about his shoulders as he fought off sleep, and a pair of well-coiffed yuppies in expensive three-piece suits who should have been gone hours ago, yapping at each other at a rapid, drug-fueled pace and paying scant attention to the nearly naked women pole dancing in front of them, who in turn performed with undeniably less enthusiasm, the prospect of good tips being low.

"Ready to go into back?" Svetlana asked.

I gulped down the remaining half of my drink, deciding if I wanted to or not.

"I'm always ready."

"Karasho."

The back is a series of dim, claustrophobic cubicles lining both sides of a long and narrow corridor where the girls take their clients for private dances, at the end of which lies a larger, dimmer room with an outsized L-shaped microfiber sectional sofa of indeterminate color lining the two far walls, and a few nondescript chairs lying about pell-mell. Patrolling the room was Jessie, a gigantic American Indian with a pair of long black braids hanging down onto his chest and a studded leather vest over a sleeveless Slayer concert tee. I've never seen him talk to or acknowledge anyone, neither clients nor fellow employees, and his deadpan demeanor rarely changes. I know his name only because I've heard Svetlana and the other girls greet him upon entering, in response to which he just stands there blankly and lets us pass. Though I've been there numerous times, he never shows the barest wink of recognition and hardly looks at me when I enter. I have no doubt, however, that if I ever crossed any lines with the girls, he wouldn't hesitate to introduce himself.

I always enjoy a good lap dance, and Svetlana is an adroit practitioner. A virtuoso, really. There is much more to a quality lap dance than a little teasing, shaking, bumping, and grinding. The real pros almost make you believe they are enjoying it as much as you are. Of course, as with even the finest fiction, a little suspension of disbelief is necessary to heighten the experience. This time, after dancing on me for two complete songs—though I asked only for the first and wasn't sure if the second one was on the arm or if she expected payment for it—she sat down next to me on the sofa and lit a cigarette. The room was empty except for us and Jessie's looming presence darkening the entryway. She put her sparkling silver top back on, took a deep drag, and squinted at me. She was always squinting, and I couldn't figure out whether it was a nervous tic or the need for corrective lenses.

"You are sad," she said, almost haughtily, confident of her insight.

I felt ambushed and a little offended by her surety. She was asserting, not asking.

"And you squint a lot."

Unruffled, she squinted even more. "I cannot wear my glasses to work."

"I think glasses are sexy."

"Yes. You seem like you would."

"What about contact lenses?"

"They hurt my eyes."

"I see."

The stub of her cigarette burned bright orange and then slowly smoked down to black. "Why are you sad? So young and so sad?"

I could see there was no way of steering out of this line of questioning, and besides, I wasn't quite ready to go. There were still several bills weighing down my wallet, and I saw one last lap dance in my immediate future, depending on whether or not I was paying for the extra one.

"You think I'm sad?"

"Yes. This I can tell. I know sadness when I see it."

"And young? I never thought of myself as young, even when I was."

"But you *are* young, still," she persisted. "There are many years in front of you."

"That's part of the problem. 'Life is very long.'"

She took one last drag, dropped her cigarette onto the floor, and smashed it flat with the sole of her peep-toe pumps. "Only to the living."

I watched her foot swivel back and forth over the crushed butt. "I think Jessie is looking over here. Maybe we'd better—"

"Is not good to be sad." She ignored my attempt to drop the subject. "I know sadness, and I know that being sad does not change nothing. Just make you more sad." She pouted her lips and wrinkled her nose fiercely. "Sadness is not to be proud of. It does nothing to make relief. It does nothing but make more sad. Nothing." She pronounced this last word with disgust and made a spitting sound.

"Maybe sometimes all you want is to be sad, because that's all you have."

"Pshaw!" She reared back and turned her nose up. "This is stupid American thinking. Back in Russia we had one loaf of bread for week sometime, no toilet paper, dirty water, no heat in winter..." She gazed off into space, perhaps stepping back in time and reliving an instant of those bad old days before snapping back into the present. "But being sad did not help. Sadness did not fill bellies or heat house. We could not help being sad sometime, but it did not make better." She studied her cigarette plaintively. "And these were hard time, believe me. Harder than you will ever have to know here in U.S. Imagine to worry if you can eat and where you have to sleep each night, about how you are going to live."

"There are worse things." I realized this sounded insensitive, but it was already said and I didn't feel like justifying it. There's no room in me for hard-luck stories or motivational tales of transcendence through sorrow, and I take no solace in the sliding scale of suffering. To each his own pain.

"Yes, there are always worse things," she said, and put her hand on my leg. "But they don't stay worse forever. You must remember this."

"A kiss is still a kiss," I semi-sang.

"What?"

"Nothing."

Her eyes were hypnotic black orbs, so close I almost had to turn away, but I didn't. I am no longer nervous or shy or reticent with women, maybe because the only ones I'm around are usually at least half-naked and specifically charged with the duty of making me feel unshy. She motioned to Jessie, who left his post without a word. We were alone.

Her hand moved from my thigh to my coarse, unshaven face. She smelled like shea butter moisturizer and perfume. In a different world, I would have accepted the embrace she was ready to offer. I would have lain my heavy head on the beautiful bare shoulder of this erotic foreign fairy, this sultry stranger, this exotic being from another country and culture. I would have cried at the strange warmth of a welcoming body next to me, would have gladly capitulated to the rare opportunity to forget myself for a short while in the arms of another and savor even the flimsiest foretaste of love, however brief and artificial. But as much as I might have wanted to, as aroused as I was after the lap dance, I remained remote and statuelike as her hand inched up my thigh like a caterpillar, still and stoic as she searched my eyes for some semblance of an invitation, and finally pulled away when she brought her face in close to mine.

She was desirable, especially in that light and atmosphere, but I had no desire. Some things require more than low lighting and an erect penis. She withdrew her hand, placed it atop the other in her lap, and sat back, staring at me with an expression of deep understanding and no sympathy.

"You are very sad. Very sad." She was simply stating a fact, a flat and emotionless fact. "Even more sadder than I thought."

The muffled music pounded in the other room and vibrated the entire place with each electronic pulse, and we sat on that plush, pilling couch without saying anything for a full two or three minutes. Severine was right: I am indeed gifted at creating awkward moments, or at finding myself in them.

Our speechlessness withstood the background ruckus and somehow even seemed to suppress it, as though the banging bass and synthesized whirs and screeches were nothing but contextual flourishes to the silence. But it had gone on long enough.

I was about to get up and return to the bar when it happened. The pale light struck her head at just the right angle, brilliantly illuminating her long blonde Russian hair and casting her profile in a deceptive light that made her seem like someone else for the flash of a second, before she moved and the dimness blended her back into obscurity. I reached out and touched it—so soft, hair I'd seen before, felt before—and then I pounced on her. I swept her to the floor, kissed her shoulders and neck feverishly and slobbered all over her, fondled her firm little dancer's breasts and tight, smooth stomach, fingered that moist pit of infant skin under her arm with its vague scent of rosewater talcum powder and deodorant and its small, hard sprouts of stubble. My mouth and hands worked at a frantic pace as I pulled at her skirt and nibbled at her neck.

But it still wasn't desire; it was an attempt at relief, simple, radical relief from physical agony, and it was enough.

"Wait," she said. I kept going. "Wait." Not *no*, but *wait*, a protest not out of fear—there was no resistance, no rebuff. So I stopped. "Wait. Is fifty dollar."

"What?"

"Is fifty dollar," she repeated.

I pushed myself off her and onto my knees, caught my breath.

"You're serious."

"I am sorry, but I have husband and daughter, you know. I like you, you nice guy, but I must make money. I must make money for to live."

I'd had no problem paying for sex before, when I expected to, but this time was different. I zippered my pants and buckled my belt.

"Yeah. We all must for to live."

"Usually it is hundred-fifty dollar or more, but I like you."

"Of course you like me. I am nice guy," I said in my best rendition of her accent.

She leaned up on her elbows and watched me as though struggling to make out the image on a poorly received television station. I got up and brushed myself off. "I am sorry, Peter. Fifty is really good bargain."

"I can imagine."

"It is almost free."

"The best things in life are."

"Okay. We make compromise. We say forty, yes?" Her bid was sprightly and glib, as though she were peddling tchotchkes at a flea market.

I arched my head and pretended to think about it. "Thank you. It's a kind offer, very kind, but I don't have it on me."

"Is too bad, you know. I like you. I like your sadness."

She liked me, for the third time.

"How about another lap dance?" she proposed as consolation, slipping her bare foot up under the cuff of my jeans and caressing my shin with her toes. "I think will do you good, yes?"

I declined. It was late and I was tired, and her last-ditch overture offered little enticement, only the likelihood of deeper disenchantment.

She pulled back her foot and was silent. I think she might have been considering fucking me for free, just because she liked me and found my dysphoria charmingly pitiable, a refreshing departure from typical American exuberance. If so, she decided against it. She looked crestfallen, that strong, proud Russian stripteaser who had survived starvation and privation and the soulless severity of the Soviet regime, now dispirited over a sad suburban kid—who was so miserly he wouldn't cough up forty bucks for a once-in-a-lifetime lay—in a deserted strip joint on a torpid early Tuesday morning. But at this point, even if she had offered a freebie, I don't think I would have accepted. I was past it now and glad to see her in a state of befuddlement. This was my true consolation.

I paid for my lap dance—just the one—left the bar and drove to the supermarket, bought a box of Hostess cream-filled chocolate cupcakes and a half-gallon of skim milk, and headed home, hurrying so that the milk would stay cold and the cupcakes wouldn't harden with chill. It was well after 4, but the night felt incomplete, and I wasn't yet ready to turn in. I already regretted not fucking Svetlana. Maybe she would have taken thirty dollars if I'd haggled; Russians probably appreciate a bit of good old-fashioned dickering. Or maybe she would have sucked me off for twenty-five, conceivably twenty, if I'd held out for it. I was annoyed at myself for giving up too easily—regardless of how I had felt at the moment—but found quick reassurance in the knowledge that by this time it would have been over and done with anyway, the ephemeral pleasure lasting at most a few intense seconds, and the only difference would have been the amount of money left in my pocket. Good. Okay. Now I could go home with no regrets, eat my cupcakes, masturbate, and try to keep to my sunrise bedtime.

Almost home, and there is this guy on the road, walking along the unpaved edge of the left lane of the service road of the highway, right near my house, about a hundred yards west of the overpass from which my grandfather took his fateful fall, close to where Severine left the car the night she died. It is highly unusual that anyone would walk this road, let alone at this time of night. During the day, there is always a steady flow of cars, but at night it is very low-trafficked and poorly lit, especially at the stretch close to my home, making it extremely dangerous for anyone on foot since cars zoom by even faster when there's less traffic. There is no footpath or shoulder, only a grassy patch off to the side and a 50-foot-high wooden wall separating the three-lane service road from the highway—a noise barrier, they call it, constructed to minimize the constant clamor of traffic for those houses that back up to the roadway, as mine does.

I'd seen an occasional bicycler or a motorist changing a flat tire, maybe a cop giving out a speeding ticket, but in the twenty-odd years that I'd lived there, the thousands of times I'd been on that road, I'd never seen anyone walking it, and yet here is this kid, a high school kid, sixteen or seventeen, strolling breezily in the same direction as I'm driving, and treading a narrow path between the road and the grass. I slow down to see him better, slow to a near crawl, click on my high beams, which confirm that he is young, perhaps even a bit younger than I'd originally thought. What is he doing out so late on a school night? Did he sneak away for a quick teenage tryst with his girlfriend? Maybe he'd had a squabble with his folks and stormed out of the house to simmer down before returning home to finish the fight with a slightly cooler head. He turns and squints briefly into the lights, then unconcernedly turns back around and keeps walking, arms swinging, hastening his pace only a bit so as not to disclose his mounting nervousness and seem overtly suspicious of the creep-ing car behind him. He is a fair-skinned, fair-haired, lanky kid. His cheeks are ruddy from the cold. Or maybe that's just his normal complexion. He is wearing a long-sleeved black shirt, baggy camouflage cargo pants, and mid-calf olive-drab combat boots. On the back of the shirt is a large male face with long hair covering one eye, and when I get closer I see that underneath the face is written: KURT COBAIN 1967–1994, in big block white letters that glow off my headlights. The kid's hair is shoulder length and stringy, like the dead idol on his back. The shirt is hooded, and the kid puts the hood over his head and slips his hands into his pockets. He is carrying a skateboard under one arm and has a red and black checkered flannel shirt tied around his waist, which looks like a kilt. I imagine he must be cold and wonder why he chooses not to wear the extra layer.

Coming almost to a complete stop, brights still on the kid, foot applying just enough pressure on the brake to keep the car moving as minimally as possible, I turn on the radio to find the *Goldberg Variations* are just beginning. It's been some time since I've heard this composition, and I like it very much, so I raise the volume and slow down. There is no rush to get home. Nobody is waiting up for me. The milk and cupcakes will hold.

I'm wondering if I will jerk off to Svetlana tonight. Yes, probably. While the image is fresh.

I think about that forenoon in the hospital when we sat in the mirthless waiting room while my grandfather lay dying, and Severine explained to me with early-onset disillusionment why it is impossible to experience one's own death. This little girl who rarely played with dolls and read books almost too heavy for her to hold up was sitting there telling me how disheartened she was about this, because she would have liked to know what death feels like.

The things you miss in life.

I am about thirty feet from the kid when I jam my foot on the gas pedal, knuckles clenched white around the wheel. The tires spin like mad but don't screech as I thought they would. Nonetheless, the car roars as it bolts into motion. The kid doesn't take off into the grass where the car can't follow him, doesn't even change his pace, just keeps walking normally. Doubtless he thinks I am going to blow past him, to scare him at the most, maybe skid out a few yards in front of him and brazenly rev my engine before taking off into the anonymous night, leaving him unscathed except for some befouled underwear and a little dirt sprayed up onto his face; doubtless his heart rate elevates and his palms get clammy, but soon the car will be well past him, and he will continue his solitary walk along this dark, quiet, lonesome road until he is back in the warm safety of his own house with his parents. And maybe his sister. He has no reason to suspect what is going through my mind.

And what is going through my mind is how easy it would be—hardly any effort at all, the merest flick of the wrist—to turn the wheel and feel that solid, reverberant thud of bone against metal, hear his skull smash against glass and watch his front teeth collapse into his mouth. I visualize it all, every part of the scene before it can happen, but my eyes closing just at the point of impact do not see his face flying at me lightning-like, crashing into the windshield and staining the shattered glass with blood, or his body bouncing backward off the car and arcing through the stream of my headlights, soaring through the air and landing half on the road and half on the grassy patch that he should have run off into, lying there still and broken, legs bent and twisted in ways legs should never bend or twist. It would be easy. Too easy. But for some reason I want to. I don't know why. I just want to. Just to do it. There is no reason. Just to do something that has come into my mind. To bring a thought to fruition. To exercise an impulse. My heart is pounding and my hands are slippery on the wheel.

And then there's the other choice. The colossal tree on the opposite side of the street. Also easy. There are a good many trees bordering the road, but this one stands out for its imposing height and massive girth, dwarfing its companions so they seem like saplings in its presence. The titanic trunk surely wouldn't offer much give, probably wouldn't even suffer significant damage from the impact with my little Japanese economy car. I am not wearing my seat belt, so it should be quick and efficient and hopefully not that painful. A broken neck and instant death. A sliced jugular as my head is jolted through the windshield, chest caved in by the steering wheel. Thrown clear out of the vehicle and cranium crushed against the mammoth tree or impaled on one of its many low-hanging branches. But that would be too facile an ending for me, and much too easy to explain.

Those are the choices, and a choice must be made. The kid or the tree. It's him or me. Somebody has to go.

The tires finally screech when I brake and cut the wheel, and the car fishtails sharply, its back end swerving into the right lane and stopping perpendicular to the dotted yellow line, four feet from my intended target. I feel his presence but refuse to look up at him, focusing instead on the immobile speedometer dial. Stretched seconds pass. I shift to park, keep the engine running, and eventually look up. The kid is centered in my high beams, standing there with his ashen face turned toward me, a helpless animal, a bewildered creature, no different from me, neither more nor less terrified than I am.

There is no one else on the road. I stay there a few seconds, looking at the kid frozen before me as if we are involved in a bizarre staring contest, judging who will blink first, though I don't think he can see much of me with the lights in his eyes. The first *Goldberg Variation* ends. I turn off the stereo and flicker my headlights. The kid makes no response, so I repeat the signal. He takes a single step in reverse, hesitates, then slowly moves back and away, out of the line of my lights, without ever taking his eyes off me. I straighten the car, flip the high beams down to low, put the stereo back on—the second variation, my favorite, is now playing—and continue on my way.

I find myself shaking when I get home, but not as much as I would have expected, just a little, as you do directly after a quick adrenaline rush that can often do a world of good for getting to bed once you come down off it. Before going upstairs, I sit at the kitchen table with two cupcakes and a large glass of milk in front of me. The cupcakes are very soft and fresh, but the milk is not as cold as I prefer, and though it smells okay and the date is fine, it tastes sour, and I will not eat cupcakes without milk, so I put them back into the box and empty the glass in the sink, rinse it, refill it with tap water, place it on the counter, and let it sit there until the liquid looks as still and solid as the glass that contains it. I reflect that though the water seems ordered, its plane calm and its consistency uniform, this is only appearance, only how it appears within the confines of my optical perception, because nothing is ever completely at rest; neither the water nor the glass is actually solid or still. Inside, it is chaos, its essence turbulence, aswarm with the madness of unrelenting motion. If I could peer into its molecular structure, I'd see a tumult of colliding atoms, churning protons and neutrons, flashing electrons and spinning bosons and eddying quarks, a storming interaction that cannot be divined by the naked human eye, which sees only an illusion of clarity and peace. I take my glass to the table and sit back down and watch the bubbles circulate toward the surface and settle at the meniscus, and I wonder through whom these H_2O molecules have passed, hoping at least one of their uncountable number might have made it through her.

Spoiled milk or not, it doesn't matter. I can't eat a thing. My stomach is a lump of inextricable knots. Suddenly, I have to throw up. I run to the bathroom and make it to the toilet just in time, managing to lift the lid and accurately spew inside without the aid of light. No one comes to see if I'm all right, though they probably didn't hear me. I'm kneeling over the bowl, elbows on cool white porcelain, wiping a web of vomit that drips from my chin, waiting for the next round of retching and thinking about how I had wanted to kill that kid, how I had wanted to see him dead and splattered across the road with pieces of him stuck to my car, to erase his existence and prove to myself in the most dramatic and visceral way that life really does not mean anything, and therefore, neither does death; two sides of the same worthless coin. I wanted wisdom from experiencing firsthand what I've always been taught, that it is all *de trop*, we are all *de trop*. I had wanted to snuff out his young life so that I could then snuff out mine, so that I would finally be forced to do what should have been done long ago. His death would have cleared the path for mine. His blood on my hands would have drawn out my own blood. But I couldn't do it. Despite everything, I cannot conquer this obstinate and baseless belief in the intrinsic value of life. Even if I were to cross the line, the line would still be there, with or without me. Now I know that I will never kill myself, that suicide is not an option. I want desperately to live. I always have. I just don't know how.

I clean up the bathroom and return to the kitchen, throw the full box of cupcakes into the trash bin and sit at the table, in the chair I've sat in for twenty-five years. I sit there alone, just me and the glass of water, and finally I cry.

11

Epilogue

We have nothing more to search for — the heart
is full — the world is empty.

— Novalis

My father had Severine's room completely redone. To this
he would hear no objections and sanction no interference, nor
did he offer any reasons. If he felt any need to explain or justify,
he did not bend to this need. One morning, about two months
after her death, when the belated vernal warmth had finally cast
anchor—with summer hot on its heels—the doorbell rang and a
bevy of workers strode in, a full-service crew of eight burly men
who did their job with professionally detached competence. Half
of them started removing the larger stuff—bed, dresser, night
table—which they took to the Salvation Army. My father had
made arrangements for this in advance. Meanwhile, the other
four ripped up the rug in sections, which they wrapped into
long, tight cylinders and shoved into the back of a beat-up green
moving van. Then the bare hardwood floor was sanded, stained,
and shellacked, the walls patched and primed and painted with
a mild eggshell, and the ceiling finished in flat white. The shades
were torn down to expose the naked windows, which were
washed so thoroughly that when they were placed back in their
frames the glass didn't appear to be there. The room had never

seen so much light; its surfaces seemed to shrink back from the fulgent June sun, surrendering grudgingly to the bath of brightness given by those overlong, overluminous pre-summer days.

The renovation was an arduous process, and by the end of it, the room bore no evidence of her whatsoever, as though it had never been the room of a little girl, a teenager, *une jeune fille en fleur*. There was no way to tell she had been there. It could have been a spare room. A guest room. It smelled of sawdust and fresh paint and polyurethane, the latter stinking up the entire top floor for days, though it wasn't so repellent to me, as I've always had an odd affinity for those types of acrid, vaguely toxic scents, e.g., acetone, gasoline, formaldehyde. The plan was for this room to become a second study, with laddered, floor-to-ceiling bookshelves to relieve my father's downstairs office of its overflowing stock. He went so far as to hire an interior decorator —a strapping Austrian émigré named Günther, who specialized in psychologists' offices and wore a vintage pince-nez—to work up the layout, which included a sleek custom cherry computer workstation and a long leather daybed with an attached bolster pillow and high-gloss chrome legs. The roller shades would be replaced by mini blinds, and since there was no need for closets, the proposal called for getting rid of them to add more space. My father was skeptical about this, as it required structural changes, but Günther insisted that it was the right thing to do. "You'll be surprised at how much this will open things up," he said with an imperious Teutonic accent, holding out his brawny arms as though embracing the space. "It will be an entirely new area."

Area, the man said. My sister's room was not even a room anymore; it was an *area*.

The blueprint was impressive, but it never went further than the conceptual stage. Four years later, the room remains preserved in barrenness, its pristinely painted walls yellowing with neglect and the once shiny varnished floors dulling and dusty.

There is a faintly familiar yet unidentifiable scent in front of the door to this *area*. Some days it's stronger than others, but even when it's weak, I can still sense it. The door is always closed, and no one considers entering, as though there were no room behind it, just a void, an ineffable no-man's land that exists in a kind of timeless vacuum. The house is more than spacious enough for three adults and a dog, but if the room were needed for some unforeseeable reason, I would almost see us moving out before putting it back into use.

My mother kept the sheets from Severine's bed. And her clothes. She insisted. To this *she* would suffer no objections. They are downstairs in the storage room of the basement, boxed up along with Severine's jewelry and other personal belongings. I have her books. Her journals were never found. She must have destroyed them or taken them into the water with her, all but the pages she sent to me.

The piano is terribly out of tune. I randomly pressed a few keys the other day, and the sound was offensive. She would hate it. No one plays the untended instrument, so there's no reason to keep it tuned. It is basically a piece of furniture now. But it's clean. My mother dusts and vacuums the entire house every day—except for that room. Every single day. She never misses. All the surfaces are spotless and sparkling and smell like Lemon Pledge or Lestoil or Windex or antibacterial bathroom detergent. Cleanliness is good.

When he's not sealed in his study, my father spends week-ends weeding through old junk. He threw away those cracked plastic toboggans that were hanging on the wall in the garage, unused for so long. We had gotten too big for them anyway, and winters are not as snowy as they used to be. In the past few years, there have been only a handful of middling storms and a few weeks of real bitter cold. I sometimes miss those single-digit temperatures and snowfalls you could measure with a yardstick, though I'm sure I would hate them if they returned.

I have heard it said that now is the best time in history to be alive and young. The world has so much to offer in the spring-time of life. It is *our* tomorrow. Youth is the future. But I have no stake in the future. At twenty-five, faced with this wondrous world of opportunity waiting for me to pick its ripened fruit, to harvest its mature crops, I am the one who is waiting, watching and waiting as my field goes fallow and my days dry up and die on the vine. And although I've tried to convince myself that I have a lifetime ahead of me, my best years in front of me, I can't believe it; I just do not believe there is enough time to forget, enough future to erase the past, to balance what has been. And I know she's not waiting, even if she could. It's my place to wait. So I'll wait. For nothing. I'll wait a lifetime in bed because there is no place else, and there is nothing to do but sleep. There is nothing, but there is sleep. And if I do not think — if I sleep — then I am not. Therefore, I am not — except in the early evening, when the house is not yet dark but darkling, the silence not yet morgue-like but promising, and my thoughts stray to that warped wooden playhouse in the backyard, from which I never returned, that abandoned little log cabin surrounded by tower-ing oak trees and overgrown with creeping ivy, dandelions, and wild white clover, its musty plywood planks rotted and infested with termites and dressed in full decay, dead and still dying, that rickety old ramshackle hut echoing the treble voices of two small children who once believed that whole wide worlds were present within its scant space, that an independent existence was circumscribed by its borders. I imagine it will be there until it can no longer stand, until it can only collapse and disintegrate, the decrepit rafters toppling down and the unsound walls finally falling in on themselves, its moldering timber frame welcomed back into the earth.

And then, maybe, I can get up.

Acknowledgments

A mountain of thanks to: Catrina Neiman for her thorough, thoughtful editing; Sandy Lu for her endless encouragement; Richard Woodson for his keen copy editing; Albert Fayngold for the *artist's eye*; Joel Plotch for believing from the beginning; Bonnie Timmermann for her unflagging advocacy; Geraldine Lau for her brilliant work on the cover; and to Laraine Cassese for a lifetime of support.

www.ingramcontent.com/pod-product-compliance
Lightning Source LLC
Chambersburg PA
CBHW031425200626
46814CB00016B/1776